Praise for THE LILAC PEOPLE

* * *

"With exquisite attention to historical detail and deep compassion, Milo Todd brings to life a story that feels both urgent and timeless. From the streets of prewar Berlin to the isolation of rural survival, we follow characters forced to choose daily between truth and safety. Through Bertie's eyes, we witness how quickly hard-won freedoms can vanish, and how the bonds of chosen family become both sanctuary and salvation. A profound and riveting story of identity and resilience, *The Lilac People* reclaims a powerful piece of trans history."

—CHRISTINA BAKER KLINE, #1 *New York Times* bestselling author of *Orphan Train*

"In *The Lilac People*, Milo Todd brings to life the hope, joy, and complexities of trans identity and community in Weimar Berlin and beyond. At once a celebration of what becomes possible when humans truly accept one another and a stark reminder of the precipice between personal freedom and catastrophe, the story of Bertie Durchdenwald's fight for autonomy, dignity, and love cuts through history to underline what's at stake in our present moment." —JASON LUTES, creator of *Berlin*

"Through deft world-building and astute characterization, Milo Todd's *The Lilac People* transports readers to WWII-era Germany, where queer and trans people were subjected to a world that worked overtime to snuff them out, eerily similar to the world we live in today. Through this book, I was reminded of the timely history that it depicts, and I was delighted by Todd's intentional, careful prose. If you want to read a book that accurately depicts trans people of this period wholly, pick up this book." —KB BROOKINS, award-winning author of *Pretty*

"Remarkable and urgently needed. Milo Todd breathes life into erased histories, resurrecting trans history with heart, humor, and love, showing not only how people survived, but offering hope for how we will today. Meticulously researched and enchantingly written, *The Lilac People* is a book I will cherish."

—ALEX MARZANO-LESNEVICH, award-winning author of *The Fact of a Body*

"*The Lilac People* is at once a poignant ode, a powerful testimony, a rousing anthem, a timely warning, and a gripping heart-in-throat novel that is as richly rendered as it is urgent. All fiction should aspire to as much."

—NAWAAZ AHMED, author of PEN/Faulkner finalist *Radiant Fugitives*

"Todd's debut is a moving and poignant reminder that, even if we imagine ourselves finished with history, history is never finished with us. *The Lilac People* is a bravely, brutally perfect companion for those desperate to survive our darkening century."

—PATRICK NATHAN, author of *The Future Was Color*

"With *The Lilac People*, Milo Todd brings to life an almost-forgotten chapter of World War II. With this remarkable story rooted in history, the author speaks to the urgency of our times where the rights of trans individuals are steadily being robbed by right-wing extremists. It's a stunning feat of storytelling."

—S. KIRK WALSH, nationally bestselling author of *The Elephant of Belfast*

"From its thrilling first pages to its elegiac yet buoyant close, *The Lilac People* is a fully immersive reading experience filled with indelible and achingly human characters. A masterful debut, and a treasure of a novel."

—CHRISTOPHER CASTELLANI, author of *Leading Men*

the Lilac People

the Lilac People

A NOVEL

Milo Todd

COUNTERPOINT
CALIFORNIA

THE LILAC PEOPLE

This is a work of fiction. All of the characters, organizations, and events portrayed in this novel are either products of the author's imagination or are used fictitiously.

First Counterpoint edition: 2025

Library of Congress Cataloging-in-Publication Data
Names: Todd, Milo, author.
Title: The lilac people : a novel / Milo Todd.
Description: First Counterpoint edition. | California : Counterpoint, 2025.
Identifiers: LCCN 2024061935 | ISBN 9781640097032 (hardcover) | ISBN 9781640097049 (ebook)
Subjects: LCSH: World War, 1939–1945—GermanyFiction. | LCGFT: Queer fiction. | Historical fiction. | Novels.
Classification: LCC PS3620.O3214 L55 2025 | DDC 813/.6—dc23/eng/20241230
LC record available at https://lccn.loc.gov/2024061935

Jacket design by Farjana Yasmin
Jacket images: person © Magdalena Russocka / Trevillion Images;
sky © iStock / DmitryPK
Book design by tracy danes

COUNTERPOINT
Los Angeles and San Francisco, CA
www.counterpointpress.com

Printed in the United States of America

10 9 8 7 6 5 4 3 2 1

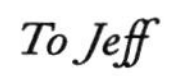

To Jeff

Das war ein vorspiel nur, dort
wo man bücher verbrennt,
verbrennt man am ende auch menschen.

That was but a prelude;
where they burn books,
they will ultimately burn people as well.

HEINRICH HEINE (1820),
plaque at the Sunken Library
in Bebelplatz, Berlin

Contents

the Lilac People

Please note that all terms used in this novel reflect the story's era. Terms such as *transvestite* are outdated and should be avoided when referring to transgender people of today.

We've received word that the liberation of the camps is not the celebration we'd hoped. The Allied forces are sending all pink triangles and any qualifying black triangles to jail to start the sentence for their crimes. All other categories of identity, crime, or marker have been liberated, for the Allies feel they have suffered enough.

We repeat. All inverts, transvestites, and lilac people who survived the camps have been sent to jail. If you avoided detection during the War, you are still not safe. We repeat: you are still not safe.

To any left out there, be safe, be well, and look after one another. Our sun will shine after this night. Thank you and goodnight.

1

1 • Ulm, 1945

IT WAS SUNDAY NOW, NEARLY TWO WEEKS SINCE THE WAR ended, a breezy-aired morning in mid-May. Bertie had been harvesting the potatoes, pulling them up by satisfying fistfuls when Sofie heard it over the radio, calling out as she ran to him. She left the cow half-milked, he the last row unharvested, as they dislodged the flag from their doorstep. They tore it that night, burning the scraps in the fire pit behind the house. She wondered if the news was false, more propaganda spread by the Nazis to punish those who were not true believers, who were hiding in plain sight like them. He wondered if they could soon use their real names again in public.

They had ridden out the length of the War in Ulm on a little farm that was not theirs, less than two morgen large, and in an arguably undesirable spot. They were in the hilly part, more than half of their ground useful only for heartier crops, and a quarter of it ended in a forest of five-meter conifers that ate both space and sunlight. Oma and Opa had surely built the house by the edge of those trees as a way to content themselves. But what that contentment was, Bertie was still not sure.

It was a Schwarzwaldhaus, what they had built, a wohnstallhaus cowshed made of dark wood from the Black Forest. The shingled roof was steeply hipped and near black, sloping down to the ground floor. When Bertie first arrived, he felt it all gave the look of a foreboding fairy tale, sticking out oddly dark against the sunshine and rolling hills, the chirping birds and greenery. But he had learned the intelligence behind it all. The wood was sturdy, splitting the heaviest winds and snowfalls. The roof was angled to work with the sun, shading them from its summer height and warming the walls when it hung low in the cold. During the early part of the War, Bertie helped Opa convert the roof from thatch to shingle. Bertie slid off twice.

The farm was close to where the Blau and the Iller joined the Danube, but not too close. It was as safe enough a place as possible to survive the War. They knew they were long since surrounded by dead vineyards by now. Only them and their most immediate neighbor, Frau Baer, were left from the original small grouping of farms, far as they could gather.

Bertie sipped his hot water and placed the teacup beside him, his folded paper rustling in the light wind. He looked out over the farm. It was hilled in places, flatter in others, but he was proud to maintain such neat rows of rich green and brown. He had recently finished planting the carrots, their tiny seeds light as air and frustrating. He had once sneezed and lost the worth of an entire bed. It was impressive how much life could fit in the palm of a hand. He would soon need to choose which ones to uproot so they did not choke one another. He did not like that part. He did not like what he worried it represented, if the path from plant to person was a short one, if there was something in his blood to be terrible, deciding what lived and what did not. But the seedlings were too young yet to poke through the mounds, for now just rows of freshly turned earth, darker than the dirt around them. The pumpkins and squash would be next, planted in a few more weeks.

The hilly parts, he had been taught, were perfect for root vegetables. The drainage was natural and the soil was sandy. Root vegetables did not bring much on the market, but they kept Bertie and Sofie well fed during the War. They did not have to deal with ersatz meat or many of the other substitutes the townsfolk paid for with their ration cards.

Bertie closed his eyes and breathed. The sun felt warm and good on his eyes, painting the backs of his eyelids a deep pink. Some birds called in the distance. The chickens absently glucked among the crops, pecking at beetles and grubs that caught their eye. He had to throw only a handful of feed at them in the morning, mostly the bits and ends and peels that Bertie and Sofie did not eat themselves, and they were fine. A soft plop of liquid dripped to the ground every few moments behind him, from the lump of cheesecloth Sofie had squeezed tight and left high on a nail an hour earlier. She had become quite good at making simple cheeses from vinegar and salt. Bertie caught a faint whiff of sharp, damp curds when the breeze turned. The air felt light and clean, the sun smelled like the sun. He did not believe a person would understand what he meant by that until they lived here.

He opened his eyes. Despite his careful planting, the asparagus made things look wild. Each crown grew at its own pace, but as soon as they started, they became eager. Some were still just baby stalks, poking out of the ground obscenely at first with their pale skins and distinctive heads. Others were already ferning, sprouting big and bushy far as they could reach. Some of the berries on the delicate fronds had already gone red as cherries and heavy with seed, others still green and new. By the end of the season, the ferns would be nearly as tall as him. An achievement for a plant, though perhaps less so for a fellow person.

Spargelzeit was his favorite season. He loved how easily the beetle eggs fell off with a tender skim of his thumb, he loved parting the tickling fronds to check the crowns beneath, he loved the juicy snap when he broke off a ready and eager stalk. He always chewed a spear raw as he harvested the others, the pale skin tender and woody on his tongue. Some mornings sprouted so many spears that he could barely make it to town at a respectable hour, other times there were only a few to be had. He and Sofie simply split those while breakfasting. They were not worth the trip.

Their crop was old, older than life, Opa had claimed, planted back when his own grandfather first bought the land. Long before this War, long before the one before that, long before the Treaty or the Inflation or the Crash or the Nazis or any of this. Long before Opa had been born, or Oma, or Bertie, or Sofie. Or Gert. The asparagus sprang up every spring without fail, an old friend, a capsule of history from when life kept growing, birthed from a better time. What they ate came from the same roots that fed people who had long since lived and died. It was the exact same asparagus that Gert had eaten. With such love over generations, the crop was wild and plentiful with Bertie barely trying.

But he worried. The current beds were slightly younger than Bertie, as Opa had said they needed to regrow crowns from the berries every forty years or so. Opa himself had done it only once, under the instruction of his father. But now Bertie feared the time was soon to do it again. He was not quite sure how it was done. He did not know if knowing mattered.

During those precious ten weeks of Spargelzeit—easily Bertie and Sofie's most lucrative time of year, particularly since the rationing—he was crowded by people the moment he stepped into Ulm with his cart. Oftentimes, he made all his trades before he even got to the stores. If there was something he and Sofie needed—flour, shoes, soap—now was always the time. Sofie called it white gold. Spargelzeit always felt like the shortest season of the year.

Bertie took another sip and placed his teacup back upon his neglected newspaper. He had bartered for the paper with that morning's crop. A paper outside of Deutschland, from Amerika, was a coveted treat, no matter that it was already two weeks old. Such things had gotten difficult to find as the War stretched on, even on the black market, no matter how much asparagus he offered. But now with the surrender, the Allied forces brought some things with them worthwhile.

He picked up his paper, slipping it from beneath the scissors. Sofie was still inside, writing another letter to home with increasing angst. They had some time left before church.

The fronds of the asparagus ferns swayed in the breeze like lace, those with berries beginning to hang from the weight. They took to wind well. Always bending, never breaking. They danced unconcerned.

Sometimes they could forget the War entirely. The sun was nice on good days, the farm quiet, the labor working them into both distraction and deep sleep. They did not feel the sting of ration stamps. As more men of any age were drafted, Bertie dodged the draft, not only as a farmer, but also, surely, for having long since been declared dead. Still, the War was never far away. He and Sofie often rushed into the root cellar following the false alarm of the Klaxon. Only three air raids ever struck Ulm, all in the final months of the War. The first and worst hit that past December, the third just last month. The bombings had left most of the city center in ruins, but their farm was too far out to feel the effects beyond stunted trade and their spooked cow not giving milk for days.

They were poor, they were careful, they were hidden in ways most would never know. Bertie sometimes felt ill at ease with their fortune, but they had made it to the end of the War. They had endured. If Bertie sometimes forgot who he had been in his twenties and thirties—his suits and ties, his assistance of Doktor Magnus Hirschfeld at the Institut, his leisure time drinking beer with his friends at the Eldorado—at least he had Sofie and their life together. His only keepsake from the past was a thick album full of photos of his friends, clippings from newspapers from Amerika, and his own transvestite card.

He was forty-seven now. There was always dirt under his fingernails, his hands rough and callused, his cheeks beaten by weather. He wore a flat-cap and working trousers in dark gray, his braces frayed, a dirtied white button-shirt, collarless and currently rolled up to the elbows. He still combed his brown hair from a side part, but without the shiny pomade of his youth. His hair looked fluffier and less refined. The gray did not help.

He felt his stamina wane among the other slow signs of aging: the weakening of his eyes, the one varicose vein that ran the length of his left leg, the modest ridge of fat around his middle that no amount of farmwork could strip away. These were the things his body wanted to do, and so that was what it did. But one of the wonderful things about being a man like him, he assured himself, was he would likely never lose his hair.

He finally unfolded his paper from the top down, straining to remember his stunted English. The headline was unsurprising, joyous news of the Deutschland surrender, of the end of the War for Europa. Amerika was still fighting Japan, but they had already secured their part of Deutschland, which included Ulm.

Bertie did not know what to expect from the occupation. In his latest trip to town, he heard the rumor that a ship bound for New York City was leaving Amsterdam in three weeks. He and Sofie discussed the possibility of leaving. But it would require hurdles—stealing away into the night, risking their lives while the Allies continued to attack civilian vessels, being arrested or sent back if Amerika found them out—and they did not know if it would be a necessary feat, starting life over yet again. For now, they put it aside.

He gave a start when he thought he heard a faint knock on the front door, but he quickly dismissed it as his perpetual worries of being caught. He opened the paper and skimmed over the smaller headlines with disappointment. It was not until the end of the paper, near the bottom of the second-to-last page, that he saw something to finally add to his old collection:

> THE GIRL WHO "MARRIED" A GIRL
> The astonishing case of a pretty woman who masqueraded as a man for over thirty years and married her lover. Only to be found out after her death, her lover claims she did not know, and the deception has swept across the United States.

It was the Midwest of Amerika. It was always the Midwest of Amerika. He had been thinking about it for a long while, had been talking to Sofie about it for the whole twelve years of the War and then some, back when he had first noticed the pattern and started his collection. The place where someone like him could live with little intrusion. The amount of articles proved that sometimes one could be found out, but they also proved how many more were not. Transvestites were congregating there, a place of privacy and simplicity, of honest work and no questions, and he wanted to be there. He had always wanted to be there. At least since he and Sofie had lost everything.

He picked up his scissors and cut out the article with an old precision bittersweet to remember. The paper was left with a rectangular window. He held it before his face, slowly rotating his torso with a small smile as he looked at the world through his little picture frame. A moment of calmness for himself, a forgotten familiarity, an instant to capture when the world was in that blissful spot between one bad thing ending and another beginning.

The breeze picked up once more, stronger and shifting, and a smell slid past his nose. He wrinkled at it. Not dirt, not fertilizer, not sweat or worry. None of the smells he was used to. It was something foul, something new. Something wrong.

He placed his paper and scissors down, standing up as he sniffed. His first instinct was the old toilet shed nobody had the heart to finally break down. But when that proved as much a relic as it had been when Bertie and Sofie had arrived, he sniffed around again, craning his neck.

The wind gave another gust, and he heard the thin rustling of paper behind him. He turned to see the article take off, gliding happily through the air toward whatever freedom it sought. He swore and ran after it. He grabbed at it but missed, the clipping dodging him at the last moment like this was a game he was in the mood to play. It gained courage across the fields, tumbling, rolling, and already persistently out of reach.

It was not until he noticed the chickens gathered in the asparagus ferns that he stopped. One of the hens pecked at something hidden from view. Then again, then a third time. The smell got worse the closer he got.

It was the battered bottom of a bare foot he saw first, the toes flattened against the earth, the heel caught in a wink of sunlight through the thin leaves in the wild bushel of fronds. He feared the worst. An asparagus thief, most likely, perhaps who had gotten curious about the poisonous berries that hung from the swaying lace.

Bertie defied his instinct to be cautious. He ran to the body. "Hello?" When he heard nothing, he ran faster, squinting through his aging eyes. "Are you alright?"

He slowed to a walk. The chickens scuttled away. The foot was indeed attached to a body, equally small and pale white. The body itself was prone, dressed in the dirtied stripes of a camp prisoner.

Bertie swore under his breath, trying to remember where the nearest camp was. The prisoners had been liberated two weeks ago, all the news claimed. He dared to shake the body's shoulder. "Hey! Can you hear me?!"

There was a slight stir and that was all Bertie needed. He gently turned the body over. The cheekbones were shadowed, the skin stretched tight and thin, the peek of collarbone looking like it had been sucked dry. But Bertie barely registered the emaciation. What kept his eyes was the black triangle sewn brashly against the stripes, and the face that he was sure, very sure, he remembered. The shame choked him.

He did not bother to think of the consequences, did not bother to wonder if this was the type of black triangle he would care most about, that perhaps he was mistaken, hoped he was mistaken. He picked that body up into his arms, too light, and ran to the house.

There was a low noise from his arms, perhaps a groan of worry. An arm dangled, head cocked back, mouth slightly parted.

"It's okay," Bertie said. "I have you. You're going to be alright."

He left his teacup to go cold, left his scissors and newspaper and thoughts.

"Sofie!" he called out as he struggled inside. "Something's happened!"

A drop from the cheesecloth landed on his shoulder, and he felt the chill as it reached his skin. The floorboards creaked the farther into the kitchen he went. He was careful as he crossed over the potato planks, weaker and looser than the others, worried that this extra weight, however sparse, would send him crashing through.

Oma had showed them both how to pull up those loose floorboards to expose the earth underneath. They would bury several potatoes from the end of the season to chop and cure in the following year.

The kitchen smelled of firewood and dried onion, a hint of animal and manure hiding beneath. A potent medley of herbs accented it all from the flavors Sofie grew on the windowsills, their dark little sprouts reaching toward the sunlight. Windows were plentiful in the kitchen area, their small centers sliding open for fresh air in the coldest parts of winter. They were all currently open, bringing in the breeze from all sides, the thin curtains billowing softly.

A modest cocklestove of stone rested at the center of the kitchen to warm the rooms. Their cast-iron cooking stove was against the wall, overlooking the conifers, the low ceiling blackened above it from generations of smoke. A sturdy square table rested in the near corner, flanked by two chairs and a substantial length of bench built into the two walls.

But Sofie was not at the table, her letter to her parents already addressed and ready for the post. Katze blinked up at Bertie beside it, swishing her tail as if ready to pounce for the sake of pouncing.

"Don't you dare," Bertie said. He did not know her name, did not care to know it, and so he just called her Katze. She belonged to their neighbor Frau Baer, had no business being in the house so many morgen away, but she was always finding her way inside, surely mostly from when he and Sofie left the windows open every day for fresh air. She seemed determined to come in just to torture him every day. Biting him, clawing him, getting underfoot, chasing the chickens. She seemed indifferent to Sofie, which made Sofie find the situation all the more amusing.

Bertie hissed at her now, causing her to skitter away into the sitting room with a flurry of her nails, running across the keys of the upright piano in a discord of notes. She jumped up, nearly knocking Oma and Opa off the top of the piano before leaping to the nearest sill. As she disappeared out the window, he could hear Sofie weaving fast down the old staircase.

"What is it?" she said, as scared as he was these days of the latest occupation. "What's happened?" She stopped dead in the kitchen entryway as her eyes lay upon Bertie and his bundle. Her blond hair was much longer than it had been in the old days, her temples suggesting gray under a discernible eye. The skin at her jawline had a slight sag. Her fashion was long gone, replaced with the drab gray of worn working dresses, but she still shone in his eyes.

Bertie did not know how to address the body in his arms. "Black triangle," he managed to get out before his voice broke off. He vowed years ago that he would not cry about things like these anymore. Crying spent energy needed to do labor, to eat and to live, and these were things he could not change, no matter how much he blamed himself for them. But to not cry was a silly promise. "We have to help."

"Oh, Bertie," she breathed, the pair of them once again letting their natures slip while indoors, for it felt impossible to stop calling each other by their real names entirely. "We don't even know what type of black triangle."

He did not want to tell her this was a face he recognized. "Tell me no and I'll put it back."

"You know I can't say no."

"Neither can I."

She held herself a moment before letting her arms drop. She wore the same face she had the night they had fled, the face she wore every time they heard bad news on the radio, or worse news on the radio, or news that was good for everybody but them. "Let's draw a bath."

The galvanized tub was attached to the cooking stove by a thick pipe, a thinner one underneath for drainage. They bathed there once a week in the hotter months, usually before church, nearly not at all in the winter.

Bertie carried in buckets of cold water to fill the tub. On his first trip, some sloshed onto his sock. He let his foot squish in his shoe as he returned to the pump for more, bucket after bucket. Sofie kept an eye on their guest, who had yet to properly stir.

"Breathing?" he asked every time as he came back in, adding to the tub.

She nodded and fed cold water down the young man's throat. She had already lit the stove, warming the bathwater as Bertie went. When Bertie had brought in enough bucketfuls for ten or so centimeters, they began the undressing delicately. His body was as divulging as the peek of collarbone Bertie had seen, shadow after shadow cast from bone to hollow like bruises. This body was not quite like the skeletons Bertie had seen dangling in the rooms of the Institut back in Berlin, but to see this still frightened him. In the difference of a minute, this fate could have been Bertie's.

Bertie and Sofie were quiet for a short while, the only sounds the gentle sloshing of water from the sponge and the ticking of the kuckuck clock in the sitting room just past the open-faced kitchen. The water in the bottom of the tub quickly grew gray and cloudy. Just when Bertie wondered if they should drain it all and start fresh, the man stirred. A small grunt, a flutter of the eyelids. And then suddenly, awareness as if he had just come up from drowning. His hand shot out, gripping onto Bertie's forearm, his eyes wide.

Bertie looked closer at those eyes, the recognition stronger now. He did not want to remember. He would not remember. The difference of one minute, the neglect that sprang from his own selfishness and fear.

He would finally start to make amends. He would not let the young man know, but he would make amends.

"It's alright," Bertie said with a calm voice. He thought a moment of his next words, for they were the kind of words that could never be taken back. But he was sure he knew him. "I'm a transvestite. I am Berthold Durchdenwald. And this is Sofie Hönig, my lover. We're called Goss and Ina Baumann here in Ulm."

The grip of their guest had loosened upon Bertie's wrist as soon as the word *transvestite* was uttered. "Me, too," came the worn and dusty voice. And then he took a moment, as if he could not remember. "Karl Fuchs."

"A pleasure, Karl. I'm going to get you some clothes and then we'll make you something to eat."

Karl nodded, finally releasing his grip from Bertie's arm and sinking into the water as if it were filled to the brim and still warm. Sofie brought the cup back to him and Karl took it into his own hands this time. He drank in loud mouthfuls until there was none left.

"Why were you still in those clothes?" Bertie asked. "Didn't the Allies liberate the camps weeks ago?"

Karl's voice lowered, as if using it suddenly tired him. "You haven't heard." He looked down at his wet hands. "Nobody's heard."

"Heard what?"

"The Allies." Karl picked at his fingers. "They sent all the pink triangles to jail. And all the black triangles that qualified the same."

Sofie suddenly stood, dripping sponge still in hand, as if she planned to do something. "What for?"

"To start the sentence for their crimes."

"That can't be true. They wouldn't do that." Bertie looked over at Sofie. "Would they?"

Sofie dropped the sponge and gathered Karl's clothes. "We need to burn these immediately."

Bertie nodded and began to tear up the camp wear. The fabric was so threadbare that he wrenched his arm backward with the first fistful. The rest took almost no strength at all. He took the scraps out to the fire pit and set the flame.

He stood with the flats of his palms against the small of his back, looking out across the farm as he made sure the clothing all took. Parts of the Alps were visible in the distance. The apple blossoms were beginning to show on their three trees at the far edge of their land, pollen spilling out as they blushed. The spiky white flowers of the wild garlic had also arrived, sprouting past the bushels of thick green leaves that coated their territory, stretching out from the forest. Bertie left those alone, for wild was wild, and he liked the carpet of greenery that licked his ankles. Their two hazelnut shrubs loomed naked and imposing near the garlic, closer to the forest edge, finally showing peeks of leafing. They would not be ready until fall, and they would likely produce poorly. Bertie swore he could already smell their earthy sweetness on the air.

But now, it all felt different. He thought about what Karl just said. When he was sure all the scraps had caught fire, he returned inside.

Sofie was finished washing Karl. She picked up the final bucket, still cold. "Sorry," she said simply before dumping it over his head. Karl closed his eyes against the cascade, but he did not seem to mind the cold. His shoulders slackened against the rush, head tilted toward it like the sun. He swallowed the water that trickled into his mouth. When it was over, Karl opened his eyes and gave a gentle puff of exhale, the small droplets glinting against the streaming sunlight before they fell in feathery plumes. Droplets clung to his dark lashes. Bertie knew he was being watched as he went up their single wheezing staircase.

He ignored the second bedroom, door always closed, bringing down some of his own clothes instead. More working trousers and his other flat-cap, a worn button-shirt. He held the bundle out to Karl, but as Karl stood and dried off, Bertie realized the young man was smaller than he was not just by many kilograms, but some centimeters as well. Bertie could barely get by on his own with the clothes of Opa, bigger and longer than he could comfortably work in. On Karl, they would look ridiculous. He would look suspicious.

"Wait," Bertie said, his voice flatter now. The thought sank his stomach. "I have others."

He went back upstairs, put away his own clothes in the main bedroom, and stood out in the small hallway. He rested his hand on the door of the second bedroom. Finally, he turned the knob. It was thicker in there, older and dusty, the only room they did not air out. Not since they had moved into the main bedroom. It was hell for Bertie to live in here before then, and he could not, had not, stepped inside it since. He opened the curtains; dust motes leaped off and fell to the floor. He squinted against the sunlight as if he had been left there in the darkness, too.

He did not like the room's quiet. The creaks of the floorboards sounded disrespectful, like laughing in church. He knew the noises, dredged up like an old memory, and they made him sad. He surveyed Gert's small room as he filled his lungs for a sigh. The single twin bed, his wardrobe, the small desk Gert studied at in his youth, even his old toy chest filled with glass marbles and wooden planes before he left for Berlin. His life before he met Bertie. The place where he was loved.

Bertie took a moment to release his breath, to gather himself before he opened the wardrobe. As the wooden hangers wobbled, the smells of Gert wafted out, compressed and ready to pounce, hitting Bertie hard. The beer drinking, the singing, the walks around the Tiergarten, the laughing, the times they fell asleep on each other, with each other, in Bertie's old apartment. He felt a pressure surge in his head and he crouched down in a single sob. He pressed the back of his hand against his mouth and nose to keep him from biting his tongue. The fingers of his other hand balanced him in his crouch, uncovering a streak of hardwood in the dust. He breathed through his own skin, the smell of dirty fingernails and apple blossoms and feed scraps, of chores just that morning before he saw Karl, before he had to go into this room.

He suddenly was not sure how long he was taking, how long poor Karl was standing naked and cold in the middle of the kitchen. He breathed twice more, deep, before removing his hand from his mouth. He forced his knees to straighten. He took things out of the wardrobe with as little thought as he could manage. Some trousers, a shirt, a pair of braces. Socks and shoes.

He left the bedroom door open as he left. Bertie knew what keeping someone in their home would mean.

Gert's clothes fit Karl much better. Bertie helped him dress as Sofie heated a cast-iron pan, the handle wrapped thick with old fabric and twine. They did not need to discuss as she fried all three eggs the chickens had laid that morning.

Bertie went down into the root cellar, the square grids of stone smelling of damp and dirt. It was notably cooler than the rest of their home. The potatoes he had harvested when they caught word of the War's end were there, alongside their cabbage and kohlrabi from early spring. Their onion bulbs were endless. He knew he should be grateful, but sometimes he was not. The onions never stopped. They split and split and kept growing from themselves. They were like a plague. He was long tired of the turnips and radishes of winter, the beets, some of the mushrooms left from the fall forage, and was glad they could soon move on to fresher things. The fiddlehead ferns and tender green onion stems were already long gone.

He fished through jars of pesto from their wild garlic and pulled out one of apple preserves. He returned to the kitchen and set Karl a plate as Sofie warmed a thick slice of stale bread. Karl sat at the table in his new clothes. He was on the bench side, his back to the open windows toward Ulm proper, staring at both of them silently as the breeze caressed his neck. Bertie was not sure if Karl was too tired or just did not know what to say. He worried he was being watched. He worried he was being remembered.

Bertie and Sofie loaded his plate. Karl thanked them many times until they both insisted he actually eat. Bertie watched quietly as Karl ate faster than he should have, barely chewing, but neither of them wanted to lecture him.

"Where did you come from?" Sofie finally asked.

Karl slowed his chewing. A dribble of yolk leaked from his mouth and he licked it away, glancing at the table before meeting her eye. "Dachau."

Bertie gave a slight jump, like he had been stuck with a pin. He willed himself to say nothing.

"You came all the way from Dachau?" Sofie said. "Isn't that over a day's walk without rest?"

"I've been so tired and staying out of sight that it took me two weeks to get this far." Karl suddenly looked confused. "It's been about two weeks since the War ended, right? I worry I lost count."

Sofie nodded.

"Were there others like us there?" The words spilled from Bertie, his resistance weak.

"Don't push him right now, Bertie."

"Did you come across anyone named—wait, wait, I have pictures..."

"Bertie."

But he was already kneeling to the potato boards, lifting the few he needed to pull out a burlap sack, smashing his finger between two of them in the process. He pushed aside his old work satchel from Berlin and removed a thick photo album from the sack. Returning to the table, he scraped Karl's plate to the side and slipped the album, opened to a page of photographs, before him. He pointed.

"Anyone here? Karsten? Gebhardt? Markus?"

"Bertie." Sofie's tone was twice the warning it had been before.

"Wait, wait." He was talking faster now, his breathing lighter. He flipped a page until he found a photo of a younger him sitting in a chair at the Eldorado, grinning widely as a smaller man sat in his lap, holding up a passport and laughing. "Him. Do you recognize him?" He could have sworn he saw a small spark light in Karl's eyes. A slight change in the way he held his jaw. He felt both hopeful and sick.

"Bertie—"

"His name is Gert Baumann." He was tripping over his own tongue now, his voice unnecessarily loud. "He—"

Sofie yanked the album from him so hard that Karl's plate almost crashed to the floor. Karl caught it with both hands, his face still as quiet and hidden as when Bertie had started.

Sofie clutched the album against her lap, her veined pianist hands sharp as claws. "Not. Now." She stared at him until he sat back down.

The quiet suddenly felt too much. Bertie bounced his leg beneath the table, his eyes flickering to the album as he opened and closed his hands in his lap. He felt like when the War had made him stop smoking.

Sofie turned her attention back to Karl. Her voice was gentler toward him. "How did you manage to get out?"

Karl slowly scraped the plate with his fork for the last dried flecks of yolk. He sucked on the tines. "I fled when they came."

"Who?"

"The Allies."

"Is it true?" Bertie stuck in again. "They're setting everyone but us free?"

Karl nodded slowly at the table, the fork still dangling from his mouth. He kept sucking on it like a nervous tic. "Anyone with a pink triangle was taken away immediately. All those with black triangles were cross-checked with the surviving Nazi records. If you qualified, you went, too. I ran while they were checking for mine."

Sofie clutched the album tighter in her lap. "And so you just . . . ran? They didn't shoot you?"

"The only difference I've seen between them so far is their style of murder. I was surprised when I made it past the grounds alive. That hadn't been my plan. I've been wandering ever since, hiding and stealing wherever I can." He glanced at Bertie before looking back at his plate. "I was going to steal from you, too. The last few farms either just harvested their latest crops or recently planted the new ones. Your neighbor had nothing. But then I saw your asparagus ferns." His thoughts seemed to trail off as his gaze wandered to the aged, upright piano in the sitting room before finally looking back at the pair of them. "I'm in Ulm?"

Sofie nodded. It was a full minute before anyone spoke again. "How old are you, Karl?"

It was a fair question. Men like him and Bertie were often difficult to pinpoint. Sofie sometimes joked about her jealousy that Bertie was a year older and yet looked at least fifteen younger.

Karl moved his mouth as if to answer with confidence, but then caught himself. Once more, his mind seemed to trip over the question. "What's the year?"

"Nineteen forty-five."

He licked his dry lips and Bertie got up to refill his water cup for him. Karl furrowed his brow, clearly trying to hide that he was counting on his fingers. They twitched one after the other in lines as his mouth faintly moved. When he came to his answer, his face weighed heavier than before. "I think I'm twenty-seven now."

Bertie spoke again in an attempt to make amends from earlier, to keep himself from asking what Karl had witnessed while inside Dachau. "You'll stay with us in the spare bedroom upstairs. We'll just need to keep you hidden until we know what's happening with the Allies."

He did not want to say that even when wearing Gert's clothes, Karl was not immediately convincing. His manner of speech, the way he carried himself, nothing seemed to be working for him. Before '33, it would have been less of a problem. But these days, being unconvincing put all of them in danger, especially if what Karl was saying was right.

Sofie glanced Bertie's way. They seemed to have the same thought. "We can't let anyone see you. Not yet."

"And perhaps when you're rested," Bertie said, "I can teach you how to transvest."

Karl placed the fork against his mouth, his bottom lip puffing slightly between the tines. He swallowed. "I am not a man exactly like that."

"I know, but being"—Bertie cast about for the proper word—"unassuming is our only choice."

"Or you could wear some of my things," Sofie added gently.

Karl put the fork back down on the plate, his eyes now to the table. "So we have to be who we're not in order to be who we are."

"I'm afraid so, yes." He knew Karl knew it was the truth, but also knew how much he did not want it to be true. "Even before, we only got what we got as long as we didn't draw attention to ourselves. If we were respectable, if we behaved like them, then we were rewarded. It surely would've gotten better over time, and some strides were being made, but..." It was not necessary to finish his thought.

"And if either of us were to be found out, it could put all of us in danger."

Sofie nodded. "Me by association, but yes. But once you've gotten used to it, you just need to do it outdoors, among other people. Otherwise, you can stay here and work on the farm."

Karl toyed with the fork, nudging it gently across his plate and back.

His brow flattened and his mouth twisted into a grimace of defeat. "What sorts of things would you teach me?"

Before Bertie could answer, a sound hit his ear. Across that late, quiet morning, slow footsteps scraped against the dirt path outside.

"Down!" he rasped. Karl ducked beneath the table before the command was even fully uttered. Frau Baer turned onto their path just as Karl's back disappeared from the open window. Small and stooped, she patted her fraying church hat atop her cottony hair. She looked as unpleasant as ever. Bertie never trusted a lick of sweetness from her.

Sofie angled her chair in front of where Karl crouched while Bertie answered the door, positioning himself to further block her view.

"Herr Baumann!" she said in her singsong way as he appeared. Her Deutsch had such a light accent that Bertie could never quite place it. He suspected she originally came from Austria. "Why weren't you at church?"

Neither he nor Sofie realized how much time had elapsed since they found Karl. "Oh!" He reminded himself to resonate his voice, to draw the breath from his stomach. He stood straighter. "I was feeling ill."

"But you've never missed church." Frau Baer attempted to peer over his shoulder, so Bertie angled himself further in the opening of the door to block her view. "You even hobbled in that time you twisted your ankle in a rabbit hole."

Squeezed between the door and the frame, he surely made a poor show of looking relaxed. "Yes, well—"

"You should be careful," she said. She leaned in slightly, as if intending to lower her voice, which she failed to do. "Appearances are everything, you know."

He thought about her words, how she always talked like this, something between a signal and a threat. He and Sofie had always concluded the latter. She had taken her flag down as quickly as they had. But that could mean anything. She was nosy, and nosy types were the ones looking to grab information.

"Indeed," he said. "Appearances are quite important. But I fear I must go now, Frau Baer. Must continue to rest. We thank you for your concern."

Frau Baer blocked the door with her fragile foot, and for a brief moment Bertie considered slamming the door on it, to hell with the consequences. "Quite something, the end of the War, isn't it?" It was the fourth time she posed the question to him. In the last two weeks, she had visited three times, forever unannounced, to ask the same thing.

"Why, yes. Yes, indeed it is."

She seemed to wait for more from him, but he did not give it. "What were you burning out back? So early to be handling debris, and on a Sunday no less. It smells like it may have been some sort of cloth?"

Bertie was unsure if this meant she had been sneaking around their property that morning. Perhaps it was something she had done before. Though, surely she would not have done so in her Sunday clothes. But if she had, perhaps she overheard them talking with Karl.

"Your cat let herself into my house again during our fresh-air time," he said after a pause, attempting to pull anger into his voice. "Keep her on your own property. And while I'm so unwell, too."

"How can one control a cat? And she's such a sweet thing. If she doesn't like you, it's your own doing."

Bertie opened his mouth to respond, to readily engage in their usual bicker, but she was not so easily taken off the scent. She ambled several paces to the side, craning around the corner of the house. Bertie was unsure what was wiser, to stay put or to stop her.

"It looks like your teacup is still outside," she finally said, coming back to him. "And a paper. It's like you suddenly abandoned everything."

"Yes." Bertie shuffled, wanting to remove himself from the door immediately. "Well, that was when I suddenly took ill and had to lie down."

"But—"

"Oh! Frau Baer!" Sofie called cheerfully from behind, squeezing through the sliver of open door to appear out in front. "I didn't know you came calling!" She smiled wide. "Thank you so much for coming to check on Goss! But I'm afraid I must insist he return to bed. He's doing much better and I intend for him to stay that way. You know how men are!"

Frau Baer's body slumped lower than its usual stoop at these words, at the indication toward her own late husband and his illness. It sucked the wind from her.

"Indeed." Her look lingered at the pair of them before she finally nudged her chin toward the front of the door itself. "It would appear you've received an order, too."

Bertie frowned and looked at the door as Frau Baer turned away and down their dirt road. He ripped the folded paper that had been nailed to their door. So that explained the knocking he thought he heard earlier before he found Karl.

They both went back inside and closed the door. Bertie watched through the window to ensure Frau Baer was indeed walking home instead of around to the back of their land. Sofie turned to the table.

"You said you went by her farm first?" she whispered.

Karl remained beneath the table, waiting for a signal from Bertie. "Yes."

"Did she see you?"

"I don't think so."

When Frau Baer disappeared down the road, Bertie gave a small twirl of his wrist near his waist and Karl came out and stood.

"How do you know for sure she didn't see you?" Sofie asked.

Karl shrugged. "I can't." He sat back down at the table. "Why is she so suspicious of you?"

"We took the names of the couple who lived here," Sofie said. "We hoped it would hide any question that the farm was ours. And we're so far on the outskirts of Ulm, only one person would've known."

"Frau Baer."

Sofie nodded. "Honestly, we didn't think she would live for so long. It was a chance we took."

"So why has she never turned you in? Why does she play along?"

She paused. "We still don't know."

As they continued to talk, Bertie opened the piece of paper. It was in English, but that was not what slowed his reading. He read it once, paled, and read it a second time. On his third time, he knew that what he was seeing was true.

Mr. and Mrs. Goss Baumann,

By order of the United States of America, you are hereby notified to report to the Oberer Kuhberg camp on the first of June to begin your compulsory labor. You will work no less than twelve hours each day, at which point you may return home. Any person who does not report for duty will be imprisoned until deemed suitable for work.

—Lt. William Ward, United States Army

It all ran through his mind at once: They would be found out in the camps, surely. Even if they both managed to be unassuming the entire time. And then there was the matter of Karl, who, with his inability to transvest, had suddenly become an even heavier risk than earlier that morning. They could not subject him to the camps again. They would not make him go back. Neither would they end up in a camp themselves after all they had done to avoid one. They had to flee. That boat in Amsterdam was leaving for New York in three weeks, but they needed papers, and they needed reason to be let into Amerika. These were things they could never get. They could not stay, and they could not leave.

"Sofie," he said simply. He handed over the order for her to read. "Things have just become quite difficult."

2 • Berlin, 1932

IT WAS EARLY WINTER, NOT FAR INTO DECEMBER, WHEN Bertie walked to the Eldorado his first evening out since his recovery. The club was on the corner of Motzstraße and Kalckreuthstraße, in the Nollendorfkiez neighborhood of the Schöneberg district of Berlin, within walking distance of his apartment.

In that winter chill, Berliners clutched their overcoats up to their chins, their hatted heads ducking into their collars as they rushed to wherever they wanted to go. They crossed the streets however and whenever they wished, the autos stopping, honking, starting, swerving between each daredevil dash, every cocksure stride. It was an intimate dance that left the ausländers bewildered and easy to spot in their unfamiliarity.

The city's drone pierced with enthusiastic life: an excited greeting, a whiny horn, a laugh, a strangled chug from an auto, a shout from a protestor, the rattle-rattle-rattle of the collection boxes from the brownshirts. Bertie ignored one of them as he walked past. They seemed to be popping up everywhere with each passing day, becoming more aggressive, especially since they had lost two million votes and thirty-four seats in the November election. With their slip, it seemed, they were shoving their collection boxes into the faces of people on every corner, as if their open palms would smooth over their angst-riddled shouting and luxurious promises built on the backs of scapegoats. They were just streetcorner spinners with uniforms.

The streetlamps dripped a pale yellow against the night sky, polishing the wet cobblestones. The cobblestones were always wet at night; Bertie did not know why, as if it rained like clockwork and he always missed it. The lamplights were blurry suns in the haze of smoke and exhaust, coughing from auto pipes, billowing from sewer grates, drooling from manholes. The thin fog parted and curled as people sliced through, as autos turned a corner, headlights winking. It melted upon all of them, invisible in the daytime, and Bertie found it as comforting as a blanket. You are here, the city said, a world within a world. And at night, you can be whatever you want to be.

Past the earthy tobacco burning from his lips, he smelled it all: the damp stone, the auto fumes, the thick odors of sauerbraten and kartoffelpuffer billowing cleverly from lokals. It made him hungry, all the sweet gravies and fried oils, potatoes and breading. The open businesses shone bright and white from their display windows.

He could see the lights of the club before its dark brown walls in the evening haze, darker and more alluring than the rest of the wide intersection. ELDORADO, it declared from the front of its diagonal cut, its neon red bleeding onto the street. Bright light spilled out of the windows of all five stories, those on the ground floor plastered with posters for privacy and enticement. Balconies graced both sides of the higher levels as the building fanned out from its corner like a flock of geese. A long strip of mural wrapped itself around the east side between the ground and first floors: people holding banners, dancing, and having a good time.

Under the neon buzz of ELDORADO were sturdy cutouts. A young woman with a dark bob smiled coyly behind a translucent folding fan, a large question mark printed upon it. Beneath her, just above the doors, were the faces of a man and woman on the left and right, his dark hair slicked back, her blond waves ending just past her ears, both wearing gloss and shadow, both grinning and winking. HIER IST'S RICHTIG! was the proclamation between them. Here it's right.

The slogan repeated itself directly beneath, wedged into the thin strip of the overhang, to make sure you saw, to make sure you did not forget. For anything worthwhile was also worth repeating.

Bertie glanced at the little kiosk nailed to the left side of the doors, full of advertisements and pamphlets and show schedules. Sometimes he refilled material from the Institut there himself. It looked fit to burst for the moment, with used copies of papers and journals by the third sex from all over Berlin.

He squinted as he looked for a copy of the latest *Das 3. Geschlecht*, but of course it was the only one not in stock. He would have to buy a copy at the newspaper stand tomorrow on his way to work.

He checked to make sure his transvestite card was still safe in his jacket pocket and pushed against the metal bar of one of the double doors, the windows shrouded with curtains. The noise of life hit him instantly.

The main room was a grand hall with high ceilings, arched windows hanging above the long single balcony that overlooked the dancing area. A parkett of wood squares both light and dark scraped beneath his feet, still shiny at the edges. The center had grown scratched and dull over the years from dance.

But the dance area was as empty as ever these days given the recent new laws, surrounded by its usual little tables, naked and circular, sitting four if you liked one another. All of them were full with the stepchildren of nature.

A small stage graced the far end, elevated to the height of a man, an upright piano settled directly before it upon the floor. The small tables were crowded there, chairs scraping into one another. Drunken apologies were often made.

The stage was predictably bare now, just the teases of pulleys and curtains up high, revealing a tragic belly of mediocrity. There was no show, no table linens, just the strums of talk and laughter bouncing off the grand walls, the music no more than the comfort of the third sex settled within itself.

Since the Inflation and the Crash, the Eldorado was more dependent on tourists. They mostly came from England and France, Scandinavia and Italy. But most especially Amerika. The Amerikan men in particular looked for loose boys and fast drugs, or maybe it was the other way around. The women in furs just wanted to try cocaine.

It was an understanding in silence, when the normally sexed arrived.

Especially if they had the stink of money. People would jump up and start dancing, purposely woman to woman, man to man. The most gleefully dressed—usually someone with the soul of a woman—would get on the stage and would sing and dance while someone else hopped to the piano with the first jaunty tune to come to their head. Sometimes the performer onstage did not know the tune and faked their way through; sometimes the player did not even know the tune and faked likewise. Sometimes neither could meet in agreement and they would trip their way together through an unintended duel. The wild applause of the normally sexed was often underscored by the stifled grins of the regular patrons.

If a band was lazing about, they would get to their corner and strike up to the beat of the dancers, a new competition of noise that only added to the image of a grand time for wild stories. It was always jazz.

Zigarette boys and girls would come out of places unknown, walking directly to the rich tables with their flirtations and trays. If fellow patrons moved fast enough, table linens were spread, creased at the folds and smelling somewhere between soap and storage. Linens were set up only when the normally sexed arrived, and such folks never seemed to notice that only their tables got them.

By the looks of things, there were no ausländers yet that night, and likely there would not be. Nobody wanted to tour or travel or gawk in the middle of a workweek. For stories could be told most deliciously only over the weekend, and those stories had to be fresh.

Bertie preferred it this way. He did not appreciate the normally sexed categorizing his own as part of sightseeing. A topic for colorful stories back home, as if the visitors had been on safari, narrowly surviving animals in their natural habitat in acts of heroism they had willingly put themselves into. Sometimes, when he had had a bit much to drink, he wanted to go over to them and ask: Had they never seen joy?

He checked his coat and got a beer for himself, walking across the grand room to the congested stage area. He found his table of four, making them five. It was just as well with Gert forever running around and Markus forever fidgeting with his camera. The place smelled of beer and cigarette smoke, the sweat of bodies and harsh perfume.

His friends rapped their knuckles against the table at his arrival, and he gave a bashful wave and smile, ducking his head a little when he saw the noise had caught the attention of a few neighboring tables, including one with a certain young woman. His nerves failed to meet her gaze once again, and Gebhardt and Karsten shifted their glass mugs over as Bertie squeezed in. Before he could place down his own mug, a painful flash took his eyes. He grunted with a snap of his head like he had been hit. He felt the lukewarm dribble of beer slide down his knuckles as he pinched the bridge of his nose with his other hand.

"Scheiße, Markus."

"Sorry." Markus tucked his chin as he got his camera ready once more, a pleased little grin on his lips. He liked to commemorate everything, and that certainly included the return of Bertie. He hissed and snapped his wrist when he touched the bulb and proceeded to make a show sucking air through his teeth as he unscrewed the flashbulb in short bursts with his fingertips. He opened his case for another.

They were doing alright for a country torn to pieces. Poverty had bloomed alongside the immediate Inflation. Wheelbarrows full of marks could not buy a newspaper. Fortunes were lost, the poor got poorer, and the wealth gap that managed to remain grew wider. People became more violent and desperate, and by '23, it took one trillion marks to equal one Amerikan dollar. Bertie had managed to survive because Doktor Magnus Hirschfeld had liked the look of him and the insight he could provide, and gave him a job as his assistant at his new Institut für Sexualwissenschaft. What Bertie could not get through his modest salary, he got through trade. He most often would expose himself in the slaughter room of the local butcher in exchange for meat.

When the Crash happened in '29, Deutschland collapsed alongside the United States. Bertie was saved because he had never invested his life into those stocks, but plenty of people even poorer and more desperate than himself were not as lucky. Some of the rich who had invested everything took their own lives in the shock of the resulting days. Most people had been tricked into investing whatever they had in Amerikan stock, no matter how much or little money they possessed.

And so here they were, hurting again, though in some ways not as bad as the last time. The Deutsch hardiness proved itself once more, and the country was already showing signs of improvement just these few years later. Everybody found work where they could. Karsten picked maggots out by hand at a slaughterhouse, giving his friends discounts and information on availability whenever he could. Gebhardt sold decks of cocaine to ausländers the moment they walked through the door, sometimes cigarettes with a little extra kick, and always had something on hand for the rest of them. Bertie had powdered his nose more than once, maybe a handful of times, and Gert had found it only slightly more interesting than he had.

Markus wanted to do more with photography, but he at least had a job as a gaffer at a local theater on play nights. When the theater showed films, he always had tickets for the rest of his friends, particularly for the invert and transvestite films. Old or new, silent or sound, they did not care as long as it nodded toward their kind. Especially trouser roles, even if the endings or morals were not always what they wanted. They were eagerly anticipating the release of *Viktor und Viktoria* next year.

Doktor Hirschfeld had helped create *Anders als die Andern* back in 1919, the first homosexual-positive film, but it was banned soon after release. Doktor Hirschfeld managed to argue it was educational, however, and at least was granted permission to show it within his own Institut. It was during one of those showings that Bertie and Gert had met Markus, Gebhardt, and Karsten, and their small group had formed. They since dedicated themselves to meeting a few nights a week to drink and talk. The Eldorado was their favorite spot because it welcomed transvestites without being exclusively for women.

There were clubs and meeting spots all over Berlin for what seemed every type of the third sex. Half the time Bertie could not name all the ones still open despite the latest laws. There were events and shows and parties given frequently by the Transvestite Association D'Eon, the Deutscher Freundschaftsverband, the Bund für Menschenrecht, and his own Institut für Sexualwissenschaft. But out of all of them, the Eldorado was his home. And now, he was back among his friends, and could just sit and have a beer.

"Did you hear Gert's news?" Gebhardt drawled, his pupils suggesting that he may have already sampled his own wares with the lack of ausländers coming in.

Gert suddenly came out of nowhere, flying into Bertie so hard he nearly knocked them both to the floor. He wrapped his arms around Bertie's neck, half-sitting on his lap. "Did you hear my news?!"

Bertie loosened his joints at the sight of him. Gert was what would happen if a scamp fell in love with a pixie. A gentle face with a wicked smile, with all the compact charm of a farm boy. He was still wearing his dark work trousers and gray knit sweater, fraying at the collar and stubbornly clutching a few stray woodchips. His flat-cap was already missing, his sideswept puff of wavy blond hair making him look centimeters taller in his tiny frame. Bertie was never quite sure how he managed to stuff it all beneath his hat.

Gert mostly made his way as a carpenter's assistant, though he sometimes made extra on the side—he claimed accidentally so—when he would bird at Noster's Cottage, an invert pub near the working-class district of Hallesches Tor. The more knowledgeable ausländers were known to stop through, particularly Amerikans. They were quite aware of his biologic type, but this seemed the opposite of a deterrent for many of them. They affectionately called him Dreilochhengst. The three-holed stallion.

He never visited the Cottage without leaving with at least two good stories. And if tourists happened to offer him money for being adorable, who was he to deny them? He was going to have his fun either way. Bertie had gone with him on multiple occasions, and while he, too, had found his fun, he mostly preferred people he knew rather than those he did not.

Gert had looked after Bertie during his first two weeks of recovery. When it seemed Bertie was able to care for himself as long as things were left at elbow-level, Gert still visited each evening for an hour of company. It was only the last week that Gert had finally started to leave him alone for longer stretches of time. Bertie was admittedly surprised that Gert could have any sort of news that he would not have heard first.

By the smell of his breath and the flush in his face, he knew Gert was already drunk. His heart warmed. "I already know about your American companion." Bertie had not met Roy yet, but that was partially his own doing. The man had finally returned to Deutschland while Bertie was recovering, and Bertie had not wanted to meet him in such an intimate state.

"Yes, but look!" Gert dug into the inside pocket of his jacket and pulled out a passport, opening it up to a rubber-stamped page. "It's official! I'm a citizen!"

Bertie tried to keep the grin on his face, to show Gert excitement, but it was slipping between his fingers like sand. He knew this was coming, he knew it was in the works. He had helped Gert with the paperwork himself. But now that it was real, all he could think about was himself. And it made him feel terrible.

"That's wonderful!" he said.

"Oh, Bertie," Gert said, resting his face into the crook of his neck. "I'm never going to *leave* leave. It just makes it easier to go back and forth with Roy, especially for men like us. As an American citizen, I can stay in America for as long as I want. And as a former German citizen, I can stay in Germany for as long as I want."

"Well which one do you want more?" Bertie had meant it as a joke to ease the tension, but he realized he meant it more than intended.

Gert grabbed both sides of his face and kissed his forehead. "It's not perfect. But we'll get used to it."

Bertie sighed. "You won't have to wear a skirt anymore when you travel?"

"I won't have to wear a skirt anymore when I travel."

Bertie kissed his forehead back. "Then it was worth it."

"Hey, Gert!" Markus called out. "Hold it up!"

Gert grinned his biggest grin. Still on Bertie's lap, he held up his passport to the citizenship page, his other arm around Bertie's shoulders. Bertie likewise smiled, more genuinely this time, one arm around Gert's waist, the other draped across his legs. They squeezed each other, their heads touching.

The spark of light seared their eyes and Bertie grunted like always.

A whiff of burning filament passed by. Gert tucked his passport away, using his other hand to rub the spots out of his eyes.

"Nobody do anything else important tonight," Markus said, hissing through his teeth as he unscrewed the hot flash. "I'm already out of bulbs."

* * *

"To Berthold!" Gert shouted for the seventh time that night, standing his small frame up atop his chair. "May his scars always give him pride!"

And for the seventh time, they all cheered so loud that the room gave shouts of "Prost!" on happy instinct.

"To Gert!" Bertie replied, a bit too wobbly now to stand. "May his go just as smoothly!" He gulped from his mug and bopped it down in the sticky rings of glasses gone by.

Gert sat back down with a large smile. Although he did well pretending to hold his beer, the flush across his nose gave him away. "I can't believe it's just one more month! Do you think it'll go well, Bertie?"

Bertie took a drag and tapped the ash into a tin tray. "They've been doing surgeries for us for almost thirty years now. You'll be just fine." One of the perks Bertie got from his job was easier access to the medical interventions. He had already used his position with Doktor Hirschfeld to fast-track the applications for name changes and transvestite cards for his friends, and now Gert was next in line for a surgery. It usually cost five hundred marks, but just like with himself, he had managed to convince the Institut to waive the fee.

"I'm so glad you've done it already," Gert said. "It makes it less frightening."

"Does Dr. Hirschfeld do it himself?" Gebhardt blurted. He had breathed enough snow by this point that he was only partially following the conversation.

Karsten shook his head. "He's not a surgeon."

Gebhardt suddenly squinted at Bertie. "Did you go back to work already? You're pretty dressed up for someone to just spill beer on."

Bertie smoothed his palm down his striped tie and black shirt. His braces were white, and he had painstakingly polished his dark shoes, which he paired with his gray trousers and suit jacket, his homburg hat atop his slicked-back hair. It was the most fashionable attire he owned. "Not until tomorrow. I've just been cooped up for so long and this is my first real night out." He tried not to let his eyes flicker to the young woman some tables away. He was certain Gert caught him. Gert caught everything.

"She's been asking after you," he said.

Bertie felt his face warm, and he tried to hide his smile. "She did not."

"No, she really did! She came over last week and asked where you'd gone. She wanted to know if you were coming back."

Markus craned his neck. "The blond one over there? She plays the piano sometimes during the silent films at the theater. You should talk to her. She seems nice."

"And is hot stuff," Karstan said.

"Yes, and is hot stuff."

As if feeling the conversation about her, she looked over from her own table of friends. She and Bertie caught eyes and she gave the smallest smile. He had always been too shy to approach her, but now with feeling a new home in his body and a belly full of beer, he got up.

"Remember to enunciate!" Karsten called after him, and the table laughed.

Like a proper Berliner, Bertie slurred his words and chopped off syllables. He overpronounced some letters, mispronounced others, and threw away whatever was left. He had no concern for grammar. His friends teased that he sounded both in a hurry and drunk, perpetually pissed by everything in even his softest voice.

"You're destined to be an old man yelling at courtyard children," Gert once concluded.

Bertie responded that if he talked like the big city, then Gert sounded like a cow town.

Bertie could clean it up when he wanted. He just did not want to. But now, he worried the woman across the room would find his Berliner dialect rude or dumb or both. So he cleaned it up.

He weaved himself around people and tables, thrice knocking into one or the other and twice remembering to apologize. She rose as he arrived, standing maybe five centimeters taller than him in her flats. He worried this would repel her.

"I've had a lot to drink," Bertie said by way of introduction. "So if I'm misunderstanding you, I'm very sorry."

Her friends shared something between a giggle and a laugh among themselves, but she smiled so wide that her cheeks dimpled. "You're charming even when you're not. Have you been out of town?"

She wore her hair in a curly blond bob that stopped just shy of her jawline, the hint of her nape exposed in the back. A slight frizz made it poof on the sides. She kept the swoop out of her face on the left side with two barrettes, shaped like three interlocked silver diamonds. Her brows were darkened with pencil, pink placed upon her eyelids and edged with silver. She had given her lips a dusty rose that weakened him when she smiled. A single freckle teased just beneath her right cheekbone. She was daring enough to wear slacks, a wide-legged and high-waisted black with white button fasteners on the side. Her white-buttoned shirt was a deep peacock blue, gathered at the cuffs and tucked in at the waist.

Bertie was not quite sure how she could be presumably unattached, and if so, why she would talk to the likes of him.

He shook his head, offering her a cigarette from his emerald-green pack of Ecksteins. "Surgery."

"Oh! I'm so sorry!"

"No, no, a good surgery!"

An understanding appeared on her face. "Oh, I heard about that when I visited the Institute for Sexual Science!"

"Yes! I work there!"

"Really?! Which part?!"

"I'm assistant to Dr. Magnus Hirschfeld himself!"

"Really?!"

"Yes!"

Bertie was not sure how they had started shouting into each other's faces. He realized from the flush in her cheeks that perhaps she had indulged in a few drinks herself. He took a moment to regain his breath, pulling out his lighter as he thought of something gentlemanly to say. "It was nice of you to ask after me."

She stopped before her cigarette hit the flame cupped in his hands. Her smile thinned slightly, her brows giving a small, polite wrinkle. "What?"

Bertie stared at her a moment before heat surged through his face. "Please excuse me while I go kill my best friend."

"Oh please don't go," she said as she caught him at the crook of his arm. "I'm glad you came over. And I like that you didn't find it threatening when you thought I'd made the first move."

Bertie faced her again, the embarrassment still hot in his cheeks. "Honestly, I was relieved."

"I don't know what the rules are yet. I used to only go to the Toppkeller. Until they closed."

His shoulders sank a little at this. "Oh."

"Please don't misunderstand me," she said quickly. "I like men, too. I just meant I didn't want you to think I was rude."

"You're not rude." The beer parted within him enough to remember he had yet to introduce himself. He held out his hand. "Berthold Durchdenwald." He slightly shrugged. Mentioning his name suddenly made him more aware of himself, self-conscious of the fact that there was finally nothing left to change. "Bertie."

"Durchdenwald. That's uncommon."

"I gave it to myself." It was not that he did not love his parents, but rather he had long become a different person since last knowing them.

She took and held his hand rather than shaking it. "Sofie Hönig."

The warmth of her ran up his arm, and he tried to keep his wits about him as the floor opened beneath his feet. "And what is it you want to do in the world, Fräulein Sofie Hönig?"

"I have an interest in worker's rights and take odd jobs here and there, but I'd really love to teach piano."

"You enjoy playing?"

She gave a polite shrug. She had yet to let go of his hand. "I really do. And I enjoy helping people. I believe music can heal. And you?"

"I certainly could believe that, yes."

She smiled wide again. "No, I meant what kind of life do you hope to live?"

"I'm quite close to already living it." He meant in relation to his job and friends and body, but her blush indicated she took it as a suggestion toward her presence. He was proud of himself for his accidental smoothness. "If it's not too forward, I would enjoy the chance to talk with you sometime in a quieter place and with a more sober brain."

She grinned again, finally shaking his hand like they had made a deal. "I would like that, too. But will you promise me something?"

"Anything."

"Don't try to hide your accent. I think it's cute."

Of all the words to describe it, *cute* was not one he would have ever thought. "You don't think it sounds, I don't know, low-class?"

She shook her head. "I like how comfortable you are with yourself. You don't hide anything." She tugged on the arm of his jacket then, biting her bottom lip, and Bertie was quite certain now she had had many drinks. Part of him wondered if she would have anything to do with him by the next time they met.

"Oh please," she said, "say something in full Berlin."

Bertie tongued his cheek a moment in a smile. If he could have only this moment, then he would at least have this moment. "Icke? Na, as pretty of a schnieke ische you are, we seem to've had too much pee lemonade tonight, wa?"

Sofie clapped her hands. "That's it! I love it!"

"Everyone!" Gert called out to the entire room. For someone so small, his voice was a force. He muddled his way to the empty stage, and with the fresh beer in his fist, Bertie was certain the alcohol had finally hit him like a brick. "Everyone!"

The room quieted as they all turned to Gert. It took him three tries and a shove under his backside from the nearest stranger, but eventually he made it onto the stage. "Everyone! I want to make an official toast—"

"Oh no," Bertie groaned, covering half of his face.

Sofie tugged on his jacket once more, laughing as she looked at Gert. "He yours?"

"—to one of my dearest, the one who has made me most happy to be myself—"

"Never seen him before in my life," Bertie replied.

"—Berthold Durchdenwald—"

"He seems sweet," Sofie said.

"—who has, quite recently, conveniently misplaced his breasts!"

There was an uproar of cheer at this, mugs and glasses held high in the air across the large room. Everyone rapped their knuckles in a rolling drum of applause. The noise was so loud that Bertie felt his eardrums rattle. His laugh was lost within it.

Gert raised his own glass. "Prost, Bertie, prost! I love you!"

"Prost!" came the roar from the crowd, mugs now tipping for a mouthful.

Gert downed his glass in one breath. "And now," he said, placing his foam-tickled mug by his feet upon the stage, "a song!"

There was another cheer around the room as knuckles rippled across tables.

"What shall it be?" Gert teased, cupping his ear as if to better hear the answers.

"'Das Lila Lied'!" the call resounded from at least a dozen spots at once.

"What's that?"

"'Das Lila Lied'!" came the cry again, louder this time with all the might of a singular force.

"Oh, alright," Gert said. "If we insist on something new!" Some more laughter sprang from this. "Who would like to play the piano?"

Several hands shot up, but Bertie made a scene of pointing at Sofie and grinning.

Sofie gasped and gave him a playful smack on the shoulder. "How dare you!"

"What? Now everyone will know how good you are and pay you to teach them."

Gert immediately took notice of Bertie and grinned at Sofie. "Yes you, Fräulein! Please come up!"

To the cheering of all, Sofie rolled her eyes with a smile before walking to the foot of the stage just below Gert. She sat at the piano. Bertie left Sofie's friends to their joyful laughter and returned to his table where Karsten and Markus had their eyes fixed to the stage. Gebhardt had since fallen asleep upon his own arms.

Sofie and Gert exchanged a cue, and Sofie began to play the introduction. She was boisterous on the keys, expertly loud as she announced the jaunty foxtrot pace. While Bertie had always loved when a full band was around to play the song, Sofie could certainly put them in the shade as a solo player. He felt the warmth begin to fill him again as he witnessed the full-throated pride she had for their anthem.

Gert began the first verse, though he was soon joined by many others from around the room. When the song rounded to its slowed chorus, the room suddenly grew quite loud. For even the drunkest of them knew the lyrics by then, however slurred they may be. Their contributions lessened into the second verse as some of the more alcohol-riddled folks could not remember the correct words.

But as they rounded back to the chorus, Gert got off the stage, still singing, and made his way toward Bertie, who lit a fresh cigarette as if this would somehow stop the inevitable from happening. Gert pulled him to his feet and onto the stage. He protested as the rest of them laughed. Sofie glanced up from the keys, grinning that wide grin of hers, and as Gert put his arm around him, Bertie decided to lose himself in the moment. Their anthem pounded in his ears, the words like a declaration of might, the joy and laughter filling him.

Sofie finished the final notes in a flourish. The crowd cheered, some getting to their feet. Sofie joined them onstage, hand in hand, and took an uncoordinated bow. Gert faltered and knocked into Bertie. The two of them fell to the ground in a heap. Sofie clapped and laughed along with the crowd.

* * *

Bertie and Gert staggered home, wrapped shoulder to shoulder within one another, slurring "Das Lila Lied" at a medium volume. It was only just past the twenty-second hour. The clubs usually did not get going until two in the morning, midnight at the earliest. They used to stay out as late as three or four, sometimes through to six before going home to wash up, nap for thirty minutes, and get ready for work. But the Catholic policies of the new Papen government had implemented in July their "extensive campaign against Berlin's depraved nightlife," including "all amusements with dancing of a homosexual nature." The twenty-second hour was a curfew now for all related bars, clubs, and dance halls. Then two months ago in October, the Chief of Police ordered a ban on third sex dancing in public.

It was frustrating at first, the curfew. But now all it meant was they drank the same amount of beer in a third of the time.

The two of them repeatedly forgot what they were doing as they walked to Bertie's apartment in the northern section of Schöneberg. It had snowed while they were inside, and the thin coating of white proved slippery. They lost their footing more than once on the uneven cobblestones, nearly going down if they were not already holding themselves up. They continued to laugh, making quite the ruckus as they fought the road, the curb of the sidewalk too much effort to climb. The lamplights still smiled like yellow orbs, and the cold bit just enough to feel on their cheeks, but the dusting of snow had sucked away all the usual exhaust and smoke. The stars looked clean and friendly.

"Why Gert?" Bertie asked.

"What?"

"Why did you choose Gert instead of Gerd? Everybody chooses Gerd."

"That's exactly why."

Bertie slipped a little, his free arm arcing toward the sky, and shifted more of his weight on Gert until he righted himself. "But there's plenty of Gerts, too."

"But this way, we can always be Gert 'n' Bert."

"Nobody calls me Bert."

"But if they did, we'd be Gert 'n' Bert."

"I've never gone by Bert in my life."

Gert poked him in the shoulder. "You will when I say you will."

He walked into a trash can and Bertie started laughing, the sound of the tin lid hitting the ground echoing down the quiet street. Gert laughed, too, until the two of them were shushing each other quite loudly.

"What's going on here?" a voice boomed, shooting through their fun and causing them to stand more upright. They ceased moving as an officer approached. "What are you two doing out so late? You're disturbing the residents."

Gert started to giggle again, and the officer shined his flashlight into both of their faces, back and forth. Gert stopped laughing and squinted against the harsh light. The man took in their close embrace. Bertie felt the beer settle into his feet as he saw the officer reading them. It was a terrible place to be caught between, those two laws. If they were not found in violation of §175, a sexual offense of intercourse between men, then they would automatically be at the mercy of §183, a sexual offense of public indecency by crossdressing. The only real difference was how much time they could spend in prison if Bertie did not gather his wits. Six months if §175, one year if §183.

"Ociffer," he said. He realized it was not coming out right and tried again. "Oriffcer. We have . . . have . . . ähm . . ." He thought hard a moment. "Cards!"

"Cards?" the officer asked.

Gert nodded with a big grin.

"Yes," Bertie said. "Travesh . . . tratish . . . transveshesit cards."

"What?"

"Hirschfeld!" Bertie suddenly shouted, quite pleased with himself for managing to get a word out correctly.

Understanding dawned on the officer. "You have transvestite cards from Magnus Hirschfeld? The doctor?"

"Yes!" Bertie said, increasingly happy with their conversation. "We can show you."

They both reached into the inner pockets of their jackets and brought out their slips of paper, both folded in half and getting more worn around the edges with each passing day. They handed them to the officer, Bertie's card on top. It was signed and dated with a picture of him from the waist up, dressed as himself, looking directly into the camera with a serious face. It was taken at the Institut as part of the agreement Doktor Hirschfeld continued with the police. Stamped in purple, inked with black, the message was brief:

The worker Berthold Durchdenwald, 30.8.1898 Berlin born, residing in Schöneberg Nollendorfstraße 17, is here known as wearing men's clothes.
—Kriminalkommissar

The officer was silent a moment. "You're right down the street. And where are you coming from?"

Bertie and Gert both pointed behind themselves, necks craning. The red neon of the Eldorado could still be seen in the distance. Bertie lived a five-minute walk from the club. He could not remember if they had walked in circles for triple that time tonight or were just quite successful at being loud. The beer in him wanted to laugh, but his last bits of sense made him clamp down on his lips.

"We're going directly home, Herr Polizei."

Gert cackled in two short bursts at the name, burying his face into Bertie's jacket to get himself to stop, biting the fabric. He took in a deep breath through his nose before standing back upright.

"Do that," the officer said, handing them both back their cards. "There are some brownshirts skulking around looking for trouble. And I don't want to hear another word out of you, or I'll bring you both in for disturbing the peace."

Gert saluted dramatically.

Bertie chuckled out of relief. "Thank you occifer . . . orrifcer . . . erri—"

"Just go."

The two of them returned to staggering down the street, quieter now as they linked their arms back around each other's shoulders.

"That was the first time I got to use my card!" Gert shouted into his ear. Bertie shushed him as they walked down the right side of the tree-lined median, the branches bare and clutched for the winter, the light brown bark of their tall trunks stripping away to patches of white. The buildings were the same on either side, long lines of red brick covered in lime and cement, styled with white stucco that had grayed over the decades. The street was once a place for the rich, but as the years went by and Inflation set in, many of the landlords rented to whoever would take those apartments. Bertie managed to snag one with the help of Doktor Hirschfeld, a particularly small space that likely had been for a servant or two.

Bertie fumbled with his keys, dropped them twice in the thin snow, and barely felt the cold melt on his fingers as he finally succeeded in his task at the thick double doors.

They went up the stairs, their hard shoes clacking more than they needed to. Bertie's small apartment faced the backside and was four flights up, but at least it was one floor less than dealing with roof issues. He unlocked the heavy door.

He flicked on the switch and an overhead bulb came to life in a slight hum, further prickling the unnecessary heat already smothering him like an old blanket.

"Did I tell you," Gert said, his voice finally an acceptable volume, though his words still sounded like unbaked bread, "that I finally sent enough for Oma and Opa to get electricity? They're going to have an indoor toilet and everything. One of the perks of living near a city center as large as Ulm."

"They still arriving tomorrow?" He was sure Gert was nodding behind him. He remembered how much angst Gert had felt for them when the Hinterkaifeck murders happened in '22, though that had been over a hundred kilometers away. "It'll be nice to finally meet them."

The mention of plumbing reminded his bladder that he wanted to use the bathroom, but it was at the other end of the hallway and he did not have the energy to leave the apartment after he had just succeeded getting into it.

His space was two rooms separated by an old linen curtain in a doorway. The main area contained a hat rack and coat hanger by the heavy door. There was a square table for two in the center of the room, a few lightened circles in its finish from watermarks. A small woodstove in the corner was decorated on either side with shelves of spices and plates for four. A dry sink with washbasin followed, a wrinkled hand towel flopped over the little rack, his razor and lather brush dried and tucked away. He had set up his small desk as close to the window as he could, opposite the door, attempting to overlook the narrow stone courtyard four flights down. The radiator was otherwise in the way. It clanged terribly in the winter, was clanging right now. He opened the window to dispel some of its unbearable heat and fill his lungs with the crisp sting of outside. His laundry, long since dried, dangled low across the center of the room from a piece of twine.

Behind the curtained doorway was the bedroom, barely fitting a three-quarter bed and a small wardrobe. Two mismatched nightstands wedged themselves into the corners on either side. Bertie often banged his elbow on one of them in the night. The single other window overlooked the same courtyard, the smells of fires burned by the less fortunate often wafting up to him while he slept. He could not sleep without the windows open.

Both rooms had the same wallpaper, beginning to curl in places, a pattern of tiny blue flowers. Both were littered with papers and books, some for pleasure, some for work that he took home in his leather work satchel. On the hardwood floor and on available surfaces and anywhere else they seemed ready to topple or spill. It was an organized sort of chaos. A small banker's lamp was crammed with the radio on his desk. Everything smelled of him. The last few meals he had cooked, the ink of pens and rubber stamps from work, the clean soap of his laundry and shaving cream. Airing the place eased some of it, but not entirely. It was not possible to eliminate the smell of living.

"I have to say, Gert," he said as he flopped widthwise across the bed. "Our government may be chaos and our money may be worthless, but I've never been more content."

Gert landed on top of him in a diagonal fashion and Bertie grunted. "I can't wait for next month." Bertie patted him roughly, but Gert did not move. "Can I see yours again?"

Bertie groaned a little as he shoved Gert off him. He sat upright on his second try, head swimming slightly, and took off his suit jacket. Gert waited as he slipped the braces off his shoulders and unbuttoned his shirt, forgetting to pull the tails from his trousers as he removed it.

"Yes, exactly!" Gert shouted and Bertie shushed him once more. He did not want to rouse his neighbors. But he smiled as Gert put his hands to his chest, his fingers lightly tracing the scars, a thick line a couple centimeters under each nipple.

"And the scars stay?"

"They'll lessen a bit over the years, but yes, they will stay." Some days, it bothered him. But other days, it was a deep sense of pride of who he was and what he had overcome.

"Reminders to never forget our strength," Gert said. "I like to think there's beauty in such a thought." He began to take off his own suit jacket, unbuttoning his shirt until it pooled around him. He pressed himself flat while still looking at Bertie. He looked down, then looked back. He smiled. "Yes, that is what I want."

He released himself, unselfconscious of his nakedness in front of Bertie, and the two of them piled against each other back upon the bed.

Bertie was still not sure who started their first time a few years back. They had looked at each other after a night of drinking and slowly moved closer until they were kissing soft and sloppy. They opened their mouths more, roamed their hands, laid themselves upon the bed. Bertie had felt the blood rush between his legs, and just as it began to ache, Gert indulged him. He had slipped Bertie's braces off his shoulders, a tug on the front of his trousers as he slipped his hand through. Bertie breathed against his mouth as Gert began to tease him with his juices. He felt himself slowly get close, closer, until finally he held Gert by the wrist and pulled away from his face.

Bertie rolled atop him instead of letting him finish. He kissed Gert down his shirted chest, taking off his trousers in short tugs once he got to them. Gert parted himself as soon as his legs were free, opening himself up with such a trust that Bertie fell in love in a way he never had before. He took Gert in his mouth, slicking his chin with joy until Gert moaned and clutched the back of Bertie's head with one hand, twitching against his tongue. Gert caught his breath before finishing what he had started, sealing his lips around the throb of Bertie as he hithered his insides with one finger, then two.

Bertie was a third off the mattress by then, the world upside-down and without leverage as Gert toyed with him. Faster, slower, faster, making his eyes roll back until the swell of his pleasure finally burst. He bucked against Gert in surrender. They lay upon each other after, catching their breath, the room full of beer and heat and wet fallen leaves. It was the first time either of them had experienced it with one of their own.

"When does Roy come back?" Bertie asked now. He knew Gert would be interested if he initiated, but he suddenly felt too shy to do so. His beer bounced between giving him confidence and stealing it away. It was not so much that he feared Gert would reject him, but rather knowing that he was not as interesting or desired in the world as Gert was.

Gert sighed. "A couple of weeks. He had someone pass away, a great aunt he didn't know well, but he felt it was best to make appearances at the funeral." He had met Roy at the Cottage one night several months back. Bertie sometimes wondered how things would look now if he had not declined to go that night.

"It feels glamorous to have an American boyfriend. And from New York City, no less."

"It does." The smile could be heard in his voice. "I really love him."

"I'm glad."

"And you have a new lady friend." Gert lifted his head to see Bertie better, now grinning quite large. "It's about time."

Bertie gave a small shove to Gert's head and tried to fight his smile. "We don't know that yet."

"But you like her?"

"I do."

"I'm very certain she likes you, too."

He sighed and patted Gert on the back of the shoulder. "Will you take me to New York the next time you go? I would love to see America." Bertie was in the process of getting his transvestite passport. It would not be terribly helpful outside of Deutschland, perhaps, but he still wanted it. It could still help.

"New York is far from the Midwest," Gert said. "You still doing your album?"

"I am." He rolled Gert off him as he reached for the nearest nightstand and put the album into his lap. He opened it as Gert looked over his shoulder. The first several pages were different mixes of the five friends, many of them taken at the Eldorado, as well as the parties the Institut threw for transvestites and inverts. The biggest collection was of Bertie and Gert together.

As Bertie flipped the thick pages, he came across the clippings he took from overseas newspapers whenever he found them. "Nearly all of them are around the Midwest," he said, "but New York sounds like a wonderful place to arrive."

Bertie was still smiling and pointing, sometimes tapping the clippings as he read their headlines aloud, but then he noticed that Gert's face had sagged. "What's wrong?"

Gert took his turn tapping a few of the articles, their headlines all boasting marriage and lovers in plain sight. "No matter where I go, I'll never be able to marry. You could. You like women as well as men. But I don't."

They were both getting pulled under by the beer again, but Bertie hitched their naked torsos together. Gert rested his head on Bertie's shoulder.

"There's more than just marriage to show how much you care for someone."

"Like what?"

Bertie was feeling foggy. He was unprepared for the question. "Oh, I don't know. How you treat them every day, little gifts you can give them . . . ähm, let's see . . . telling them you love them . . . taking care of them when they're sick . . ."

"I've got it!" Gert straightened his neck, taking his head from Bertie.

"What?"

"A tattoo!"

Bertie lit up as much as Gert. "Yes! A tattoo!"

"Put his name on me!" Gert shouted as Bertie went to his desk in the other room. Gert flopped back down onto the bed, sounding sleepier by the moment as Bertie got foggier.

After some rifling, Bertie found a fountain pen and a sewing needle. He returned with them to the bed. There was suddenly a flicker beneath the beer. "Should we be giving you a tattoo? Isn't this what criminals do?"

"Put it on my back," Gert said, trying to point behind himself while rolling over. "That way, nobody can ever see it without a mirror."

This felt quite logical, and so Bertie poised himself above Gert's bare back. "Wait . . . what's his name again?"

"Roy Collins!"

"Roy Mullins?"

"Roy Collins!"

"Ray Collins?"

"Roy!" Gert shouted. "Don't ruin my marriage, Bertie!"

"Roy Collins," Bertie said to himself with a nod. "Roy Collins. Okay, I got it."

It took less time than Bertie had thought and less pain than Gert made known. Though Gert fell asleep in the middle of it, Bertie finished without him, feeling it important for their friendship to do the job he had said he would do. When he completed his task, he nodded happily to his success, put his tools on the nightstand next to his album, and fell asleep beside him.

3 • Berlin, 1932

BERTIE GROANED AT THE BIRDS SINGING NEAR THE WINDOW. A string of morning light bounced through the open glass, hitting him cruelly across the eyes. It was a bloody pink through his eyelids, the birds a mockery of the sleep he had chosen to forsake.

He tried to roll over but felt himself weighed down by something. He opened one gummy eye to Gert asleep upon him lengthwise. He was prone, still breathing long and heavy, arms crossed beneath himself as a pillow.

Bertie twisted to grab the key clock from his nightstand. He had less than an hour to get to work and the walk took forty minutes. "Scheiße," he muttered. He smacked Gert's rump with the back of his hand twice. "Gert, wake up. Wake *up*, Gert."

Gert snorted. He took a moment to slowly rub his eyes, the sound of his lips dry. Bertie jiggled his legs to get him to move. But when Gert tried to roll off him, he grimaced and groaned, returning to his stomach.

"My back hurts."

"Ähm . . . yeah." The blurry inking stared up at Bertie from his lap. He tapped a safe distance from it, the edges a blushing pink as it healed.

Gert flopped his head back into his arms, his voice muffled. "Scheiße, I remember." He tried to crane his head over his shoulder. "How does it look?"

"Oh. Hrm."

"Please tell me you spelled his name right."

"No, I did. It's just that it's a bit . . . crooked."

Gert groaned and pulled a pillow to his face. His voice could barely be heard through the feathers. "Remind me to never drink with you again."

"Deal. Now get off me."

Gert suddenly sprang into a sitting position, wincing a moment before getting off the bed. "I'm supposed to meet Oma and Opa at my place!" He picked up the clock before plunking it down so hard it pinged. "I'm late!" Gert dug around the floor for his shirt, slowing down only when it graced over his back. "It figures this would happen. The first time they travel all the way over here for an entire day and I'm already wasting their time." He buttoned the buttons, messed up, and had to do them all over again. "Scheiße, scheiße, scheiße."

Bertie yawned as he got up himself. His shirttails were still tucked into his trousers. He pulled them out, letting his shirt fall to the floor. "To be fair, farmers have half their day done before the sun has even risen," he said, while rummaging through his dresser drawers. "Can you imagine?"

Gert was already headed toward the door. "I need to go."

"Drinks in a few days?"

Gert grinned and nodded, slipping on his jacket and trying desperately to stuff his hair back under his flat-cap as he jogged to the door.

Gert's retreating scramble was marked by his hard shoes clomping against the old wood steps and the front door slamming. It left the thick kind of quiet that always came when Gert had gone, settling like dust.

Bertie moved faster now. The pulse in his head was dull at best, his mouth the usual amount of fuzzy. He leaned over his basin and poured a pitcher of cool water over his head, letting it run down over his eyelids and drip off his chin. He combed his hair over and back, the teeth spitting flecks of water with each rake. He dumped the rest of his pitcher into the basin for a quick shave, more to get the scent on him than anything else, removing the soft hairs with long, easy strokes. The water quickly turned cloudy, burbling every time he swished his razor through it. His nose filled with oakmoss and lavender, citrus and anise. The chill of water and metal licked him. He dreamed of one day trying a hot shave but worried who would be on the other end of the razor.

He toweled his face and put on a dark suit with a white shirt, a light gray sweater vest slipped over his black braces. He made sure his transvestite card was in his jacket pocket before heading out.

Leather work satchel in hand, he began his walk north toward the Tiergarten. The sun was peeking out in the short month, tossing long shadows and flashes of rays between buildings. The snow dust was disappearing in assaulted patches. Lamplights loomed over him, tall and idle on the wide streets. The people were back, had never left, but they were different now. The laughter had turned to grumbling, the excitement of a destination to the haste of being late, the lokal food replaced with breakfasting families. He had not breakfasted.

Programs for papers, beer mugs for coffees. The daytime returned to the smell of sunshine and exhaust, deceptively clear to the eyes. The blanket of sultry-gay lilac night was once more invisible. It was hot in the shine and Bertie considered removing his overcoat as he walked briskly to the Institut. But when he hit an unending line of street shadow, of so many buildings attached at the hip, he reconsidered. Little boys dragged sticks along brick and mortar as they held their mothers' hands. Paperboys shouted the latest headline, waving a copy above their heads like a greeting. The honks of the autos were more forceful in the morning hours; trolleys clanged in the distance. The bloody strike had ended the day after the November election. Posters were still pasted everywhere, nestled into the grooves of brick and stone; VOTE COMMUNIST, VOTE SOCIAL DEMOCRAT, VOTE NATIONAL SOCIALIST, ABOLISH THE ABORTION PARAGRAPH, ABOLISH THE HOMOSEXUAL PARAGRAPH, JEWS CONTROL YOUR MONEY, WORKERS' RIGHTS NOW, BRING BACK THE KAISER.

Wooden wagons were unloaded of their wares, bicycles already parked in long lines of racks. People sold this and that out of handcarts. The poor congregated on patches of street. They held up signs looking for work: WILL SEW ANYTHING, WILL REPAIR ANYTHING, WILL WORK FOR FOOD, WILL DO ANYTHING FOR ANYTHING. Men on crutches sold last week's news; houseless children held out their dirty palms. Veterans missing limbs sat on blankets and wooden boxes in the platzes and busy intersections, singing for pfennigs. Bertie tossed a few into each cap.

He hurried over the footbridge of a southern fork of the Spree, played courage with autos on main roads like Tiergartenstraße, clomped over a thin, dripping finger of Tiergartengewässer, before finally entering the Tiergarten itself. He stopped along the way only for a copy of *Das 3. Geschlecht* and some toast. The former took longer than he expected, with nearly thirty different Deutsch-language journals for the third sex sitting on the outside racks of the newspaper stand. Some of the more inconsistent issues were hanging on from nearly a year ago, their covers fading in the sun, their edges curling in the elements. Some had clearly been vandalized. Above their slots, the morning papers hung folded from clothespins.

He finally saw a copy of *Das 3. Geschlecht* and paid. It was his favorite, focused on transvestites, written by transvestites and those who supported them. There were stories both personal and imagined, declarations of joy ("My First Outing as a Woman"), broadcasts of frustration ("The Desperate Struggle of a Male Transvestite"), poetry, advertisements, and information on the next hot social event, where to find clothes in your size, places for medical care or makeup tutorials or voice lessons. And so many wonderful pictures.

He put the journal in his satchel, the toast back in his mouth. Gert, newly worldly after a visit to New York, said the Tiergarten was like the Central Park of Berlin. Only, after Gert explained it all, Bertie still thought the Tiergarten was more special.

The frantic noise of Berlin dulled as he stepped into the trees. He walked his favorite footpath, nearly a straight shot to the Great Star and parallel to the busiest road that cut through. Birds chirped more, autos honked less, and people slowed a little as they took in the nature around them. Its lush magnificence was bare for the moment, the winter sucking away the flowers and leaves. He missed the greenery that filled his eyes like soothing a flame. But it was still peaceful in the winter, still calmed his heart. The light snow had made the gnarled branches pretty, sheets and speckles of brilliant white against all the dead brown. The sky was barely visible through even the leafless branches, dense as the trees were.

It was a scenic place no matter the season. Countless paths and footbridges and unending stone statues erected in Deutsch pride. Queen

Louise, King Frederick William III, Johann Wolfgang von Goethe, Richard Wagner, the Composer Monument memorializing Ludwig van Beethoven, Joseph Haydn, and Wolfgang Amadeus Mozart. Statues also commemorated the history of the Tiergarten, stone animals and huntsmen portraying its birth as a fenced-off hunting ground for the rich and privileged before it was handed over to the people.

Bertie passed by clusters of trees, small islands surrounded by lakes, wide-open grass lawns, and stream after stream yet to be frozen over. It was hard to walk fast through the Tiergarten, to keep the desire to reject a moment of peace. He had since finished his toast.

He rounded at the Great Star and took a right, soon following the lower bank of the Spree proper, the sun-dappled water rolling calmly. And there, just a lick before emerging out of the Tiergarten on the other side, just before leaving the woods entirely to return begrudgingly to a harsher world, the Institut für Sexualwissenschaft emerged.

It was a major tourist attraction the world over. If one wanted to learn anything about sex, the Institut was the place to go. It was two buildings pressed together on the corner of Beethovenstraße and In den Zelten. The original was the building on the right, white stone and stucco nodding back to its birth as a villa for violinist Joseph Joachim. Its square floorplan was chopped in the front and back for garden areas, pinching the building into a fat-knotted bowtie that centered its rooms around what used to be a grand music hall.

The building was surrounded by a waist-high wrought iron fence. Grand windows blinked out from the ground and first floors, as big as the main door and draped gently inside with gauzy white curtains. Windows half their size settled in the attic and peeked out from the basement. Evergreenery held fast wherever there was space, bushes and ivy and all that thrived in a Deutsch winter. The flowers would return in the spring. Tall elm trees graced the perimeter, two particularly large ones reaching past the building itself, artfully planted in the front-facing cutout of the bowtie. A flight of thin stone steps rounded up the left side to the elevated rotunda of the front entrance. INSTITUT FÜR SEXUALWISSENSCHAFT, it stated above the door.

At the edge of the property perched a wooden box. It was where curious individuals could slip in questions and concerns anonymously about sex and abortion, transvestites and inverts, and pleasure and venereal diseases. Bertie grabbed the new strips of paper every morning. Every two weeks, the Institut invited the public in for an evening of sexual education, during which the compiled questions were answered.

Doktor Hirschfeld himself lived on the first floor of the main building, along with his lover, Karl Giese—who Bertie and the rest of the inner circle affectionately called the woman of the house. Both Doktor Hirschfeld and Herr Giese opened their private chambers for smaller parties and social gatherings. The ground floor held a living-cum-dining room and a small lecture hall.

The building on the left was darker stone, a deep gray and brown from its past as a restaurant and stable. Unlike the first building, it was a solid square, taking up all its property among more trees and wrought iron fencing. Its entrance was large, its windows plentiful, generous balconies hanging over the far end of each floor, all resting on an indoor porch at the ground level. Its dark stone towered an extra floor and a half over the original building, its roof steeped instead of flat. When Doktor Hirschfeld purchased the second building, the ground floor was converted into exhibition rooms for tours, and the restaurant above was changed into a larger lecture hall, seating two hundred and named after biologist Ernst Haeckel, of whom Doktor Hirschfeld was a great admirer. It was here that most education happened: evening classes, weekend and weeklong workshops, lectures in which research findings were passed on to academia and the working class alike, and the anonymous questions that were answered to the public every two weeks.

Workers and friends of the Institut resided in the second building, whose rooms often led into some of the housed sections of the archives. The attic housed rooms for people sent to the Institut for expert assessment in criminal court matters, usually sexual crimes from a range of definitions. When they were around, plainclothes detectives positioned themselves opposite the building to make sure none of them left the premises. Forensic fees provided a major source of income for the

Institut. To a lesser extent, the Institut also got by with other paperwork services: written court assessments were 150 marks, transvestite cards 50 marks. In '21, the Prussian Ministry of the Interior began to permit name changes for transvestites who underwent a medical assessment, though such changes had to be reported in the official gazettes, including dates of birth and home addresses. Bertie hated how his personal business required broadcast. It felt both unfair and unnecessary.

The rest of the Institut's matters scattered themselves throughout the two buildings. Consultation rooms, treatment rooms, surgery rooms, reading rooms, exhibition rooms, offices, a moving picture projection room, a ballroom, and the large library and archive. Even the departments were known to shift and restructure based on which doctors and staff members were currently practicing. Archives management and financial administration offices were a constant, alongside departments for research, sexual counseling, physical sexual ailments, psychological sexual ailments, forensics, eugenics, sexual reform, and public sex education. Homosexuals, transvestites, and hermaphrodites were a particular source of study and outreach, alongside abortion access, understanding fetishes, and avoiding and curing venereal diseases.

Bertie pocketed the few folded papers within the question box and went inside. The violinist's old music hall now served as the Institut's grand entry room. It was also used for their biggest and most famous parties for the third sex. Visitors already flooded the place, forming lines for the first tour of the day. Others gazed and pointed at information hung on the walls. Dark frames coated everywhere space could be found on a beginner's array of sexual topics. Quotations by Goethe and other spiritual giants were included throughout the Institut, and signed portraits of famous scientists hung in the stairwell.

"Good morning, Herr Doktor," Bertie said to the bust of Doktor Hirschfeld that greeted everyone at the door.

Light spilled in through the large windows, draped in rich curtains. All double doors leading into public areas of education were already wide open. Dora Richter, one of the hauskeepers, was always first to air both buildings out for a new day. She lived in the basement, working in exchange for the first vaginoplasty known to be performed. Though the surgery was since paid off, she continued to stay and work. Bertie sometimes spotted her and the four other hauskeepers with the souls of women sitting close together, contentedly knitting and sewing during their off hours as they sang old folk songs. Doktor Hirschfeld and the surgeons frequently said they were the most hardworking and conscientious hauskeepers they ever had.

The grand hall had a wooden dance floor not unlike the Eldorado, but most of the other rooms were covered with a plush, dark carpet. The ceilings were high and the sounds of excitement and awe bounced pleasantly within it. The wallpapers varied from solid light colors to dark and rich patterns of fleur-de-lis. Dark display cases were scattered across the premises, containing objects ranging from contraceptive devices to pleasure toys to materials on the struggle against the antiabortion paragraph. The examination and surgery rooms, white-sheeted and sterile, were the only ones closed off from the public. But even the consultation rooms were pleasant and homey, often indistinguishable from private chambers at first glance. Fine wood furniture and plush armchairs, grand Oriental carpets and framed artwork. The entire place smelled of the biting peppermint of antiseptic and the comfortable musk of a lived-in life.

Bertie nodded a polite greeting to Helene, a widow who had originally been a tenant at the Institut. When she saw what she felt was disorder, she put a desk in the entrance hall, connected an internal telephone, and from that day on made sure nobody entered without an appointment. She did not care that she was not on the payroll. Bertie suspected she just wanted to feel purposeful.

He acknowledged a few more workers as he wove through the crowd and took the staircase to the first floor. He opened the last glass-paned door on the left. DR. MAGNUS HIRSCHFELD, it said in block letters.

Bertie's mahogany desk was the first thing to greet him, so familiar and yet so odd to see unchanged since his weeks away. He realized it was the lack of dust that surprised him among his immaculate stacks of papers. Doktor Hirschfeld likely dusted the desk himself for his arrival. Or, at least, Dora did. Doktor Hirschfeld's key aphorisms and maxims for the Institut hung in a black frame behind Bertie's desk, above his many file cabinets, for all applicants to see while sitting with him:

1. To love one's neighbor, one has to respect his love.
2. Instead of asking "Who's to blame?" rather ask "What's to blame?"
3. Both predisposition and circumstance mold mankind.
4. All attraction in nature rests on laws—so does love's attraction.
5. To every law an exception, to every exception a law—everything is determined.
6. Love is the transformation of latent into active energy.
7. Just as love sprouts life, so life lets spring forth love.
8. Whoever stems from both sexes possesses a union of both.
9. The concepts *supernatural*, *unnatural*, and *contrary to nature* are signs of a deficient knowledge of nature.
10. Manners and morals change according to time and place.
11. A naked human being is not undressed, but rather not dressed.
12. Freedom obliges.
13. To prejudge is to judge by proxy.
14. *Per scientiam ad justitiam*—Justice through science.
15. Science does not exist for its own sake, but for people's sake.
16. True purity is pure truth.
17. Truth—more than anything.

"Herr Doktor!" Bertie called out. "I'm back!"

"Ah, my boy!" came his booming voice, somehow always soothing. He appeared in the doorway of his office only steps from Bertie's desk. He grinned wide and brought Bertie a hug that was notably lighter than usual against his healing chest. "How are you feeling?"

"Quite well, Herr Doktor, thank you. And you'll be pleased to know that I had to use my card late last night and it worked as well as always."

"The police are still honoring it? Good. Did you happen to catch the officer's name?"

His memory flashed to Gert biting his overcoat to keep from laughing and he suppressed a grin. "I didn't, no."

"Pity. I'd like to report back to them whenever I can, good or bad." He nudged him with another smile. "Celebrating, were you?"

Doktor Hirschfeld reminded Bertie of the jolliest walrus. He was a short, thick man in his sixties. He wore a full mustache shaped like the handlebars of a bicycle. Once black, it had since gone gray, alongside his hair, which also sported a significant bald patch in the back. His round, wire-framed glasses hung over his generous ears and seemed to catch every glare from a camera, which often washed the thick lenses into shining white orbs in photos. But behind them were the kindest brown eyes. He dressed exclusively in three-piece suits, save for the times he indulged nudist colonies. He had long since acquired the invert moniker of "Aunt Magnesia." He made Bertie think of a solemn old professor who happened to find joy in smiling.

Bertie smiled back. "Perhaps. I met a young woman, too. We'll be seeing each other again soon."

Doktor Hirschfeld grinned wide again. "Well if you ever need help with marriage, you let me know. I'll see what I can do."

Bertie gave an embarrassed laugh and waved a hand in front of his face. "Much too soon for that, Herr Doktor, but thank you."

"Would you indulge me in another interview later about your recovery? Potentially more photographs if there's any documented change?"

"Certainly, sir. Anything I can do to help." He went to his desk and sat down, the familiarity again feeling odd in a pleasant way, as if he had never left. "In the meantime, what would you like me to help with? Have applications been backing up?"

"Actually, Bertie, I have a favor to ask of you. Rüdiger has taken ill and the woman of the house is currently tending to other matters. Would you mind doing the next tour or two until I can find someone else? Are you feeling well enough to be a guide?"

Bertie hesitated before giving a small shrug. "It's been quite a while since I last led one, but I'm sure I'll remember. If you don't think they'll mind a lesser quality."

"Oh you'll remember, son, you'll remember. You know everything about this place. You'll tell me if you feel fatigued, yes?"

"Of course, Herr Doktor."

"Wonderful. I'll call you back up if I need you. There will be plenty of applications to process when you return, but for now, it's more important to educate the masses."

Doktor Hirschfeld returned to his office, keeping the door open. Bertie smoothed down his sweater and checked the lay of his jacket. He hung open his jaw and massaged it, then stretched out his tongue as far as it would go. It had been some weeks since he had truly used his trained voice. He worried he did not have the energy to indulge it, would not sound convincing enough and end up a poor representation of Herr Doktor's accomplishments. The man never put such a pressure upon Bertie, but he knew outsiders and ausländers scrutinized him for flaws or differences when they realized what he was, and if these showed through, the city could very well turn on the entire Institut. He wanted to transvest as well as he could, even if it was not always all him. He felt it was a noble sacrifice for those after him. If he had to transvest in public further than his comfort so that others could have the chance to tranvest at all, it was worth it.

When he felt ready, Bertie returned to the main floor. The first tour of the day was already five minutes late in starting. The sizeable crowd gazed around, some looking unsure, others nervous. Most simply looked in wonder. Bertie liked to think that while tourists often visited the Institut as if it were some sort of zoo, an idle curiosity to kill an afternoon, they would leave seeing sexual intermediates as something more.

He stood in front of the crowd and smiled broadly as he raised both his arms in welcome as far as his healing would allow. "Meine Damen und Herren! Thank you for your patience and welcome to Dr. Magnus Hirschfeld's Institute of Sexual Science! My name is Berthold and I will be your guide this morning. As a transvestite—" there was the usual murmur of awe and disbelief at this, the sudden scrutiny of his height as he was shorter than a decent portion of them, his voice, his unshadowed face "—I'm thrilled to show you the many wonders and humanities Dr. Hirschfeld and his team have developed and provided for not only people like myself, but also inverts of all types, third genders, and even for people like you, such as sexual practices, indulgences, safety, childbearing, family planning, and many other knowledges vital to each and every one of our livelihoods."

The crowd of thirty or so had gone rapt and quiet by his second sentence. Even after thirteen years, the Institut managed to pull in locals and tourists by the dozens every day, even more on weekends and during tourist seasons.

"Dr. Hirschfeld bought this first building in 1919 for four hundred marks and the Institute opened that sixth of July. We bought the second building next door and expanded in 1921. By '22, Dr. Hirschfeld had already convinced the police to sympathize with transvestites, and they published a document that instructed their own officers not to arrest us simply for wearing the clothes that we wear, stating that 'The still commonly held view that people who dress up are clandestine criminals is outdated.' Dr. Hirschfeld did and continues to dedicate a significant portion of his time educating the police, often using real-life examples. I've myself volunteered as a subject for such seminars twice."

He did not mention how he would have preferred not to, how he was not particularly fond of disrobing in front of strangers, in the middle of a lecture hall's stage, to be looked at in such ways, however briefly. But he had, indeed, volunteered of his own volition. He felt the need to be on his best behavior at all times in their world. He knew a single bad example could ruin opportunities for the entire community. With all the progress they had made in such a short span of time, the situation remained precarious. It could all tip backward quite violently with the weight of a feather.

"The Institute of Sexual Science is the first of its kind anywhere in the world," he continued, "and has been unique in its role of advising, researching, and treating people of all sorts, but most especially inverts and transvestites. Dr. Hirschfeld is the first known person to start a movement for the human rights of our kind. We've seen as many as twenty thousand people from across Europe and have gained accolades and support from such scientists as Dr. Albert Einstein." He automatically paused for the customary ripple of awe through the crowd. "We're additionally a primary archive and pseudo-university for anything related to sexual intermediates. Our library houses over twenty thousand books and journals collected from around the world, at least half of them rare or the only known surviving prints of such works both by and about inverts and transvestites. We've also collected over thirty-five thousand glass photographic slides of similar excellence. If you're looking for anything that proves, explains, or shows our existence, here's where you'll find it." He gave a small smile then. "It's my favorite part of the Institute."

The crowd chuckled at this and he continued. "More than forty people work here, nearly all of us sexual intermediates in one way or another, from our housekeepers and cooks all the way up to Dr. Hirschfeld himself. We also operate as altruistically as we can. We don't work with profit in mind, and instead rent out rooms on a sliding scale for those in need, sometimes for free, as well as offer free services and treatments to our most impoverished clients. Dr. Hirschfeld recognizes how many sexual intermediates are in poverty, often due to a lack of employment when people realize what we are. This is also why so many of us are employed here."

He finally extended his arm out toward the walls around them. "Let's begin our tour right where we are. If I may direct your attention to the walls that so many of you have already been admiring, you'll notice countless framed photographs and explanations, most involving inverts and transvestites." The next usual murmur was uttered through the crowd. "Yes! This may surprise you to hear! In fact, one of the main reasons Dr. Hirschfeld not only allows these tours but encourages them is to promote education and understanding about people who are different from one another. As you'll soon understand, transvestites and inverts may be different from you, but at the same time, we're also quite the same."

He saw some heads nodding at this, others still digesting what he told them. A select few eyes had since lit up and he knew them to be one of his own kind. It was a type of joy and relief that he knew too well, and he had to often look away from such visitors before he felt emotional. He remembered his own first time learning that there was nothing wrong with him. And that he had the chance to attain the dreams he had always wanted. It was a theme heard frequently by patients and visitors, how monumental it was to learn that there were others out there like them.

Bertie took a breath, quickly swallowing the thickness in his throat before he continued. "Dr. Hirschfeld was the first doctor to differentiate inverts from transvestites, as he realized there was no automatic relationship between homosexuality and transvestism. Rather, he believed the urge to cross-dress came from a discrepancy between an individual's mental and physical condition. As a doctor, he felt he was not only justified but obliged to provide proof of a patient's need to re-clothe themselves, to transvest, as part of preserving and improving their physical and mental welfare.

"The first known chest surgery upon those with the soul of a man was performed by our own Dr. Ludwig Levy-Lenz, in 1926. The first for the soul of a woman was done in 1931. We're in the process of developing hormone treatments, but we believe we're still a few years away from a decent breakthrough. But we'll get to all of these things in more detail as we move through the exhibition rooms. So if you'll indulge me in walking this way, we'll start with contraception and abortion access..."

Bertie continued in this manner for multiple tours. The library, the exhibition rooms, the endless hallways of photographs. A highlight of the tour was the Institut's famous Picture Wall of Sexual Transitions. At two meters tall and four and half meters wide, it showcased nude bodies, before-and-afters, male-versus-female presentations, surgeries immortalized in motion, and closeups of genitals of every sort alongside explanations of Doktor Hirschfeld's theory of gender. It ran nearly the entire length of the wall, unashamed in its size, unapologetic in its subject matter. There was something powerful, Bertie had to admit, about seeing his community displayed so large and exposed. They were worth an entire wall. They were a force. Look or not, the wall said, but we will not budge.

Bertie fielded countless questions. Some personal, some quizzical, some insulting in their innocence, none of them a surprise to him these days. By the end of each tour, he brought the group back to the main hall, showing them where they could donate money and grab free pamphlets on information of all sorts, including their next public education evening.

"Tell your friends!" he always ended, giving a smile and a wave. At least half of any given group, often starting off so shy, would happily bid him goodbye in turn. He thought of mentioning to Doktor Hirschfeld again about starting to charge admission, but the man was firm on his stance. While they could always use the money, keeping the knowledge accessible to the masses was key for changing the world. It was why Doktor Hirschfeld left so frequently on tours across the globe. Anybody who was learning about inverts and transvestites, they were learning about them from here.

By lunchtime, Bertie was beginning to tire. He was about to slip back upstairs, about to ask Doktor Hirschfeld to switch him out with someone else, but then he heard his name echo across the entrance hall.

"Bertie!"

He turned and smiled. Gert was running up to him. They both went to hug each other at top speed, but then skidded to a halt. Bertie for his chest, Gert for his back.

"I didn't expect to see you here today," Bertie said instead, patting him on the shoulder. Gert responded in kind.

"Oma and Opa said they wanted to see the Institute." An elderly couple made their last steps toward Gert. "Bertie, I'd like you to meet Goss and Ina Baumann."

Bertie extended his hand to each of them. "A true pleasure to finally meet you. Gert talks about you all the time."

"Likewise, Berthold," Ina said. She was wearing what was surely her best dress, and her gray-streaked blond hair was up in a bun. She had wonderful laugh lines around her mouth.

Goss had warm brown eyes and the compact strength of one who worked on his feet. He took Bertie's hand and held on to it a moment longer with an extra shake. "Gert is much happier these past few years, more than we've ever seen him. We're excited to see the place and the people who helped make that happen. And to learn more about him, too."

"I was hoping we'd find you," Gert said. "But I didn't expect it to be so easy."

"I'm doing tours for the morning. The usual man is ill today."

Gert's face fell a moment. "Oh no, did we miss your touring time?"

Bertie shook his head with a smile. "I was about to see who I could switch out with and take a break. But if you'll permit me to sit and have some lunch first, I'd be happy to give you three your own personal tour."

Ina and Goss looked quite pleased at this, and Gert appeared ready to burst on the spot.

"Thank you, liebling," Ina said. "We'd love that."

"So important, what you do here," Goss added. His brow suddenly darkened and he leaned forward a little, lowering his voice as if each sound did not bounce across the entrance hall. He thumbed the front door, and it was only then Bertie registered the familiar protest shouts and rattle-rattle-rattle of collection boxes bursting a moment as the door opened and closed. "We don't like what those people are saying about you all. What do they call themselves . . . the National Socialists . . ."

"Just call them Nazis," Ina said. "They hate that."

"Yes, Nazis. I don't like them."

"He spat at one on the way in."

A pleased smile came to Goss's face and he shrugged. "I'm an old man, I get away with it. But I worry what could happen if they got a firmer foothold."

"We would go out in a blaze of glory if we were younger." Ina suddenly looked ashamed. "I wish we could do something. When people hurt bad enough, they'll grab any idea to make their own lives better, no matter how illogical. It's been tough since we lost the War. And they're quite alluring in their promises."

Goss huffed. "They're pandering to the people who were already hateful and looking for reason and protection to be so. I just didn't realize there were so many of them. It makes me ashamed of Germany. Going after your kind and homosexuals, saying Jews don't belong here. It's ridiculous. Some of the most patriotic Germans I know are Jews."

"The Nazis' numbers are declining, though," Bertie replied. He suddenly was feeling less hopeful since the November election.

"Exactly. They know their grip is already slipping. And they're going to do everything they can to gain control no matter what the public wants."

"Hindenburg is holding firm," Bertie tried feebly. "He refuses to appoint Hitler as the new chancellor no matter how much they lobby him."

Ina shook her head. "Hitler and Chancellor Papen are more alike than gives me comfort. They both want to keep the Communist Party from getting any bigger, they both want to do away with anyone not like them, they're both antidemocratic. All the conservative, monarchical, and corporate interests could make a coalition government between them quite possible. Those parties could all work with Hitler. Scratching backs and such. They'll combine seats until they get as close to absolute majority as they can, and then Hindenburg can't refuse them."

"Papen already used emergency powers to dissolve Prussia's state government after the reds and browns got into all those street fights in the summer," Gert added quietly. "That's why the Eldorado has a curfew now and we have all these renewed censorship laws and vice crackdowns against our kind." He locked eyes with Bertie a moment before looking back down at the floor. "Dr. Hirschfeld doesn't have the influence he had with the older police forces. They might soon see him as someone in the way, if they don't already."

Bertie was not sure how his day was going sour so fast. He had had a good morning, his first day back, feeling so light after his evening with Sofie and the weeks finally finished recovering from his surgery. This was supposed to be the start of the next phase of his life. But not like this. He did not say anything, the sounds of the excited visitors and tourists around him becoming a pressure in his ears.

Ina spoke again, softer this time. "We want Gert to move back to Ulm with us."

"I won't suddenly be immune there," Gert said with a factualness indicating that they surely had had this conversation many times already.

"But if something bad happens, it'll take longer to get to you there than if you stay here. There, you'll at least have some warning and time to consider your options."

The option, surely, was Gert fleeing to Amerika, staying with his new boyfriend Roy. But Bertie was not sure Gert would leave everyone and everything behind. Not Bertie, not Gert's Oma and Opa. It felt like such a drastic solution to a situation that was still so small. Not even real.

Plenty of inverts in the community were not yet panicked. They saw themselves as Deutsche first and homosexuals second. It seemed unlikely anything would happen to them. Even Hitler's own close friend and commander of the brownshirts, Ernst Röhm, was a known homosexual. Perhaps that was partly why Bertie did not feel too worried; such inverts indulged in many of the same parties and places he did. In a world where anything could go wrong, their calm was soothing. Not even the fact that anti-Nazis frequently branded the Nazis as homosexuals as a way to humiliate and discredit them seemed to bother the inverts.

"You have a beautiful city," Goss said, "but that's the problem with Berlin. You take nothing seriously. Everything's a joke."

Bertie tried to shrug off what he knew was true. "Everything's just so hard. It's how we get through life, laughing it off."

"But sometimes it's not a good idea. I worry this is one of those times." He locked eyes with Bertie, the lines of his face deepening as if he had learned this lesson himself the hard way. "Never laugh in the face of villainy."

Bertie's chest was sore and his legs ached from standing all morning. He had already spent more time thinking about these unpleasant things than he cared to for one day. He unlocked his jaw, rounded his shoulders, and gestured toward the courtyard exit where the protesters never thought to gather. His smile forced more of his muscles than he wanted to admit. "I don't know about you, but I'm famished. Would you care to join me for lunch?"

4 • Ulm, 1945

THE THREE OF THEM FACED EACH OTHER IN THE SITTING room. Sofie sat on the bench, her back to the piano. Bertie and Karl shared the small old couch. Karl already looked more in the pink of health since his meal. The urn rested behind Sofie on the piano, just to the right of her head, and Karl glanced at it multiple times.

Bertie still held the order in his hand. "I think this is it for us. We need to do something. We need to leave." He felt silly saying such a thing. Where did you run when nowhere would protect you? If there was somewhere they could go, they would have done it long ago.

"We'd talked earlier about that boat leaving for New York," Sofie said with a sigh and rubbed at the bridge of her nose. "But I don't know what plan we could have in place for when we get there. I can't imagine Americans would be particularly welcoming to German immigrants."

"There are already so many of us there, especially in the Midwest," Bertie insisted. "A large German population from before the first War. And plenty of transvestite men hiding in plain sight. All those articles I clipped out, almost all of them were in the Midwest. Not to mention all the farming jobs that would be available there. And in the meantime, I could write to Roy Collins."

"Who?" asked Sofie.

"Gert's lover from before the second War." To say Gert's name aloud once again felt like a summoning, like a foreign word he was just learning. Out of all the times he thought of Gert, he could not remember the last time he had spoken his name to another person before today, not even Sofie. His essence hung in the air.

"How in the world do you remember that?"

"Oh, I remember." There was a spark of joy in his mind as he thought of that late night of drunken choices, but it was quickly cut by hurt. "The letter would get there before we do. If he's still alive and still lives at his old place in New York and has it in his heart to help us, then he could meet us at the docks. It's a long chance, but it's the only chance we have."

"But what if he doesn't arrive? Or what if the letter doesn't get to him in time?"

"Then I guess we just show up at his address and find out for certain."

Sofie nodded but also hung her hands from the back of her neck. So it was decided. A simple enough decision. Stay and surely be found out or take their chances on Amerika.

"I just wish we had something safer." Her eyes flicked over at Karl and Bertie knew what she was thinking.

Karl had said nothing since Bertie discovered the order. He had moved with them from the kitchen into the sitting room, but otherwise continued to stare at the uneven planks of the floor, his hands folded in his lap.

He held himself in a way that felt peculiar the more Bertie stood in his presence. It was not wrong, exactly. More like dulled and muted, gagged when one was screaming. Like he had been picked clean while swallowing the world at the same time; like he wanted to learn how to be human again, but also did not ever want to be, not after what he had learned. He could inflect, he could gesture, but there was a slight slackness to the expressions in his face. He could frown, but not far enough. He could show quickness and surprise, but these emotions were contained only to the required body parts. He had yet to smile.

He presented himself as blank and emotionless, nothing beneath the surface, yet a swallowed world pressed outward from all sides, clawing and heaving against his skin as it tried to rip through, bursting forth with things that Bertie did not know, that maybe Karl did not know. It was this thought that caused Bertie the most angst. Bertie was certain Karl would never hurt them. But this presence, this unpleasant truth of humanity, was still uneasy to be around. Karl served as a reminder of the cruelty of people, and as such had to suffer doubly for it.

To his earlier vow of protection, Bertie added that he would never shy from the presence of Karl. He would love him for surviving.

"Karl," Bertie said. "You should know the risks involved with this. There are people who will inspect us if they think we're sick or hiding something. We both need to be convincing."

Karl lifted his head up, lips slightly parted. "I don't think I can do that. I'm not convincing."

"I'll teach you how to transvest," Bertie insisted. "I've had a lot of practice." He almost said more about his time at the Institut but stopped himself. He did not want Karl to start putting the pieces together.

"These aren't the Ellis Island days," Sofie said. "They're not going to just flip up our eyelids with a buttonhook and then let us on in. There are procedures. Papers. It'll be impossible to become citizens, even if we make it onto the boat and step foot in their country. And if they find out about either one of you . . ."

Bertie sat down beside Karl. The weight of Sofie's words sank into him. He thought a moment before uttering his favorite English word. "Fuck."

"I sincerely appreciate your willingness, both of you," Karl said, his eyes fixed on the floor. "But I'm not worth it. I'm not worth the sacrifice of two lives that survived this long from the War."

"And you haven't survived this long, too?" asked Sofie.

Karl did not move. "I'll ruin everything."

The usual stubborn flame in Sofie was lit by this talk. "You have just as much chance as either one of us. After everything we've all been through, it's nonsense to simply give up now. We have to try. We have to figure out something."

Karl lifted his head to look at her. "Who will we say I am?"

"My nephew," she replied. Bertie felt his heart miss a beat at her words, but she was purposely looking away from him, concentrating on Karl far too hard.

"Why your nephew?" Karl asked.

"Because we don't look terribly much alike, but we at least have the same hair and eyes. And the less connection made between you and

Bertie, the better. We'll just say you're my nephew and that should be convincing enough. Though honestly that's the least of our concerns right now."

Again Bertie felt the uneasiness inside him, but he knew better than to say anything. Sofie knew the choice she was making.

Karl looked a little more convinced, but not much. "But I have nothing to barter my way onto the boat."

"We have a few things around," Bertie said. "It's not a concern. The only things you need to concern yourself with are looking healthy, behaving like any other young man, and keeping yourself hidden away until we can come up with a plan." Bertie stopped to think a moment, counting on his fingers. "Okay. So the boat leaves in three weeks, but it comes out of Amsterdam."

Karl's eyebrows rose. "But that's clear on the other end of—"

"I've heard folks in town say that a ferry sometimes leaves from Stuttgart. The Rhein flows right into the North Sea. At least one ferry will be planned in time for that boat. I can trade for information tomorrow to make sure. So that'd be maybe one or two hours by drive, Stuttgart. Then the ferry ride would probably take ten days. And we also want to leave before the Americans come to collect us for the camps on the first of June, but not so soon that we have nowhere to stay in Amsterdam or get caught."

Sofie rubbed her temple with two fingers, her arms crossed, as she summarized. "So, we plan to flee to a country that hates us, and will likely do terrible things if they find out we're lying, by a boat that may not arrive or leave when it says it will, after taking a ferry that we don't know will exist at all and will have to go through both the French- and British-occupied territories, with no papers or plan—"

"And with me not at all good at transvesting," added Karl.

"Yes," Bertie said.

Sofie stopped rubbing her temple, her wrist hanging limp near the side of her face. "How much time does this give us to figure out a plan?"

Bertie looked up from his fingers. "Eleven days."

All three of them were silent. Just when Bertie was finally going to speak again, to say that they could at least prepare as if they were leaving and hope they could figure out a plan by the last day, a particularly loud low rumbled from nearby. Karl jumped to his feet and turned around, backing away from the latched wooden door that he had just been sitting beside.

"It's okay," Sofie said quickly, standing to meet Karl. "It's just the cow."

The livestock area was behind the sitting room, under the same roof and separated by only a wall, taking up half of the ground floor. Oma and Opa had never been much for livestock, and these days Bertie and Sofie were down to just the one cow and five chickens. But Bertie liked to hear them glucking and muhing from not far away, their sounds rising gently during the quietest times.

"I think she's lonely again," Bertie added, thinking about the others they had slaughtered for food. They had since sold her calf. "She heard us talking."

Karl relaxed his shoulders, though still did not look entirely convinced. He likely was not familiar with the wohnstallhaus structure.

A wry smile formed on Sofie's face. "Tell him what you named her, Bertie."

Bertie knew she was trying to ease the tension, to help Karl relax, but he gave her a glare anyway. When she held his eye, he finally lowered his head in defeat. "Muh."

The corner of Karl's mouth twitched. "You named a cow—"

"I'm not very good with names."

"Tell him what you named the chickens, Bertie."

Bertie gave an exasperated sigh, drowned out by another low from Muh. It sounded like her head was against the door now. He looked up at the ceiling. "Ki, Kiki, Kiker, Iki, and Kikeriki."

There was a longer pause this time. The corner of Karl's mouth twitched again, his voice nonetheless flat. "That's a rooster."

"Oma and Opa thought it was hilarious," Sofie added.

"I need to spread ashes on the asparagus." Bertie began to leave the room but stopped when he noticed the sudden look of pain on Karl's face. He thought at first that his embarrassment at the situation had come off too harshly, but then he saw Karl's eyes flick to the urn.

"Wood ashes," Bertie explained, "from the stove since breakfast.

Not human ashes. Asparagus is one of the few plants that thrives on wood ashes. Human ashes contain too much sodium to be helpful to plants; it actually keeps them from absorbing nutrients. If you toss human ashes around, you may as well be salting the earth so nothing ever grows again."

An understanding that Bertie had not intended spread on Karl's face, and what little joy he had gathered from barnyard names was sucked from his eyes. They all went quiet. Even Muh stopped lowing.

"Actually," Bertie said, trying to lighten his tone. He suddenly did not want to leave Karl with his thoughts. "Let's get started instead."

"With what?"

"Your transvesting lessons. We only have eleven days. Come along."

Bertie grabbed his album and weaved up the tight stairs, the walls narrow enough to serve only one person at a time. Bertie was never quite sure how the furniture had arrived up there, and he suspected Opa had made it all in his workshop on the same floor. These days, they used that space to store firewood.

Karl trailed behind him into the spare bedroom. Bertie hoped that it would be harder to see through the windows on the higher floor, should Frau Baer come by to stick her nose in their business again, which she certainly would.

They stopped in front of the door. While he had left it open on purpose, Bertie had trouble once more stepping into it. And in that moment, it was as if something slipped in the air.

"Goss and Ina Baumann," Karl said softly, remembering their conversations from that morning. "Gert Baumann." He looked at Bertie directly now, right in the eye, his face as bare as ever. "This is his room."

For Karl to know this made Bertie feel exposed. "Yes."

Karl held his gaze. "This room will only know respect from me. These clothes . . ." He looked down at them and back up at Bertie. "The highest respect only."

Bertie felt pressure surge behind his eyes. He wiped at his face roughly before any water could come. "Thank you," he said. "Thank you. That means, ähm . . . thank you." He cleared his throat and stepped inside. With Karl trailing behind him, it suddenly felt a little easier. He placed his album on the nightstand. "Now you're already dressing the part," he began. "And that's half of the battle. But we'll also go with it as far as we can. First, standing and walking."

They went about this way for nearly an hour. Bertie demonstrating, Karl mimicking. Bertie analyzed each move Karl made with the eye of a perfectionist and frequently corrected him. The corrections seemed small to the untrained eye, but they were necessary. Bertie could tell that Karl was becoming frustrated from the constant need to fix himself.

"I'm trying my hardest," he finally said, in what probably passed for him as exasperation. "And you don't stand and walk this way yourself."

"Not when I'm in my own home," Bertie said, his tone still even. "But out there in the world, it's very different."

"This is exhausting."

"Yes, it is."

Bertie put a hand on his shoulder to correct him yet again, but Karl jerked his arm away. "I can't do this. I told you."

"This is only your first lesson. You just need to keep trying until it becomes more natural—"

"It will never be natural, don't you understand that? It's not in me. I'm not as lucky as you are."

"Karl—"

Karl gestured at him. "You're ignoring the obvious problem here. You look the way you do, and I look the way I do. It's not fair, but it's the way it is. Not all of us are as lucky as you." His face sank, his eyes lost within himself. "Were as lucky as you . . ."

Karl quieted, and Bertie dared to place his hand back to his shoulder. "Do you want to talk about it?"

Karl moved away from him and faced the opposite wall, speaking softer this time. "And maybe I don't even want to."

"Talk about it?"

"Be convincing. Make it seem or feel natural. There's transvesting for myself and then there's transvesting for everyone else. I don't care how other people think they see me. They're wrong."

"You know there's a difference between being wrong and being wrong with power," Bertie continued gently. "They could hurt you,

Karl. They could hurt us. And this?" he gestured to himself in an up-down motion. "Some of this was luck, but the rest has all been training. This has never been easy for me, either. But we're stuck, okay? We're stuck. We either do this or die."

"Maybe I'd rather die."

"If you did, then you wouldn't be here right now."

For a long moment, Karl did not speak, and the quietness of him was unnerving. "Many of the ones that died were convincing. More convincing than either you or I could ever hope to be."

"I didn't mean it like—"

"But they were found out anyway. While you've be sitting here on your farm warm and fed—"

"I just meant that you're a fighter, Karl."

"They were fighters, too." Despite his words, his face continued its stoic stance. "I'm not supposed to be here. I'm supposed to be dead."

Bertie did not say anything.

"That's the worst part," he continued. "Trying to make sense out of who died and who lived. But I was there. And I can tell you that there is no sense to be made. All that death was meaningless." He breathed out. "I'm here and I hate it."

The room was silent. Calm as Karl's voice remained, Sofie surely had heard, but she was choosing to leave them to it.

"I'm sorry," Bertie finally said. "I wasn't thinking."

Karl cast his eye to the album that Bertie had left on the nightstand. "Your album," he said, softer now. "Is it happy pictures inside?"

"Very happy. Before any of this started."

"I'd really like to see us happy."

Bertie sat down on the bed, patting beside him so Karl would join. He placed the album on his own lap, the front of the cover resting upon Karl's knees as he opened it.

"Sorry," Bertie said quickly, "wrong side. These are just old newspaper articles about us that I collected. Most from America." He flipped the album around to its correct side and opened it again. "Careful. This is some of the only history we have left."

Karl simply nodded, now looking down at the sepia photos of people he did not know. The spine crackled lightly as Bertie slowly turned a few of the thick, stiff pages every couple of minutes.

"My transvestite card," he said simply when they arrived to it, tapping the loose paper between the pages. It had turned a deeper shade of mottled brown over the years, the crease so worn it likely would tear the moment he tried to pick it up.

"I always wanted one," Karl said. Bertie held his breath, but Karl did not elaborate. He gazed at it without touching. He had yet to touch anything in the album, his palms pressed into the bed at either side of him, only the front cover resting in his lap.

Bertie slowly continued to flip the pages. "Some photos from Dr. Hirschfeld's parties . . ." He finally stopped at some of his favorite photos, the times he and his friends would go to the Eldorado. "You ever been there?"

Karl shook his head.

"Oh, it was wonderful. One of the most popular clubs for us in all of Berlin, if not the world. It was a magical place. Singing, dancing, drinking. Just a good time."

"Could people be however they wanted there?"

"Oh yes." He began to point at the different pictures now, smiling to himself. "This here is Markus. And that one there is called Karsten. And then there's Gebhardt, of course. You can see in the background there Sofie playing the piano. She hated having her picture taken." He smiled wider, his eye falling to a picture of the group of them, save for Markus, who was likely behind the camera. "Ah. That's a much younger me." He chuckled a little. "But right there, that's Gert. My best friend."

He turned his head to Karl for his reaction, beaming now with the memories. But his smile faded, for what little pink Karl had gained since breakfast had left him as he stared at the photo.

Bertie's breath caught. He remembered the promise he had made to Sofie earlier, to not interrogate him, but he could not help himself. "Do you recognize him?"

Karl said nothing, his eyes widening slightly.

"Did you know him? Gert Baumann," he repeated, as if Karl did not already know his name. He waited only a moment for a reply. "Karl, please answer me."

Bertie had felt a renewed dread all day, ever since Karl said that he had come from Dachau. If something really had happened to Gert that night, if he had not been able to get out, then he would have either been killed or sent to Dachau. The timing lined up perfectly. It was the first and only camp open then and had originally been designed for only two types of people: political opponents and sexual intermediates. They were considered the most immediate threats to the plans of Hitler.

"I'm quite tired." Karl's voice was dry. He broke his gaze from the photo. "I need to rest."

Bertie swallowed, feeling pulled in two directions at once. He finally nodded. "Yes. You've had a long day. Rest as much as you need, and I'll bring dinner up for you later."

He stood, clutching the album in his hands as he left Karl to curl atop the covers, facing the wall.

5 • Ulm, 1945

KARL HAD ALREADY GAINED WEIGHT IN THE TWO DAYS SINCE he had arrived, and more color was returning to his face. He still did not ever smile, but his blue eyes had become less dull. Bertie had not bothered him about the album again. He did not know how to bring it up without feeling like a dummkopf, so he instead returned to their lessons.

"Shaving is important," he instructed in the little room, holding up a small mirror as Karl tried for himself. "Removing even just the soft hairs of your face gives the indication of someone who needs to shave, and the use of shaving cream provides a scent that helps others assume you to be a man. You may be tempted to go heavy on it, but trust me that the lighter the scent, the less people will notice how it's shaping their opinion of you."

"Everything is a mirage," Karl said flatly.

"It is, yes."

Karl continued through their lesson stiffly, perhaps even more than the last time. It seemed like the performances were already weighing on him. Bertie worried what this could mean when they arrived in New York, if they ever got to leave. But they at least managed to get through the lesson without an argument. When he was about to leave so Karl could have some morning rest, the younger man spoke up.

"May I please borrow the album?" His tone was less dreary than it had been for the past hour. "I'd like to look through it before I rest, if you'll allow it."

Bertie felt a surge of protection for his album, as if Karl would rip it to pieces the moment he got his hands on it. But after all Karl had been through, Bertie felt it was not in his nature to deny him such a small gesture. He nodded and returned with it.

"Thank you. I enjoy seeing us happy. I wish I could've been there." When Bertie handed him the album, Karl curled up on his side on the bed, facing the door, the album cradled in his arms like a cherished stuffed toy. Again Bertie worried that he would somehow fall asleep and crush it, and again he chastised himself for wanting to snatch the album back to his chest.

He left Karl alone upstairs, going to send their mail to the post. It was five letters now that Sofie had written to her family since the War ended, every few days despite knowing she likely would not have received a reply from the first one yet. Bertie had also since written to Roy Collins, careful in his wording, as he did not know if the Allies were surveilling letters like the Nazis had. His written English was as stunted as his speech, and it took him considerable time to write:

Dearest Roy,

To long, it is being! We miss you much and we are finding soon: Was it a dagger or a cross? We ask June 1st. We answer by 10th. Your sunny-set will say.

Loving,
B.

He was sure Roy would know what he meant. He had to. It was the first night the two of them had met, at the Silvester fest.

"Karl's resting," he told Sofie now.

She nodded at the kitchen counter as she wiped the eggs of their last surviving chickens. "I'll check on him anyway."

He kissed her on the cheek and left for town on the main dirt path at the front of their home. The selections were slim at the shops, even less than they had in the last few years of the War, but he was able to barter some asparagus for flour and another Amerikan newspaper. There were posters plastered all over town. REMEMBER THIS! they said in English, covered with photos of dead, emaciated bodies in lines and piles. DON'T FRATERNIZE!

Bertie looked away.

He asked around quietly, to only those he knew he could trust, though he now wondered why he could trust them. Was there a ferry leaving soon for Stuttgart? There was, just in time to catch the ship in Amsterdam. He was not sure if the townsfolk knew that there was a ship, what this ferry meant in its timing, but he was certain it was not a coincidence. It soothed him. It was one less thing, this ferry in Stuttgart.

He returned home by early midday, the sun high in the sky. There was still plenty of time to clean out Muh's hold and weed the crops.

"I'm home, schatz!" he called out. He smiled as he saw Sofie standing near the throughway between the kitchen and sitting room. He held up the newspaper in a small victory. But instead of showing happiness for his habit, her eyes were wide and she was shaking her head in quick, small jerks as if trembling from the neck up.

A man dressed in Amerikan military clothes clomped up from behind her. In his hand, he held one of Oma's porcelain figurines from a shelf in the sitting room. The one of the little boy feeding the pigeons. He wore a scoffing smirk as he looked up at Bertie. "Goss Baumann, I presume," he said in English.

He was a tall man, his brown hair cut short beneath his olive green crush cap. His stately nose and defined jaw would have served him well in Deutschland during the War.

Bertie swallowed. "Yes," he said carefully. His accent was thick. The English Gert taught him evaporated as he tried to make sense of the situation thrust upon him. "I am Goss Baumann and this is my woman, Ina."

"But that's not what you called her when you came in."

"It was not?" Bertie already felt unsteady. He was so used to calling her by her real name in the house.

The man continued to stand just behind Sofie. He surely must have only just arrived. Sofie was usually the better of the two of them when it came to coming up with plans, to keeping themselves safe. Bertie then realized what else might be giving her angst: Karl was likely fast asleep upstairs, unaware of the situation.

"I call her what?" Bertie asked, trying to buy time. He was worried he had just stood in too much silence, but then realized no time had passed since he had last spoken.

"Something that sounded like . . . shucks? Shooks?" A mocking grin hinted on his lips. "Shits?"

The bubble Bertie held in his chest released some of its pressure. "Ah. You are meaning 'schatz,' yes?"

"Yeah, that."

"That is a . . . how are you saying . . ." he wished he could remember the right words. "A nice thing you are calling someone you love. A . . . a petting name. It means 'darling,' maybe. Or 'sweetness of heart.'"

"A term of endearment."

"Yes! That. Endear-ing term. Thank you."

The man did not look convinced. He walked the rest of the way into the kitchen and put the figurine down on the table. "Lieutenant William Ward of the Army of the United States of America. My troop is occupying this part of the American section of Germany."

"Happiness," Bertie said. Before he could say more, Muh must have heard their voices again, and she lowed by the door in the sitting room.

Just like Karl, Ward was unprepared. He twisted quickly. "What in the hell was that?"

"Ähm . . ."

"Was that a cow? Do you have a *cow* living in your goddamn house?"

Bertie was not sure how to explain the logic of the farmhouse structure to him, Deutsch or English. He simply nodded with an embarrassed shrug.

"No wonder it stinks in here." Ward swiped a hand under his hat in disgust. "I swear, you fucking Germans. Between your cabbage and the manure and your sexual impulses, your entire country reeks."

Bertie tried to swallow it all down, coming up instead with a small, polite smile. "May we getting you something for eating or drinking?"

He gestured to the table for him, this Offizier Scheißkopf, to sit. But instead the man yanked the paper from Bertie's grasp.

"What's this you got then?"

"Oh, a zeitung from—"

"A what?"

"A, ähm, how does it go . . ." Bertie squeezed his eyes shut a moment to think.

"A news," Sofie piped up from the throughway. Her English was worse than Bertie's, as it was Bertie who had taught her, but she could catch enough words to knit together an understanding of what someone was talking about. Her voice came out quite even and her face had finally regained its usual composure, though she had yet to move.

"A news, yes. Thank you, schatz." He added the last word for emphasis. "From your own Nordamerika."

"From my what?"

"United States," Bertie tried again. He swallowed as he chose his next words. "Thank you for saving Deutschland."

Ward tossed the paper onto the table, knocking into the figurine and skittering it a hand's length. He looked Bertie in the eye the whole while. "Listen here, we're not here to make friends. We're here to stop you fucking Germans from killing millions of Jews."

"Yes, this is very important."

"So you admit it."

"Admit it?"

"To killing Jews."

Bertie stammered. "Naja, not me persönlich."

"But you didn't stop it, either. You were complicit."

Bertie could not remember what *complicit* meant, but he was certain that it was not good. All he knew was the man was now before his face and at least twenty centimeters taller than him. He blinked, trying to think of the proper thing to say. "How I stopping it? I am one man."

He had not meant for his words to sound contrary, but Ward did not seem to appreciate his response. He shoved him at the shoulders. Startled by the force, Bertie was knocked backward by two steps before the small of his back smacked against the heavy wooden table.

"Bitte!" Sofie called out, finally stepping into the kitchen. She stood an arm's length from the lieutenant. "Sir. Our English bad. He say no hate."

"You keep your distance," Ward said. "I'm more than happy to hit a Nazi, man or woman."

"We are being not Nazis," Bertie said sharply, straightening himself from the table. "We hate Nazis."

Sofie nodded, but Ward scoffed.

"Yeah, that's what you all say. That you were forced. That you never wanted to do it. All I know is you all scattered like cockroaches the moment you lost the War, and now suddenly nobody is a Nazi, everybody hates Nazis. Germans are saying they had nothing to do with it and yet are fleeing left and right to other countries. Why didn't you leave before? Why start now? It's because you lost. And now you don't want to face the consequences of what you've done."

He spat on Bertie's shirt. Bertie simply stood there, missing some of the words Ward had said but following his meaning nevertheless. He could not say that they did not know. Because they had known. Everybody had known for the past six years, for the entire War. Plenty of people who benefitted celebrated it. It seemed the ones who wanted to stop it could not, and those who could did not want to. There were plenty in between who did not care beyond what it meant for them. He thought of Karl upstairs and felt the shame choke him all over again. He did not know anymore which one he was.

"You're to report to the Oberer Kuhberg camp on the first of June. I'll see to it personally. And in the meantime, I'm going to weed out as many Nazis as I can find. So you won't mind if I look around your home."

"Please not," Sofie said quickly. Bertie grimaced as Ward turned to her.

"And why not?"

"It is being a old house," Bertie replied for her. Whatever plan she may have had in her head, he worried she would not be able to say it right in English. "Many places are not safe for walking."

"Bad floors," Sofie added.

"We are not wanting seeing you hurt, sir. You save our country. You are being a hero."

This did little to smooth over Ward. After looking at Sofie a moment, he turned back to Bertie. "You're hiding something. You're scared." He gave a long, loud sniff at him. "I can smell it on you. And I'm going to find out what it is."

"We hide nothing, sir," Bertie said.

There was a loud, single thump from upstairs. All three of their heads shot upward. Bertie felt his face drain.

Ward flashed his teeth. "And what is that?"

Bertie said the first thing he could think of. "It is only Katze."

Ward took Bertie by the shirt. "Who is that? Who are you hiding up there?"

"Katze," Bertie tried again. He could not remember the word and neither, apparently, did Sofie. He could swear he was pronouncing it right. "Only Katze."

He shoved Bertie back against the table. "Out of my way, kraut." He shouldered Sofie to the side as he quickly walked toward the stairs. Bertie glanced at her for guidance, but her expression conveyed only panic.

"Sir, the floor!" Sofie said as she stumbled, but Ward kept going.

"Katze!" Bertie shouted. "It is only Katze!" They followed directly behind him. Bertie grabbed Sofie by the upper arm as they pressed themselves together in the tight stairway. She put a hand over his.

"Sir, please," Bertie said simply. "This is no need."

The door to the smaller bedroom was still closed as Bertie had left it. Ward opened it with more force than necessary, and it banged against the little wardrobe nearby.

Bertie and Sofie shuffled in quickly behind him. It was difficult at first to see over his large shoulders. But when he did not give an immediate reaction of triumph, they breathed a sigh of relief. The room was empty. There was the rumpled bed and an open window. And there in the middle, to Bertie's surprise, was indeed Katze. She hissed when she saw him, but as he stood behind Offizier Scheißkopf, it was clear Ward thought it was for him.

"*Cat*." Ward kicked in her direction with some sort of Amerikan grunt, and she scampered back out the window. He turned to Bertie. "It's *cat*, you idiot. Not cat-*zuh*. Learn to say it right."

There was quiet in the room. Bertie was not sure if he meant he wanted him to say it right now, but he was also worried that too much quiet would make more noises known. He did not know where Karl was. He did not want to make Ward madder.

"Cat," he said as firmly as he could, putting extra emphasis on the *t* to keep himself from saying the rest of the word.

Ward smirked before he looked back around the room. He checked under the bed and opened the wardrobe, patted the walls and tested his weight on the floorboards. Aside from the creaking of old wood, there was nothing to be had. He pointed to the window.

"Why is this open?"

Bertie could not remember if the window had been open before or not. "Frisch luft."

"What?"

"Fresh, ähm . . ."

"Wind," Sofie said.

"Yes! Wind!"

"Air," Sofie suddenly corrected, for it was indeed the better word.

"Frisch air," Bertie said. "It is a Deutsch ding."

"*Thing*." Ward pressed his fingers to the bridge of his nose. "Reading American newspapers, and you can't even learn some damn English."

Ward stuck his head out the window and looked down. Bertie held his breath. Ward brought his head back in and looked around once more, determined to find something. "Is this your bedroom?"

"No." Bertie was trying harder with his English now, but it seemed to be making him worse. All the words he knew were flying from his head at an alarming rate. "It is für gäste. *Guests*," he added quickly.

Ward pointed to the bed with its rumpled blue-and-white pinwheel quilt. "This bed has been slept on."

Bertie felt the room thin again as he tried to come up with an answer.

"A fight," Sofie said evenly. "I . . . how you saying it . . . kicking him out."

"Why?"

"Saying mein cook ist bad."

"You kicked him out of the house?"

"Bett. Before night. He sleep hier."

"He waited until bed to say you were a bad cook?"

There was a pause here as Sofie either tried to find an answer or tried to find some English. "Kicking out house. First. Then coming back, trying bett. I kicking him out bett."

"You only slept on top of the bed?"

"I was trinking, and not sleeping well without my woman," Bertie added.

They waited for the reaction Ward would give. To their surprise, he began to laugh. It was a cruel one, but still a laugh.

"For someone as short as you," he said, "you should try harder to please your *woman*. You're lucky to have one at all, let alone a pretty one."

Bertie first worried about his emphasis on *woman*, as if implying something about Bertie himself, but then he realized he must be using the word wrong. He did not like how Ward called Sofie pretty. It was not a compliment.

Offizier Scheißkopf walked out of the room, his boots clomping the whole way with such force that Bertie worried that the floorboards would actually fall through.

"Goss and Ina Baumann of Ulm," Ward said to himself, his back to them a moment as he filled the doorway. He turned around. "If you're not Nazis, then you have nothing to be afraid of."

They both stood in place, listening as he walked back down the stairs and let himself out the front door. They could hear only their own breath after that. Bertie waited a moment more before he spoke.

"Ina?" he asked quietly in Deutsch. He was afraid to say her real name just yet.

"I'm alright." She came over, putting both her arms around him and resting her face into the crevice between his shoulder and neck.

"You were brilliant."

She held him tighter. "Do you think Frau Baer said something to him?"

"It'd be a fine way to get them off her own scent." Bertie was not sure what else to say.

A new thump downstairs, quieter this time, made them both startle within each other's arms.

"He's back," Bertie whispered. They went down, skulking as if he would jump out at them. "Sir," he called out in English, "are you needing help?"

They heard a shush. When they rounded the corner, they saw Karl hunched in the far corner of the kitchen, the album clutched to his chest. They both went to him quickly, kneeling beside him on either side.

"Are you alright?" Bertie asked.

"I'm so sorry," Karl said quickly, still breathless. "Katze came into the bed and woke me up and then I heard the officer downstairs and then she leapt off and landed on the floor and then I heard him coming so I just grabbed the album and went out the window."

"You jumped from the window?"

"More like dangled and then let go. I had to throw the album out first. I'm sorry, Bertie, it's dirty now. I'll clean it."

"No, it's alright."

"You're lucky you didn't break your neck," Sofie said.

Karl gave a small shrug. "I didn't know what else to do. The Allies, they look everywhere, but only for what they want to find." His breathing was slowing into something normal now. "So I grabbed the album and went around to the other side of the house and hid under the kitchen window. I waited until he was gone and then climbed back in."

"Are you sure he's gone?" Sofie asked.

"I saw him walking down the road. He only stopped and looked back once."

"Do you think he saw you?" Bertie asked.

Karl shook his head, still clutching the album. "He'd be back already if he had."

"Well, he's going to be back regardless. He's here to make sure his labor orders are followed."

"What does that mean for us?"

Bertie took in a breath and held it before releasing it. "It means we have nine days left to get to Stuttgart."

II

We've received word that the Allies are occupying their territories without any known regulation. The French occupation has expelled more than 25,000 civilians from their homes to clear minefields in Alsace. The British are forcing prisoners of war and civilians into reparations work, as are the Americans with all inhabitants in their zone aged fourteen to sixty-five. The food situation is dire in all territories.

But the Russians . . . reports are coming in of mass murder and rape. No German is being spared by gender nor age. Some are even Russian themselves or refugee survivors trying to get back home. Elderly civilians are being killed as a form of entertainment. Mothers and children as young as six are being raped by groups of soldiers at a time, often for hours, in front of one another. Many victims have died of their injuries. We will spare you further details.

To any of us left out there, be safe, be well, and look after one another. Our sun will shine after this night. Thank you and goodnight.

6 • Berlin, 1932

BERTIE HAD TROUBLE CATCHING A FREE MOMENT WITH Sofie. He called her two days after their introduction at the Eldorado, and they had gone to a café, opting to warm themselves at a small outdoor table with teacups of chocolate. The steam curled eagerly from each of their cups, a smell of nuts and roasted coffee, of malt and cream, cutting through the raw weather. They had a wonderful conversation, sharing interests and jokes and thoughts. When Bertie realized he had been neglected a spoon, Sofie offered to share hers instead of bothering the waiter. The spoon swapped between their saucers. He noticed she would always lick the spoon clean after each use, and Bertie felt a particular warmth when she would lock eyes with him, sucking on the tip a moment longer than required. Bertie hoped the blush in his cheeks could be explained away by the cold.

She had agreed to a film afterward, and after discussing it for nearly two hours when they stepped out, he decided to end their date before she became sick of him. He kissed her lightly on the cheek. She appeared surprised by the move. Whether it was too much or not enough, Bertie did not know.

But he had not managed to see her since. Three times he tried to make plans with her and three times she canceled quite late, sometimes the same day as they were supposed to meet. He worried that his fears from their first night were right. She had been drinking, she was not interested when sober, their singular date had been out of pity, or perhaps not a date at all. The spoon sucking, a lustful projection of his imagination. But then he reminded himself that each time she canceled their plans, she made an effort to create new ones. It was the only reason he was still trying, this endless cycle, but his doubts were winning. He should probably stop soon. One more try and then he should stop.

It had been two weeks since they first met. December had reached its most bitter part, and his thoughts turned to the upcoming Silvester fest celebrating the end of the year.

On his walk to work, the air was predictably biting, and a light snow had started to fall. He walked with greater care than usual over the slippery, thin slush blanketing the cobblestones. The Tiergarten was once again majestic. The small flakes fell slow and lazy, coating everything with silence. He collected papers from the question box in front of the Institut and walked in, past the gathering crowd, and up the stairs to the first floor. But as soon as he sat at his desk to file applications, Doktor Hirschfeld emerged from his office.

"Good morning, Bertie! How are our party plans coming along?"

"Quite well, Herr Doktor. The band you like has confirmed and the team will begin decorating early morning on Silvester."

Doktor Hirschfeld was known for his parties at the Institut for transvestites and all manners of invert, but his year-end fest was the biggest of them all. He became giddy when it drew near.

"And the guest list? How is that coming along?"

Bertie gave him a pleasant smile. He was accustomed to this pestering for things to go as joyfully as possible. "Everybody is on it, sir."

Doktor Hirschfeld wrung his hands a moment before releasing a sigh and grinning. "I just want everything to be perfect. I want everyone to have a good time."

"We always do, sir."

He seemed to sense now that he was bothering Bertie and switched tactics. "And how is next year's world tour coming along?"

Bertie sorted through some papers a moment until he found the list inked in his own hand. "Everything is shaping up well. You're going to have a very full travel schedule." He paused here. "Actually, Herr Doktor, this reminds me. May I apply for a transvestite passport? I believe it's the last thing I need."

For a moment, Doktor Hirschfeld looked alarmed. "What would you need the passport for? You're not planning on leaving, are you?"

"Certainly not. But Gert would like me to visit New York City with him in the future. And, well, I've always wanted to."

Doktor Hirschfeld nodded. "They're a tricky thing. We can barely get the cards to work in Germany anymore, but the passports in the rest of Europe, not to mention America?" To his credit, he did not ask if Bertie would be willing to do the obvious, to dress as a woman. "Fill out the paperwork and I'll take it from there. But remember, it'll take me a while to convince the powers."

"Thank you, sir."

Doktor Hirschfeld cheered up. "Perhaps if it comes through in time, you can assist me on my tours."

Bertie brightened at the thought. "I would like that very much, sir, thank you."

* * *

It was already getting dark out as Bertie made his way home in the evening. He longed for the languorous, sun-drenched days of summer. He currently felt like he was barely living between waking up and work. He pulled the neck of his overcoat closer, watchful not to slip on the cobblestones. A cloud of shouts grew in the distance before him, false light warming his eyes. When he turned onto Klingelhöferstraße, he was met with a crowd of people. There was much shouting and pointing. All seemed to be toward the line of men at the front, trying to yell slogans and demands in their brown uniforms, clicking their heels and giving that straight-armed salute, the purpose of which seemed nothing more than to incite the crowd to anger.

The brownshirts had been a growing problem. Bertie had first cast them off as common troublemakers, as young and angry men, most less than thirty years old, who wanted an excuse to beat people up in alleyways. But they grew quickly after the Crash, vastly outnumbering the Deutsch army. Papen's government was not regulating them at all. They ran around and caused destruction, harassed and wounded people, picked on Jews and Communists and inverts and transvestites, simply because they could.

Based on the clothes and armbands now, it looked most likely that a Communist crowd was protesting against a demonstration by the Nazis. Bertie could not make out much within the shouting, but he was certain he heard "Juden" more than once. He thought of Doktor Hirschfeld.

When he was certain he heard "transvestiten," he turned around to avoid Klingelhöferstraße and take the long way home. The Weimar Republic had existed for only fourteen years, but in that time transvestites had made so many positive strides. He did not like the worry that prickled up his spine. Now that people knew his kind existed, he feared a backslide would be catastrophic. It would be so much worse than before.

A gunshot rang out behind him, and he threw himself to the ground. His hands covered his head, his face stung against the cold of the cobblestones. He grunted as pain jolted through his chest, part still recovering, part unused to hard contact without padding. Screams echoed behind him as more shots followed. Something heavy fell near him and he dared to turn his head. A worker's body unmoving on the ground, splatters of red in the snow. He caught a glimpse of brownshirts continuing to open fire onto the scattering crowd.

His first thought was to stay still so he would not get hit. But as he heard the thunder of footfalls cresting behind him, he worried he would be trampled instead. He got up and ran. More shots rang out and he ducked, his overcoat open and flapping. He had already lost his hat.

Large gasps of cold air stung his lungs, the heat escaping from him in great plumes. He worried that his breath would make him easier to track. Him breathing, him existing. His brain was not able to piece together what had just happened. All he knew was he needed to flee from the crowd.

He had heard so many stories about the increasing violence of the brownshirts, of them not being regulated no matter what they did. He had believed what he had heard, but now that it was happening to him, he found himself wanting to deny it. On his walk home from the Eldorado with Gert, the officer had said brownshirts were around, looking for trouble. What would have happened if it was Gert and Bertie the brownshirts had found?

He turned into a thin alleyway and flattened himself against the wall. He was panting, his breath smoking out before him. The taste of metal filled in his mouth. He must have bitten his lip when he threw himself to the ground.

People continued to run past him down the main street. Some looked to be unrelated civilians who had been as unlucky as him, but most were armed with Communist bands. Someone passed that he thought he recognized. He doubted his recognition at first, but when he saw her blond hair, he was certain.

"Sofie?!" he called out.

She stopped and turned around. A man shouldered her hard as he ran past, and she almost lost her footing. She swam against the people and slid into the alley with him.

"Bertie, I can explain."

"Take that off immediately," he whispered loud, though she was already stuffing her Communist armband into the pocket of her coat.

Her eyes were wide, and she was breathing as heavily as he was. "Please don't tell anyone, Bertie, please," she hissed back.

"I won't."

She shook her head. "I never thought they would just start to shoot us like that. Never. The police have been shooting at us since '29. They slaughter us like birds when they're in the mood. But I'd always believed they were provoked first. This time they just . . . felt like it."

"Where are you running to?"

"My first thought was home, but I'm worried it could cause trouble with my family. I don't want them to get hurt."

Bertie turned to face her as best he could in the small alley. "Are you a registered Communist?"

She took a moment before shaking her head. "I was worried about putting anything down in writing."

Bertie breathed in relief. "Okay, good. You might be okay then. But I agree it's best to not go home tonight, just in case you were recognized."

The crowd was beginning to thin, which meant either many bodies had fallen or the Nazis were close.

Bertie grabbed her wrist and pulled her down to the other end of the alley. "Come. You need to go somewhere they won't think to look for you."

He felt the instinct to run, but once Sofie fell in step with him, she slipped her arm into his and slowed their pace.

"It'll look suspicious if we run. We'll walk the rest of the way as lovers who don't know what's going on."

Bertie's mind still reeled, but he was glad that he was not expected to think of everything, nor her likewise. He nodded and tried to slow his breathing. "Yes. Good."

* * *

He handed her a cup of instant coffee and she nodded her thanks. They were both dressed in dry clothes, Sofie in a set of his, though they were almost too short for her. Her underthings hung from the line above their heads as she sat at the little table in the middle of the room. Bertie avoided gazing at the unrestricted curves of her body showing faintly through his white shirt. It did not help that she left some buttons undone. Why had he given her a white shirt of all things? He offered her the bedcover. She accepted and draped it over her shoulders.

Bertie sat sideways at his desk. Snow fell lightly past the window as the rest of the sun disappeared. Thin flakes caught the dull lamplight against the dark sky. He worried that diving onto the cobblestones had undone something from his surgery, but the pain had since quieted into a dull ache. It would likely bruise at worst, and he made a note to tell Doktor Hirschfeld about it for documentation and likely an evaluation. He was surprised to feel anything, seeing as how he had yet to regain sensation. It seemed cruel and mocking that pain was the first and perhaps only thing he felt there again.

He shifted in his rickety desk chair. She held the coffee with both of her hands, and it steamed her face as she looked out the window with him.

"You can stay here as long as you need," he said. "I don't know what happened out there or what it means for us now, hopefully nothing, but the offer is there."

She nodded. "It might need to be a few days. I'll keep my ear to the stations. You have a radio?"

"Of course."

"And I'll need to write to my family so they don't worry. Would you mind going to the post tomorrow to deliver it?"

Before Bertie could tell her it was no trouble, she scoffed.

"They're going to love this."

"What do you mean?"

She looked away from the window. The shadows of the weak lamplight drew circles under her eyes. "They've seen me as a screwup for years now. Ever since I was a child."

"How can that be? You're smart, you're pretty, you play the piano wonderfully, and you stand up for what's right. Do they not approve of your love life? If you bring them to the Institute, we'd be happy to talk with them."

She was silent a moment before she walked past the throughway curtain and sat down on the bed. Bertie leaned back on his chair, craning his neck. She patted the space beside her. "You don't need to sit over there, Bertie."

Bertie sat beside her on the edge of the bed. He was grateful for the invitation. The chair had already started to hurt him.

They were quiet then, both sipping their dull coffees as they looked out the smaller window. It was many minutes before Sofie spoke again.

"I had a nephew. I was fifteen, he was eight. We were close. I already knew piano and I would teach him whenever he was over. We were from Bavaria. It was summer and I begged our mothers to let us swim in Lake Starnberg. I promised that I would watch him." She shifted where she sat, adjusting the bedcover closer around her when it began to slip. "There was a boy there I liked. He smiled at me and it made me feel warm. Nobody talked much about inverts yet and it scared me, the feelings I had, and I hoped that me liking him proved that I wasn't an invert at all. I flirted with him as my nephew went into the water. I let him go in. I let him go in and then I turned my back. I heard splashing a few minutes later but thought he was just having fun. Seaweed had tangled his foot and pulled him under. By the time I dove in for him, he'd already used most of his fight. I tried to free him, but I couldn't. I kept trying. But then—" she stopped there, taking a moment to swallow "—but then I ran out of breath. I swam back upward. I left him because I needed air. And even when I did it, I knew that he would be gone by the time I came back down. I'm certain that was the last thing he saw, me leaving him."

She was quiet. Bertie tried to think of what to say, of what would help her to hear. But then he realized that there was nothing. So he simply rested his hand atop hers. "I'm sorry."

She made a sort of noise like it did not bother her, but her eye had returned to the bedroom window. She glanced at him after a moment, turning her head to the side. She did not move her hand away from his. "What about you? What's your family like?"

"My father died in the War when I was sixteen, my mother from that flu a few months later. I was on my own after that. Dr. Hirschfeld gave me lodging at the Institute and a job soon after. I've been working for him ever since." He took a sip of his coffee, the heat running down his throat. "So I guess you could say he's my family these days. Him and Gert and all of my other friends. We all look after each other."

Sofie gave a small hum. The corners of her mouth twitched in a smile, and a warm light sparked in her eyes behind her sadness. "That sounds nice."

Bertie felt the air around him slow. He seemed to be leaning toward her, or perhaps she was leaning toward him. Either way, the closeness was stirring the deepness of him. But he did not feel his sexual desire was appropriate in the moment. He stood and stretched, placing his cup on the desk and sitting down beside it.

"We should get some sleep. I have work in the morning."

Sofie placed her cup on the nightstand and started to curl onto one side of the small bed, but then stopped. "You're not planning to sleep there all night, are you?"

Bertie stammered. "Well, I—"

"Just come over here, Bertie. I know you're sweet." She looked a little self-conscious then. "And to be honest, I wouldn't mind being held tonight. Please don't misunderstand me, I like you very much," she said quickly. "But this isn't intended to lead you to anything else. Not tonight."

Her final words caused the stirrings in him again. He once more quieted them, for even if she had been interested tonight, he felt he would be too tired and too distracted to enjoy it. He did not want it to feel hollow. "There are different types of comfort appropriate for different occasions." He tried to give a small smile. "And you are permitted to kick me if I ever choose the wrong one."

She pursed her lips in a muffled grin and scooted over so they could both lie down. They faced each other, his chin resting on her head, her arms wrapped around him, their legs tangled. It was the way they would fall asleep for the next thirteen years.

7 • Ulm, 1945

FOUR DAYS HAD PASSED SINCE THEIR SCARE WITH OFFIZIER Scheißkopf, four more letters Sofie had written, and four more lessons Bertie had given Karl. They had yet to come up with a plan for fleeing beyond praying. Bertie tried to mask his growing concern when giving Karl his lessons, as if circumstances had not forced the young man to develop the survival skills to notice everything.

"The handshake," Bertie said. Today's lesson concerned greetings. "A silly thing and yet considered so important. Fellow men will gauge you based on how well you do it."

Karl rolled his eyes. "Who made up all these ridiculous rules?"

"They did, I suspect."

"This is all just to keep as many people out as possible. It's a miracle anyone gets through."

They were in the small bedroom again. The window remained closed against another Katze scare and to prevent their voices from carrying. During sunlight, Karl ate downstairs with them and engaged in limited socializing. But at night, he had to eat upstairs in Sofie and Bertie's bedroom, shades drawn. He could engage with his own bedroom only in darkness.

He had milked Muh every morning since his arrival. Sofie twice caught him lying against her thick side in the night, eyes closed. He opted to clean when he could, but he was forbidden from standing by any windows, and this proved difficult for most of the indoor duties. Bertie noticed he made his bed impeccably smooth every morning. Sofie believed Karl's secret was he never slept in it.

"Why do they do it?" Karl asked. "Keeping everybody out?"

"Power, I'm sure. If they're to decide that those with the most power are them, then logically they'll want as few people like them as possible. The few in control decided that all the correct traits were what they already had. The rest of us have been left scrambling, transvestite or otherwise. What we need to emulate aren't things that men naturally have."

"This is all a game."

"It is, yes."

Karl sat on the bed and rested his head in his hands. "I don't want to do this anymore."

"I know, I know." Bertie sat beside him. "But we don't have a choice. It's temporary, I promise you."

Karl looked at him, his tone flat. "Is it?"

"Well, maybe more like occasional. We'll need to be constantly unassuming during our voyage, but as soon as we've found a safe place to rest our heads, we'll only have to do it when we're out in public. That's something, at least."

Karl shook his head. "You don't understand. I'm not like you."

Bertie was about to remind him that they had already had this conversation, but Karl stopped him.

"I like other men, Bertie. Not women. You'll always have it easier because of that. You were always going to be safer than me. I spent my whole life not living as myself and now I have to not live as myself all over again. No matter where I go, no matter how much people see me as a man, I will always have to choose between living a lie or living in fear." His mouth made what passed for him as a smirk. "Silly, isn't it? If I were a woman, this wouldn't be a problem at all."

Bertie felt many emotions rush up to meet him at once. To his surprise, he chose the one he knew he should probably leave most alone. "First of all," he started in a clipped tone, "don't assume that just because I'm with Sofie, I don't like men, too. Second," he held up two fingers, as if this helped make his point, "I have to hide as much as you do. Did I get lucky, falling for Sofie? Yes. But to only call it luck, to conclude that I don't suffer, too, it's demeaning and disrespectful to both me and her. And lastly," he held up a third finger, his speech moving faster and faster with each word, his breath coming shorter, "what makes you think I didn't fall for a man in the past? If things had—"

He suddenly stopped himself, realizing what he was about to say. Bertie and Sofie had never talked about it. Not really. His old feelings of guilt and shame reacquainted with him. Sure, they had dated before the War, they had flirted. They had shared a bed together and had been intimate. They still did. But what were they, really? They surely enjoyed each other's company well enough, they genuinely liked one another, but they had been thrust together into this situation early in their relationship. Was all this simply convenience? A necessity for survival? An outlet for loneliness and compassion and bodily need? What would, who would, either of them have chosen if they had been given the freedom to do so from the start? He was sure neither of them ever talked about it because after all the intimacies they had shared over the years, the answers could make the rest of their survival together impossible.

Bertie looked at the floor, drifting away from the bed, from the room, as thoughts of Gert returned to him. For the first time, he began to wonder if that was part of why he had gotten out and Gert had not. He had thought perhaps it was what he did that final night at the Institut, his desperate bid to keep himself safe, but he could not be sure. Paragraph 175 had been explicitly about upholding male homosexuality. Transvestites were somehow lumped in based on how they were treated, but how exactly? What upheld male homosexuality and what did not? Did both people need to be male on their birth certificate? Many of them had successfully changed their birth certificates, including both Gert and Bertie. Or did both of them just need to present themselves as male? What about the surgeries? What about one surgery but not another?

People seen as women were not on the books for their homosexuality. An attempt had been made years before. The only reason it did not go through for proper consideration was the first War and then the Treaty and suddenly Deutschland had much bigger problems to worry about. The Nazi Party considered women valuable incubators that could not be spared, so female homosexuals were prosecuted at much lesser numbers. And what of the Allied forces? Would Bertie be seen as a man or a woman to those in control? What about Karl? Did it matter? How could Karl be seen as a woman and a male invert at the same time? How could he be both a threat and not a threat for reasons that contradicted themselves? What about Bertie himself? It all suddenly hurt his head. It did not feel like anybody had ever decided on the rules. They could all be destroyed on a whim, with reasoning that refused to emerge from wet clay, and that was frightening.

But no, Gert could still be out there. He could surely have gone off with Roy to the United States. He could surely have changed his name or lived in peace, just like Bertie had always wanted to. For all of their protection, Gert could surely have never written to them. Bertie had written to Roy only once back when he and Sofie first arrived to Oma and Opa, when Gert continued to not come, but he never heard back. As Hitler grew worse and the War began, he was afraid to try again.

"Are you okay?" Karl asked. He had dropped his frustration.

Bertie took in a breath, blinking rapidly to bring himself back to the room. It was a difficult process, his spirit fighting him to be pulled back into his body, to think and work for him like it always had. It seemed to feel quite tired. He let out his breath and gave a thin smile to Karl.

"If they want to get us, they'll get us. But I want us to try and make it as difficult on them as possible." He swallowed. "If it helps, I believe everyone is acting in one way or another in this world. We're all afraid to be ourselves. And the saddest part is that fear is unnecessarily genuine."

They were quiet for a short while. Karl stared at the far wall, giving a big sigh before speaking again. "Do you think every man is miserable, Bertie?"

"Some more than others. But yes, I believe every man. None of us naturally fits every criterion demanded of us. But some of us have to work harder at it than others because some of us have so much more to lose if we don't."

Karl fixed his gaze on the midday sun reaching the top of the sky. His voice sounded tired. "I think it may be time for my rest again."

"Please rest," Bertie said simply. He stood and took two steps to the open door, but then turned around. "I hope you know that I don't do any of this to you to be cruel. I do it because I want you to live. I want you to be happy, even if it's not completely. But at least happier than you are now."

Karl's head was already on the pillow, his eyes closed. "And it's not my intention to cause you trouble in return. I have a lot inside of me right now. I'm sorry for what I said to you."

"That's alright."

His eyes remained closed. "I'm afraid of what could happen if I finally let it out. And I'm afraid of what could happen if I never do. Poison has been swimming inside me for the past eleven years. I'm worried I'll poison you, too."

"If we haven't been poisoned yet, then it's not going to happen." Bertie forced a smile then. "And good luck trying to poison Sofie. When you're ready to let it out, we'll be right there to bring you back to the world."

Karl managed a small grin then. It faded. "Thank you, Bertie. You two have—" his voice broke a moment. "You've reminded me what kindness is. I just hope I can repay you someday."

"You already are." He was not sure what he meant, but he felt like he and Sofie were a bit brighter despite the scare. Karl reminded them both of people they missed. "Have a good rest."

He walked the few steps out. He was about to close the door behind him when a loud pounding hit their front door below. He heard Sofie startle, dropping a plate as she finished the wash.

"Open up!" came the shout in English. It was Ward.

"Scheiße," Bertie hissed. He turned back around. "Karl."

But Karl was already slithering into the wardrobe after smoothing the bedcovers out. Bertie gave a simple nod to him before leaving, daring to keep the door open to save face from the last time Offizier Scheißkopf had come knocking.

He thumped down the stairs quickly, not wanting to make Sofie answer the door alone. She was still standing near the kitchen sink, toweling her hands anxiously.

"Open up!" Ward continued to pound on the door.

"B—Goss," Sofie said.

"I know, Ina." He put his hand on the knob and opened the door. He flinched as he came upon the raised fist of the man, ready to hit the wood again. He put his arm down.

"You two are coming with us."

"Where?" Sofie tossed her threadbare apron over a kitchen chair as she came to the door. Some locks of her hair had come loose, and she quickly put them back up. Bertie thought Ward's eyes may have lingered on her neck a moment too long.

But the officer said nothing, instead turning around and walking away toward a group of thirty or forty Deutsche, flanked by armed Amerikan soldiers. Bertie recognized many of the people from town. Frau Baer was among them, looking as wilted as ever in her bent little frame.

"They've come to collect us early," Sofie whispered. "They fooled us into thinking we had more time."

"Baumanns!" Ward barked when he saw they were not directly behind him.

They both tossed off their indoor shoes, grabbing their farm boots from just outside the door. They jogged to the group in their bare feet. The pebbles hitched against the underbellies of their feet, the dirt powdering their soles. The Amerikans ordered the group to march before they could do more.

Bertie hopped on one foot as he tried to get one of his boots on. One of the Amerikans knocked him with the butt of his gun hard enough that he fell into Sofie.

"Hurry up!" the soldier shouted.

"You don't like it when the tables have turned?" said another with a grin. "Schnell! Schnell!"

"We're in trouble," Bertie whispered breathlessly in Deutsch. "We're in so much trouble."

They quickly detangled from each other, Sofie already with a strip of dirt against the length of her arm. She slapped it off the best she could. Bertie resisted the urge to look back at the house, to see whether Karl knew what was happening. He worried the Amerikans would raid them while they were gone and find him.

Despite the shove, they both dared to finish putting on their boots. Bertie glanced around at the other Deutsche. Some of them refused to meet his gaze or give a nod of recognition; others walked as if this were a pleasant daytime stroll, smiling and giving the occasional laugh with their loved ones. He did not understand if they did not know where they were going or just did not care. Frau Baer, her face as inscrutable as ever, struggled to keep up with the pace. He could not decide if he wanted to feel bad for her or not, to protect her from the worries of falling too far behind. One of them was shoved every so often, Bertie more than once, but nobody seemed to be bothering with Frau Baer, maybe because she appeared to be making an effort, shuffling faster than Bertie had ever seen her before.

"We're certainly headed toward Oberer Kuhberg," Sofie whispered.

"This is madness." His words, his anger, tumbled out in a hiss. "The Amerikans waited two years to join the War, and that was only for revenge after Japan attacked them. They never cared what Hitler was doing. Great Britain invented the camps in South Africa. And the Russians are raping children so badly that they're killing them. If Hitler hadn't double-crossed them in Poland, they never would've joined the Allies. It was all for revenge again."

Sofie shushed him as she patted his hand. "I know, schatz."

"All this superiority. The Americans and everywhere else ignored all the Jewish refugees. The Jews were sentenced to death by indifference."

Sofie gave up trying to quiet him. At the very least, Bertie kept his voice to a mutter.

"The entire world had the Summer Olympics here. Everybody saluted him. His salute."

One of the soldiers shoved him. "What're you saying, kraut?"

"I asking where we go," Bertie said in a low voice, keeping his eyes to the ground.

The solider smirked without answering. He looked around the heads of the group. "If I hear any more talking, you're going to regret it." The frivolity from the smiling ones continued despite this threat, yet they were left alone.

As much as he did not want to admit it, Bertie knew that they, civilians, had all known for a long time now what Hitler had been doing. All the death and carnage and mass murder, especially of the Jews. They had known and many of them had convinced themselves that this behavior was good and rational. It could not have been done without their cooperation. They could have stopped it if enough of them had banded together early enough. Surely they could have.

Bertie was innocent, yet he felt very much not. Could he have done more? Did it excuse him for hiding, being one of the heads on the chopping block? There were so many emotions swirling inside of him since '33, he did not know how to even begin sorting them. All he knew was he felt sick. He always felt sick.

After nearly an hour of walking, Oberer Kuhberg began to peak in the distance. The camp was closer than he wanted to admit. They approached it from behind, embedded into the rolling hillside of bright green grass and white dandelions. Tall trees flanked its front on the other side, while parts of Ulm could be seen far off behind them on the horizon. The structure was almost ninety years old already, first built as a fort before the Nazis turned it into a camp for political dissidents during the last couple years of the War. Its limestone walls had long since begun to crumble in a speckle of black decay. The roofs of the alcoves were terra-cotta, but the main structure still carried its strong greenery on top, rendering it nearly imperceptible from overhead. The radio once said it held nearly six hundred people during the War, but now it looked deserted.

Bertie had heard that Oberer Kuhberg was an imprisonment camp, not even a labor one. Perhaps they were being lured to their deaths. Would they do what the Nazis did, make them first dig their own graves?

Sofie slipped her arm through Bertie's and squeezed it harder than usual. He patted her hand. Would they separate the two of them before they were shot? Or would they make one watch the other? He suddenly had so much left he wanted to say to her and wondered why he had never taken the time to do so. They had talked so much over the years, and it no longer felt like it had been enough.

"Go in," Ward ordered when they arrived at the gates.

Inside the grounds, tables had been set up, almost as if it were a nice picnic for them. Bertie felt uneasy. How far would the Amerikans imitate the Nazis in order to punish civilians as such? The laughing Deutsche continued to titter quietly to themselves.

"Don't eat or drink anything they give you," he whispered to Sofie, but it was clear Sofie was already having the same thoughts.

But as they approached the tables, Bertie realized that it was various items on display, not food. A flutter radiated from his chest. He worried he knew what might be on those tables, was not sure he knew for certain, and also did not ever want to know at all.

The soldiers halted the group. The breeze was warm and gentle, the dandelions soft beneath their feet. Bertie could only look down.

Ward turned to face the crowd. He crossed his arms in front of his chest and dug his boots into the soft earth.

"This is Oberer," he said, bungling the pronunciation as his voice carried over the breeze. "This was one of the many camps you people built to imprison, torture, and kill millions of Jews." He paused for effect, but none of the different moods of the Deutsche changed. "Terrible things were done to them, gleeful things, and you allowed it to happen. As the first part of your reparations, you will now look at each item in turn and read the associated card explaining said item. You will go through the entire setup no less than three times."

The flutter returned, and Sofie looked gray. Neither of them wanted to see what was on those tables. Nevertheless, they were made to line up. Sofie clung close behind him. The first table contained several metal instruments, some glinting in the sun as if never used, some stained and dirty.

The Nazis often experimented on their prisoners in an array of ways. They never used anesthesia. Many died on the tables or soon after from resulting infections.

Most of the cards were labeled "Dachau" at the bottom. The Amerikans must have brought in items from the nearby labor and death camps, for Dachau certainly had plenty while places like Oberer Kuhberg had not. Bertie thought of Karl.

They took their required several minutes, reading each individual card per item, which gave significant detail to various kinds of experimentation that had taken place. Bertie tried to keep his face impassive. He was stuck between wanting to mourn these people and refusing to give the soldiers the satisfaction of getting to him. He was afraid to look back at Sofie.

They moved on to the next table, which had mostly prisoner clothing like Karl had worn, all of it threadbare and faded.

The Nazis labeled prisoners with various colored triangles based on their crime. The Jews in particular were forced to wear a yellow star.

Bertie set his teeth as the line moved achingly slow. He did not want to look but knew he had to. He did not want to think of Karl, but he did. He did not want to notice that the pink triangles were missing, that the black triangles were not fully defined on the cards. His thoughts returned to how the United States had rejected, continued to reject, Jews desperate for safety or a chance to start a new life. As angry as he was at the hypocrisy of these Amerikans, his anger did not take away what his country had done.

The third table was covered in framed photographs of bodies. Naked bodies, emaciated bodies, skeletal bodies, piles of bodies, dead and dead and dead.

The level of mass murder by the Nazis accounts for at least 11 million people. Since they tried to destroy most of the records before they were caught, we will never know how many died by their hands. Due to so many and a lack of identification, they had to be buried in mass sites.

Bertie had long since begun to feel sick. He still could not bear to glance over his shoulder for what Sofie might show on her face.

Not all seemed as affected.

As they moved in grim silence, he heard laughter and casual chatting from at least half of his countrymen. He could not look up. He had done business with these people, had been kind to them during the War. These were the Deutsche the Amerikans were making them all pay for. Plenty of them had not been as scared as he or Sofie, not until the War was surely to be lost, and it was sometimes impossible to tell until it was too late.

"These are lies," he heard one of them say in Deutsch. "We made homes and jobs for them. He had his reasons to do this."

"If they didn't want to be punished, then they should've obeyed the law," someone else agreed. "The only ones he got rid of were the ones hurting Germany."

Bertie felt a deep sense of shame for his country. This was not the people he felt they were. He could not understand how one could have their head twisted so terribly. Or perhaps they had always been this bad. He wondered how much of what Hitler said had changed minds, and how much of it was simply what people wanted to hear. Had not many countries fallen to such a fate in some way throughout time? The only difference was Hitler had gotten further than most.

Bertie could reject them all he wanted. He could say they were not his people. But they were still his people. And what others did could not excuse what his people had done. He had tried to distract himself from the truth, that these people represented his country just as much as he did. But in front of the tables, the truth was impossible to ignore. In some ways, he too was responsible, he bore culpability.

Bertie glanced toward the front of the line, where Frau Baer looked at objects with her hands clasped behind her back. Her face remained impassive, but she was leaning toward the items too closely for his comfort.

Bertie slowed down as he approached the fourth table. These artifacts were mostly made of some sort of leather, though often slapdash with garish sewing jobs on the bigger pieces. He reached behind him and clasped Sofie's hand.

The Nazis sometimes skinned the dead and made items from the leather. Many of these items became home décor and trophies for Nazi officers and their wives.

Bertie swallowed. The first item was a lamp clasped in beige, wrinkled fabric with numerous large, black stitches in seemingly random lines.

This lamp was found in the home of an officer's wife. The shade required a larger quantity of skin than a singular piece could provide. Notice the stitching of multiple pieces sewn together. It is unknown if the pieces came from different people.

The chill ran down Bertie now like egg yolk. He began to sweat despite the pleasant weather. He was not sure if he started to grip Sofie's hand harder or if she was doing it herself.

"Ina, I can't do this," he whispered.

She squeezed his hand harder. He could see now that she was ashen. "Just one more table after this and then we don't have to study everything as hard the next two rounds." Her voice sounded hollow and distant, unfamiliar.

He eased a little at the last table, which held more simple artifacts, nothing but shoes and glasses and hats. Photographs showed more of these artifacts in clumps so large they looked like mountains.

The Nazis stripped people of their belongings, living or dead. They kept or sold anything worth money. The rest was gathered in piles sometimes in the thousands.

One of the flat-caps struck him still. A small piece of something peeked from beneath its brim. He dared to lean in. Sofie pulled on his hand, either to keep him away or to make sure he did not yank her with him.

"What are you doing?" she whispered quickly. "Goss, please."

He released her hand and clasped his own chest, unintentionally reaching for his heartbeat. A surge of unwellness washed over him. Yet he could not look away.

"There's something there," he said simply. He squinted.

Sofie breathed. She suddenly sounded quite scared. "I don't understand."

He slowly reached out and picked up the cap with both hands. Behind him, Sofie gasped. He did not know why he was doing this, yet he could not stop himself. He felt the gentle weight of it in his hands. This cap, unassuming against all the others, yet his fingers felt at home as they grazed over the fabric.

"Something's stuck to it," he muttered again, more to himself. "On the inside."

He turned the cap over and plucked the small something from the fabric. It was hard and sharp and rolled into his palm to rest. It was a woodchip.

Bertie dropped the cap to the table as if it had bit him. It landed with a slap. His throat closed up.

"Gert." He was not sure he managed to choke out his name before he ran from the table and toward the clearing. His hand over his mouth, he barely fell to his knees in time before he heaved. The vomit splattered on the soft grass in three or four retches, drowning the white dandelions in brown muck. Behind him, Ward laughed along with some of the other Amerikans. Sofie remained at the table, stiff, though she was fully turned his way. She was afraid to leave her spot. Frau Baer merely glanced at him as she rounded back to start the line all over again.

Still bent over and with the laughter of Ward in his ears, Bertie wiped at his mouth before pressing the heels of both palms into his eyes. The acid from his stomach burned them.

"Please no," he whispered. "He's too sweet."

He wanted to go back to the table, to make sure he was wrong. But he knew. It was impossible to not recognize Gert's favorite flat-cap, the one he forever wrestled his hair into. He released his eyes and slumped to all fours. His hands slid in the hot vomit as his tears fell.

"He's too gentle. Not like this. Please."

Sofie must have been released by Ward, for she was suddenly kneeling by his side. He folded into her. She did not mind the vomit as her arms and shadow covered him.

"Gert," was all he said. He refused to cry in any audible way, not in front of them. But he worried he would burst.

"The Nazis must've collected thousands of hats," she said gently. "Millions. The odds of that one being Gert's..." she tried to find the right words. "It's just like any other cap. How could you know for certain?"

"I know."

"Come on," she said just as softly, though he could hear the strain in her voice. "We're allowed to leave."

The hour walk was long and silent. Neither of them spoke, and Bertie continued to stifle his tears. Not yet, not until they were inside.

But once they arrived home, once they had taken off their farm boots and walked inside, Bertie ran up the stairs. He burst into the spare room and wrenched open the wardrobe.

He grabbed Karl by the collar and yanked him out. He pushed him against the wall. He did not care that Karl had been cowering for hours. He did not think.

"What happened to Gert Baumann?" he yelled. He shook Karl when no answer was forthcoming. "What?!"

But Karl continued to stare, unresisting, his face as stoic as ever. His voice was soft and even. "You already know that."

8 • Ulm, 1945

BERTIE SAT OUTSIDE FOR A LONG TIME, IN THE SAME CHAIR he had sat in before he first spotted Karl. He sat until the sun went down, until he could no longer see the fresh green sprouts of wild garlic, until the asparagus bushes wafted vaguely in the breeze like ghosts, until the sounds of Sofie cooking dinner had long come and gone.

All those years he had believed Gert was alive. He was sure of it. He had felt it in his body. Yet all those years, he had been wrong. What he had felt did not exist, for Gert no longer existed. All those years. Bertie wondered what else he had been wrong about with him. About their friendship. He did not know how he could call himself a good friend, a true friend, if he had been wrong on something as fundamental as his life. How he let him go that night even when he felt it in himself to grab his arm and never let go. How he could have protected him so quickly, so easily, through the Institut, but had failed. Just like with Karl.

Bertie was a selfish person. He was a frightened person. He had worked hard only for what he wanted, and after that only for his own survival. He made efforts toward the people he cared about, but when he was forced to make the choice, he chose only himself.

And now here he sat, thinking only of his own sorrows. He had told Karl nothing. He did not help Sofie with dinner or the cleaning. He knew she looked out the window from time to time, the only curtain not yet drawn against the lamps. Her shadow cast over his side, waning after a pause, a single step away that felt like loss. He knew he was letting her worry.

He wanted to know. He wanted to know why he had lived and none of his friends had. He wanted to know why Karl survived Dachau and not Gert. He did not understand why some people got spared and others did not. To survive made him feel worthless, for he felt the pressure to become something extraordinary to justify his fortune. He did not feel extraordinary. He worried he never would be. To not be extraordinary would mean he forsook Gert all over again. And Gebhardt and Markus and Karsten and so many others.

God had given Bertie a gift. God had also made a mistake.

What would they do with it, Gert's hat? Burn it the way so many people had been exterminated? Throw it away to fester like trash? Put it in a museum for people to stare at for generations, a perfect insult of both anonymity and humiliation, of identity misinformed? He wasn't sure which was worse. He wasn't sure what other options there were. He thought and thought and could only come up with what Karl had surely known this whole while: there was nothing.

The only reason Bertie got up from his chair was because he could not stand the pain in his back anymore. He stretched with a grimace, the blood returning to his legs. He did not know what time it was. He walked inside.

"Bertie," Sofie said as soon as he came in. She and Karl sat at the kitchen table in silence, the curtains firmly drawn. Karl looked at him as Sofie rose to embrace him.

"I'm sorry to make you worry," Bertie said into her shoulder.

"I choose to worry." She let him go but squeezed his hand. "Are you hungry?"

"No." He sighed.

Karl's voice drifted from the table, soft and even as always. "You already knew Gert was dead."

The quiet in the air got thick. Bertie felt something terrible hit his heart. Sofie swung around to face Karl, her mouth already twisting with words. But before she could say anything, Karl spoke again. He locked eyes with Bertie. "You didn't write that letter to Gert. You only wrote it to his lover."

Bertie felt the terribleness hit his heart again, begin to grow. His voice rasped a moment. "I only did that because I thought maybe he had been captured."

Karl's tone was still quiet and firm. "No, you didn't."

Bertie suddenly had the urge to hit him. "Then why would I tell myself otherwise?"

"Because you worry that means you gave up on him years ago." He cocked his head. "And that somehow, it would mean you played a part in his death. Or at least weren't a very good friend."

Bertie swiped at his nose with the back of his hand. He said nothing.

"You want to know why I lived and he didn't." Karl blinked, impassive. "You resent me."

"I don't resent you." But as he heard Karl saying these things, he was no longer sure if it was true.

"Survival means nothing, Bertie. Just like death means nothing. To die doesn't mean that one has given up or quit or wasn't strong enough. To survive doesn't mean one is smarter or better or stronger. It's neither fate nor luck. All it is, is horrible."

Karl rose and walked slowly over to Sofie and Bertie. "Come," he said, taking Bertie's hands in his and leading him back to the table. "I'd like to tell you my story now."

Sofie followed, caught somewhere between angry and thoughtful.

They said nothing, the curtains still drawn. Karl took in a breath, then began, his words painfully slow.

9 • Ulm, 1945

"THEY TOOK ME DURING THE NIGHT OF THE LONG KNIVES. IN 1934. June. The thirtieth. It's seared in my eyes. They came in the middle of the night. They did that on purpose. I was in bed. Fast asleep. It was more cruel that way. It was the point. I heard the footsteps and thought it was another boarder. They broke down the door. They didn't even knock. They just came right in. No hesitation. No thought. They pulled me out of bed. I hadn't even sat up yet. I was still waking. They moved so fast. And then they were on me. I could've yelled. I was afraid to. Nobody knew about me. I didn't want them to know. I didn't want them to see me like that. The humiliation and the knowing. I couldn't take both at once. So I stayed quiet. I didn't want to lose my room at the boarding house. My job. I was afraid to be seen. I didn't get my papers. I wouldn't get my papers. The Institute. I fought back a little. But it was more for show. For myself. To say at least I'd tried. But I knew they would have me. And they had me. And they laughed. I thought it was a robbery. I thought they saw me on the street and followed me. Planned. Knew I was small. Easy to steal from. Then maybe they realized more. And wanted their fun. I thought soon it'd be over. They would tire. They would take my money. They would leave me on the floor. I wondered when it was. When they saw me. What I had done to alert them. What small thing. What small slip I had done. Where had I let my guard down. It was always so exhausting. I knew it was exhausting. And yet I hated myself for the slip. Whatever it was. I was pulled by the arms. I was dragged across the floor. Watching my room get smaller. I was dragged through the building. Through the street. Naked. It was almost funny. I had been afraid to yell. To be seen by one or two. And yet here

I was on display. It was late. Nearly nobody out. Others were also being dragged. I didn't understand. But surely it wouldn't be much longer now. They pulled me into an enclosed motortruck. Like they use for prisoners. I thought a law had changed overnight. Paragraph 183 maybe. I would serve a year. Maybe more. Just like that. No trial. But the lamplights. They were SS men. Not police. They dragged over a man. Also naked. Said he could live. He just had to fuck me. The man didn't want to. They laughed at him. They called him a warm brother. It made more sense. But still not enough. I could've run. I could've tried. They had guns. But no hands were on me. I was afraid to run. I was afraid of yelling for help. I was afraid of being seen. Being seen was worse. One more time and it'd be over. It'd be fine. I could go back home. He did what they told him. He turned away as he did it. He never looked at me. He finished. They pulled him away. They checked me. They laughed. They shot him in the head. They left him on the street. I knew soon it'd be over. Soon it'd be my turn. But they brought more. Same promises. Same gunshots. Sometimes. Not always. I don't know why. Me and the last men were taken to a cattle train. Were put in naked. Many others were there. Some clothed. Some not. Some with blood. Some didn't make the trip. The men who'd had me. They went to other corners. They wouldn't look at me. They didn't speak to me. The faces melted together. They were nothing to me. A few days. I don't know how long. I don't know why. Hard to tell. No food or water. Only one bucket. It was dark. It was always dark. Slivers of light through the cracks. No ventilation. We didn't know where we were going. Someone said a camp. We didn't know what that meant. We arrived. We were pulled out. They dragged me. It was muddy. They said Dachau. The first camp. Hitler's biggest enemies. A threat. Some were shot. I was still dragged. They let go. I stood with others. We marched in lines to a building. We were examined. Some were taken away by doctors. All were stripped. All were shaved and deloused and doused with cold water. It was so cold. A doctor looked at me and marveled. He measured my parts. He wanted me for that other room. I did not understand. The officers said no. I was young and pretty. I was given clothes. Thin and striped. Much too big. Others got shirts with a pink triangle sewn in. Some a red one. I got black. I did not understand. We did not understand. There were no Jews yet. Would never be many. We were a work camp. Not a death camp. I was sixteen. The pinks were separated from the rest. They thought inverts were contagious. They put me with the pinks. Like a joke. Conversion for all. Large buildings of small wooden beds. Two to a bed meant for one. I shared with Otto. It was cramped. He was nice. I reminded him of his lover. He asked to hold me at night. He left me alone. They left me alone. I learned some weren't men. They had the souls of women. But Nazis saw them as men. They got the pink triangle. They were treated the same as the men. Some others like me came. Not many. The pinks left us alone. Otto always held me at night. For me. For him. I don't know. The pinks sometimes disappeared and didn't return for a long time. Sometimes they didn't return at all. We heard the stories. Experimentation. Conversion. Sometimes they were just tortured. Some used for target practice. They purposely aimed at their triangles. I saw Gert once. Maybe. Seemed scared. Tried to smile for me. They came less for him than me. We lined up one day. SS officers were picking us out. One pointed at me. And an argument started. A coin was flipped. One of them grinned. Took me to his quarters. Had his way with me. He did not laugh. He did not say cruel things. He said sweet things. But they were still cruel. He gave me a piece of candy. He smiled. He said I should say thank you. I did. He sent me back to my building. Otto said they picked out pipels. It happened to the pinks too. Many officers were inverts. Small and pretty was most sought. I was now a pipel. He said to play it. He said it would save me. He said I was lucky. That I got an SS man when most got only kapos. That I was like a pink now. I knew only boys were pipels. I was a boy now. They finally saw me only so they could make more reason to hurt me. Months passed. Then years. Many more arrived. Pinks arrived. Reds arrived. Blacks arrived. I learned black meant many things. Including boys like me. Some Jews arrived. Then gypsies. And criminals. And murderers. And thieves. People just disappeared sometimes. Too many were coming. It blurred. Many didn't make it past nine months. The officer sent for me often. He had me. He whispered sweetness to me. He told me his secrets. He told me his dreams. He gave me food. He had me eat it there. He watched me eat it. He worried pinks would kill me for it. Anyone would kill me for it. I thanked him. I would try to smile. He did not know the difference. He talked of love. He thought it was love. He kept me alive. I stopped thinking. We heard about more camps. We heard about gas. We heard about fire. We heard about experiments as bad as our own. We heard of worse. We heard about a war. The officer was gone one day. Just gone. A new one claimed me. Then a third after that. I lost track of time. They talked of love. They all talked of love. They gave me food. They gave me better labor. I was not for torture. I was not for experimentation. They kept me alive. I thanked them. I would try to smile. I ran out of officers. I was still young. Young enough. But not young enough. Fresher and younger came in every day. Otto disappeared. Just disappeared. A new pink was in my bed that same night. He did not speak to me. It all blurred again. We heard we were expanding. We heard we were winning. I was getting older. I wasn't pretty enough anymore. I wasn't good enough. Not anymore. They'd brought in women by then. I was moved. I was reassigned. They called them the special buildings. The special task forces. I was taken to a new building. The medical area. I was scared. It was my turn. It was my time. But they only examined me. Took a smear. Drew my blood. Gave me food. A calcium injection. A disinfection bath. Sat me under a sunlamp. We were given makeup. Others helped me put mine on. They taught me. They took us to a new building. It was nice there. Pretty. Tables and chairs and benches. Windows. Even curtains. Good food and drink. I was assigned a room. All my own. I was to live there. I was given no clothes. They said no need. I was confused. We were confused. There were not many of us. A handful. Most of us German. A few Polish and Soviets. Nearly all of us black triangles. A few I'm certain like me. We were told we would be fine. Just do as told. With my first time I realized. They had built brothels. I was in the best one. The one for SS men. The officers arrived when they wanted. Did what they wanted. I was kept alive. Time passed. I was declared less pretty than before. Older. I was demoted to the soldiers' brothel. They arrived when they wanted. Did what they wanted. I was kept alive. Time passed. I was declared ugly. Old. Useless if not for who I was. Boys like me. We were viable incubators. We could get pregnant. Rehabilitation was always believed for us. A condition that was curable. Pregnancy would help. They tried to impregnate us. To fix us. Almost none took. Some of us had been sterilized before arriving. The rest of us were infertile from camp life. The few that got pregnant. Black triangles that weren't like us. Unintentional pregnancies. They were either shot or sent for abortion. It made no sense. I was kept alive. I was taken to my last chance. The prisoners' brothel. Good prisoners got rewarded. If you weren't Jewish. The men could go in and have someone. Officers watched through spyholes. They gave me back prison clothes. Little food. We cost two marks. They were given a ticket. They waited out in the hall. Waited for their number called. A different number each time. Rushed into their assigned room. They had fifteen minutes. Exactly fifteen minutes. They had to take off their shoes. They weren't allowed to speak unless necessary. Only the matrimonial position was allowed. They tried to look at me. I didn't want them to look at me. They asked why I didn't smile at them. Some couldn't perform. They were too weak from camp life. Some just wanted to be held. Everything blurred. Time blurred. So many people wanting. They wanted comfort. They wanted closeness. They wanted relief. Why should I be the one to give it to them. Where would I find it. I had none of my own. They gave them disinfectant ointments before and after. They continued to smear me for gonorrhea. To take my blood for syphilis. Pinks were still made to go. More corrections. Once a week at least. That was the treatment. One didn't comply and was shot. More men. Night finally ended. The body still there. Not gone by morning. Still there. Went through the day. Him beside me. He was frozen. He stared at me. He looked sorry. Soon it'd be over. It couldn't be much longer now. It couldn't last forever. They told the girls that they'd be let go if they worked there. They said six months was all they needed to give. I knew as I worked. I heard the gunshots. It was an expiration date. Exactly six months. They were taken out by the back wall. I waited my turn. I counted the days. I knew they counted with me. It wouldn't be long now. But the officers began to laugh less. They grew in worry. They were quieter. They yelled easier. Discussions became hushed. They fell in number. They ran off. Calls of cowardice. Some still stayed. Some carried on. I waited for my six months. The Allies came. They came five months. Nineteen days. I didn't care. Soon it'd be over. It was almost over. They told me it was safe. They told me there was no more worry. They told me I was free. I asked them the year. They told me the year. I was twenty-seven. I'm twenty-seven. Eleven years. But now they had come. Now we were free. They opened the gates. They told us we could walk out. Walk to where? Nobody knew. But we were free. This was supposed to be a good thing. And yet nothing waited for us out there. They had helped us. But didn't give us help. What more could they have done. I don't know. They seemed to want thanks. Some of us did. I was stuck in my head. I couldn't get out of my head. But the gates were open. It wouldn't be much longer now. But then I saw it happen. I saw them take the pink triangles. Some of the black triangles. They released the others. I heard them check files. To start our sentences in jail. For being inverts and transvestites. They even let the thieves and murderers go. They had served their sentences already. Being in the camps. They were punished enough. I wouldn't do it. Not anymore. Not again. I ran. I wanted them to shoot me. They didn't. They let me run. I didn't know what to do. I hadn't planned. I was so sure. And it didn't happen. I walked. I hid. I stole. I was so hungry. I was thirsty. I saw your farm. I waited to steal. I waited to rob. I was weak. My body gave. I collapsed. I allowed stillness. I felt relief. Soon it'd be over. It was all over now. And then you picked me up."

Karl finally looked up from the table at them, slowly. His face remained even.

"I don't tell you all this to shock you. I tell you because I need someone to know."

10 • Ulm, 1945

BERTIE AWOKE IN THE NIGHT, STARTLED BY A NEARBY SOUND. Sofie shifted beside him. He had slept poorly after what Karl told them. Both of them had.

"Sofie?" he said softly. She raised her head from her pillow. Her vague outline was all he could see in the dark. She did not say anything.

He got out of bed. She did, too.

The sound returned, the light plink of a piano key. He thought maybe the sound was from Katze. Perhaps the creature had come through a window earlier than usual, or maybe the morning was arriving faster than it could tell him. He wiped at his eyes.

He slunk through the dark room, Sofie's hand in his. They knew every creaking floorboard, everything that could stub them. Bertie turned on the hallway light. A note sounded again, followed by others, played soft and slow, over and over. It sounded like something familiar, but he could not quite place it.

Bertie rounded the bottom of the stairs, muscles coiled and ready. He was unsure what he expected to find—a musically inclined intruder, a surprisingly talented Katze. Karl sat slumped upon the bench, enveloped in night. He pressed his index finger lightly on each key, slowly, gently, holding his finger down just enough to hear the chord vibrate before letting it go.

"Mozart's No. 21 in C major," Sofie said.

Karl startled, his eyes squinting against the light. He relaxed when he saw them.

"I didn't mean to wake you," he said. He looked embarrassed. Or perhaps ashamed.

"Couldn't sleep?" Bertie asked uselessly.

A small, sad smile broke through the shadows of his face. "I don't sleep." Hay clung to his back and he carried the faint smell of manure. He likely had been lying against Muh again.

Bertie bit on his impulse to scold him. To be out of bed, to be out of his room, to be downstairs and making noise, however softly.

"I know I shouldn't be down here," Karl said, "but I just couldn't stand it tonight, alone with my thoughts. I needed a distraction. Anything. I was worried I might otherwise scream."

"Why don't you?" Sofie asked. "Into a pillow, perhaps."

He shook his head slowly. "Because if I do, I will scorch the earth." He looked up at her, locking his gaze as he had earlier that evening. "Do you ever feel like that?"

She faced him, her palm tracing lightly across the top of the piano. Oma and Opa stood as solid as ever, watching them. "Do you know how to play?"

Karl thought a moment before finally surrendering. "I had some lessons before that night."

Sofie had an urge in her voice that Bertie had not heard in a long time. "Would you like to learn?"

Karl's eyes brightened, though the rest of his face remained still. "You know how to play?"

Sofie tried to coax a smile out of him. "You sound surprised."

"No, I just," he looked bashful, "I just thought the piano was already here when you arrived."

"It was. But I also play." She turned on a sitting room lamp and sat beside him. "I'm happy to give you a lesson every day, perhaps after your lessons with Bertie."

Karl looked over at Bertie, who simply nodded his head.

"I'd like that very much," Karl replied.

"But for tonight, let's just make it fun."

"How do we do that?"

She smiled genuinely now. "I'm going to teach you a song."

She showed him some notes. Bertie knew her to be a disciplined pianist, but tonight she would just show him the keys. To hell with posture, to hell with sight-reading. She chopped out the notes, a slow, simplified chorus. When Bertie recognized the tune, he felt the emotions crawl up his body like hands from the earth. He could not remember the last time he had heard the song played. He did not want to remember.

Sofie finished her simplified notes and asked Karl to repeat them. He did his best, and then she showed him again, and back and forth they went. They seemed at it for an hour, just those notes. Bertie continued to stand there by the piano.

Karl's face remained impassive, but it seemed more in concentration now. A light grew in his eyes as he hit each proper key.

"Wonderful," she said. "Now do that a few more times until you feel you've got it."

He plinked out the notes, soft and slow and cautious. She waited before critiquing him. She stayed quiet as his choppy mimicry hit the air.

He stopped mid-melody, his finger resting lightly upon the next chord. "I'm worried I'll be mad forever."

"Then be mad forever," Bertie said.

He sounded unsure. "But I have so much anger."

"Because much has been done upon you," Sofie said. "The Nazis have made us scared of anger, made us believe that anger is bad. Anger is not bad. Anger is how we tell ourselves that we've been wronged, that we've been mistreated, and that it's not okay. Anger is a beautiful emotion. We just need to express it properly." She pressed her finger down on a random key. "In music, we call it passion."

The lamplight was dim, and Karl's expression was shadowed. They were all quiet. Oma and Opa kept watching.

"Your family," he suddenly said softly. He looked at Sofie from the side. "You write to them often. You don't know if they're okay?"

Sofie opened her mouth to reply, but then closed it. She gave a small smile instead. "Something like that."

Sofie did not volunteer more, so Karl returned to plinking keys. "What am I playing?"

"'Das Lila Lied,'" Bertie said. "The anthem of our community. Do you recognize it?"

He shook his head. "We have a song?"

Sofie could not help smiling at the memory. "Oh yes. We loved it. We sang it at every party, every burlesque, wherever we could get away with it. Kurt Schwabach and Mischa Spoliansky created it in honor of Dr. Magnus Hirschfeld. Do you know him?"

Karl's face darkened a moment. He did not say anything. Neither did Bertie.

"I'm sorry this is the only lilac life you've ever known," Sofie continued. "There used to be so much joy."

"I wish I could've felt some of that joy. I never got the chance." Karl hesitated before continuing. "My parents didn't approve of me, so I left. I went to Berlin. I heard you could get papers and surgeries there. If I hadn't . . ." He stopped, swallowed, once more looked torn about what he should say. And this time, he skipped something. "I just wonder. I always wonder. If they had loved me, where I would be right now. What would have been different. It would've been so different."

Sofie and Bertie waited for him to say more, but he seemed done talking. He folded his hands in his lap and gazed down.

"I remember when Gert sang while you played." Bertie broke the silence. "The night we met."

"Perhaps we should do that now," Sofie said. Karl nodded and Sofie smiled. "Want to do the honors, Karl? You'll learn the words as we go along."

Karl was slow in his notes, and missed his cues, and he fumbled often. But over and over and over he played his part. And over and over and over they sang, and they smiled, for they each sang for something, even if sometimes it was just for themselves. They did not care about making noise, about daring to show happiness. If they would be caught, then this was the night it was worthwhile.

11 • Ulm, 1945

IN THE EARLY MORNING, AFTER SOFIE AND KARL RETIRED to bed, when the sun had yet to rise, Bertie left. He walked down the main dirt path. He walked until Ulm proper emerged, kept walking through the sleeping town—silent save for the sounds of bugs singing fiercely—kept walking until the city thinned, kept walking until Oberer Kuhberg peaked like a dagger in the distance.

The tables were still set up. His group had not been the entire city. The grim parade would surely continue, handfuls at a time, until all had reported for reparations.

He walked to the table with the cap. He rolled it up, stuck it in his jacket, and rearranged the items to fill the gap he had made. Then he walked back home.

12 • Berlin, 1932

THE JAZZ BAND PLAYED AT THE FAR END, BEATING AGAINST the air above their heads, the horns bounding around the Institut like deer.

Bertie and Sofie were in the main hall of the ground floor. Paper streamers hung from the ceiling in grand arcs and thin curls of ribbon draped haphazardly from every table and houseplant for the Silvester fest. A shower of shiny confetti already littered the polished hardwood floor. People were dancing, talking, having a good time. Empty bottles were growing comfortable everywhere. The huge tannenbaum was still up in the corner, bushy and healthy, silver tinsel cascading from its branches. Someone had lit its candles.

Bertie felt he had assisted in quite the good job. The place was bursting with the third sex and their loved ones. Everyone from Berlin and beyond built their calendars around the parties of Doktor Hirschfeld, but nothing triumphed over the Silvester fest.

The large room was heavy with hot breath and the scent of food. Pfannkuchen piled on tables, their granule coatings sparkling in the lights, faint whiffs of fried oil wafting from their cooled bodies whenever someone walked by. Brezeln and raclette were served hot from a station to the left, the air full of salt and cheese and meats.

"It all looks wonderful, schatz," Sofie said, kissing him on the cheek. She was dressed in a shiny gold flapper dress, her hair adorned with a large feathered clip. She had returned home a day after the incident with the brownshirts. Nobody had bothered her family, and while she felt it best to not tell them what happened, she nonetheless was insulted by how they got over it so easily, like it was expected of her, this disappointment. They asked her only when she planned to get married.

In those two weeks since, she visited Bertie often, and they had made love almost constantly. The past weekend, she told her family she was going to a lake house with friends. She and Bertie never left his bed. Bertie could not remember the last time he had been so dehydrated.

He was dressed now in high-waisted tails, his shirt, waistcoat, and bowtie all a pristine white. A near-empty glass of warmed glühwein was in his hand, a cigarette protruding from between his fingers. Clove and orange filled his senses. "It seems like everyone's having a good time."

He smiled despite the dull ache that remained in his heart. Just the past week, the current police chief ordered the closure of all "homosexual dance pleasures." More than a dozen of their clubs were forced to shut down, including the Eldorado. Rumor had it the owner of the club, Ludwig Konjetschni, was so afraid for his life and family that he handed the premises over to the brownshirts.

Bertie could not believe that the last time he was there, the last time he would ever be there, was when he met Sofie. He wished he had known somehow, had felt it coming. He had kept making excuses about going back. It was too cold out, he wanted to spend time with Sofie, he had a backlog of transvestite applications to tend to, he had to help plan the Silvester party. He would return as soon as those obligations were out of the way, as soon as he had more time, as soon as it got less bitterly cold. He did not like this feeling, not being able to say goodbye, not knowing that the end was the end. To not see it one more time felt somehow like his own fault. It made him feel foolish, to believe so readily that he could step out that night and step right back in at his leisure.

Sofie tugged gently on his arm, and he shook his head free of those thoughts. He looked at her and smiled. Doktor Hirschfeld waded through a throng of well-wishers to greet Bertie. "Guten rutsch, sir!" Bertie raised his glass to him. "I don't think I'll be making it to work tomorrow!"

Doktor Hirschfeld laughed. His big mustache widened above his teeth, his glasses once again catching the overhead lights in a white flash. He bit heartily into a pfannkuch and the crowd around him cheered when the filling came out jelly.

"Bertie!" Gert frantically waved above the heads of partygoers as his small frame pushed through the crowd. A man trailed behind him, nearly dragged by the wrist. The man was the tallest of their group by a head, his dark brown hair expertly styled for the evening with pomade. He was undeniably handsome in that rugged Amerikan way. He and Gert were dressed almost identical to Bertie, save for black bowties instead of white.

"Guten rutsch!" Gert kissed both Sofie and Bertie on the cheek. "This is Roy!" He pulled him in to complete their circle of four.

Roy broke from his trance, eyebrows now up, suddenly aware that he was in front of people. He shook Sofie and Bertie's hands while chewing frantically. He smiled big behind closed lips.

"Hello," Bertie slowly got out in English. "I am called Bertie. This is Sofie. You are good?"

"Oh, no need, no need," Roy replied in proper Deutsch. "It is wonderful to finally meet you. Gert talks about you all the time." He shoved the rest of a raclette-slathered potato into his mouth. He looked up at the elaborate stucco of the ceiling dreamily. "Is there anything better than melted cheese?"

"He's already burned his tongue twice," Gert said.

"This is my first Silvester!" Roy sucked on his cheese-greased fingers. "Why do you call it this?"

"The feast of St. Silvester," Bertie replied. "It was always on the thirty-first, and when the Gregorian calendar also made the thirty-first the last day of the year, I guess it stuck."

Sofie waved a hand in front of her face. "It's originally pagan, schatz." She looked at Roy. "Based on Rauhnächte. The twelve days. You Americans have that little Christmas song of yours to thank us for."

Roy looked confused before realizing what she meant. "Oh! You mean as in, a partridge in a pear tree?"

"Yes! That!" She took a gulp of her glühwein and threaded her arm through Bertie's. Her cheeks were starting to blush with alcohol.

"Where are the others?" Gert asked. "I'd love for them to finally meet Roy."

Bertie gestured vaguely toward the various oracle stations toward the back. "I think they're still in line somewhere. You already go?"

Roy excitedly pulled his piece of lead out of his jacket pocket.

"We went first thing to beat the lines," Gert said.

Bertie glanced up at the bleigießen line and wished he and Sofie had done the same. People were still circled around the table heads deep, melting their little lead charms on spoons before dropping the liquid metal into bowls of cold water.

"What shapes did you get?" Sofie asked.

"Pretty sure mine is a fish," Roy said, once more as giddy as a child. He held his outward in his palm. "Gert says that means people have been talking about me." He looked at him with a playful smile. "Big surprise."

"What about you, Gert?"

Gert gave a shrug that was almost convincing. "I don't put too much into those silly things."

"Oh, come on," Bertie said.

Gert rolled his eyes and pulled his out of his pocket. Bertie came to his side, looking over his shoulder.

"I think it's a cross." Gert shrugged again, trying to say it casually. "But it's just superstition."

"But here, see?" Bertie picked it up, only to turn it around and drop it back into his palm. "Now it's a dagger. Victory is in your future." He grinned and clapped Gert on the back.

Gert rolled his eyes but looked more relieved.

"What do we say to some pfannkuchen?" Sofie interrupted. "The smell has been spinning me all night."

They each grabbed a donut, still soft and yielding to the touch, from the nearest table.

"The rule here is we all need to take a big bite together," Gert said to Roy. "On the count of three. Ready?"

He counted down and then they all bit. They all laughed when they each came up with jelly, but it was drowned out by louder laughter halfway across the room. It looked like Rüdiger, the usual tour guide, got one of the mustard ones. Bertie could see him laughing hard along with his friends as he spat out the mouthful into a napkin.

"What happened?" Roy asked, having already inhaled his pfannkuch.

"A few of them are filled with mustard," Gert said. "It means bad luck for the year, but it's all in good fun."

Bertie finished his drink in a last swallow. "I think it's time to change to feuerzangenbowle."

Roy stopped licking his fingers. "Pardon?"

"Feuerzangenbowle. It's like glühwein, but with more kick. Come, it'll give us a chance to get to know each other better."

Roy sputtered his lips as if his arm were being twisted. He grinned. "Why not?"

They walked to the long drink table, leaving Sofie and Gert to chat excitedly about workers' rights. Large punch bowls of glühwein and feuerzangenbowle flanked endless bottles of beer and sparkling Sekt.

"So, Roy," Bertie said calmly, filling both of their glasses from one of the rum-soaked punch bowls. He handed Roy a glass. "You love him?"

Roy abandoned his look of wonder and set his eyes firmly on Bertie. "I care deeply for him, yes."

His academic Deutsch was clear and precise like cut crystal, though his care slowed his pace by a beat and a half. Bertie found himself mimicking him, though he did not know if it was from camaraderie or infectiousness. He knew Roy would have trouble with the Berlin accent.

Bertie took a sip. The heat of the rum trickled down his throat. "I'm only going to say this once. Gert seems to think the world of you. He talks about you all the time. He has dreams for his future, okay? And so far, I like you, too." He moved in a little closer, lowering his voice. "But if you ever hurt him, you better pray I never visit America."

Roy did not waver. He gave a single nod. "Gert is a treasure that I have no intention to waste. In fact—" He placed his glass upon the table and pulled out a pen. He scribbled on a napkin. "Here is my address. If I ever hurt him, you can stab me in my sleep. But I hope, in the meantime, you and I can be friends."

Bertie took the napkin with a small smirk. He clinked his glass against Roy's. "Treat him well and we will be."

Roy's face softened into a smile. "Remind me. Are you not the one that tattooed him?"

Bertie took a drink, mostly to hide his face. "Shut up."

Gert came over. "Hearing you two talk to each other is like watching the world in slow motion." He tugged on Roy's sleeve. "So are you coming back over or should me and Sofie see our plan through to elope?"

They all talked for some time more, eating and drinking until glasses of freshly poured Sekt passed into their hands. Doktor Hirschfeld got up onto the stage. The band stopped playing and the crowd quieted for the first and last time of the night.

"Everyone!" he said in his booming voice. "Thank you for coming!" A great cheer rose, and Doktor Hirschfeld flapped his raised hands for quiet. "But now it's time for the countdown! Ready?"

He checked his watch and began to count from thirteen. Once he got to ten, everybody joined in, growing louder with each tick downward. At one, the fest exploded in riotous mirth.

"Prosit Neujahr!" came the unanimous call from all corners, overwhelming even the band as everyone cheered and beat against the floor. Glasses were raised.

"Happy New Year!" Roy exclaimed in English. He laughed and kissed Gert on the lips.

Bertie and Sofie embraced. He looked at her and sighed quietly. "I'm really glad you're in my life."

Sofie grinned and kissed him again, putting her hands to either side of his face. She released him. "Let's make this our year."

The band struck up once more in "Das Lila Lied," and the crowd joined in song. But even their noise was no match for what had already started to rumble outside. They could feel it through the floor, eating into their feet.

Gert took Roy by the hand and began to tug him toward the stairs. Sofie and Bertie quickly followed. "Hurry, Roy, you'll want to see this! We need to go up!"

They traveled three flights of stairs before they stopped, now breathless.

"This should be good enough," Bertie said, knocking first even though he knew the room was not currently rented. They went through and out onto the balcony. The sound of the band and the crowd in the grand hall lessened beneath them, but a fresh, bigger burst of noise greeted them outside.

"Good Lord!" Roy said in English, laughing.

People had spilled out of every building and home. The streets were suddenly choked with bodies. People danced, they shouted, they celebrated. They banged on pots with kitchen utensils. They beat on drums. They dangled from roofs, from balconies, from courtyards and windows and terraces. Far as the eye could see, Berlin was coated with joy. Church bells rang in the distance, faint against the onslaught.

But the greatest sight was the fireworks. Already they were set off from every direction, bouncing across the street, flying into the air, shooting between streets and buildings, tails glittering, flashes blazing, colors bursting. Cracks and bangs and sputters and whistles. The city of Berlin was already setting off its carefully coordinated display, but the citizens gave a gleeful challenge themselves with their own crackers and bangers, home concerts to the main orchestra. They shot from beer and Sekt bottles, aimed without thought or intent, ricocheted off windows. The great billows of purple smoke were already wafting up to their own balcony.

"I have never seen anything more un-German in Germany," Roy said in Deutsch after a long silence.

Bertie laughed. "We may be a highly disciplined breed, but give a German a firework and we become the most reckless people you've ever met."

"Everything we do," Sofie said, "we do with passion."

They all continued to watch. The sky became a sea of light and smoke.

Bertie sipped from his glass of Sekt, his arm around Sofie, Gert close at his other side. Berliners continued to run through the streets, setting off fireworks, banging on pots, laughing, yelling, and doing all possible to drive out evil spirits. They were loud. The transvestites and inverts downstairs were loud. It would be the last time Bertie felt they ever made noise. It would be silence ever after. In death, in hiding, in mourning, in denial of their selves and their community. The bleigießen of Gert had been a cross. It should not have been a cross, not ever. Crosses meant death.

Bertie kissed Sofie and laughed with Gert. He gave a respectful nod to Roy and raised his glass. He looked out over the street, heard the church bells, smelled the smoke, felt the bubbles of Sekt burst on his tongue. The scene soaked him. And through it all, the band rose up from downstairs, the Institut drowning out all else in "Das Lila Lied."

13 • Ulm, 1945

BERTIE SAT AT THE KITCHEN TABLE AS THE SUN ROSE. HE had not slept at all. He already weeded the entire field. He already snapped off the asparagus crop for the day. He was going to milk Muh, but she was still sleeping, Karl resting against her. One of the chickens nuzzled herself up against his leg, her neck melting into her fluffy body.

The sky stretched in purples and pinks. Bertie thought about how Sofie would be up any moment, just before he heard her footsteps creak above his head. She had still not heard from her parents. She was hoping to find where they were, if they were still at home. If nothing else, she wanted them to know she was okay, that she was alive. And once she was safely across the sea, she wanted them to know where she'd be, that they could try to come over, too.

Bertie did not know what he would do with the hat or how he would explain it to Sofie or Karl, but he knew it did not deserve to be in the hands of others. After returning from Oberer Kuhberg, he pulled up the potato planks and slipped the hat inside the burlap sack containing his scrapbook and his leather work satchel. He willed himself to look at it one more time. The hat was tattered, and it was old. It certainly looked like Gert's, but that could mean anything, and in the light of day, he was not convinced it was even Gert's. That hat could have come from anyone. As Sofie had said, there were surely thousands just like this one. What were the odds? Karl said he had seen him, maybe once, maybe not at all, he was not sure. It had been years and memories failed, especially under duress. Maybe Gert was still out there. Maybe he got out, maybe he fled to Amerika and was still living with Roy, maybe he was hiding in plain sight in Deutschland just like Bertie was. It was partially why

Bertie had never left, why none of them had left. They were all waiting for Gert to arrive; they were all waiting for things to get better. "Let's wait and see" was the mantra. "Let's wait and see." And then Gert kept not arriving, and then transvestite passports were shut down, and then other passports were shut down, and then the Deutschland borders were closed, and it was illegal to leave.

He slipped the hat into the burlap bag and, by unsurprising reflex, pulled out the photo album from his old work satchel. At the kitchen table, he slowly turned the pages, soaking in every picture of Markus, Gebhardt, and Karsten. And Gert. His favorite picture of them both was on the final page of photos, two-thirds full, mostly images of their last time at the Eldorado when Bertie had returned from surgery. Gert sitting on his lap, holding up his passport, smiling his biggest smile. Had Bertie known this would be the last true time they would be together, he would have been happier for him. Perhaps he would have made more of an effort to be intimate with him that night, just to have one last time.

What was the last thing Gert ate? Breakfast that morning, maybe a quick lunch on a haphazard break? Had he neglected dinner again in exchange for fun? Did he have a chance to drink a beer, to kiss a man or two before he had to flee Noster's Cottage? What tastes lingered in his mouth? What were the contents of his stomach? When was the final time he relieved himself? His final orgasm? When were the last times he did any of it, and did he know, deep down, that these were the final times he would use his body in these ways? Did Karl really see him in Dachau, was that really his cap now beneath the floorboards? Or had they killed him during the pogrom? Bertie did not know why he was asking these questions, he did not know why they mattered. All he knew is that they did.

Everything mattered and nothing mattered. He finally let the other thought in, the thought he had been resisting since Karl told them his story. It was some of the medical experiments he mentioned, the pellets of testosterone they had forced on invert men. They were Titus Pearls, those little capsules implanted under the skin. They were patented by Doktor Hirschfeld, they were his. Bertie was ashamed to say it. The Institut also had a department that studied eugenics. The Nazis had been inspired by Doktor Hirschfeld's own work. They must have visited the Institut, gone on the tours. Bertie may have led those tours himself, fed them information, put ideas in their heads. The Institut was complicit in the slaughter of his own people. He was complicit in the slaughter of his own people. He had felt the shame of this for a long time, but he had never truly realized the scope of it until now. He felt the sharp twinge of acid gathering at the backs of his cheeks.

He rested his hand in his lap, staring at it for some time. He thought about the tiny lead cross Gert had held in his palm. Where had that omen gone? His mind flashed with images of Gert throwing it out as soon as he got home, of losing it after keeping it in a sock as a memento, however macabre in his sentimentality. Perhaps he dropped it during the party, during all the noise and jostling, perhaps trampled by festivities. Swept away, fallen into a gutter, forgotten. Where was it the fateful night of the Institut? Where was it the Night of the Long Knives? Did it puddle and warp in the heat of the sun? Was it buried under the rubble of bombings? Had it been collected in scrap metal, boiled into Nazi ammunition? Here too Bertie felt responsible. He had been the one to arrange the lead for the party. Such a tiny thing, such a silly thing. Yet suddenly it was all Bertie could think about. Where did it sit, what had it seen?

He wanted to blame the cross. It felt so much easier than blaming everything else.

He wished he could go to Gert's old apartment in Berlin—Who lived there now? Was the building still standing?—wished he could gather some of his clothes or his aftershave or anything adult-age Gert held dear, anything he had touched. He just wanted a memento. But it was all surely gone by now. Sold or burned or used or discarded.

Bertie wiped at his eyes and closed the album in a thump. He rested his face in his hands as the soft footsteps of Sofie came up behind him.

"You look terrible." She leaned over to wrap her arms atop his. She kissed the back of his head.

His shoulders relaxed against her. "You're just saying that to get me into bed."

She gave a squeeze before letting go. She scooped up the small pile of asparagus Bertie had put on the table. "I say we start keeping all these for ourselves. Fuck it."

Bertie gave a weak chuckle and nodded.

Karl came in from the cowshed, holding a chicken. Bertie did not have the energy to correct him and Sofie seemed to have the same thought. If he wanted to hold a chicken in the living quarters, let him hold a chicken in the living quarters. The chicken twisted its neck around in sharp little jerks, gave a few soft clucks of awe at this forbidden place, but otherwise remained docile. It was difficult to tell if Karl looked any worse than usual.

"I milked Muh," he said. "Wanted to check for any scraps to feed the chickens."

Bertie nearly asked him to just let the chickens out to roam free but then remembered how risky that would be for Karl. He instead stood and handed him the pail of weeds and food scraps that had accumulated since yesterday. "Bring us back the eggs and we can all breakfast."

Karl noticed the asparagus Sofie was already throwing into a skillet and his face allowed a flicker of excitement. He turned around with the bucket in one hand, the chicken in the other, and elbowed his way back into the cowshed.

* * *

"Stretch your tongue out, far as you can, good." Bertie did it himself, too, counting to ten with his fingers.

They were continuing their lessons in the smaller bedroom. This was their third voice lesson. It was, Bertie had been honest with Karl, one of the biggest improvements he needed to make. Karl begrudgingly accepted this fact even as he resented the timing. He wanted it to be for him, not anyone else. If they got to Amerika, Bertie promised, he could alter his voice however he wanted and at his own pace.

"Okay, good. Now massage your jaw muscles with the heels of your hands. Downward motion. Good." He did the same alongside Karl. "Remember that we need to stretch out and relax everything from the ribs up. Try to remember to breathe and keep your heart rate down. The more tension you have, the higher the voice naturally becomes."

Karl finished his stretches and huffed for the hundredth time in the past week. "That's just mean." He mocked in a voice that Bertie assumed was meant to represent people at large. "Don't have angst or you'll die. No pressure. It's not like you're fleeing for your lives or anything."

Bertie simply nodded. Karl was, after all, right. Gert had been the same way.

"Now I want you to repeat after me and remember to breathe in from your belly. Bring your voice up from there. Remember it's not so much pitch as it is resonance. You want it to vibrate from your chest, not your head. And end each sentence a note lower than you used for the syllable before it. All these little things add up." He could see Karl resisting the urge to roll his eyes. Karl knew all this already, some of it long before his lessons with Bertie. Like any of them, he studied the normally sexed closely. The problem was that it was a lot to keep in one's head and took a lot of energy to perform, especially in the early days. "Okay. So. Repeat after me."

He went to open his mouth with his prepared sentence, but then he stopped.

"Oh my God," he said softly.

Karl raised one brow. "Okay . . ." He cleared his throat. "Oh my God."

Why it struck him now and not earlier that morning, Bertie did not know. But after seeing the hat and thinking so much about Gert and looking all the way to the end of the photo album, staring and ruminating and trying to soak up every last detail he feared was lost to his grief and aging memory, suddenly everything fell into place.

Bertie dashed out of the room. "Oh my *God*."

"Wait, what's happening?"

Karl trailed behind as Bertie descended the winding stairs and entered the sitting room. Sofie poked her head in from the kitchen, confused by the noise. Bertie rooted through a side table drawer until he pulled out a magnifying glass.

"I'm such a dummkopf!"

"Bertie?" Sofie glanced at Karl, who shrugged.

Bertie knelt and raised the potato boards. He extracted the album from the satchel, careful to keep the cap hidden, then replaced the boards. He opened the album on the kitchen table to the final page of photos. He hunched over with the magnifying glass. Satisfied, he stood back upright and held the magnifying glass in place. "Look!"

Sofie leaned over first and then Karl. They shared a glance, but neither understood the meaning of the photograph. "What are we looking at, Bertie?"

"His passport!" Bertie picked up the album and pointed to the photo of Gert on his lap. "Gert's passport! He became an American citizen that night!"

". . . So?"

The thought raced through his mind like a bolt of lightning, and he felt like he might burst for it. "We make our own passports!"

Sofie and Karl both gave a loud, involuntary groan, twisting away in the ridiculousness of the moment.

"Bertie, be reasonable," Sofie said.

"That'll never work," Karl said.

Bertie lowered his voice. He worked to slow his breathing. "No, think about it. We act like it's such a big thing, but it's all so trivial. Some paper and cardboard, a little ink and rubber. What it comes down to is the manner you present it. What matters is who we get sitting across from us at that immigration desk. Significance is only worth what someone puts into it."

"But to fool an entire country . . ."

"We're not fooling an entire country. All we have to fool is a single person who decides whether or not to let us in."

Karl remained unconvinced, but Sofie followed the thread of Bertie's logic.

"Okay then," she said. "Cardboard, I take it?" She pointed to the broken-down boxes near the door from Bertie's last trip to town.

Bertie nodded.

"And I guess we have ink."

Bertie nodded again, his excitement growing.

"But what about the paper?" She examined the photo with the magnifying glass. "That's some sort of patterned paper."

Bertie put the album down and flipped further back to a blank section. He carefully ripped out a page with its light, patterned background and held it up.

Sofie squinted. "That paper isn't exactly the same as in the photo."

"No, but it's close."

"And how would we explain that?"

Bertie shrugged with both hands up in the air. The paper flapped and he put it back on the table. "Rationing. Shortages. There's been a war. And everything's gotten bombed over here, especially Berlin. How many Americans in America have seen a Nazi passport, anyway? Even if they work in immigration?"

Sofie said nothing and Bertie shook his head to put his thoughts back in order. "It's less about the materials and more about this." He held up the photo again, tapped on the passport open in Gert's hand. "The most important piece, the only thing that'll make this work, is the citizenship stamp. And we actually know what it looks like." In his excitement, a hard pang of sadness hit his heart. Gert had, once again, saved their lives.

Karl finally spoke up again. "But materials *are* important here. Where are we supposed to get the stamp?"

"We make it."

Sofie and Karl again groaned together.

"With what?" she demanded.

"Rubber."

"Rubber?" Sofie scoffed. "And where exactly are we supposed to get rubber?" She pointed to the photo. "Or these date stamps? Or these number punchers?"

Bertie went back to the floorboards. He pulled out his work satchel. He dumped out the contents from the bottom. Mostly, it was old work supplies of little consequence, but among the supplies were a date stamper and a number puncher. All the things he had ever used to file paperwork and applications.

Bertie picked up two flat pink erasers and pressed them together in front of their faces. "If I carve the stamp out of these, it should be about the right size. Then we can stamp all three passports and I'll fill out the lines with a regular fountain pen. Just like in the photo."

Sofie's eyes widened. She was quiet a moment as she thought this through. "Scheiße."

Bertie grinned big.

"How do we know the stamp hasn't changed over time?" Karl asked.

Bertie's grin slipped a little. "We don't. But again . . ."

"War."

"Yes, war."

"The last piece is knowing what the cover of a Nazi passport looks like," Sofie said. "Anything else would have expired by now."

There was silence a moment. Bertie had not thought about that part.

". . . I've seen them," Karl said quietly. He swallowed. "I was around a lot of SS officers. I visited their camp homes for years. Theirs are a little different, but their wives and children . . . it's just a plain brown cardboard cover, really cheap looking. Really simple. They weren't giving out a lot of passports once they closed the borders. It just has the Nazi eagle painted on the front in black with the words *German Reich* and *Passport*. And some numbers punched out at the bottom." He glanced back over at the broken-down boxes near the door. "This really could work."

It looked like Karl was officially interested in trying, but Sofie still hesitated.

"There's one last problem. We can give them the most believable passports possible, and they still might assume they're fake simply because they're letting in so few Germans these days. Especially not the working class. If a family of German farmers suddenly show up with not only passports but citizenship that's impossible to get, they're going to know something's wrong. They're going to check with the American embassy in Berlin."

"Remember what the radio said? Not only has Berlin been bombed into ruins, but everything is so chaotic right now." He took a breath and looked at Sofie. "The Allies are like dogs trying to catch a car. They moved so quickly without definitive plans that they cut up Berlin wrong. The American embassy is in the Soviet section."

Karl took in a sharp breath. "You're joking."

Sofie looked past Bertie's head, thinking.

"I'm not saying this is a perfect plan, schatz. I'm just saying we actually have a chance. If we present ourselves right, if we play the part, they might just wave us in. They may not see us as worth the effort of proving us wrong. Germany is done with the War, but America is still fighting it with Japan. They're distracted. They'll be looking for reasons to do less work, not more."

"But that also means they could send us back just as easily," Sofie said. "Not worth the effort, like you said."

"It'll all come down to who sits on the other side of that desk. But it's not impossible."

"What happens if we're caught? In any sense?"

"We get sent back," Bertie said with a resigned shrug. "Or we're put in one of their jails for an unknown amount of time, possibly forever because we'll be easily forgotten, or we're made to do reparations work alongside the other Germans."

"With their prisoners of war?" Karl looked genuinely frightened at the thought of doing camp work alongside Nazi soldiers and SS men.

"Or German Americans. Either."

"So our choices are those fates there or the same fates here?"

"Here, it'll definitely happen. But there, we have a chance that it won't. That we can just disappear and start over. I've wanted to see their Midwest for a while now. There's a lot of German immigrants who have settled there since the end of the century, and a lot of farmland. It'd be a little piece of Germany, doing work that we know how to do, and maybe they'll take more pity on us than anywhere else in the world. As Germans, at least. The rest we'll still have to keep indoors."

Karl shook his head, but it looked like more for putting things in order. "You really think we can do this in four days?"

"If we split up the work with what we do best," Sofie said. "I can make the covers and inside papers, Bertie can cut the stamp and fill out the final information—"

She stopped there. They both looked at Karl, neither of them wanting to say what needed to be said.

Karl glanced at them both before dropping his shoulders. "I'll ink the Nazi eagle on the covers."

Bertie reached out and squeezed his shoulder. Sofie took his hand and bent her head to catch his gaze. "We can do a piano lesson in a few minutes," she whispered. "You can play 'Das Lila Lied' again."

Karl nodded and stood more upright, though his face was once again stoic. Bertie released his shoulder, careful to keep his tone even, less excited.

"We have to be careful because we have very limited resources, but I really think we can do this. This is it. This is how we get on the ferry, this is how we get on the boat, this is how we get through the French and British territories and into the Netherlands. This is how we get out. Four more days, and we're on that ferry to Amsterdam."

It didn't seem real, this sudden change, like they were all just fantasizing or playing a game. It was the first moment since thinking this idea that Bertie felt some fear.

Sofie added a moment later, "Remember that you need to carve it out backward."

14 • Ulm, 1945

AS PROMISED, SOFIE WORKED WITH KARL ON "DAS LILA Lied," only this time it was a slower, more structured lesson. It was Sofie's way of teaching Karl to sight-read each note. Bertie sat on the couch and listened. Afterward, the three of them went up to the smaller bedroom to work on the passports. The task would have been easier at the kitchen table, but they could not risk being spotted, not being able to clean up quickly.

Bertie and Sofie sat on the bed with the photo and magnifying glass between them. After slipping out the necessary photo, they had left the rest of the album on the kitchen table downstairs. Sofie scrutinized the size and shape of the passport in the photo, while Bertie examined the stamp. They'd been at the task for hours, and the effort was taking a toll. Bertie's back ached, and carving such small details backward into rubber was making him think he was starting to lose his eyesight. The quilt was covered in tiny pink shavings. These were the only erasers they had. Probably the only rubber in all of Ulm by this point. He took the time to carefully sketch it all out first and was not even a quarter of the way through carving. He was too afraid of making a mistake to hurry.

Karl sat on the floor with his back against the bed, practicing stencils. The insignia was of a swastika clutched in the talons of an eagle. Every so often, he lifted up his work for their approval.

"We'll be in so much trouble if anyone finds these," he said, starting on a fifth iteration.

There was a pleasant knock at the door downstairs. They all froze, staring at each other.

"If that's Frau Baer . . ." Sofie sighed. She squeezed Bertie's shoulder before standing.

"We better clean up," he said.

Karl nodded. "Go. I'll take care of it." He was already swiping eraser shavings into his palm.

Downstairs, Bertie sat at the kitchen table, as if relaxing after a hard day's work.

"I'll get rid of her as fast as I can," Sofie whispered.

Sofie glanced at him before approaching the door. She turned the knob and immediately stepped back. The door swung open as Ward strode in, a grin plastered on his face.

"Officer," Bertie said in English, quickly standing. The chair legs skidded jerkily against the uneven floor. "The hour is much late."

"My apologies," Ward said. He continued to grin. "But I wanted to clear up a confusion I have."

"We are much happy helping you." He glanced at Sofie. Her eyes were fixed on something behind him and her face was pale. He realized he had neglected to put the album away. It was within two steps of Ward, within a swipe of his arm. He tried to keep his face pleasant.

Ward had not yet noticed. "You're Goss and Ina Baumann, yes?"

Bertie felt uneasy. "Yes."

"Of Ulm, Germany, yes?"

"Yes."

"And you own this farm, yes?"

"Yes." He slowly took a few steps away from the kitchen table toward Sofie. Ward turned to face him, his back now to the album.

Ward dug into his military jacket. "Interesting. Your names are on the deed to this land." He pulled out a few pieces of paper, old and yellowed and folded. "But your parish records of birth . . ." He unfolded the one and then the other. "Goss Baumann, born 1865 in Ulm. Ina Graf, born 1864 in Ulm. And your marriage license, 1884. Again in Ulm." He held the records open in one hand, pressed together by his thumb. "And what year is it again?"

Bertie swallowed. "Nineteen and forty-five."

"Nineteen forty-five," Ward repeated. He tucked the papers back into his jacket. "Wow. I must say, you two look wonderful for your age. What's your secret?"

Bertie stammered, backing away from the table. Ward calmly matched his pace. Sofie slunk toward the album. But Ward caught her by the upper arm.

"Or more importantly," he said, still looking at Bertie, "what did you do with those poor people? Because I'm not seeing any burial records."

Bertie held his gaze. He swallowed. "We have doing nothing."

"Did you kill them?"

He took another step back. "We are innocent peoples, sir."

"Then why are you hiding?" He took a step closer, pulling Sofie with him. "Innocent people do not hide."

Bertie did not know what to say. He did not know if he could somehow still convince Ward that they were Goss and Ina, that he had made some sort of mistake. He did not know how to explain that Goss and Ina had taken them in, that they wanted them to have the farm. How with every year that Gert did not arrive, they seemed to crumble that much more. How they had died naturally, each in their own time, halfway through the War. How they had made Bertie promise that he would never abandon Gert if he was still out there somewhere, would give the farm to him if he ever arrived. He did not know how to convince Ward that innocent people had many reasons to hide.

Sofie looked ready to strangle Ward. She could save herself, she could tell Ward about Bertie and claim she was a victim, that he had threatened her for years and she had been so scared and thank God he was here to save her. But she did not. Bertie nearly wished she would. At least she and Karl would still make it.

He suddenly felt mad at her for not doing it, for staying quiet. But he was staying quiet, too. He could turn himself in. Yet he was not.

After Bertie's long silence, Ward released his tongue from the roof of his mouth in a single, wet snap. He looked at him like a disappointed schoolmaster. "That's a shame." He turned to Sofie, then, her arm still stuck in his grasp. She kept her head cocked away from his gaze. She was dressed in her graying nightgown for the evening, slightly sheer in the wear and evening chill. His eye lingered.

Sofie quickly crossed her free arm over her chest. She still did not look at him. All Bertie could think about was the stories they had heard over the radio, about the Amerikan soldiers who plastered their posters everywhere about not fraternizing, about how they withheld rations to the Deutsche as low as seven hundred calories a day, and then turned around to offer pretty girls food and cigarettes to bird them. Frau bait, they called it. Bertie knew the babies would be denied, as paying support to the mothers would equal aiding the enemy.

Bertie hated himself for having that album, hated himself for everything that was happening to them, how he kept getting them into danger. He hated how Sofie paid for it again and again. If he had put the thing away, she would not have gone toward it, Ward would not have caught her by the arm, maybe would not be eyeing her.

Bertie did not know what to do. He stood like a fool. Innocent people hiding. He watched as Ward pulled Sofie closer to him.

"We are Juden!" The words were out of his mouth before he could think on them.

Ward halted, looking at Bertie in surprise.

"Jews," Bertie said.

Ward's face recovered, quickly becoming wiser. "Jews," he repeated simply. He let go of Sofie's arm and walked toward Bertie.

Sofie immediately slunk to the kitchen table and picked up the album, wedging it out of sight.

"Why didn't you tell me sooner?" Ward said.

Bertie kept his gaze on him. He thought, tried to mask it as caution. "We hiding for years. Who is safe telling? We do not trust."

"But I'm an Ally." Ward sounded almost insulted now. "The Americans are part of the Allied forces."

Bertie was not sure what to say to that. He did not know how to explain such a thing to someone who already did not understand violence.

What little chance they had was quickly waning in Ward's eyes. "If you're Jewish," he said, "prove it."

"Prove it?"

Ward brought back his old grin. It slowly grew on his face. "If you're Jewish," he said slower, "then you're circumcised."

Bertie did not know this English word. It was not until Ward brought up his hand, waggling his little finger with a deepening grin, that it finally made sense.

Bertie was certain he whitened as much as Sofie. He took a step back. "This is not necessity, sir."

Ward stepped into the empty space between them. "But it is."

"Sir, please."

"Plenty of Nazis have said they're Jewish to get out of punishment. It's terribly cruel. Are you a Nazi, kraut?"

"We are not Nazis." He kept taking steps back and Ward kept filling the void. He thought he heard a muffled thump outside.

"Then let me see."

"Sir."

Sofie gave a loud, sudden gasp from the other side of the kitchen. She flailed dramatically, falling to the floor in a particularly loud thud. She purposely took out the nearest chair on her way down. But her acting was wholly ignored.

"Show me you're circumcised and then this all goes away." Ward flashed his smile wider. "Unless you're not."

Bertie's back pressed into the wall as Ward placed his palm against the wood. The much taller Ward towered over him.

Sofie quickly got up off the floor. She picked up the fallen chair by its back, holding it upside down with both hands. She crept toward Ward. They were out of ideas, but she was trying. At least they could tell themselves that in the end. He wondered if she could knock him out, if she could hit him just right. But what then? What would they do with him before he woke? Could they bring themselves to do terrible things, even if they were for good reasons? Were they good reasons?

Ward leaned in. His hot breath caressed Bertie's cheek.

"Show me, kraut."

"Sir, please."

Sofie raised the chair above her head. A hearty knock at the door arrested her motion.

Ward spun around, and Sofie quickly placed the chair down and sat. Ward took no notice of her. He walked to the door and flung it open.

Karl stood on the other side. He was dressed in one of Gert's nicer three-piece suits, holding a travel suitcase.

Sofie and Bertie stared, wide-eyed, and said nothing.

"Oh hello, dear sir!" Karl said in nearly perfect English, bringing his breath up from his belly. "I was wondering if my aunt and uncle were in." When Ward did not reply, Karl let go of his smile, feigning concern. "Do they not live here anymore? Goodness! Has something happened to them?"

"Karl!" Sofie ran to him, pushing Ward aside quite roughly to give him a hug.

"So glad to see you, Tante!" He looked over her shoulder to Bertie, who was still pressed against the far wall. "Onkel, you are well!"

Sofie let him go and he stepped inside. He put down his suitcase before turning to Ward, clasping his hand in both of his own. "Oh, good sir. Thank you so much for keeping them safe until I returned. You are a blessing."

Ward stayed silent a moment, allowing his hand to be shook up and down. His brow furrowed slightly. "You're, ah . . . welcome."

Bertie dared to remove himself from the wall, standing a few paces behind the rest of them. He recognized the luggage from under Gert's bed. He recognized how heartily Karl shook the hand of Ward, how straight he stood, how well he had tied his tie. His voice resonated from his chest, and he ended nearly every sentence with a note lower than the syllable before it.

Karl finally released Ward's hand and looked at Bertie. "I trust you've told him, yes? He knows about us?"

Bertie was about to answer, but Ward silenced him. "Know what?" His back was straight, and the glint returned to his eye. He suspected something but couldn't prove it, so he was testing them, seeing if their stories matched.

Karl widened his eyes. "Oh my, they haven't told you." He glanced back and forth between Sofie and Bertie. "I'm so sorry, I—" He cut himself off, taking in a breath. His tone softened. "Well, if we can trust anybody, it would be the Allies. And especially the Americans, no less." He paused, taking in a bigger breath than before.

Ward leaned in. He gestured for Karl to continue.

Karl released a breath. "We're Jewish." He began to talk fast, then, as if worried Ward would condemn him for this truth. It succeeded in making him sound younger than his years. "It was during Kristallnacht and my parents had long died and I was living with Tante and Onkel and they gave me everything they had so I could flee to Switzerland but then they were stuck in Germany and I couldn't get them out because I couldn't find work fast enough and then they fled out here to Ulm and dear Goss and Ina Baumann took them in and hid them in the attic from the Nazis and then they died and Tante and Onkel took over the farm and I worried for years that they'd died until I finally got a letter from them and I'm so sorry they lied to you, sir, we never would've done it if we weren't so scared but you never know who might side with Hitler." He blinked up at him, now allowing his voice to rise slightly, a gamble of indicating innocence. "You don't side with Hitler, do you, sir?"

Ward's squint lessened and tightened in various intensities as Karl spoke. His shoulders lowered. While he did not seem sure if this was the truth, he equally did not seem sure how to say otherwise. He stared at Karl in a long silence. Bertie thought of all the questions Ward could ask, all the holes in the story Karl had just told him. He knew Ward could still ask for either Bertie or Karl to show themselves to him. But now, it suddenly seemed quite silly, quite inappropriate. Quite cruel.

But Ward continued to stare, and Karl continued to look at him with awe and thanks. Bertie felt a flash of what Karl must have had to do with so many officers in Dachau. Many things passed through his heart at once.

Ward finally cleared his throat. "I most certainly don't side with Hitler."

Karl's body slackened as if releasing a large weight. His tone reverted to the lower octave. "That is a relief, sir. Thank you for looking after Tante und Onkel. I'm alive because of them."

Ward tightened his eye again. Perhaps it was the slip into Deutsch, perhaps it was the fluctuation of the tone Karl used. Ward grabbed the suitcase beside Karl and slammed it upon the kitchen table. He opened it. It was stuffed with clothes, albeit quite messily, all from Gert's wardrobe upstairs.

Ward grunted. He closed the suitcase more gently and handed it back. He again looked like he wanted to say something, and again seemed unsure of how to begin. Everything hung somewhere between coincidence and fate.

"What's your name?" Ward asked.

"Karl Friedman," he said without hesitation. "And they're Jacob and Sarah Friedman. We're from Teltow, near Berlin."

Ward stared at them all a moment more. As his gaze lingered on him, Bertie felt his chest tighten. He was not sure how to hold his face in that moment. He did not know how it looked right now. It seemed every expression would be understandable as much as it would be damnable. It came down to what Ward would decide to believe.

"Say your name again."

"Karl Friedman," he answered pleasantly, as if happy to meet Ward all over again.

He pointed. "And them?"

"Jacob and Sarah Friedman."

"And you're from?"

"Teltow, just outside of Berlin."

Ward's expression did not change, and yet he also did not move. They all stayed quiet as he looked down at his hands, as if counting off something.

Karl looked to Sofie. "May he stay for abendessen?"

Ward snapped his head back to him. "Is that a Jewish thing?"

"Dinner," Karl translated with a polite smile. "Won't you stay, sir? It would be an honor to have a hero sit with us."

Ward remained skeptical, but Karl was smart to make the invite. He had taken control of the momentum of the moment and forced Ward into a choice: to stay or to go.

"Yes, Offizier," Sofie added in her heavy accent. "Bitte."

Ward stood a moment longer. "No," he finally said. His tone was flat. "I have important matters I must attend to."

"Of course, sir," Karl replied. He shook his hand again in that hearty way. "Thank you again for everything you have done for us. Please come back to visit anytime."

They were so close. Bertie could almost catch his breath, but then a look flashed over Ward's eyes. It happened so quickly that Bertie almost missed it, but it was there: a realization, an awareness. It was a look he had seen before, back in the earlier days, back when he must have done or said something, such a small and slight something that betrayed himself. The look that made him feel like a failure and a liar even if all he was showing was the truth.

Such a look always either landed or passed. And in this moment, it was the latter. Ward seemed to cast it away from his mind as soon as it arrived, knotting in the tangles the evening had already brought. He let go of Karl's hand. Without another word, he stepped away from the younger man, looked at no one else, and left.

Sofie eyed Ward through the front window as Bertie shut the door. He did not know if he should praise Karl or scold him for his recklessness. But he had saved their lives and Bertie was suddenly too exhausted to do either.

Instead, he whirled back around to Karl. "You know English?!" he hissed under his breath in Deutsch.

Sofie slinked around to the side of the kitchen, still following the windows.

"I learned it in school," Karl said. "Didn't you?"

Bertie had left school early and Sofie was particularly working-class. He said nothing.

Sofie pressed herself against the far wall of the kitchen. "He's not leaving."

Bertie resisted the urge to join her. "What's he doing?"

"He's just . . . looking." She swallowed. "Looking around. Quite carefully. He's near the fire pit now."

Bertie had burned Karl's prison clothes well and good to ash. But he did not like Ward lingering. The man had not been convinced, not entirely, and now he was looking for anything to twist his thoughts into what he wanted them to be. He wanted Bertie and Sofie and Karl gone. All he needed was a reason. They all knew he would be back, that their final few days may have just become their most dangerous.

Sofie moved away from the window, turning off the lights and drawing the curtains. "It will be more difficult for him to see in the dark."

"The album," Bertie muttered. He quickly scooped it up and put it back beneath the floorboards. He then went to Sofie, bringing her into a hug as they both sat on the floor. "I'm so glad you're okay. I'm so sorry."

Sofie said nothing, just leaned her weight against him, so he kissed the top of her head and rested himself there.

"Karl," he said, unsure where he was in the dark, "you did wonderfully."

Karl slowly creaked toward them and placed a hand on Sofie's. "If you ever need a music lesson," he said softly, and simply stopped there.

Sofie gave what first sounded like a sob, but it quickly turned into a weak chuckle. She squeezed Karl's hand and nuzzled herself against Bertie. Karl eventually rested himself on Bertie's other side. They stayed like that until they were too tired to keep their heads up.

15 • Berlin, 1933

A MONTH HAD PASSED SINCE THE SILVESTER FEST AT THE Institut, and Sofie and Bertie danced slowly in his apartment as the radio played a casual foxtrot.

It was Monday, and Bertie had put in his usual full day before returning home. It still felt a little odd to be home. For one, Sofie was now a part of his life. She did not officially live with him, but she may as well have. Her clothes hung from the line, her toiletries mingled with his at the basin. They made love constantly.

But also, this was the first week Bertie had returned home like it was home. Gert got his surgery not long after Silvester. Besides some pain, he recovered well and was in high spirits. Bertie and Roy had gotten to know each other better as they cared for him. Bertie was beginning to like the Amerikan. Roy had yet to leave Gert's side.

Bertie let the music lull him as he felt the warmth of Sofie's cheek pressed against his. Her hair smelled like almonds. They clasped cigarettes between their fingers, two curls of smoke forming a thin circle around them as they slowly turned in place. Bertie had long since converted her to the Ecksteins brand.

"Gert and the boys wanted to get together at a pub this weekend if he's feeling well enough," he said in a quiet voice. "We'll have to blend in, but it'll still be fun. Want to bring your friends?"

He could feel her smile from the stretch of her cheek. "That'd be nice. We never get everyone together."

"We could go for a late dinner tonight, just the two of us."

"I'd like that." She moved her cheek away from his, kissing him on the mouth. Bertie took her hand and placed it flat against the central bone of his chest. He held it there.

The music cut out in the middle of a final, lingering note.

"We interrupt to bring you important news," the radio said. "President Hindenburg has just appointed Adolf Hitler as the new chancellor of Germany. Papen will serve as vice chancellor."

They stopped dancing mid-sway. Bertie blinked, quite certain he had heard wrong.

"Those pigdogs!" Sofie spat, removing herself from him. She pointed at the radio as if it knew what it had done wrong. "Papen and his associates only want him because they think they can control him! They want him to be head puppet for the people! I'm telling you, that's not going to happen! Scheiße!" She slammed her foot against the floor. "Why do they have to be so goddamn greedy?! Don't they know what this will do to Germany?! Do they even care?! Most of the country didn't even vote for him! Fucking coalition government!"

Sofie continued to spit profanities. All Bertie felt was cold.

We've received word that as one of the first orders of business, transvestite cards will no longer be granted. All persons currently in possession of a transvestite card will have it revoked. We repeat, transvestite cards will no longer be granted nor honored. We're also receiving reports that most new name changes for transvestites are being rejected. Take heart, fellow souls. Let us hope that this dark day is short.

We've received word that many transvestite name changes long since granted are now being rescinded. Many transvestites are being ordered to no longer live as themselves, and some have had their homes searched to ensure they no longer own any articles of clothing deemed inappropriate. Hold on, friends. Let's hope this spreads no further.

We've received word that an unknown party has set fire to the Reichstag. The building of our parliament is in flames. While Hitler is already blaming it on the work of Communists determined to destroy German government from the inside out, some eyewitnesses have said it was brownshirts they saw entering the building just before it caught fire. This is a terrifying event unfolding before our eyes. Please look after one another, lilac people.

We've received word that Hitler has demanded President Hindenburg exercise his constitutional authority and issue what he calls the Reichstag Fire Decree, to protect Germany from the Communists. Hitler's government now has the legal right to arrest and imprison opponents and suspected enemies of the state without trial. The press is also censored, and many civil liberties and protections are now suspended. This is distressing, friends. Keep your heads up. The sunlight will one day shine upon us once more.

We've received word that Hermann Göring, cabinet minister to Hitler, has ordered the full and permanent closure of all remaining clubs, bars, and social spots related to inverts and transvestites. Reports are already coming in that inverts and transvestites are now being routinely arrested and imprisoned. Hold steady, fellow lilac people. We will see this heartache through.

We've received word that a prison has opened in Dachau. They're calling it a work camp, specifically built to house transvestites, inverts, and political opponents of Adolf Hitler. Rumor has it there are plans to build many more as time goes on. Be careful out there, friends. Do not draw attention to yourselves. Do not give them reason to harm you.

We've received word that the Eldorado has been taken. They've torn down the signs and banners, hung up their swastikas, and are now using it as a local headquarters for the brownshirts. The only visible remnant of the Eldorado is the banner above the front door: Hier ist's richtig. *We believe this was intentional, and the photograph circulating in their current propaganda appears to be staged to make a statement. They are aware of the symbolism at play. We understand how disheartening all this news has been. Please take care of yourselves. Please look after one another. Please keep your heads down.*

We've received word that the Enabling Act has passed the Reichstag and has been signed by President Hindenburg, surrendering the Reichstag's legislative power to Hitler. In addition to being chancellor, Hitler has the aforementioned legal right to imprison opponents without trial and to censor the press, and he now has the power to personally enact laws without need of the legislature. Sources believe he's in the process of creating a one-party state. All of this has been done through legal, constitutional, and democratic means. This is a particularly distressing day. Stay vigilant, friends. Blend in.

We've received word that people are indeed being transported to this work camp in Dachau. We don't know yet what the conditions in the prison are or if and when people will be released. A recent report confirmed that Kurt Hiller, one of the heads of Dr. Magnus Hirschfeld's Institut für Sexualwissenschaft, has been arrested and taken to Dachau. Take heart, fellow lilacs. We understand how distressing this has been for you. It's been less than two months since Hitler became chancellor.

We've received word that the Hitler government is now encouraging a countrywide boycott of all Jewish businesses, starting in April. Our hearts go out to our Jewish brothers and sisters, especially those who are lilac.

We've received word that a sterilization law has been enacted, the Law for the Prevention of Hereditarily Diseased Offspring. Starting July 14, all those with genetic blindness or deafness, manic depression, schizophrenia, epilepsy, congenital feeblemindedness, Huntington's chorea, alcoholism, or other related conditions will be forcibly sterilized. Do not draw attention to yourself, friends. Be well, be safe.

We've received word that all surviving lilac journals and newspapers have been forced to fold. There is nothing of us left.

We've received word that the police have been ordered to supply the Gestapo with lists of all men engaged in homosexual activities. We are not sure what this means for transvestites.

We've received word that President Hindenburg has died. Hitler has appointed himself as head of the German state.

Adolf Hitler has declared Dr. Magnus Hirschfeld "the most dangerous Jew in Germany."

16 • Ulm, 1945

THERE WAS NO LONGER ANY NEED TO HIDE KARL'S PRESence. They could socialize by open windows. They could eat together in the evening, and he and Sofie could continue their piano lessons in daylight. There was no more fear of being overheard. The lessons from Bertie, however, continued in the smaller bedroom with the curtains drawn, as well as the work on their passports. The day after the latest scare, Sofie had already finished the covers and inside papers and Bertie was halfway through carving the stamp. The effort strained his eyes and caused more exhaustion than he wanted to admit, but he could not afford to take a break with the deadline only three days away. He could surely push himself just a little longer. There would be time enough to rest on the long crossing to Amerika.

With Sofie's contribution finished, Karl had started carefully outlining the symbols and lettering of the covers in pencil. He held them up to the light after every small stroke to check his precision.

"I'm so proud of you," Bertie told him once again. "You were so convincing."

Karl offered only a thin smile at this praise, a cockeyed nod of his head that looked more like a defeated shrug. Bertie understood. To be praised for not being yourself was never praise. It was not something to celebrate. But for now, it meant survival, and Bertie was determined for them all to survive.

After working on their passports, Karl plinked out notes on the piano following Sofie's demonstration. Bertie rested his legs on the couch. The farm still required tending if only to keep up appearances. Karl had insisted on helping. He wanted to make use of himself, to pay his way.

Bertie and Sofie worried that the labor would trigger something in him, but he seemed eager to get out of that room, to go outside and exist in the sunlight.

Bertie enjoyed showing Karl how to shake the potato leaves above a bucket of water so the beetles would drown, how to use a thumb to scrape off the bright orange eggs that looked like caviar. He excitedly explained the history of the asparagus bushes, how their lineage went back generations, feeding people who had lived and died before they themselves had even arrived on this earth. He showed him how to keep an eye out for the fallen berries. They contained the seeds of the plant but were poisonous. To fail to pick them up risked the chickens eating them. He had watched with some amusement as Karl diligently checked every bush, kneeling to plop each little berry into his bucket, the chickens following him from behind with soft clucks like he was their best friend. Karl stopped to look over his shoulder at them every so often. It was the closest to a smile that Bertie had seen from him, but it was bittersweet. From behind and from a distance, in Gert's old clothes and one of his old caps, Karl looked almost exactly like Gert.

Even with the help, Bertie needed to move slower. He was getting older. He was still strong, he was still capable, but the work did not come as easily anymore. Each passing year, he performed less and less. Should they make it to the Midwest of Amerika, he feared what it meant for their prospects of starting over from scratch. He could not entertain such thoughts. Not when their future was still so precarious.

Bertie sipped his hot water, listening to the plinking piano keys from Karl, the gentle corrections and encouragements from Sofie. If he closed his eyes, he could pretend everything was okay.

When he opened his eyes again, he saw Frau Baer's form come into view against the hot yellow sun. She did not turn off the dirt path and continue toward town. Instead, she was walking to their home.

"Scheiße." He put his teacup down and stood. "Frau Baer is coming," he said quietly as he passed the piano.

Sofie and Karl stopped playing. Bertie opened the door. The cooling spring air hit him at the doorstep, the sky settling into purples and pinks.

"Ah, Frau Baer," he said, as if he had only been stepping outside for some air and had not expected to find her on his path. "To what do we owe the pleasure on this fine evening?"

Frau Baer did not bother acknowledging him until she stepped onto the porch. She looked over his shoulder without apology. "I hear you have a guest."

"News travels fast." Bertie tried to stay calm. He gave a pleasant smile. He was more certain now than ever that Frau Baer and Ward were in conversation with each other. Perhaps she was selling out her neighbors and peddling lies to grant a pardon for herself.

"Who is he?"

"Our nephew." He did not bother to say which of theirs he was. But he knew that if she had heard about Karl, surely she knew the rest of it. She was checking up on them. She was checking their story.

She looked back over his shoulder again, her eye on Karl at the far end of the sitting room. His back was turned to her, trying to continue his lesson as if nothing was the matter.

Bertie waited a moment in the silence. His legs ached. "May I help you with—?"

"You're planning something."

Bertie's mouth went dry, but he snorted. "We're certainly not."

She took a step closer to him on the porch. "I saw him go out the window."

Sofie stopped playing behind him, a thickness in the air pressing against his back.

Bertie straightened his shoulders, trying to stand to the top of his short height. He made his voice stern. "Frau Baer, you are mistaken. And I don't appreciate anything you're implying. We are good, decent people and are just trying to live our lives beyond this damned War."

"Twice." Her stare was hard. "And they were both when the American came to visit."

"Your age is starting to show, Frau Baer. Our farms are certainly not that close together."

"The window to your spare room faces my home. I saw a form drop from it two times."

Bertie crossed his arms. "Your eyes are failing. It was probably two of the many times I threw out your cat." He knew his argument did not make much sense and he tried to distract from it. "Do you watch our home every time? Or just when the officer has finished visiting you and you know we're next? I don't have time for your senility."

Frau Baer pursed her lips and took a moment to think. She looked uncertain for just a moment but then regained herself. "Why'd you get sick at Oberer Kuhberg?"

"Who wouldn't?"

"Many didn't."

"Including you."

Frau Baer ruffled. "What are you implying?"

"I'm just saying that there are people in this world who wouldn't get sick and people in this world who would."

"You were the only one that did. You had a particularly strong reaction."

Sofie stood from the piano bench. She walked to his side and slipped her arm through his. "He wasn't feeling well that day. The march exhausted him. The heat, you understand. It can be harder the older you get."

"It was quite pleasant that day. Even I could keep up."

Sofie shrugged. "He's an ailing man. These have been trying times for all of us." She squinted. "No matter which side you're on."

Frau Baer looked both insulted and curious. "What are you implying?"

"I think you know what I'm implying."

Bertie, however, had lost the thread of who was implying what, and he was not very sure Sofie knew, either. He realized she was likely attempting to talk Frau Baer into circles until she tired. But they both knew Frau Baer never tired.

In their fresh standoff, Bertie thought. He felt that if the lie bought them time before, perhaps it would again now. Perhaps it would lock it in better when she and Ward swapped stories. "We're Jewish."

"No you're not."

The bluntness of her answer silenced him a moment. He stammered. "Of course we are." He straightened his back then, telling himself that she could not be as much of a danger as he worried she was. "And what does it matter to you, anyway? We're Jewish and the Americans will protect us now."

There was a jostling behind him, the piano bench quickly scraping against the worn floor. They all turned to see Karl give a grunt of exclamation as he lunged at the top of the piano. Katze was upon it, jabbing at things with her paw with a steely stare. Karl managed to grab the urn of Oma and Opa before Katze could knock it off.

"Frau Baer!" Bertie suddenly shouted. He pointed behind him. "When are you going to keep your cat off my property?!" He felt a tickle against his leg and looked down. Katze swished past him with her tail up high, sitting down when she reached Frau Baer.

Frau Baer ignored Katze. She pointed over their shoulders at Karl. "He looks nothing like either of you." She glanced down at the doorstep before looking back up at them. Her lips were a thin line. "Your mail is here."

She turned and walked off their porch, Katze following by her side, taking the left down the dirt path toward her own farm.

"I swear that cat's a spy," Bertie muttered to Sofie, stooping down to pick up the letter. He shut the door before looking at the address. "It's for you."

Sofie took it from him. Her eyes lit up. "It's from my old neighbor in Arnstadt."

She immediately sat down at the table, opening the letter so quickly she tore it. Bertie sat by her side. He could already feel the dread building in his belly, but he tried to fend it off with possibilities. Karl stood a couple paces away, having returned the urn to its rightful spot.

Bertie watched the shifting of Sofie's face over the next few seconds. The excitement, the pure hope. As her eyes slid over the lines, the corners of her mouth began to sag, her eyebrows frozen in their place of hope now looking like desperation.

She shuddered out a breath, her body tremoring from it until it left her completely. And once it was gone, it was as if she had no air left.

"Oh Bertie," she said. She put her arms around him, burying her face into the crook of his neck. Her fingers dug into his back so hard he was sure he would bruise.

Bertie pressed her into him as he looked over her to what he could see of the letter.

saw your letters
hope you don't mind
so glad to hear
miracle
weren't the same
condolences
three years ago
bombing
did not leave
do not know

"I'll never forgive myself," Sofie said into his neck. "It's all my fault."

"It's not your fault," Bertie said softly. He rubbed her back. He tried to fight away the thoughts, the thoughts that told him the blame was squarely on him. That she would be much happier if they had never met. That she would not be here, right now, in any of this.

"They died thinking—" She hiccupped then, burying herself harder into his neck. Her breath began to shudder again, each one an effort. "I'll never forgive myself."

Karl put a hand upon her shoulder. He squeezed.

17 • Berlin, 1933

THE WORLD HAD CHANGED OVERNIGHT. AS SOON AS HITLER was appointed chancellor, there were celebrations from the loudest, complete with marches and torches and salutes, and it seemed as soon as Bertie stepped out of his building the next morning, the city was already draped in swastikas. Bright red flags hanging, flapping, lolling like dead tongues from every corner shop, from every flagpole, from every window and balcony. Berlin was bleeding from the inside out.

The charity boxes rattled everywhere, even more than before, and there was considerable pressure to put something in, even if you had just donated to the one several paces behind. Nazis patrolled every street.

Bertie kept his eye out these days on his way to work. It was only May, the sixth of May precisely, only three months and one week since Hitler had become chancellor. The transvestites were some of the first people Hitler went after, starting with their cards. It was one of his first orders of business. Many of their other rights followed. Now every time Bertie stepped outside, he was breaking the law.

The snow had long since melted away, the ice nothing but a memory, yet Bertie walked more carefully than he ever had in winter. The young sprouts of spring looked ill and wilted between the cobblestones. The wet earth of the season smelled more like decay than rebirth. He did not like this world.

He kept his head down as he walked, not daring eye contact. He hunched his shoulders whenever he passed someone who was doing quite the opposite. Beware the ones that were happy, he knew. Beware the ones that felt invigorated. They were lethal.

He walked into the Institut. Its morning bustle was not such a thing these days, waning so quickly since the end of January. He never thought he would see the day. They were still in operation, but some of their practices had become restricted by new laws. Visitors had become so sparse that Rüdiger was instructed to give a tour only once a day. Brownshirts sometimes came in with stern faces and asked about Doktor Hirschfeld's whereabouts. The police sometimes did house searches of workers who were still in support of Doktor Hirschfeld. Bertie had yet to be among them, but he feared the day. A handful of the Institut's staff openly declared themselves Nazi sympathizers or members of the party, such as Helene Helling, the front desk widow who had settled herself in one day and never left. Such folks were still working alongside everyone else, which made things tense.

Dora Richter greeted Bertie. She was scraping the last dribbles of hardened egg off one of the front windows. Faint crudeness showed on the white stone no matter how hard the hauskeepers tried to wash off the paint.

Bertie walked up the stairs to his floor, slower than usual, seeming to be slower every day. His shellacked shoes tapped against the hard floor, echoing off the walls. It made him feel hollow. He and Sofie had tried to keep hope, but as time went on, as the reports kept coming in, as he saw the halt on the transvestite cards and worried about the future of his own and now could not get his passport and could not see his friends as much as he used to and passed the Eldorado with all the swastikas hanging over the windows, they both nearly all but stopped discussing it entirely.

"He's doing their bidding for now," Sofie had said, one of the last comments she gave on the matter. "And they're happy for now. But hear me, they'll regret it soon enough. People who start attacking at the bottom never know when to stop climbing. They eventually eat their own. It's not a sustainable practice."

Bertie knew she was right. Bertie also knew that it was of no comfort.

"It might be time to think about going somewhere safe," Bertie had said.

"The only safe place would be out of Germany. And I'm not leaving you."

It was a difficult call to make yet, whether anyone who could leave the country should. There was so much disbelief, so much incomprehension of what was happening. Surely things could not happen this way. Surely things could not happen this quickly. Perhaps they would be safe. After all, the inverts argued, Ernst Röhm was one of them and he was Hitler's right-hand military man. He would never forsake his own kind. Hitler would never go after inverts if one of his top team was one. But what protection did transvestites have, Bertie wondered.

He dragged his feet up the final few stairs and into the office. His desk looked as neat as ever. It was his attempt at stability. He sat down and sighed, the one wheel of his chair squeaking as he took a moment to place his face in his hands.

"Is that you, Bertie?" Doktor Hirschfeld called out.

Bertie removed his hands from his face and looked up. Herr Doktor had another black eye.

"Are you alright, sir? What happened this time?"

Doktor Hirschfeld simply shrugged, trying his best to give his usual walrus grin.

"Was it the brownshirts again? I thought you'd been changing your route home every night."

Doktor Hirschfeld let his smile wane. "At least it wasn't too bad this time."

The worst was so bad that Herr Doktor had read his own obituary in the paper the next morning. Bertie had worried that the injuries were so grave that he would lose his eyesight, that he had punctured organs. It was all broken bones, all deep cuts and swaths of bruises, and a fractured skull. But he had slowly recovered. And then he just kept on trying to make the world a better place for the third sex.

"Why do you do it, sir?" he asked. "I know you'd look after your own kind, that makes sense. But why do you do so much for transvestites, too?"

Doktor Hirschfeld looked away, as if ashamed. He seemed to be choosing his words. "If I'm being honest, Bertie, my reasons are quite selfish." He paused a moment, finally faced him. "Do you know about the canaries?"

"The little yellow songbirds?"

"For twenty years now, miners in Britain and America have taken cages of them down into the mines while they work, to detect carbon monoxide. Carbon monoxide is odorless, tasteless, cannot be seen. It'll also kill you in an instant. When a canary stopped singing, when it became ill or acted unusually, the workers would flee back aboveground. When we started using mustard gas during the War, their soldiers once again brought canaries when they tunneled."

Bertie did not know why he was telling him this, and he did not like being reminded about the mustard gas. "Why canaries? Why not another animal?"

He shrugged. "They were the most vulnerable."

Bertie waited for more, still not fully understanding.

"A country is only as strong as its most vulnerable people. And you, son, if you may forgive me for saying, are on the lowest rung of the ladder. You're a canary, Bertie. Transvestites are the canaries of the world. You know from our own library that bad people always go after transvestites first, no matter the country or culture. They are the first ones removed when an environment turns poisonous. What makes it more worrisome is you represent everything. You represent housing and job security and access to healthcare. You represent workers' rights and voting rights and full stomachs and freedom. And perhaps most importantly of all, you represent the right to body and personhood. You represent a country not owning you, not using you however benefits a select few at the top. You represent a country of a people, not a country of the dominant. If transvestites are under attack, then the whole of the country is on the brink of destruction. If transvestites are cared for, the rest of us are cared for. You touch everything a strong society has to offer. We could work, we could eat, we could be healthy, we could live in safe homes, we could decline to fight in unnecessary wars. Our country would be honest. We would no longer be tricked. Our country would take care of us and we, in turn, would take care of our country. So as long as transvestites are okay, we know society is, too. That's why I'm here for you. Because I love my country."

"That's terrible, though," Bertie said. "Being forced into a cage to see if you die first."

Doktor Hirschfeld nodded a quiet agreement. "If it helps, they love those birds. Having them around brightens their spirits and they carry them out with them during a scare to try and resuscitate them. They searched for them through the rubble after bombings. It's not a perfect analogy, but it's something that's stuck in my head for a long time."

He sighed. "What I'm saying is, don't regard me too heroically. I care about you because I care about everyone. Nothing I'm doing here is noble or generous. It's simply common sense. It's simply humanity. No person should encourage the suffering of another. There's already too much given by nature. And when a person encourages the suffering of another, you can bet they won't stop there. They want to see it because they hope it will fill the emptiness inside themselves, but it won't, because it never does, and so they'll look for the next one, and the next one, and the one after that."

Doktor Hirschfeld looked out the window a moment, at the large elm rustling in the late spring breeze. "Any invert who thinks Hitler will stop at transvestites is a fool. And any person who thinks Hitler will stop at inverts thereafter is just as foolish. They try to convince people that you're the only group they're after when really you're just the first one. They look for the first domino to knock down, the one people will give the least resistance to, the one they care about the least. And once they've done it, it might be too late for everyone else."

He took in another big sigh and waited. He finally spoke again. "Have you finalized my world tour?"

Bertie realized he must not have spoken for several moments since Herr Doktor had stopped. He cleared his throat and picked up one of the top folders on his desk. "You're all set, sir. The boat for New York leaves this afternoon. Then the tour moves to Chicago, Kansas City, Los Angeles, and San Francisco. Then it's Tokyo and Shanghai, then Canton, Manila, Bali, Singapore, Colombo, Calcutta, Bombay, Cairo, and a few stops around Palestine, Greece, Austria, Switzerland, and then you finish in France. I have your ticket here, as well as your itinerary and your prepared notes."

He took the folder. "Thank you, Bertie. I don't know how I'd run things without you." He gave a small nod, his lips tight beneath his graying mustache. He looked about to say something more but instead turned away.

Bertie took a moment before standing. His voice was still softer than usual.

"I wish I could go with you, sir. I've always wanted to see the world. Especially the United States." He trailed off, for they both knew the answer. Doktor Hirschfeld had been working on his transvestite passport. And now that it had been halted, now that it could never be a thing, he was stuck.

Doktor Hirschfeld cupped a warm hand against Bertie's jawline. He smiled his usual smile, a real one. Bertie could not tell if his eyes were sad or it was the pain of his bruises. "Take care of yourself while I'm gone. I don't want to come back and find you hurt."

"I'll be careful, sir."

"Promise me."

"I promise, sir."

He gave a small smile, again both sad and genuine. He gently patted Bertie's cheek and turned to go back into his office. Bertie grabbed him in a hug. He buried his face into his waistcoat, his words muffled.

"Thank you, sir."

Doktor Hirschfeld chuckled. Bertie felt his chest bounce against his own.

"You act like I'm leaving forever." He gently pushed Bertie away and grasped his upper arms as he looked him in the face. "I'll be back. One of the most important things we can do right now is keep educating people. Other countries will understand, even if Germany won't. But Germany did before and Germany will again. It's a dangerous game of time and energy and setback that we play, but we must play it. It's the only way forward."

Bertie swallowed and nodded, trying to give a smile for his sake. But he knew the truth, he had seen the notes on Herr Doktor's desk. Part of his world tour was to educate the masses, yes. But he was also spending so much time in Amerika. He was not leaving just yet. But eventually, he would. The worst part was Bertie could not blame him. Nor for why he would not yet tell him his plans. It was difficult to admit leaving someone vulnerable behind.

The man gave Bertie's arm a squeeze, then retreated to his office.

Bertie returned to his desk. Not a minute later, he heard a timid knock upon the open door.

"Excuse me?" A boy stood just in the doorway, absently clutching one hand against the other. He seemed afraid to step in any further. "I'm sorry to bother you, but the people downstairs said I should come up here. I don't have an appointment."

Bertie took note of all the attributes that told him what he was likely here for. He pushed past his own hurt and put on his friendliest voice. "Please come in. I'd be happy to help you."

The boy timidly stepped the rest of the way toward Bertie. He looked no more than fifteen. Bertie gestured toward the chair opposite his desk and the boy sat.

"I was wondering if you could help me with the paperwork for a card and a name change."

Bertie tamped down his old joy of helping with such matters, of his immediate instinct to congratulate him and inform him of every opportunity available. "I'm sorry, but please know that transvestite cards are no longer being granted. Nor the passports."

The young man did not seem surprised by this. He leaned forward in his chair. "But not the name changes yet, right? Or the medical things?"

"Not entirely yet, no."

He sat back against his chair, a small sense of relief on his face. "I was hoping if I got those started immediately, I might manage to get them in time." He looked unsure of this. "I owe it to myself to at least try."

Bertie nodded. "I'd be happy to help you every way we still can." He meant his words, felt the old rush of belonging and purpose. He told him how Doktor Hirschfeld would want to take a long walk with him in the Tiergarten, ask him all about his childhood and hobbies and family. No, there was no right thing to say or correct answer Doktor Hirschfeld wanted to hear. Yes, he simply took one's word for it. There was nothing to prove. It was not so much an evaluation as a collection of information.

No, he did not know what he was looking for. Hence all the information. He wanted to understand. He wanted to see if there were any patterns. Bertie told him how there would be an examination of his body, nearly everything about him quantified, measured, and cataloged. He would be photographed. Yes, Bertie could stay with him in the room during all of that. He would ask him various things, measure his ring finger against his index finger, see whether or not he could whistle and how well. He told him Doktor Hirschfeld believed that careful observation and talking at length with patients, often over long walks, were vital to establishing a theory. He was a man of logic and reason. He believed nobody knew them better than themselves. It would feel, Bertie assured him, like talking with a friend.

The boy seemed convinced of all this. Bertie pulled out a fresh folder of forms and opened it upon his desk. His fountain pen hovered over the first form.

"What's your name, my friend?"

He looked hesitant. "The one I want?"

"The one you want, yes."

He glanced down at the floor a moment, giving a shy smile. He seemed hardly able to contain the pleasure of declaring it. "Karl Fuchs."

18 • Berlin, 1933

BERTIE WORKED LATE THAT NIGHT, AS WAS OFTEN THE CASE when Doktor Hirschfeld left for his tours. He made it his priority to have the office running as smoothly as it could in his absence. He filled out forms, finished paperwork, and penciled appointments. Karl Fuchs's application was still atop his desk. He had liked talking with the young man, liked to see the hope that was in his eyes. It was nice to still see someone with hope.

It had made him feel better, that look. Like he was still making a difference. Like their world still had a future. It had been a terrible few months, and Bertie had not seen as much of Gebhardt, Karsten, or Markus. Socializing was out of the question. They were all afraid to gather, to be seen too much in public. He had seen a bit more of Gert, but even with him it was far less than customary. Home to work and work to home was what they had largely reduced their lives to. It was unclear, now, what exactly could happen to them, what exactly was allowed. But they knew the consequences of being themselves. Arrest, beaten to death, dragged to the mysterious and frightening Dachau. Every step outside was a danger.

It was dark, and Bertie was hungry. He had missed dinner. Sofie was good about these longer-hour days, often waiting up for him reading or practicing songs on a piano board she drew on pieces of cardboard, attached longwise with staples.

He stopped to rub his blurring eyes with his fingers. He rested his face a moment, both elbows upon his desk, and breathed in the ink of the room. A soft breeze rustled the tree outside. The clock above him continued to tick. Just a few more papers and he would pack up, turn off the lights, and go home.

He heard something outside then. Faint. It slowly grew louder, a deep beat keeping perfect rhythm, feeling both familiar and foreign at the same time. His mind knew it was something he knew, but it was not where it should be, like a bedroom pillow in a bathroom. It was a moment more before he recognized the sound as a brass band. It was playing a jaunty tune, sounding as if it was coming down the street like a parade. Louder and louder it became with each tick of the clock.

"What the hell?"

He got up from his desk and peered out a window. It was indeed a brass band, followed by over a hundred people. Most of them looked to be young men, perhaps sport students. Several of them hauled empty carts. Others carried torches and flags.

As he squinted, he finally recognized their uniforms from the German Student Union. Young Nazis. Bertie wondered if they had been drinking, if they were celebrating all the rot they were forcing upon Deutschland, strutting through the Tiergarten. If they wanted to make a spectacle of all they had done. Wake people up, disturb the peace, make sure nobody forgot. Surely they felt cocky these days.

Bertie continued to watch as they walked up the street. But when he expected them to pass on by, they stopped. They cordoned off the front. The band continued to play.

He moved closer to the window, his forehead nearly touching the glass now. He squinted against his own reflection illuminated by the office lights.

"Death to Hirschfeld!" someone suddenly screamed from the crowd.

"Oh my God." Bertie felt the blood drain from his face. A roaring cheer rose from the mob as they began to beat on the main door, the thump of the brass band continuing. The pounding on the front door boomed up the stairs. A few heads looked up at his window.

He stepped backward so quickly that he tripped over himself. He landed with a grunt before scrambling back to his feet. He continued to back away from the window, breathing heavily. His office lights were on. They would have seen him looking out. They would know exactly where each of the few workers currently were.

He did not know what they planned, but he knew what they wanted.

Bertie felt caught between feeling grateful that Doktor Hirschfeld was already at sea and wishing that he were still here. There was no telling what these people would do when they could not find him, but it would not be anything good.

The band went quiet. The silence built a pressure in his ears. He strained to hear, too afraid to move back to the window. He waited.

A single trumpet call bellowed out.

"Death to Hirschfeld!" someone shouted again. It quickly turned into a chant. They became loud as fresh air, already breaking through the door. They got through surprisingly quickly. So many fists against the wood. He could hear their fast footfalls on the floorboards downstairs, the echo of their screams blurring into nonsense against the majestic walls.

They scattered below. He could feel them flocking everywhere beneath his feet. He could hear shattering and crashing. And soon, he could hear laughter against a chorus of screaming. Somewhere, the band resumed playing.

"Oh my God," Bertie said again. His throat seized him. He tried to think.

The footsteps came up the stairs, past his floor, onto his floor.

Someone down the hall started to yell, guttural and wordless. It was Rüdiger. Bertie knew what they were doing to him.

Screams from other familiar voices slowly ate up the hallway, rising from the first floor. He thought he recognized the voices of Dora Richter and some of the other hauskeepers below. And the brass band continued to play.

Bertie locked the door and looked out its small window, his breath fogging the glass. Rüdiger was far down on the left. Some men held him down and apart while another had his way. Others shoved one of the radiologists into a nearby room, already pummeling him.

One of the Nazi students near Rüdiger caught sight of Bertie and grinned, standing up from his crouch.

Bertie jerked away from the door as two of them began to bang upon it. With each hit, the thin glass rattled in its frame.

He surveyed the office. A desk, a chair, files. Nothing but files. He ran back to his desk and yanked it toward him, feeling the muscles in his back spasm from the force. He gritted his teeth against the pain and shoved the desk against the splintering door. Files spilled off like ocean waves.

There was no other door out. He was trapped.

"Come along, warm brother," someone called, their voice muffled by the door. "Don't you want to play?"

The room had only four windows, two overlooking the street and a couple facing the alley. The front had the mob. The back had a tree.

He ran toward the back windows but immediately slipped and fell against the papers strewn about the floor. He staggered back up as the door continued to splinter behind him. He could not leave. Not yet. He ran to one of the filing cabinets behind where his desk had been. He rifled through, cursing the seconds, cursing the clock above him, cursing every tick above the door as the brass band kept the beat below. A crowd gathered outside, watching curiously. He finally pulled out the file with his own name.

The glass of his door shattered. He lit the file with his lighter and dropped it into his wire wastebasket. The flames grew in concert with the screams of Rüdiger, Dora, and so many others he could not bear to identify. Only a thin wall separated him from the rest.

Bertie dashed to one of the rear windows. It was stuck. He beat against it as the office door wilted from the force of the men. The sounds of the hallway grew louder.

He shifted his efforts to the other window. After he heaved with all he had, it sprang open. He crooked one leg out, straddling the sill. The lights of the office beamed behind him. He tried to make out the tree in the dark, tried to remember just how far away it was from him, what was shadow and what was a branch. Were he to miss, he would surely break his legs on the ground and be easy prey.

The door gave. The desk skittered across the floor. Bertie jumped out.

He tumbled, his other leg catching before finally clearing the window. He worried in a moment that someone had grabbed him, but it was just the sill. The catching did not make him leap so much as fall. He tried to grab a sturdy branch and climb down the rest of the way, but he was too far away, the outmost parts of the branches too thin, and they broke beneath him as he fell. He could barely see, his eyes still adjusting to the dark. Stars winked at him as they played coyly in the leaves. Branches cut his face and hands.

In a moment, he was on his back in the grass. His exclaim was short and deep, the impact knocking the wind out of him. A pain shot through his wrist.

He lay still a moment, unable to move. He tried to catch a breath, but nothing filled him. Worse than breaking his legs, he worried he had paralyzed himself.

He could not tell if his eyes were open or closed until he saw a head jut out from his office window.

"I think that one's dead," they muttered after a moment. They poked their head back inside, seemingly disappointed in this news. He heard a laugh.

Bertie waited a moment more before trying to breathe. When he was sure that the men had moved on, he slowly sat up. His wrist throbbed, but that seemed the extent of the damage. He struggled to his feet and glanced around, crouching near the wall of the Institut. It was hard to get his bearings in all the commotion. He could not tell which way was safe.

But the back end of the Institut was dark and barren. The mob had overtaken only the front of the two buildings.

Half-crouched, he walked the length of the back end toward one of the nearby side streets. If he sprinted at the corner of the building, he might make it without anyone noticing him. He heard the breaking down of doors, the smashing of medical equipment, the scattering of papers and books as they were tossed out of windows. The students outside piled them high into their carts.

He saw the shadows of people inside, could hear the yelling and the destruction over the band. He glanced into one of the library windows and stopped dead. Dozens of people were tearing it apart. Pages were ripped out of books by the handful, pieces of photographs thrown into the air like confetti. Papers and documents and history were heaped into looming piles on the floor: the entire life's work of Doktor Hirschfeld, the first tentative steps of tolerance toward the third sex, the history of a community gathered from every corner of the world.

Bertie realized then what he had always known deep down. The immobility, the existence of being stuck between two difficulties. He understood what Doktor Hirschfeld was trying to do, for the only true way to gain rights was to show you existed. To create outreach and educate the public, to build awareness. But by showing they existed, not yet gaining the rights to back them up, they had made themselves targets. Visibility without protection only encouraged violence.

He thought about all the times he had adjusted his voice, his clothes, his mannerisms to gain favor, all the times he consented to undress in front of strangers or have his picture taken, his body cataloged, every private detail of himself made public, all in the name of outreach and education, all for the good of future generations that were like him. It had all been for nothing, his sacrifices. They had not accepted him, they had never intended to accept him. And now, with any hope of humanity toward him gone, he had to continue the adjustments of himself simply to survive.

The weight of the devastation was too great to bear. Bertie shut his mind to the horrors unfolding before him. He needed to look away. He needed to leave.

He ran off down the side streets. When he was far enough away, he stopped to catch his breath and then behaved much like he and Sofie had the day of that bloody protest. He played it casual. The farther away he got, the more disillusioned he became that the world could keep turning despite these events. He refused to let the truth of it enter him. Not yet. It was not safe yet.

In the distance, he could hear their brass band break out in "Burschen, heraus." Fellows, come out. Their mockery had no limits.

"Sieg Heil!" came the bellow from a hundred throats over the brass. "Sieg Heil! Sieg Heil!"

Bertie's legs weakened the closer he got to home. As he climbed his stairs, he worried he would not make it all the way up.

Sofie was reading a book in his desk chair with her feet propped up on the table when he entered. Her smile washed away the moment she saw him.

Bertie held his wrist to his chest. The cuts on his face and hands stung. Before he could even close the door, he dropped to his knees.

Sofie leapt up, her book falling to the floor as she rushed to him. "Bertie, what happened?"

"It's gone." The hopelessness finally took him, drowning him in an instant. "I didn't . . . It's all gone."

19 • Ulm, 1945

BERTIE WALKED OUT LATE THE NEXT NIGHT, LONG AFTER Sofie and Karl had gone to bed. His arms were full as he clutched his history against his chest. He knelt to the fire pit. He took a breath.

Under the waning full moon, he gently placed his album into the pit, then his transvestite card. The ghostly shadow of his younger face stared up at him in the small photo. He looked singularly fixed in that moment, staring directly into the camera as if daring it to challenge him, serious despite the relief and happiness he surely felt. He could not remember anymore what he had been thinking that moment. He hated that he could not remember.

He struck a match, the pungent whiff of sulfur taking his senses in the fine spring air. The sudden flicker of orange light illuminated the photo of his card. It now stared directly at him, through the camera, as if knowing all those years ago that he would one day be disappointed in him.

He was burning himself. He was burning all of them. With all that had happened, this felt particularly cruel. It felt like betrayal, but he did not know what else to do. He could not bring it with them, and he could not leave it behind. The album was a threat to their survival. He had given up so much already, what was one more sacrifice?

Fire, the purest form of destruction. Everything had burned in that pit. Karl's prison clothes, the flag they were forced to hang by their doorstep for years, Oma and Opa, all the wood they had ever burned, worrying when the War would be over, worried what would happen next. And now his album, his card, his friends would all be added. The ashes of everything mixed together in the pit. It meant everything or it meant nothing, and it bothered him that he could not decide which.

Everything had burned, ever since that night at the Institut. First the twenty thousand books and then the thirty-five thousand photographic slides and then the countless people and then the proof that any of it had ever happened at all. It was a threefold devastation. Generations of history gone, the people still living killed, the Nazis eventually destroying all the evidence of their crimes that they could, now backed by the Allies who were throwing their few survivors into prison, upholding the Nazi versions of these laws, the final stragglers too afraid of further retribution to speak up. They would all die out not speaking up. Even after all they had survived.

An erasure of history was an erasure of personhood. It seemed like every last one of the normally sexed was in on it. No matter their differences, this was the one place they all found agreement. It hurt his heart.

These memories were precious. And just like Gert's hat, he refused to leave them vulnerable in the hands of those who would never understand, who did not want to understand. At least this way, it could not be weaponized against them. Why, then, did he still feel like a hypocrite? Like a traitor.

He had held on to it all to remember his friends, to remember his community, to remember who he was. That he had once been happy. That he had been himself, that they all had been themselves, and how it became less sensational with each passing day, and yet every day, it still was. But that was a long time ago. He had managed to hold on to them this whole while, against all odds. But now, their time was up. He had not quite made it. He had not quite been clever enough.

The match burned down as he held it above the pit. The heat of the tiny flame grew hotter, licking closer to his fingertips. He continued to hold it. His vision blurred as he looked at the album, at the card, at the photo of himself. It continued to stare at him. He wished he could say something comforting to it. He did not know what comfort he could give to it when he had none for himself.

The flame began to burn his fingers. He finally released the match, letting it fall into the pit on its own. He could pretend it was not entirely his doing. It was gravity. It was the world. Of course it was the world.

The match simply lay there a moment, atop his own younger face.

But soon it caught, soon it spread. The dry and yellowed paper of the card lit easily, charring and curling as Bertie watched himself burn, the thin line of red embers crawling across his face in a slow assault. It ate him like mites, a tiny battalion gaining ground. The corner of his chin disappeared, his cheekbone, his lips, his nose. His favorite suit that he had picked out especially for that day.

He wondered where that suit was now. Had someone ransacked his apartment the year after the Institut? Had it been a soldier? Did they throw it out into the street or sell it for some quick money? Had they liked it and kept it for themselves? Was the suit he had worn now touching the skin of a Nazi, of a man who had been assigned to kill him? Or was it burned in a heap like so many other heaps? Was it rotting in trash somewhere? If it had been left to rot, how long did it take to rot?

He felt silly indulging these thoughts. Things were just things. But sometimes, things were more than that.

The fire grew as it ate, sloppy and greedy. Bertie pulled one last photo from his pocket, the one he had been inspecting for the past few days as he worked, the one of Gert on his lap, both of them grinning. He did not need it anymore. He had stenciled the stamp's design on the erasers perfectly. The carving was nearly finished. This photo, of all photos, he knew he could not bring with him.

He stared at the photo a few moments longer. He was surprised he could feel any sadder than he already was. He slowly lightened the pressure between his two finger pads, little by little until the photo broke free with a flutter. Just like the match, it fell into the pit guided only by the hand of gravity.

Bertie distracted himself until his second eye burned away from the card, the final feature of his face. Now there was nothing left to look at him, nothing left to judge him. He continued to stare as the fire took hold of the photo of him and Gert, and then the album. It felt wrong to watch it burn while it was closed, but he also did not know what else to do. He could not look at the newspaper articles he had once so excitedly collected. He could not look at his friends. He could not watch them burn.

They had burned.

He wiped the smoke from his eyes. He breathed it in. It would live inside him now. It would live in his lungs. He hoped, finally, that they would all be safe there.

He sat for as long as it took for the album to finish burning, for it to turn to ash. It was not until the last embers were flicking that he heard the side door open behind him. The footsteps toward him were equally quiet.

Karl sat beside him, staring into the fire pit. "You burned it," he said simply.

"Yes."

There was nothing further that could be said. He realized, then, perhaps that was why Karl rarely spoke.

Bertie cleared his throat. No matter how much he did it, it did not remove the grit. He did not know if it was the smoke. "I've been keeping something from you." His voice was dry and husky. "We've met before. I recognized you the moment I saw you last week. That's part of why I took you into the house. I was responsible for you."

Karl took in a breath. His eyes remained fixed on the fire pit. "You thought I didn't remember you."

Bertie blinked at him. He had not been expecting this response.

"You were the first and last transvestite I'd ever met."

"You knew the whole time you've been here?"

Karl nodded.

"Why didn't you say anything?"

"Why didn't you?"

Bertie's face fell. "Because it's my fault you ended up in Dachau." He hoped Karl would interrupt him, to ask him what he meant, if only so he could delay explaining himself a few moments more. But it did not happen. "I was working late the day you came in, when we met. That night was when the Institute was destroyed. They broke into my office. I couldn't think. I wasn't sure what their plan was, if they had a plan. But I took the moment to burn my own file anyway, to be extra careful. And then I ran."

Karl was quiet. Bertie was not sure if he was mad at him or if he did not yet understand.

"Your folder was right on top of my desk. It was probably the first one they picked up. I could've burned it faster than finding my own. I could've set fire to the whole office. My lighter was right in my hand. It would've taken seconds." Bertie slumped. "So many people died because of me. So many inverts and transvestites. They made their lists from the very papers I'd written by my own hand. I wrote down their names, their addresses. I clipped their photographs to their folders myself. My hands gave the Nazis everything they needed to slaughter my own people. And if they didn't have those lists, then a year later, they wouldn't have . . ." The smoke got to his throat, then, and he had to stop and swallow. He had to keep swallowing. ". . . Karsten and Gebhardt and Markus. And Gert. All of them." He swallowed again. "All of them. And you."

If only he had known about Karl that day, when he first arrived at the Institut, freshly parentless and alone in the world. He could have invited him to stay with him. He would have been there with them when Gert came with his warning. He wondered if fate was real, if the three of them were meant to find each other in the end. He wished he had known.

Karl said nothing in the looming quiet. But after a moment, his voice came out as even and monotoned as ever. "There are surely many reasons why it's not your fault, Bertie. But I don't know how to tell you what they are. I don't know how to comfort you because I can barely comfort myself." He took a breath, letting it out slowly. "It may look like I'm collected. It may even look like I don't care. But inside, the crying, it's all in my heart. It's in my heart every day. I cry for myself, I cry for the others. I cry for the ones I've never even met. Just because they are faceless doesn't make them less important to me. I know they were out there somewhere. And they suffered."

"I can't imagine how you're able to go on."

"Because I have to." He paused, looking out to the forest. "Some moments, I want to end things. But that would be an insult to those who did not make it. But to move forward, to move past this, to be happy, is that not also insulting?" He glanced over at Bertie before looking away. "So here I am. Suspended in motion as time rushes around me."

The pit was barren now, only ash left from what had once been Bertie's life. The proof of his happiness. The pride of his community and the love of his friends. The orange light was gone, now only the blue and white of the moon. The world suddenly looked so colorless and dull.

"The Institute," Karl said. "Besides the lists. What happened to it all?"

"It burned. It all burned."

Karl took in a breath, nodding to himself as if he were deciding a choice of beer. "Then we're all that's left of our history."

They sat, then, saying nothing for quite some time. Bertie felt the urge he always did when he was sad, which was to look through his album. It panged him even more. He did not realize he could feel hollower than he had these past twelve years.

"If you had the chance to tell your younger self what was going to happen," he finally asked, "even if you knew you couldn't change any of it, would you?" He swallowed. "I've been thinking about that a lot lately and I just don't know. I feel I would've wanted to prepare myself. I was too hopeful, too innocent. And I know that probably made things harder. I know it's not fair, but sometimes I hate him for that." He cocked his head at Karl. "What would you tell your younger self?"

Karl looked straight ahead, his face set. "I wouldn't tell him a damn thing."

The silence of the night was interrupted only by insect songs. Bertie suddenly wondered if Sofie was really asleep, if she was not unintentionally listening to them through the open window of their room.

"You know," he said. "I read plenty in those archives before they burned it all. I saw what history has seen, time and again. They may get most of us, but they'll never get all of us. They never do."

Karl seemed to consider this. "If that's the comfort we have left," he finally said, "then I'll take it."

20 • Berlin, 1934

IT WAS THE THIRTIETH OF JUNE, JUST OVER A YEAR SINCE the Institut had been attacked. It never recovered. Bertie was too afraid to return; most of them were too afraid to return. It was mostly the Nazi sympathizers and party members who had remained. A few others were loyal workers who desperately tried to keep operations running in the spirit of Doktor Hirschfeld, who also never returned. It was too unsafe for him. Dora Richter was never seen again. Nobody had seen what happened to her or where she may have gone. It was long since concluded that she was killed that night.

About five weeks after the attack, the police officially closed the Institut. The property was confiscated without any compensation. The police also urged the Minister of the Interior to remove the Institut's charitable status, retroactively declaring its tax rebates as illegal. Eight employees with salaries in arrears were never paid, the tax authorities claimed more than one hundred marks for tax payments, and both buildings were liquidated. The liquidation included the auctioning of Doktor Hirschfeld's personal belongings from his private living quarters, including his three hundred–volume library, medical equipment, instruments, and furniture. The Institut's rooms were then lent out to anti-Communist and antisemitic institutions.

It had been that way ever since. Over the past year, things had only gotten worse. With the threat of the third sex largely squashed in the earliest months, Hitler started to focus his gaze on everyone else. Sofie had been right all along. The politicians who had given Hitler his power were fast losing control of him. Brownshirts crawled over every centimeter of Berlin, aggressively shaking their collection boxes in everyone's faces. To not pay was to invite trouble. Bertie had put money in a box held right beneath his nose on several occasions, cold eyes locked to his. They surely did not need the money anymore. He wondered if this was just one more play of power they enjoyed, to remind everyone that they could make them do whatever they wanted. They often sought out the Communists they had beaten bloody the day before.

Sofie and Bertie had spent most of their time in the apartment over the past year. Neither of them left for any film or dinner, daring to go outside only to work. The Olympics were coming to Berlin in two years, and they took odd jobs preparing the city for the summer welcome. Bertie often scrubbed graffiti; Sofie swept sidewalks. On the days they did not find Olympics work, Sofie washed clothes while Bertie cleaned up after horses. They took whatever they could find.

Nobody asked them for papers; nobody stopped them in their work. As long as they were helping, as long as they did not stand out, as long as they looked Deutsch and normally sexed, they were left alone. Bertie hoped to keep it that way.

It was just as well to him to stay inside whenever possible. He stayed constantly aware that every step he took outdoors these days was illegal. He had become afraid of going out, afraid of talking wrong, gesturing wrong, standing wrong, doing anything that might tip someone off about himself and, by association, Sofie. He did not want to get her hurt. He did not want to get himself hurt. He felt naked without his transvestite card, so often nestled in the pocket nearest to his heart. The emptiness inflated like a balloon.

He wondered where everyone had scattered. He wondered what everyone was doing. He hoped they were doing better than him and Sofie, but he also did not know what that would look like. He and Sofie sometimes talked about leaving. But to go where, they did not know. To get Bertie out was a risk, nearly impossible, and they did not know if the consequences would make things better or worse than they already were. It certainly could not get much worse than it was, they always concluded, for to do so would be to tip into complete madness. A country as old and steadfast as Deutschland would never allow it.

They had pulled long hours that evening on the thirtieth of June, and both were still awake. They had not yet even bothered to change from their clothes. They just sat in the quiet, pretending to read despite the distraction of both their heads. It was late, very late, and the rest of the building sounded like it had long since fallen asleep.

"We should go to bed," one of them would say after a stretch of quiet. The other would agree. But then neither of them would move.

A knock on the door startled them. It was a fist, halting only the once before hitting and hitting and hitting until Bertie quickly went to answer. Sofie held back toward the other side, one of their eating knives in her hand.

"Who is it?" Bertie barked, trying to sound his meanest.

"Bertie!" Gert replied breathlessly. "Let me in!"

As soon as Bertie unlocked the door, he was knocked backward by Gert's compact force. Gert quickly turned around and relocked the door.

Sofie put down the knife. "Do you have any idea how late it is?"

An odd question since neither of them quite knew themselves.

Gert dug into his jacket pocket. He spoke so quickly that he tripped over his breath. "You both need to leave. Right now."

"What's happening?"

Gert went to their windows and pulled the curtains shut. He extinguished each light in the apartment, save for the dim one near the door. Bertie and Sofie followed him as he babbled, still breathless.

"It's started. It's happening."

"You need to explain to us, Gert." Sofie was always the more level-headed one.

"Hitler has ordered Ernst Röhm killed."

Bertie stopped in his stride. "What? You don't mean—"

"It's a pogrom for the third sex." He stumbled over something in the dark, regained his footing, and continued. "It's happening now. Right now. You need to leave."

"How do you—?"

"I saw it with my own eyes. I was at Noster's Cottage when they came. They were slitting throats everywhere, anyone they could grab. I barely got out in time. I saw it all along the streets getting here. They're stealing people right out of their beds. Killing some, taking others to Dachau. Checking us off the list, one by one."

"But this sounds so calculated." Bertie's insides became watery at the thought. "How would they have found an entire list of us?"

Gert paused a moment to stare at him, helpless.

"But I burned my file." Bertie felt the guilt hit him, that he had never thought to burn Gert's file, too. "They wouldn't suspect me more than anyone else."

"I'm sure they do. You were still registered as an employee there." He began to dig into his suit pocket again. "You both need to leave."

Sofie looked somewhere between exasperated and in disbelief. "But where?"

Gert pulled out a torn piece of paper. "Do you remember Oma and Opa? They'll take us in. They'll hide us in Ulm." He held the paper by the dim light of the single lamp. They both leaned over. "Look well. Memorize it. Both of you." He waited a moment. "Do you have it?"

They nodded. To Bertie's surprise, Gert ripped the paper into pieces before shoving it into his mouth. He chewed and swallowed. "Leave a suicide note signed by the both of you so they think you're dead. So they won't come looking for you. Drown yourselves. Say you were too ashamed of your lives. Get to Ulm. Drive there all night. Do not stop for anything. Do you understand? Nothing. I'll be right behind you."

"Where are you going?" Sofie grew more concerned by the moment as it sunk in. "Just come with us right now if things are so urgent."

"I need to go to my apartment first. I need to leave my own letter. Otherwise, they'll know exactly where to find us."

"What about the others?" Bertie asked. "Markus and Gebhardt and Karsten. Are they coming?"

Gert stopped his pacing mid-stride. In the dark of the room, Bertie could see that Gert was no longer looking at either of them. "There was only time to tell one person." He scratched at the back of his head at a rapid pace, his voice cracking. "God forgive me. God forgive me."

As the seconds ticked by, Bertie felt his entire world slipping away. "We're going to pack and be out of here in five minutes, I promise."

"No!" Gert turned from the door. "No packing! You don't take belongings with you to die! You must leave with nothing! Write the note only!"

Bertie nodded fast. "The note only."

"Promise me!"

"We promise." He felt the dread in his stomach as Gert turned away again. "Gert," he said simply. He put his hand out, clasping it on his shoulder. "Thank you. Truly."

In the thin light of the lamp, his best friend smiled weakly. "Gert 'n' Bert."

* * *

Sofie and Bertie wrote the note hastily, signing it and leaving it atop the made bed. Bertie looked around his apartment, a fresh batch of devastation hitting him.

Bertie did not think himself a materialistic man. But his things represented the life he had built, and he liked his life. The clothes he worked so hard to afford, that he carefully picked out for his own style and had altered to fit his body. All the knickknacks and books he collected through various adventures, through trips and birthday gifts and all the other little moments of life that made it a life. His sexual toys were sometimes an extension of himself, sometimes for pleasure of himself, and to leave behind that level of intimacy for strangers to paw through, to mock, felt unjust. He knew he could surely get new ones later, he could get almost everything later. But that was not the point.

He was leaving himself behind. The realization hollowed his insides. He grabbed his photo album, his old transvestite card inside.

"I can't not," he said simply.

"You don't need to explain," Sofie replied. "They'll never notice." She picked the framed photo of her family off the shelf. She looked at it longer than she probably should have before glancing back at their suicide note. Her voice was almost a whisper. "This is going to destroy my parents."

"Yes, but you'll be able to tell them once it's safe."

Sofie seemed to be having many of the same thoughts as she took in the room. "This is it, isn't it?"

"Yeah," he said. "It is."

She tucked the framed photo of her family under her arm, wiping the dust clean from the shelf, rearranging the other knickknacks to fill the space. "Okay."

They slipped her photo and his album into his work satchel. It had been sitting useless near the door for the entire year. Bertie never had the heart to move it, as if he would return to the Institut any day now.

They otherwise left with only the clothes on their backs. They both stopped at the door. Bertie hesitated with his hand against the wood. He looked back at the apartment.

"Sofie."

"I know."

She turned off the final lamp and they went out the door. Bertie could not help but lock it.

They got into their auto parked on the street nearby. In the distance, they could hear yelling. It sounded like only a street or two away. Bertie froze a moment as he started the auto, the night of the Institut flooding his brain. His last image of Rüdiger. He thought again of Dora.

"Bertie!" Sofie hissed from the passenger side.

He shook his head free of the thoughts, but they clutched at the back of his brain, tiny fingernails burrowing into the soft flesh. They started down the street.

They decided to drive calmly despite the late hour. Just coming off from a long day of work, they were, so determined to make Berlin shine in time for the Olympics. Was there a problem, officer? Should there be concern for that yelling in the distance?

It took longer than usual to get out of the city, Bertie taking every turn that did not appear to have someone on it, even if it meant back-tracking on occasion. They sometimes found themselves on deserted streets littered with loose clothes or broken furniture. Dark puddles all slick and shiny and new against the dry cobblestones, seeping between the grooves. A few bodies. Bertie tried to not think about how they were crossing over places that had been freshly extracted of their kind. His hands shook upon the wheel.

"Don't speed up," Sofie kept reminding him in a soft whisper. "Don't speed up."

As the buildings thinned and the landscape widened, Bertie's breath slowed. His hands did not shake as much. He could not risk himself to think about all that had just happened, and so he held on to the only comfort he had. He was safe. They were safe.

The cobblestone road turned to dirt, grass growing up around them in clumps. And then suddenly, in the distance, came the shadows of creatures in the night. A few Nazis were lined up singularly, blocking the road as they stood ramrod straight, guns clasped to their chests with both hands. There were blockades of wood and barbed wire.

"Oh God," Bertie breathed. "They're going to pull us over."

Sofie said nothing a moment, their auto getting closer. "I have an idea," she suddenly blurted.

Bertie nodded his head, but he nearly drove off the road when Sofie let out a piercing scream. With each intake of breath, she let out another. Over and over again as she curled up in her seat.

With the first scream, the soldiers turned toward their auto, guns drawn and pointed. Bertie began to slow as they got closer.

"Halt!" one of them called out, the flat of his palm facing them.

Bertie slowed to a stop. Sofie would not stop screaming. She now clutched her stomach with both her hands, wailing.

"The baby!" she screamed. "The baby!"

The Nazis who had drawn their guns seemed to hesitate, though they continued to point their guns at the auto. The one who had issued the order to stop approached the driver's window. He glared at Bertie despite the yelling.

"Why are you leaving the city so late?"

"Please, the baby!" Sofie was crying now. "Anything but the baby!"

Bertie was breathless. "Bitte, officer. My wife is ill. We're worried she's losing the baby."

The man did not seem convinced. "Perhaps she's in labor."

"It's far too early for that." Bertie tried to screw his face up into the helplessness of a father. "It's happened once before. All we want is a family."

"The baby! No!"

Bertie struggled to hear the Nazi with Sofie's screams ringing in his ears. He was certain the Nazi was feeling the same way, based on his quickly tiring face.

"Why aren't you going to a hospital within Berlin?"

"Something's happening there, officer. The roads are blocked. We had no other choice." He worried his words could be used against him and he tried to recover. "I'm sure der Führer is improving Berlin with whatever these plans are, and I appreciate that he waited until nightfall to do them so as not to disturb his citizens. But I also know he cares deeply about family. We want to do our part in producing good, strong children for our fatherland."

"The baby! The baby! Please, no!"

Bertie could not understand how Sofie was able to hold on like she was, her voice still carrying as strong as when she had started. As the Nazi continued to analyze them, Sofie broke into full, wailing sobs.

"Please, officer," Bertie tried one last time. "Please let us save our baby."

To his amazement, Sofie managed to go up another octave. The Nazi finally had enough. He nodded.

"Very well." When he gestured behind himself, the other Nazis shouldered their guns and began to move the roadblocks. "Heil Hitler!"

"Heil Hitler!" Bertie responded with his deepest voice, raising his right hand from the wheel for the salute. He worried briefly if the Nazi would not let them through until Sofie did it, too. But he began to move the auto regardless, slowly squeezing through the roadblocks. The soldiers provided only the smallest gap. Sofie continued to scream without a single hesitation.

Once the auto cleared, Bertie pressed his foot down on the gas pedal. Part for the effect of their emergency, part for his impulse now to run. They careened down the road, each bump nearly smashing their heads against the ceiling. They kicked up dust and pebbles that pinged and crackled against the frame of the auto. And still Bertie did not slow down.

Sofie continued wailing and sobbing for at least another five minutes. When her voice could no longer carry back to the soldiers through the thin night air, she suddenly stopped, slumping against her seat.

"My God, Sofie," Bertie breathed. "You were wonderful."

"My throat hurts," she rasped back.

They drove for hours after that. Bertie eventually slowed down to a normal speed when neither of them could handle the severe bumping anymore. As the adrenaline sapped them, as the road and landscape around them continued to remain unchanged, they started to take turns driving. As they approached Ulm, Bertie panicked. In the freeze of fear, he had forgotten the address. But between the two of them, they managed to piece it together.

They traversed Ulm to the farmland as the sky softened. The night was still night, but it had taken on the tinge of a new day.

"This looks like it's it," Sofie said as they pulled up to one of the farmhouses. It was one of the only things she had said since her screaming. Her voice was still hoarse.

"What if we're wrong?" Bertie suddenly worried that such a thing would happen to them. That after their successful escape, they would happen to knock on the wrong door.

Sofie pointed at the mailbox. BAUMANN was written upon it in large scrawl.

They got out of the auto, both of them wobbly in the legs. As an afterthought, Bertie quickly retraced his few steps back to the auto and bent down to smear mud on the license plate, making it illegible. They would remove it before sunrise.

Sofie then doubled back as well, scooping up handfuls of dirt. She threw them at the auto. Bertie did a couple himself until the auto looked less like the city. They approached the farmhouse once again. A faint light shone inside and a curtain fluttered as a head shuffled away from the window.

The door opened before Bertie could knock. Opa stood before them, Oma barely visible past his tall frame.

"Herr und Frau Baumann," Bertie said. "We're so sorry to disturb you like this. You may not remember me, but—"

Opa grabbed Bertie by the shirt and yanked him inside, Sofie by the upper arm. They nearly fell on top of each other.

"You poor things!" Oma said as Opa quickly shut the door and locked it. "We've been so worried about you!"

Bertie and Sofie righted themselves and brushed each other off.

"Gert called us hours ago to expect you. We've been waiting all night." She looked expectantly between the two of them, almost smiling in her concern. "Where is he?"

Bertie stammered a moment. Opa reopened the door, sticking his head out to make sure he had not missed him. He closed and locked the door again.

"He hasn't arrived yet?" Bertie asked simply. His voice sounded distressingly small.

Oma's face dropped slightly, concern growing behind her eyes. Opa folded his arms across his chest, though he looked like he was deflating quickly. He had yet to speak.

"He was stopping by his apartment first," Bertie said. "He can't be far behind us."

Opa dropped his arms from his chest while Oma began to wilt.

"An hour," Sofie croaked out.

"Yes, an hour at most."

Opa nodded. Oma wrung her hands.

They all sat. They all waited.

III

21 • ULM, 1945

IT WAS THE DAY AFTER BERTIE BURNED HIS ALBUM. SOFIE and Karl were now looming over him, frustratingly close as he spread some ink on a folded cloth. He placed the cloth in one of the frying pans, as if stains mattered.

"Okay," Bertie breathed. He held the two erasers together and pressed them gently into the cloth. A bit of ink leaked out from the sides, the cloth burbling softly. "Karl," he said, and Karl immediately moved to Sofie's side at the kitchen table, out of Bertie's light.

Sofie held open one of the passports. Bertie could hear her breath. Karl seemed to have stopped breathing entirely. Bertie was very aware of his heartbeat, was mad that he was so aware of it. He should be better focused right now. If this did not work, if he made a mistake, that was it.

He inhaled and let it back out. He lifted the erasers from the cloth, still pressed together as one, all the backward letters and lines now slick with black ink. He shook them gently for any loose drops. He hovered the stamp over the passport. They all held still.

He pressed the erasers into the passport's page, holding them only a moment before rocking them slightly back and forth.

"You'll smudge it," Karl said, a rare anxiety in his voice.

"That's the idea. Worn stamp."

He lifted the erasers from the page. They all immediately leaned over, three shadows falling upon the inking.

"This looks almost good," Sofie said, releasing what sounded like all twelve years of tension. "If they don't examine it too close, it might work."

"It looks decent," Karl agreed.

Sofie was already blowing on it, her lips barely pursing. The shininess of the ink started to dull.

"Okay, Karl," Bertie said. His heart had yet to calm down. "Hold open the next one."

* * *

The ferry was not scheduled to leave from Stuttgart until the following night, but by nightfall, they were packing. All three stamps had gone well. Once they dried, Bertie stamped the date and made up the mysterious numbers. He assumed they were a way of numbering individuals, of keeping track of how many citizenships were given out. He made an educated guess based on the number in Gert's passport and how many Deutsche he thought Amerika let in per year as new citizens. Surely he was close.

They agreed to keep their names—save for Sofie, who took Bertie's surname as her own, continuing the story of husband and wife.

"I do think it's best," she said, barely above a whisper. It was the final nail in the coffin of her family line.

She and Bertie now had an open suitcase each on the bed, Karl in the other room with the same. He had asked Bertie what he should pack. Whether it was for permission or suggestion, none of the items being his, Bertie knew the same response applied to either. Whatever Karl wanted to bring that could fit in his suitcase.

"What about Muh and the chickens?" It was the second time that day that he had genuine concern on his face.

"I'm not sure," Bertie said. "I plan to let them out and they can graze and roam until someone finds them." He did not add that whoever found them would likely butcher them for food.

There was no telling how big the ferry would be or how many people would try to get on. Nor did they know exactly when it would arrive. They had to be there early, they had to be first in line. They had to get on that ferry.

When Bertie was nearly done with his suitcase, he slipped it downstairs. He lifted up the potato boards and pulled out the flat-cap, placing it upon his neatly folded clothes. He shut his suitcase.

Sofie's footfalls sounded on the stairs, faster than expected. She quickly placed her suitcase in the sitting room. "They're here."

Karl lumbered down the stairs with his own suitcase. He placed it next to Sofie's and cocked his head, feeling the tension in the room settle upon them.

"Ward," Sofie said. "With some officers."

Karl grabbed Bertie's suitcase and put it with the others, tucking them into the sitting room against the front-facing wall. Bertie collected the passports from the table and shoved them against Karl's chest as he returned. Karl looked a moment as if he were handling hot coals, his palms out and open as he hesitated, before cramming them into one of the suitcases.

There was a hard knock at the door. Time and again he had come. Time and again he picked terrible hours, inconvenient moments, chances to trip them up and startle them into submission.

"Not tonight," Bertie moaned quietly. "We're not supposed to report to the camp until the day after tomorrow. He couldn't leave us alone for just one more night?"

The banging grew louder against the door.

"What would happen if we ignored it?" Karl whispered. "They wouldn't drag us all out with me here, would they?" He winced as the banging began to rattle the door. "They think we're Jewish."

"Fräuline Durchdenwald!" came the voice of Ward. Though it was muffled through the wood, the singsong taunt was clear, the grin audible.

Bertie's heart stopped. He felt sweat quickly collect on his body, his palms going clammy. The officer surely did not say what Bertie thought he did. His eyes shifted between Karl and Sofie. But from the look that Sofie had, he was sure he had heard Ward correctly.

It was not possible. There was no way.

"Fräuline!" Ward yelled again. It sounded now like he was kicking the door with everything he had. "Open up so we may arrest you!"

Bertie swallowed. He thought about the window, thought about his escape from the Institut. But it was not like then; it was not as easy. They were looking for him, they knew he was inside, and there was very little place for him to hide.

Without much more thought, he moved by instinct. He started to walk toward the door.

Sofie grabbed him by the arm.

"There's nothing to be done." His tone was flat and dry. "He's got me. I don't know how, but he has."

"Bertie, please don't." She would not let go of his arm.

Karl stood a couple paces away, looking quite sad.

Bertie turned to Sofie. He gently released her from his arm, then held her face in both of his hands. His tone was even, frightening himself. "You have to do something for me."

Ward's voice shot through again. "We'll beat down the door if you don't open up!"

"You have to tell them you had no idea," Bertie continued. "You and Karl both. You had no idea I was a transvestite."

Sofie tried to shake her head against this, but Bertie still held her in his hands.

"Tell them I was a liar and a cheat. Tell them I beat you. Tell them every bad thing you can think of to gain sympathy."

"I can't betray you like that."

"Please. Do this for me. I've read it many times in the papers from America. It works. I've seen their lovers do it. It's the way it is. It's the only chance you have, that you both have, to get out of here. I won't let you go down with me."

He released Sofie, who was still shaking her head. He walked over to Karl.

"Durchdenwald!" Ward barked. It sounded like the door was splintering. "You're making it worse for yourself!"

"You, too, Karl," Bertie said simply. He placed both his hands upon his shoulders. "I'm sorry for not protecting you years ago. I'm sorry for the part I played."

Karl swallowed thickly. "None of that was your doing."

"Either way, I have the chance to protect you now." He shook his shoulders gently. He looked directly into his eyes. "You deserve a second chance. You deserve happiness. Please live your life the best you can."

Karl said nothing. It seemed he did not know how to respond.

Bertie let him go and returned to Sofie. "I love you, Sofie. I've loved having you in my life. I'm sorry if I've ever made you feel otherwise."

She swallowed to keep herself from crying. "I've never regretted being with you. I love you, Bertie."

The three of them stared down the buckling door. Ward continued to yell and pound and kick. Sofie rushed to move the suitcases, to tuck them beneath the sofa. Karl helped her. They came back to stand beside Bertie.

"No matter what happens," Bertie said to them. "You claim your innocence and get out of here. Get on that ferry no matter what. I need some good to come out of all this." He turned to Sofie and hugged her, kissing her on the lips. "I love you, Sofie." He suddenly felt awful for all the times he had not told her when he could.

She buried her face in his neck, clutching the hair at the back of his head. "I love you, Bertie." She sounded about to say more, but she stopped. She still had not promised to honor his plan, but Bertie could not bear to force her. He did not want to make her admit it out loud.

They finally let each other go.

"Karl," he said to him. "I truly do love you, too."

Karl looked startled by this. He was quiet a moment. And then, suddenly, there was a rush of emotion on his face that Bertie worried would finally be released, at this time of all times. The pain of the world would finally break free. But then Karl grabbed it, tamped it back down. He let out a breath. His voice was quiet. "I love you, Bertie. Thank you for everything."

Bertie took in a big breath and stared at the door. And while by now it seemed unnecessary to act, Bertie wanted it on record, if only for himself, that he opened the door of his own volition.

He stepped back quickly as Ward burst through. He was followed by five other officers. Bertie expected the man to be angry after all his pounding and yelling; instead, he grinned as he laid eyes upon him.

From his breast pocket, he extracted a newspaper clipping in English. THE GIRL WHO "MARRIED" A GIRL. The article Bertie had clipped the morning he found Karl. He had not thought of it once over the past week, how it had blown away and he had stopped chasing it.

"Found it near the trees the other day," Ward said, putting it back into his pocket. "And it made quite a bit of sense. One of my officers overheard you talking on the way to Oberer Kuhberg, said you had a Berlin accent. Berlin accent, Berlin born. So I started checking all the Berlin transvestites the Nazis had listed, from the copies we kept while we liberated the camps. I didn't know what name I was looking for, but someone's work identification picture from that old transvestite institute looked quite miraculously like you. Someone who conveniently disappeared during the Night of the Long Knives." He clucked his tongue. "But my, how you've aged."

Bertie felt a fresh rush of despair, along with some of Gert's final words. *You were still registered as an employee*. He was listed the whole time. If not definitively, then certainly suspect. Ward had found the article, had found him, which meant he had burned his card, his album, his pictures of Gert, the remaining history of his community, for nothing. He found himself wishing that, if nothing else, Ward had arrived a day earlier.

He was also mad at himself. After all the energy he used to transvest his voice, he sometimes had nothing left to hide his Berliner dialect. He had gotten sloppy somewhere. The masking had worn a hole through him.

"You were also reported as dead by suicide." Ward glanced at Sofie and smirked. "Alongside your lover."

They had signed the suicide note together, had disappeared together. Bertie never considered the possibilities of that working against them.

"Why does this mattering?" Bertie asked in English, gesturing to himself. "This is not important."

"There are laws."

"But you having now the power. You choosing now what is laws and what is not laws."

Ward seemed unmoved by this attempt at humanity. "It's for the best of a people."

Bertie did not understand and he did not care to. "How much time?" he asked. "Six months or five years?"

"Five years," Ward replied. He gave no hesitation.

They were choosing the harsher Nazi law instead of what had been on the books for generations before them. They were choosing the Nazi law when they had chosen to not honor all those against other peoples. Bertie shook his head.

"She did not know," he said sternly in his stilted English. He did not want to mention Karl, did not want any attention drawn to him, even as he stood in plain view of them all.

Ward scoffed. "She lived with you for almost two decades, and you expect me to believe she had no idea? That's a big secret to keep for so long."

"Not that secret." Bertie was not quite sure where he was going, but he was certain confusion could help. "My other secret."

Ward suddenly looked bright in the eyes. He licked his lips. His other officers continued to stand at attention, all eyes on Bertie. "Other secret?"

Bertie nodded slowly. "Mein Englisch ist bad," he spoke slowly, purposely thickening his accent. "I know not beste vay."

Ward squinted, as if sharpening his sight would help him better understand. Bertie could see him leaning forward, if only slightly. "Try."

Bertie gave another nod. He looked down as if trying to think hard about his English words. When he looked up, his words were as slow and precise as before. "I show you. Ja?"

"Ja," Ward replied in a tone somewhere between mocking and eager.

Bertie sighed, as if in a great internal struggle. "Okay," he said. "Okay."

He walked into the sitting room, Ward and the officers following. Sofie and Karl trailed behind. Bertie led the officers past the hidden suitcases to the piano.

"Hier. I hiding it hier."

"You hide *what* here?" Ward grew impatient with Bertie.

"Mein secret." Bertie picked up the urn from the piano. It was heavier in his hands than he remembered, the weight of humanity. The weight of his own choices.

Ward bent, leaning toward Bertie not a meter away from him. His eyes were fixed entirely on the urn.

Bertie looked down at the urn in his hands. "Es tut mir leid," he said softly.

"What?"

"I am sorry."

Ward blinked. "Well . . . that's not good enough to let you go."

Bertie slowly removed the lid from the urn. He looked up at Ward. "I was not talking to you."

In a great, outward arch of his arms, the ashes of Oma and Opa jumped from the urn, spitting in the faces of the officers.

"Fuck!" Ward yelled, bringing both palms to his eyes as he reared his head back.

Bertie dropped the urn to the floor. He turned and ran to the back door as the officers spat and swore in the plume of Oma and Opa, rubbing quickly at their reddening eyes.

The urn rolled away, stopping gently by Karl's feet.

Bertie was out the back door. It swung open behind him, banging once against the wall and rebounding in a warble.

At the sound, Ward swore again. "Go!" he yelled at his men. He blinked against the ashes and squinted his eyes shut once more, sucking air in through his teeth as the burning continued.

Sofie grabbed one of the suitcases under the sofa and skidded it before two of the nearest officers. They stumbled against the suitcase in the haze of the gray dust and fell into each other, tangled.

Bertie heard them behind him, but he was already halfway toward the fire pit, headed for the trees.

Ward blinked fast again and swore at the sound of his men falling. He tried to hop over them, tried to start after Bertie, but he, too, tangled himself against the officers. As he struggled to gain his footing, he stepped down too hard. His boot went through the potato boards, sinking up to his knee. His men toppled behind him, piling up against the back door.

"We say floor bad," Sofie muttered.

Karl had crouched to pick up the urn, now on his hands and knees, frantically scooping what he could of the ashes.

Those few seconds of chaos had bought Bertie precious time. He was nearly to the fire pit now, and if he could make it to the forest, he might be okay. He did not know where he would hide or how long he could last, but he might be okay.

As he passed the fire pit, he saw the last few ashes of his photo album. Of what used to be the last known piece of their history. He could not believe all that had happened, could not believe what he was doing now. And he could not believe that, through all of this, the saplings of their new crops had barely grown. It had been only a week.

The officers sputtered and swore far behind him. Ward finally freed his leg; his men untangled themselves. He sprinted after Bertie, his officers fast behind. But Bertie was already long into the woods. They went in after him.

Sofie and Karl were forgotten in the farmhouse. And as the back door continued to bang against the wall, Karl frantically scooped every handful he could salvage of Oma and Opa.

"Come on!" Sofie yelled, picking up two of the suitcases. "We need to run!"

"I can't leave them like this!"

"You didn't even know them!"

"That shouldn't matter!"

With so much ash still scattered on the floor, with so much still hanging in the air, Karl finally admitted defeat and replaced the lid. He tucked the urn against his chest, dirtying his shirt in powdery gray smears. He picked up the third suitcase, and they ran out the front door to the old auto. They did not speak of Bertie. They did not discuss their need to bring all three suitcases to the ferry. The urn was much lighter than it used to be, and it would never be known how much of whom had been left behind, how much of whom had managed to go with them, how much had entered the lungs of bad people and how much would blow out the open doors into the freedom of the night air. It probably did not matter. For after so many years of waiting, of sadness and angst and helplessness, Oma and Opa felt they had finally done something in the name of their grandson.

22

BERTIE CONTINUED TO RUN THROUGH THE WOODS. HIS LUNGS burned from the effort, but he tried not to pant, to not make a sound. He was not sure how long he had been running. He could barely see in the night, beneath the canopy of trees. Roots tripped him while branches bit at his face. He worried he could be heard for kilometers. Their voices were far behind him, but between his fear and the way their shouts carried, he was certain they were only a step behind. Any moment, they would grab him. Any moment, it would all be over. But let not the world say that he did not resist until the very end.

His nose filled with his own sweat. Damp leaves, heavy and thick, clung to him. His mouth was dry. He could not swallow.

With so many voices trailing behind, he hoped that the officers had forgotten about Sofie and Karl. They were smart. Surely, they were far away from the farm now, safely on their way to the ferry.

Frau Baer's home peeked through the trees on his right. One of her ground floor windows was open, no doubt for fresh air. He stopped running and regretted it instantly, the burn of his chest finally catching up with him. It was a silly idea, an absurd thought, but he knew he could not run forever in these woods. He knew they would eventually catch up to him.

He dashed headlong toward Frau Baer's house and lunged through the window. Something flitted across the floor of the sitting room. He yelped. Katze hissed and smacked him across the cheek. He gritted his teeth to keep himself from making more noise. The sting of her claws lingered on his flesh. Her eyes glowed at him in the moonlight.

"Who's there?" Frau Baer turned on a light upstairs, and he could hear her footsteps coming down to the ground floor.

Bertie did not dare move from his place on the floor. "It's me," he said in a hushed voice. "Please. I don't mean you any harm."

To his dismay, she turned on more lights. "What the hell are you doing here? Get out. Get out right now."

"Frau Baer, please." He pumped his palms downward, as if this would lower her voice. He froze when he heard a banging on the door.

"Open up!" came the English of Ward.

Frau Baer moved toward the door on instinct but then stopped. She turned to Bertie with a puzzled look and then looked back at the door. Ward was banging and kicking like he had when he had arrived at the Baumann farm.

"Frau Baer," Bertie pleaded quietly. "Hide me. Please." He broke off further words. For what more was safe to say? That he was innocent? That he was a Nazi? He still did not know which side she was on. He hoped that whichever it was, she would believe he was the same. "Please," he said one more time.

She did not answer right away. Ward continued to pound and yell. After a moment, she looked right into his eyes.

"Get under the couch," she said.

Bertie did as told, curling himself small as possible beneath the dusty wood of the couch's underbelly.

Frau Baer opened the door. Ward burst in but then seemed to settle himself at the sight of her.

"We're searching for your neighbor."

Frau Baer was as uncaring as ever. "I haven't seen either of them."

"We lost the trail right near your home."

"I've been sleeping."

"Then why are your lights on?"

She shrugged. "I'm an old woman. I wake up a lot."

Bertie continued to cower beneath the couch, breathing in the dust of the floorboards. He could see Ward's boots as he walked further into the room. They were now caked with dirt and ash. He walked two steps closer to Frau Baer's slippered feet. "Are you sure you haven't seen anyone?"

"Officer Ward." Bertie could practically hear the hands on her hips. "I know you are only doing your job, but I'm certain I would know if someone were in my home. Now if someone happens by, I will be sure to alert you. But in the meantime, I'd appreciate it if I could go back to bed."

To Bertie's surprise, it sounded like Ward was backing down. "Certainly, ma'am. You have a good night now."

Bertie watched his boots clomp away, retreating with his men back out the door. He could not believe she was able to get rid of them so easily. He listened as the door closed, as their boots slowly faded into the distance outside. He heard Frau Baer casually close her windows and pull the shades.

"Why did you save me?" Bertie asked quietly as he carefully pulled himself out from under the couch. He remained low to the ground, lest the officers return.

Frau Baer looked thoughtful a moment. She sat down on the couch near him. Her gaze was fixed on the door, surely in the same concerns as Bertie of the officers coming back.

"The day they marched us to Oberer Kuhberg, you became ill. From grief," she added knowingly.

He was not sure what was safe to share. "I believe I recognized someone."

Frau Baer was quiet a moment. "I'm sorry."

Bertie continued to stay low to the floor. He wished he could have such a talk with her to her face. "Did you lose anyone?"

Frau Baer continued to look ahead. Katze jumped up into her lap. "Everybody." She stroked Katze, who began to purr and settle in. "My name isn't Frau Baer. It's Ber. I was able to prove to the Americans that I was Jewish shortly after our march to Oberer."

It suddenly made sense, how she was skeptical of them, how she always kept to herself, how she constantly spoke to them in code, hoping one of them would finally figure the other out. He remembered Opa's words. *Some of the most patriotic Germans I know are Jews.*

But now, Bertie did not know what to say beyond an apology. "I'm sorry I ever thought otherwise."

"I've been trying to figure you and your wife out this entire time. Especially back when Goss and Ina disappeared."

"They died naturally, I swear to you. We loved them. They were hiding us."

"I believe you now. They were wonderful souls."

"They were." Bertie felt his neck and back begin to ache from his position, but he did not dare get up.

She continued to pet Katze, thoughtful a moment. "It was your eyes tonight that convinced me."

"My eyes?"

"You had fear in them. Not the fear of a man who must finally pay for his actions. But the fear of a man who is innocent. I know that difference well."

Bertie said nothing.

"But I don't yet understand," Frau Ber said. "It's why I still hesitated after Oberer. If you're an innocent man, then why are you running? Why did you hide behind Goss and Ina's name?"

Bertie knew that she required an answer, that to not give her one would throw him back into suspicion. But after running all the other options through his head, all the other lies, he realized he had none left. "Have you ever been to die Institut für Sexualwissenschaft? In Berlin?"

Frau Ber shook her head. "No, but Goss and Ina told me about their trip." Her tone was as difficult to read as always.

Bertie took in a breath. If she did not approve of him, this would be it. She could call the officers right back to him and have him dragged away. "I'm a transvestite."

"Ah." She was quiet a moment. "Like their grandchild?"

Bertie felt his body depress itself into the floor. "Yes. Like their grandchild. We were dear friends."

"He's a sweet boy."

"Yes. He was sweet."

He saw her body stiffen beside him. "I'd hoped perhaps he'd left the country." She finally dared to glance at him. "What happened to him?"

Bertie did not have the heart to tell her fully. "He never came home."

Frau Ber was quiet as she let this sink in. She lifted a hand from Katze to wipe at her eyes. "The younger ones. They hurt the most for me."

Katze jumped lightly from her lap as she stood. It reminded Bertie that his cheek still stung.

"You knew we weren't them. Why didn't you ever tell anyone? Why did you play along?"

"I was afraid of who you might really be," she said. "But also, I knew the Baumanns. They were good people. And I knew their grandson." She locked eyes with Bertie. "I thought you might be like him. Maybe. But even if that was true, it didn't mean you weren't also a Nazi."

Bertie said nothing.

"You may stay with me," Frau Ber continued. "In honor of Goss and Ina, and certainly for Gert, I will hide you until my last breath."

Bertie slowly got up, his muscles yelling at him after he had held them tense for so long. "Thank you, Frau Ber." He was still getting used to saying her name. "I can't tell you how much I appreciate that. But I must leave tonight. We're fleeing the country tomorrow by boat. I'm sure Sofie and Karl are on their way, and I hope to meet them there." He stopped, thinking. "Would you like to come with us? To America?"

"America?" She scoffed. "My goodness, no. Why would I want to start new troubles at my age? And besides, now that I've cleared my name, the Americans here are being very good to me. I'm perfectly set here. I'm perfectly fine."

"I'm glad to hear that."

Frau Ber walked over to her mantle and opened an old cigar box. "That young man of yours. Karl, you said his name was?"

Bertie nodded. "He's not our nephew."

"I suspected as much."

"He's like me. He's on the run from the Allies, too."

"Ah." Bertie was not sure if this was to his answer or to whatever she just found. She walked back over and placed a gold pocket watch into his palm. "I can't let you leave without some sort of help."

"Frau Ber, I can't—"

"You can and you will. Because I said so."

"But—"

"Do you have money for a ticket to get on that boat of yours? Do you have something to barter?"

Bertie had not thought of this, not in the commotion of his escape. He had nothing on him. "No."

"Then you take this. My husband always hated it, anyway." She gave a rare smile. "It was his retirement gift and he said it made him feel old."

Bertie closed his fingers around the watch, slowly bringing it to his chest. "The farm," he finally said. "There's a cow and five chickens there, and a great crop of asparagus is still coming in. And plenty of food in the cellar."

"Oh, what need do I have of another farm."

"Sell it, then. See if you can get some money for it. The deed's in the desk in the sitting room." He could tell she did not yet seem convinced. "Do whatever you want with it. If anybody deserves Goss and Ina's land, it's you."

Her eyes became wet at this, the old rims going pink. "Thank you—" Her sentence broke off awkwardly as she realized she did not know his real name.

"Bertie," he offered.

She smiled. "Bertie." She patted his cheek, the one Katze had not scratched. "How far is the boat? I'll drive you."

"I think it's best I go by foot. I can make it in the next day and I'm sure they'll be stopping cars in the meantime. I don't want you getting in trouble for all this."

She gave a small smile, her voice now almost a whisper. "Write to me when you're safe."

"I certainly will. Thank you, Frau Ber. For everything. I'm sorry we didn't get to know each other until now."

The officers were long gone. He began to leave, but stopped at the door.

"Your cat," he asked. "What's her name?"

"Käthe."

"Oh," he said. "I was close."

23

BERTIE WALKED ALL NIGHT AND ALL DAY. HIS FEET HURT BY morning, but he did not stop, could not stop. He was too afraid of missing the ferry. He halted only a moment to remove his shoes when the pain became too much. He carried them the rest of the way. His socks were met with shiny circles of blood from ruptured blisters. He groaned and removed his socks. The dirt soon soothed him, coating his feet in a gentle film that dried him up and stopped his bleeding. It was sun-warm beneath him.

He continued down dirt roads and cobblestone paths, hurrying into tree lines whenever he heard an auto or a voice. Everyone passed by without notice of him. Or at least without care. He was surely lost to Ward and the other officers by now, but he was afraid to let his guard down. If Ward knew about the ship or the ferry, perhaps he would guess that was where Bertie would go, perhaps he would try to stop the ferry leaving.

By late midday, Bertie was hungry and thirsty. He had nothing on him. He thought of finding the nearest town, of bartering the pocket watch for some money. He could get water and some bread and save the rest for a ticket. But he was still afraid to stop for too long, afraid that if he stopped, he would somehow be caught. He did not know how Karl had done this for two weeks when he escaped Dachau. Maybe because, in the saddest way, nobody had been looking for him.

Sofie and Karl were smart people, he reminded himself. Very smart. They would have left immediately. Probably with the suitcases, probably by auto. They would have money to get aboard. They would be near the front of the line. They would have each other.

He tried to keep the bad thoughts out of his head, but with little else to think about in his anxiety, they circled and taunted him. The only thing worse than not making the ferry in time was if neither of them was there when he did. He asked himself if he would still get on the ferry. He did not know the answer.

Bertie continued northwest to Stuttgart. The sun began to set, the spring air cooling slightly as swatches of purples and pinks dappled the sky. The dirt stayed warm beneath his browned and bloodied feet.

He looked up at the sky, looking at all the colors as they formed. His mouth was dry, and he was starting to feel lightheaded. "What do you think, Gert?" he asked softly. "Do any of those look lilac to you?" He was quiet, as if waiting for an answer. "I'm so sorry."

Apologizing felt like the right thing to do. He did not know if anybody had ever said it to Gert during those years, nor in his honor after.

"I really hope you're there when we arrive," he continued. His feet hurt so much now he could barely feel them anymore. "I know you won't be, but I still hope you will."

He was too tired to stop his anxious thoughts. He began to worry that he had given up too easily on Gert. Perhaps the flat-cap was not his. Perhaps he was still out there. Perhaps he could not get to Oma and Opa safely, so he fled to Amerika. And he had never written because he was worried the letter would be intercepted, that it would put them all at risk. And now that the War was over, he was writing, but the letters were not getting in. Delivery was still a shamble. It was just like when Sofie was writing to her parents. If Bertie had waited even one more day, maybe those letters from Gert would finally start arriving.

Or perhaps he really had been taken to a camp. Perhaps he had survived. He was a clever one, a charming one. He could have made it through like Karl had. Perhaps he was on foot from farther off, still on his path to Oma and Opa. Perhaps he was arrested when his camp had been liberated. Perhaps he was simply in jail. Bertie had not checked any of the jails. He had not asked any officers. If he could not have Gert released, he could at least visit him all the time. Then he would have a friend waiting for him in another five years.

Or perhaps Karl was mistaken in recognizing his photo. There were many people in the camps. Perhaps Gert was still in Deutschland, hiding in plain sight in Soviet territory. It would take a while for him to get to the farm from there.

Bertie told himself that these were all plausible events. And his great sin, the reason he did not know which event was true, was because he had not given Gert enough time. And now, when Gert finally arrived at the farm, exhausted, he would have nobody there. After all his struggle, he would be confused, disheartened, and alone. And perhaps worst of all, he would have no answers about where the people he loved had gone.

Bertie almost stopped walking. He did not realize how slow his gait had become until he nearly tripped over his own feet. He was feeling dizzier. Part of him wanted to turn around. Part of him wanted to collapse. Squirrels were jumping along the tree lines, worrying him every time he heard a branch rustle. No, he chastised himself. He would press on. If Gert did arrive, then Frau Ber would inform him and the four of them could reunite in Amerika. With Roy.

Just then he saw it, buildings sprouting up from farther out. He was approaching Stuttgart. The pocket watch had not been wound before he left, but based on the setting of the sun, he was sure had been walking for almost a full day.

He quickened his pace. The dirt soon became cobblestones. No water source was in view yet. He put his shoes back on, much as it pained him, knowing it was best to not look desperate when he began to ask if there was a ferry. He suddenly worried about drawing attention to any ferry. He asked instead where the Rhein was.

It was surprisingly, and perhaps frighteningly, easy to find. After someone pointed him in the general direction of the river, and corrected him that it was actually the Neckar, but it flowed right into the Upper Rhein not much farther north, he could already see dozens and dozens of people lined up. They were mixed in all sorts of ways. Some were dirty, some were not. Some looked tired and hungry and thin, others had energy and smiles on their faces. There was no ferry yet in sight.

As he got closer to the fellow Deutsche, he scanned the crowd. The sun was past setting and it was becoming difficult to see faces. There were too many faces. As he muddled about, tired and hungry and lightheaded, a dark form popped up near the front, followed by a familiar voice.

"Bertie!"

He immediately turned. The crowd rippled as the form of Sofie quickly materialized before his eyes, running fast as she could through the throng. Bertie worried a moment at the absence of Karl, but then he recognized his form toward the front of the line, holding their place. Karl was standing on his toes, craning his neck in a vain attempt to see over the heads of the others.

Sofie bashed into Bertie's midsection, holding him tight. Bertie kissed her head as she gave a single sob of relief.

"We've been hoping and looking all day."

"I'm sorry. I had to go on foot."

Sofie stood back up to her full height. She kissed him on the mouth and held his face in her hands. "You're alive. You're here, you're alright, you're alive. How did you get here?"

"I'll tell you all about it. How did you?"

She gave a smile. "I'll tell you all about it." She took him by the wrist and led him back to their spot near the front.

Karl was quiet as he approached. He gave Bertie a single nod of recognition, his shoulders releasing. "It's good to see you, Onkel."

Beneath Karl's arm, Bertie recognized Oma and Opa's urn.

* * *

It was four more hours until the ferry was expected. Sofie had traded the auto for some food and water when she and Karl arrived. They nibbled on rations to keep their hunger at bay.

"There isn't enough for the whole trip," she said quietly. It sounded almost like an apology. "We didn't think to bring food. We left so quickly."

Bertie nodded. "There was no other way to leave."

"We'll be okay," Karl said simply, looking out over the dark, still water. His tone left Sofie and Bertie quiet.

As the night grew its darkest and more people arrived, Karl grew anxious. He would slowly crane his neck behind him to the crowd, his eyes darting everywhere. He could turn his back for only a minute at most before he had to check them all again. The crowd continued to grow, faster the later it got. Hundreds joined the line.

When it was a late enough hour that Bertie could no longer guess the time, a dark shape arrived on the horizon. The entire crowd stood, watching, largely quiet with the occasional murmuring.

Bertie's shoulders sagged in relief. There really was a ferry. It really had arrived. It was long and thin, an old white two-decker largely shaded by white linen as cover. It would take only moments for water to soak through if it rained.

When it finally docked, Bertie braced himself. He saw both Sofie and Karl stiffen beside him with surely the same thoughts. He was not good with estimates, but he gathered the ferry could fit maybe three hundred of them if they squeezed together. But he was surprised as people began to board quietly. There was no pushing or shoving, there was no panicking of not getting on, of there not being enough room. He was not sure if people knew such behavior would only make things worse or if they did not realize this was a ferry to the last known ship. Or maybe they were not in as much trouble as Bertie and his family.

They boarded without issue. Bertie did not have to hand over the pocket watch; Sofie and Karl had made sure to bring the suitcases, which included things they could barter. They were let on as soon as they paid their dues. As some of the first people let aboard, they secured themselves to a far corner under some of the linen, against a short wall they guessed to be a small cargo hold. They would be out of the elements and the sight of others. They could at least sleep sitting upright against the wall.

As they settled in, Sofie chuckled dryly. "I just realized. We escaped the Americans so we could go to America."

The ferry continued to fill. As they got toward the end of the crowd, Bertie saw that any clamoring to get aboard would have been unnecessary. There was enough room on the ship, just barely, though some had less than desirable spots and it appeared none of them would be able to lie down to sleep. It would be a long trip.

"I'm having some difficulty." Karl's breathing was labored. He was curled into himself, hugging his knees to his chest.

"What's happening?" Bertie asked.

"The problem with surviving things," Karl said, swallowing heavily, "is that everything reminds you of it."

Bertie looked about, at the tired and dirtied faces, at the cramped confines. The smell of so many bodies so close together filled his nose.

"We're here to travel to a better life," Sofie whispered to Karl. "We're not traveling to our deaths."

Karl nodded quickly. His breaths were still deep and quivering.

Bertie wanted to say more to help comfort him, but they were interrupted by a shout back on the piers. It was in English, the voice familiar.

"Bring your boarding ramp back down!" Ward yelled. "By order of the United States Army!"

"Scheiße," Sofie said.

"What do we do?" Bertie whispered quickly.

"I don't know, I don't know."

Karl looked equally lost. There were, after all, few places to hide on a modest ferry, especially with so many people aboard. Bertie was not certain they would manage to blend well among all the faces.

"Well, we need to think of something," Bertie said.

"Shh!"

A man nearby cocked his head toward them. He was dressed in brown slacks and a white shirt, still tucked in proper although it had become wrinkled in places. He looked to be in his thirties, accompanied by a woman, surely his wife, as well as three other men his age who engaged with him like good friends. They appeared to come from a little money. As they continued to quietly joke and laugh in their group, the man in question excused himself. He walked to Bertie.

"Do you need help, Herr?" The weak lamplights hooked around them cast shadows across his face.

Bertie was surprised a moment by the formality, but then he

remembered he was noticeably older than this man, perhaps by twenty years.

Out of options, he nodded. "They're here for me. And surely my wife and nephew will come to harm if they're spotted, too."

They could hear repeated bangs of the wooden boarding plank as the crew struggled to put it back into place.

The man thought a moment and then gestured toward Bertie. "Give me your jacket."

Bertie took it off and handed it over. But when he believed it to be nothing more than a barter, the man began to take off his own. He waved over the rest of his group, who in turn handed over their own before beginning to engage others onboard.

"Lay down," the man said. "All three of you. As tight as you can."

They did as told, quickly huddling together as they lay down on the damp floorboards. Bertie jumped when a jacket fell upon him in the dark. And then another. And on and on until he felt he could barely breathe under the musk and damp. It was unbearably hot. His hand was somewhere around Sofie's hip, and he squeezed her there. She trembled slightly. Karl had gone stiff as stone. Bertie worried that Karl had stopped breathing entirely, but then he felt the soft tickle of air near his elbow.

Heavy boots marched up the plank. Bertie was certain Ward had brought his full group of officers from the night before. He held still and listened. All he could see now was blackness. He questioned whether his eyes were open or closed.

"Nobody move," Ward barked once he arrived on deck. "We're here for a search."

The thudding of their boots ate through the floorboards as they flanked out for their hunt. Bertie shrank a little as each vibration grew stronger, coming closer and closer to their little pile. Each gait ultimately passed them, but after some minutes, one stopped directly in front of them.

"What is it you are looking for, sir?" said the man from before, his voice very close. His English was decent, though his accent was still plain. "Perhaps we could help you look."

Ward snorted. "What's all this here?"

Bertie heard a soft, sudden rustle from the coats, felt Karl roll into him tighter like dead weight. He was certain Ward had just shoved Karl in the back with his toe.

"It's all of our coats and jackets," the man said. "We've agreed this is where we'll put the children each night to sleep."

There was no answer. Bertie strained to hear something, anything, and this somehow hurt his neck. He was certain Ward was listening as intently as he was. The urge to breathe was getting stronger within his lungs. He tried to release it gently to keep himself from gasping out.

Bertie continued to wait. They all continued to wait.

It was the man again who calmly broke the silence. "If you please, sir, what are you looking for? We'd be happy to help. We're in your debt, after all."

Ward remained silent. He also did not seem to move. Bertie again withheld his breath, again it began to build in him like a bubble. He became worried not that they would be found but rather that it would be him who caused it to happen.

After long minutes, Ward's boots moved on. Different gaits clomped by, back and forth, stopping and starting as they pushed through so many people, around and around. And then eventually, blissfully, they lessened in number until there was only one pair left.

"Goddammit," Ward muttered.

Bertie heard his footsteps slowly retreat across the deck and down the boarding plank. If this was truly the last time he would see him, Bertie felt it somehow fitting that he had not laid eyes on him at all. Let him be nothing more than a faceless entity intent on haunting him.

After a few more minutes of no sound from Ward or his officers, the man gave them the all clear to emerge. Bertie and the others removed themselves from the coats. People who had contributed began to take their coats from the pile. Bertie and Sofie muttered thanks to many of them who dared to make eye contact. Most just gave a small nod before returning to their own spots on the ship. The man, however, crouched down to meet eyes with Bertie. Bertie could see now from this close range that the man was clean-shaven.

"Glad to see you're still with us, friend." He gave a toothy grin.

Bertie cleared his throat. He reminded himself to bring his voice up from his belly, to deepen it best he could without suspicion. He kept his tone flat. "That was quick thinking."

"Well, we Germans need to look out for one another." He held out his hand. "Especially now of all times. None of them understand what we were trying to do."

Bertie's heart stopped. He swallowed, hesitating to take his hand and then worrying he had already hesitated too long. He finally brought his own hand out in a hearty handshake. He smiled, closemouthed, in what surely looked like a cross between a squint and a grimace. He was grateful for the weak lamplights.

The man grinned wider and finally released his hand. He gave him a friendly wave before returning to his own group. Bertie was insulted that the man had confided his allegiance so freely, that there was something about Bertie that screamed Nazi. But then he realized it was simpler than that. With the Allied forces looking for them, it was surely easy to misinterpret.

With Ward and his men now gone, the crew of the ferry readied themselves to leave. Bertie wanted to feel relief, but he quickly became aware of Karl beside him.

"There are Nazis on this boat," Karl muttered to himself, nearly a whisper. His hands were clasped upon one another against his chest. "There are Nazis on this boat, there are Nazis on this boat, there are Nazis on this boat . . ."

"Shhh," Bertie said, fighting the urge to say it sharply. Drawing attention would help neither himself nor Karl. It was always likely that Nazis and sympathizers would be on this ferry. Or at least the boat in Amsterdam. They did, after all, have every reason to flee. He knew Karl knew these things, too. But it was one thing to know it; it was another to endure it.

"What if one of them finds out about us?" Karl whispered.

"They won't."

"What if one of them knows me? What if they recognize me?" He glanced up at Bertie, his eyes wide. "What if they worked at Dachau?"

The words were tumbling out of him now, quiet as they were. "What if they suspect me, what if I can't do it? I'm barely good at it. I can't keep this up every minute of every day. It's exhausting."

Bertie could not promise Karl that these things would not happen, any of them. There were so many Nazis and even more sympathizers in their country. So he said the only thing he knew to be true. "If anybody tried something, I would beat their face in with my bare hands. And Sofie would go for their kneecaps."

Sofie leaned over toward them both. "And in the meantime, we won't talk to anyone. We won't give anyone any information about us. Nobody will know which side we're on."

Karl began to slow his breathing. He finally looked at her, gave a last big breath, and swallowed.

Sofie smiled at him. "Here." She picked up a piece of white stone jammed against the crook of their small wall. In a width less than two of their suitcases, she began to etch out thin rectangles in white, crumbly lines. They were smaller and shorter than usual keys, but they would do. "Play our song. Show me what you've learned."

Karl stared at the drawing. He unclasped his hands from himself, shifting his rump so he could slowly stretch his fingers out to the keys. His fingers lightly began to thump against the patterns on the floor. While Bertie did not know piano, he was certain Karl was playing "Das Lila Lied."

"Good," Sofie said. "Good."

Bertie watched them, slipping deeper into thought as Karl played and Sofie occasionally corrected him in a gentle tone. He thought about many things. It was not long before he could not keep his thoughts inside himself anymore. He spoke quietly.

"Do you think history we'll remember us as bad people? For doing what we're doing?"

Karl had long since evened his breathing. He kept his eyes to the keys. "I think we'll be lucky if history remembers us at all."

"We could be reporting them, but we're not. This whole time, the entire War, we never stood up and declared our resistance."

"Because that would've been suicide," Sofie replied, though she herself looked uncomfortable with the conversation. They had talked lightly about it a few times in the past but always stopped before they could declare themselves bad people.

"All we did was tuck ourselves away and fake our way through so we could survive. It feels selfish."

"Survival is inherently selfish," Karl said.

This did not comfort Bertie. "Inaction is a poison."

Karl continued to stare intently at the keys. His fingers continued to drum, but they were slower now. "Yes. And we'll always tell ourselves whatever we need to justify our actions."

"And we're allowing it to go to America now, the Nazis with us. We're allowing it to happen."

"You talk as if America is a place of purity. Do you not believe there are Americans who agree with Hitler? They have just been quieter about it."

They all went silent after that. Bertie was not sure if this logic had bested his guilt or if he was just exhausted.

Sofie continued to watch Karl play, occasionally making a light noise of disapproval and pointing to a mistake he had just made.

"Do you think Roy will be there when we arrive?" she asked. "Do you think he got our letter?"

"If he's not there, we can go to his address."

"What if he's not there anymore?"

Bertie sighed. "I don't know."

The ferry finally began its travel upriver. There was not much to see out in the dark, but their movement encouraged a nice breeze that set the linen above them flapping gently. Sofie and Karl eventually stopped their lesson. Karl had regained his calm. They settled in, feeling the gentle rocking of the dark river water. Bertie looked around. This would be their environment for almost as long as Karl had been with them. Bertie's back would surely start killing him.

"I did a lot of thinking while I was walking here," he said. "That might not've been Gert's cap I saw. He could still be alive, he could be on his way to the farm."

Sofie and Karl said nothing.

"I'm wondering if we should be here. If I should be here. I wonder if I should be back at the farm, waiting for Gert."

Sofie edged closer to him, placing a hand on his shoulder. "Bertie, you need to stop."

"He would have done it for me."

Bertie knew it was unfair of him to put Sofie in such a position, to conclude either that Bertie was a bad friend or that Gert was a fool. But to her credit, she said nothing. She simply cradled his head against the crook of her neck.

"If Gert were alive," Sofie said quietly, "he would indeed first go to the farm. And when he saw that nobody was there, he would go to Roy."

"But this is the last ship out of Deutschland."

She held him tighter. "He's not coming, schatz."

Bertie was quiet. Deep in his brain, he knew her logic made sense. But he would not let that thought surface too far.

Karl stared at him close by. His eyes were deep, the world inside him once more urging to break out, but his voice was soft. "Blaming yourself doesn't make you more in control of the situation."

Bertie locked eyes with him. He felt he could not look away. He took in a breath. "I don't know how you do it, Karl. I don't know how you have survived, how you keep yourself so calm so much of the time."

"It's not a calmness. Whatever factory was inside me to run my grief, I had to shut it down. I will never turn it back on again."

"Why?"

"Because what has happened is beyond human comprehension. It's beyond sense. All it is, is poison. And if I want to stay human, I have to protect myself."

"That's not a happy moral."

"I've realized that the mind can do only two things: make us happy and keep us safe. But it can't do both at the same time."

Nobody offered a rebuttal. After a couple of breaths, Karl tilted his head to Sofie. "Did you hear what I said, Tante? Did you hear what I said before?"

Bertie felt her chest stiffen against him slightly. “Yes, Karl.”

“Blaming yourself doesn’t make you more in control of the situation.”

“I heard you.”

“That includes you.”

Her voice became so quiet they could barely hear it. “I know.”

It was particularly dark beneath the linen covering. They rested against the little wall of the cargo hold and tried to sleep until morning. Bertie found himself between the two of them. He put his arm around Sofie instinctively and, after a pause, pulled Karl in as well. Karl stiffened beneath his arm before relaxing slightly. He curled up tightly with his head against his chest.

Sofie fell asleep quite quickly, but Karl trembled against him, his head jerking slightly toward any small sound. He eventually succumbed to exhaustion.

24

THE TRIP TO AMSTERDAM TOOK TEN DAYS EXACTLY. THEY had anticipated delays but none manifested, and the weather remained kind. When the Rhein passed into the French occupation, they were not stopped, nor did they need to show their passports. The same happened when they moved into the British occupation. Bertie was certain the other occupations were just like the Amerikans; they had yet to get their affairs in order. They entered the Netherlands without bother. They would all simply be a problem, it appeared, for Amerika.

Children cried endlessly and there was occasional hostility for space, but there was no death or major illness. Bertie had never wanted to change his clothes so bad. The smell of body odor and lingering waste became impenetrable, even in the open. They continued their habit of sleeping against one another. Karl clung to either of them while he slept.

They managed to find and ration drinking water, but the food Sofie brought with them lasted only eight days. More was difficult to come by, and hunger soon made their awareness wane. Bertie thought about all of the food back in Ulm, down in their cellar, still growing out in the dirt. So much food wasting while so many people starved. He wondered if the side door was still open. If wild animals had since gotten in and destroyed everything. He hoped Frau Ber had taken over. He hoped Muh and the chickens were not slowly dehydrating in the hot cowshed, air and water and grass just steps past the wood that held them captive.

Karl and Sofie spent much of their time with the keys drawn on the ferry's boards. With each missed meal, Karl made more mistakes. Sofie was starting to make mistakes herself. Other passengers became interested in their activities, especially the young ones. They would watch before eventually asking if Sofie would also teach them. She did not turn any away.

Bertie took stock of the others aboard. There were families and children, friends and unusual mismatches of family members that were surely the only ones still alive. There were Deutsche, mostly, but there were also accents of Polish and Czech and Russian. Some had fled from as far as the Soviet occupation in the east. Their eyes looked particularly haunted, especially the women and children. These were the ones Sofie encouraged most to the uneven keys.

The three of them had talked little since their voyage began. Or, at least, nothing they talked about was of particular consequence. They knew they could be overheard easily, and they maintained a distrust of everyone else around them. Oma and Opa gently rocked in the swaddled nest Karl had made with his coat.

The formerly clean-shaven Nazi had many times tried to catch Bertie's eye. The few times he succeeded, he would give a small smile and a nod, an acknowledgement of brotherhood in any of its forms. Bertie could think of nothing wiser to do than return the nod, curt and smileless. As soon as Bertie regarded the man as once-shaven, he realized the risk it caused that he and Karl were not. The longer they remained as such, the more it might cause suspicion.

Nobody mingled. But from what little Bertie could overhear and could gather on appearances and spirits, he guessed that at least half the boat were Nazis and sympathizers.

Bertie's attention waned a little more each day. As his stomach remained empty, his vision would sometimes blur, or he would forget a thought in the middle of having it. Mostly, though, he just wanted to sleep. Hunger made it more difficult to keep up his appearances, to maintain himself as unassuming while keeping a tired eye on Karl to ensure he was still successfully doing the same. But with his back against the cargo hold's wall, he began to doze more frequently.

He was, in fact, napping when Sofie roused him. He opened his eyes to her weakly smiling face.

"We've arrived."

To the untrained eye, the land on either side of them looked indistinguishable from the terrain they had crossed for ten days. They docked and disembarked and were pointed in the direction of the ship leaving for New York. They had only a few hours to walk there. Though they had time to spare, they agreed to not stop for rations. They worried they would otherwise not have enough for three tickets. They hoped the rumors were true that the tickets included meals.

Even though they arrived early, their hearts sank. The people got thicker the closer they got to the North Sea. Theirs had not been the only ferry to drop people off. Bertie spotted the old double-decker steamer in the distance. It did not look like it could fit them all. There was a slight craze in some people's eyes, and he realized that the three of them might not be the only ones who knew this was the last ship for a long time.

When the ship finally opened for admittance, Bertie grabbed Sofie and Karl. "Don't let go," he said.

He pushed through the crowd, more forceful than he had ever been in his life. As he elbowed through everyone, no matter their age or need, he thought again of what Karl had said. Survival was inherently selfish. No matter what, he would get them onto that ship.

The crowd was as desperate as he was, pushing and shoving and shouting, not at all like the ferry back in Stuttgart. Karl held on to his suitcase, the urn cradled in his crooked arm as Bertie pulled him by his other wrist. Karl nearly dropped the urn at one point, nearly fell forward righting it, but he managed to regain his balance before being trampled.

They were breathless upon reaching the base of the gangway. They bartered with the ticketmaster, pulling out the pocket watch, some sterling silver cutlery, and whatever else Sofie had thought to grab on their way out. The ticketmaster seemed less than impressed, but they managed to scrape together three of the cheapest tickets. They were sent to the lowest berth. They nearly ran there, the shouting and pushing behind them getting worse with each second.

Their berth was dark and airless. There were already so many people that they were afraid there was no space left. Once again Bertie elbowed through, this time a little kinder, knowing they would be stuck up against these people for several days. They made a tiny patch near one side of the hull. But even after they settled in the best they could, people kept flowing in. It seemed unlikely there would be food provided. For the first time, Bertie grew concerned one of the three of them might die on this voyage. He worried they had been tricked. Maybe they were not going to New York at all.

"I think they're trying to not turn anybody away," Sofie whispered, though she looked as concerned as he did.

Karl had gone completely silent. It was hard to tell if he was just cramped or had frozen entirely in fear, the urn so close against him it might shatter. Bertie wished he could reach over to him for some sort of comfort, but his arm was wedged against a man with a Polish accent. The corner of his suitcase was digging into his lower back.

Once the ship weighed anchor, a great sadness fell upon him. There was no going back. Deutschland was behind him forever. He had loved his country. He felt that maybe he still did. But what he loved was what it used to be, what had been lost. The things it could have been. He had wanted to be patriotic, was proud to be patriotic, and they had told him no. And then they had ripped apart what good was left so it could be enjoyed by no one. Bertie did not understand this, would never understand this. Pride in a country was for what it could do for its people, not what it could take away. He did not find this a difficult concept. Yet here they were. And he would need to get used to it.

* * *

The crew tossed bodies to the waves, victims that had succumbed to what ailed them. It thankfully happened only a handful of times over the first week, but Karl seized every time. He would back into himself, head down, and wait until Sofie or Bertie tapped him that it was over. His shoulders grimaced with every splash by their hull line.

The smell was even worse than the ferry and it was unbearably hot. There was no air. There was food, but it was insufficient and terrible, blackened bread and broth that Bertie first mistook for cloudy water. But it was something when they had nothing, so they took it and said thank you.

Karl barely spoke. He sometimes slipped into small fits. Sofie or Bertie would hold him and stroke his hair.

"Listen to the waves," they would whisper. "They are not train tracks."

There were a few looks of sympathy, and Bertie realized that the poorest among them were the most likely to not be Nazis. A small blessing.

The stench of vomit and hot urine got worse by the hour. They were desperate for fresh air, but access to the deck was limited and mostly reserved for the rich passengers. Leaving also made it more difficult to return to their berth, to once again acclimate to the stench.

The one benefit to some of them passing away was there was slowly more room for those who were left. The moment Bertie felt relief at this thought, he felt guilty.

They had, at least, managed to get out of the North Sea without incident. They were never attacked by Ally submarines, a tragedy visited upon many ships with passengers desperate to get out earlier that year, including the *Wilhelm Gustloff* in the nearby Baltic. The radio had said the ship lost more souls than the *Titanic* and the *Lusitania* combined, many of them children.

Sofie wordlessly scraped piano keys into the wood. Karl immediately took to it, and they spent a lot of their time quietly playing. When Bertie could not sleep at night, which was often, he snuck up the stairs to the decks, rooting through the scraps left in the garbage pails of the rich passengers. He would bring the food back down to Sofie and Karl. They ate in the dark, silently, in case anybody got the same idea. The trash he found was significantly better than what their tickets bought.

Bertie was caught one night. He was rummaging through, quietly as he could, when he heard a vaguely familiar voice behind him.

"Would you like a cigarette?"

Bertie turned around quickly. The face of the Nazi smiled at him. He was once again clean-shaven. Bertie had taken to smearing his and Karl's face with a light dusting of dirt.

The Nazi held out an emerald-green carton of Ecksteins, and Bertie felt his knees weaken with craving. He found himself reaching for a cigarette. The faint smell of the tobacco was already soothing him.

He suddenly had a thought both sad and frightening. Frau bait.

He looked up at the man, but all the Nazi did was continue to smile. He did not, in this moment, in this moonlight, appear threatening. The calmness of the waves against the hull unnerved him.

As the man brought the lighter to Bertie's lips, Bertie told himself that at least he did not thank him. He sucked in the smoke and felt a relief he had not experienced in years. The pleasure ran through every part of him. He held it inside for a moment before releasing.

"I'm worried about you, friend," the Nazi said. "Aren't they feeding you?"

Bertie avoided him, looking out over the water. "We're fine."

"If you ever want some more, we've got plenty."

Bertie again resisted the reflex to thank him, if only to keep him at arm's length. He instead tapped his cigarette ash over the railing. He crossed his arms near the wrists and hunched over. The salt of the sea filled his nose, the breeze cooler than he would have thought for this time of year. Perhaps they were already farther out than he thought.

"How do you plan to get into New York?" the man continued. Bertie could not understand his interest in him. Was it really nothing more than they had been on the run from the Amerikans? Did this man think Bertie was the only friend he may have left in the world? He felt a flicker of ego at the thought that this Nazi might see him not only as a normally sexed man but an Aryan one. Again the guilt struck his heart. Pride had no place here, not even if it was just for all of his hard work over the years transvesting, all the diligence and exhaustion. His head was too mixed up.

"We got citizenship."

The man grinned bigger. "Us, too. May I see?"

Bertie worried he had said too much. But then he realized, of all the chances to try out the authenticity of their work, this might be it. If they looked fake, the Nazi would surely tell him out of concern, but also not report them for it. After all, there was no way he had real papers himself.

"I'll trade you."

The Nazi nodded and they both reached into their pockets for their passports. Bertie handed over his, the dull cardboard brown. But the Nazi had a bright red cover. It reminded Bertie what Karl had once said about officers getting special ones. This man was certainly not just a sympathizer. He was an active criminal. How active, Bertie both did and did not want to know. Had he been in Dachau? Had he tortured Karl? Had he killed Gert? He told himself the odds were low. There were millions of active Nazis.

He quickly flicked through the man's passport. The citizenship stamp was sharper and more uniform than in his own. The paper was heftier. The Nazi's passport closed more crisply as well. Dread filled him. He quickly handed it back. It was only after his own passport was safely out of sight in his pocket that Bertie realized he had not bothered to look at the man's name.

"It's quite convincing," the man said.

"Yours, too." Bertie's voice was even flatter than before. It would figure someone like him would be able to afford something better. He used the spoils of war to get out of responsibility for his spoils of war. Though Bertie did not understand why he would be so bold as to use a red cover. Perhaps it was arrogance.

Bertie took one last, long drag to the filter and flicked the cigarette over the side. He blew out the smoke.

"Enjoy your voyage," he said. He still did not thank him.

Sofie was waiting for him when he returned. He handed over what little food he had managed to put in his pockets before the Nazi interrupted him, mostly bread just starting to go stale during its time in the open air. They kept some aside for Karl, who quietly roused the moment they waved some near his face. He ate in the dark, not once speaking. Bertie was not sure if he was tired or if he had simply retreated into himself and refused to come out.

Sofie swallowed her mouthful of bread. "Where'd you get the cigarette, Bertie?" She kept her voice low.

He was not sure how to answer without babbling for the next hour, for trying to excuse himself while feeling bad for excusing himself. He sighed. "Most assuredly not a friend."

After that night, Bertie always found more food in the bins above deck, sometimes carefully wrapped, sometimes barely touched. He told himself it was simply luck.

* * *

Some days later—it was hard to keep track—Sofie was teaching a few of the children on her drawn piano keys, alongside some adults. One spoke only Polish, an elderly gentleman, and they got by with Sofie making the sounds herself as she hit the faded lines of a key. Bertie was pretending to nap while keeping an eye on Karl. The younger man was having a kind day. Despite the stink and the heat, he seemed almost relaxed. For multiple days now, a group of a dozen or so people, women of various ages, sat in a circle and traded stories. Sometimes they spoke of happy memories from years ago, but most of the stories were sad, many of them fleeing from the Soviet-occupied area. As they told their sadder stories and what the soldiers had done to them, what they had witnessed done upon others, Karl listened. He crept closer every day.

Today was the first time that he got so close that he nodded politely and sat with them. Bertie listened carefully with his eyes closed. He fought to keep a relieved little smile off his face, that this might be the start to the kind of healing Karl needed. He needed people who truly understood. He needed some kind of community.

Karl listened in his usual quiet way as the circle went around, once more swapping stories. This was another day for sad ones. The types of violence that was most often had on certain bodies and what one did once it was done.

When it came to Karl, he hesitated a moment. There was surely so much he wanted to say.

"It's all so difficult," he finally said.

He sounded proud of managing even this much. But the group simply continued to stare at him. One of the women finally cleared her throat.

"Excuse me," she said, "but you'll never understand what we go through. It's you men that did all of this to begin with."

"Mmm," he replied. He paused. "If you'll excuse me, I need some air."

He got up. Bertie quickly stood and followed him, his legs tingling as the blood rushed back into them. When Bertie reached him up on deck, Karl was already looking out over the water, the wind tossing his hair in every direction.

He put a hand on Karl's shoulder. "Are you alright?"

"This life is unfair, Bertie."

"I know."

Karl tapped out piano notes upon the railing. Bertie did not think he always knew he was doing it. "They refuse to see more than two options. Either we're women and victims, or we're men and the enemy."

"They're hurting," Bertie said simply.

"Well they're hurting in quite selfish ways. And it's not fair that it's excused just because they're hurting. To lump us in with the people who have done all they've done to us, without a second thought. To ignore all the women who were camp guards and wives of SS men and supported and loved and voted for the Nazis . . ." He stopped drumming his fingers, but he did not look up from them. "It's not fair, Bertie. What do we do?"

Bertie did not answer. He did not want to mention what Karl himself had said about survival. He did not know what made sense anymore.

"I don't like people, Bertie." Karl finally turned to him. "But I like you and Sofie."

Bertie again did not speak. He gave a grim spread of his lips and squeezed Karl's shoulder.

It was midday and the breeze was nice. Bertie worried that they would soon be reprimanded for being outside on a nice day, for being poor and content. It was not the hour for the lowest berth's deck time. But Karl said he wanted to stand out in the sun, move his legs while he still could. "I'd like some time to myself, please."

Bertie nodded and released his shoulder, turning back to the stairs. He lingered not far off the mouth to the berth. He leaned against the inner wall with his ear cocked.

Karl rested his crooked arms upon the railing and let himself feel the breeze. The sun dappled the calm waves. He closed his eyes as the ship swayed beneath him.

It was perhaps half a minute before Bertie saw the Nazi saunter over to Karl. His shadow cast over him from his side. Karl turned his head and froze when he saw him. The Nazi smiled, big and toothy.

"Good afternoon."

Karl swallowed. Without standing back upright in proper greeting, he gave a nod before casting his neck back to the sea.

Bertie felt the urge to step in, but to intervene might cause suspicion. He held his breath.

The Nazi waited for more, but Karl did not give it. He leaned against the railing on one elbow, the rest of him turned toward Karl. He leaned closer. "How are you and your family doing on the trip so far? Are you eating better?"

Karl said nothing. He shifted a few centimeters away. Bertie tensed his leg muscles.

The man filled the gap, still smiling. "I saw you learning the piano from your Tante back on the ferry. Have you been playing long?"

"Please." Karl's tone wavered. Bertie knew panic was not good for a transvested voice. "I'd like to not talk right now." He continued to look out over the water.

The Nazi jerked slightly at his words. "I'm just trying to be friendly."

"I would prefer not to talk just now," Karl repeated. His hands began to tremble, and he clasped the one over the other. He continued to try and shift his face away.

The Nazi was stiffening now, his voice carrying a tone of frustration. "I'm being nice here, friend. I just wanted to get to know you."

"I don't want to talk," Karl said again, his pitch rising. He was beginning to shrink. "Please leave me alone."

"Hey, are you okay? What's the matter with—?" He clamped his hand down upon Karl's shoulder, but the sudden response Karl gave cut off his remaining words.

Bertie was staring at them fully by this point but still was not sure exactly how it happened. With the Nazi's hand on Karl's shoulder, Karl had panicked. In a wordless struggle, he wrenched himself away from the man, thrashing like a cat.

This made the Nazi hold on harder. "Easy! You're going to—"

Either he let go or Karl broke free. And with the force, Karl was over the railing in an instant. Bertie shot out from the companionway toward them. The Nazi made a mad grab for Karl and missed. There was a thud as if Karl hit the hull on his way down. A loud splash followed soon after.

"Man overboard!" came the call from somewhere above. It was only then that other people began to move, rushing to the sides of the ship. Sofie emerged from below.

Passengers hung over the rail and pointed outward. Bertie saw him and froze. Karl was the first body to go into the water alive.

He was splashing and struggling against the pleasant waves, creating foams of white as he tried to keep his head above the water. He did not know how to swim.

Bertie saw the Nazi close by, a look of shock on his face. Bertie grabbed the man by the front of his collar.

"Did you push him?"

But the Nazi put up both of his palms. "I didn't touch him, I swear. Well, I put my hand on his shoulder, but then he just . . . I don't know. He jumped, he fell, he did *something*. I don't know what happened. And before I knew it, he was in the water."

Bertie let go of the man. Before he could figure what to do next, Sofie blurred past him in a perfect arc over the railing. A flash of her shoeless feet was the last thing he saw before she was out of sight. He heard the loud splash a couple seconds later.

"Man overboard!" came the call again, quickly followed by more gasps from the passengers.

Sofie swam directly to Karl. Bertie saw him go under twice before coming back up, sputtering. Sofie made it to him and nearly went under herself when Karl clung to her. Her old farming dress billowed around her as they came up together. She resembled a grayed-out jellyfish, a sea creature of a woman. But as Bertie anxiously watched them try to swim back, he realized they had no way to get back up. They could lose sight of them on the old steamer in seconds.

Bertie swore and looked around. Everyone was just standing, pointing and gasping. While some looked worried, others seemed relieved to finally have some entertainment. His eye finally fell to a cork life ring. He grabbed it and loosened a thick coil of rope in a pile nearby. He tied the end of the rope to the life ring.

"Sofie!" he bellowed, throwing the life ring as hard as he could. It landed a few meters to her right.

She swam to it as fast as she could. Karl clung to her back as he tried to help by kicking. Bertie fed what slack he had until Sofie finally reached the life ring and grabbed hold, Karl in turn holding on to her.

Bertie pulled quickly, hand over hand, the freed rope coiling behind him. But when he hit the end of the slack, it felt like he was trying to yank up a building. He had never thought pulling two people through the water would be so difficult. But the ocean was a force and the steamer's propulsion cut through stubbornly. He yanked as hard as he could with both hands and got nowhere. The rope slipped through his grasp by several centimeters, stripping his skin.

"Somebody help me!" he yelled. He kept his eye fixed on Sofie and Karl. "I need help!"

A tall shadow fell upon him from behind, and a strong grip took hold of the slack and pulled. The rope stopped slipping.

"Come on!" the Nazi yelled directly behind his head. His soldier friends ran to line up, each grabbing part of the rope. They all started to pull in unison with Bertie.

Bertie had no time to resist or argue. He focused on Sofie and Karl. The rope was much easier now with five of them, and with each pull, his family came into sharper focus. It was not until they were pulled from water to air that it became difficult again. Sofie and Karl dangled against the side of the hull, water dripping from them as they both now clung to the rope and each other. They were heaved upward in thick, sudden jolts.

After what seemed like too long of a time, they were nearly to the side of the railing. As Bertie and the Nazi continued to hold the rope still, the others let go to come around. One of them leaned over to grab Karl by the back of his shirt, the other two hoisting Sofie up by an arm each.

"Our apologies, gute Frau," one of them said as they yanked her over the railing in an ungentlemanly way.

The deck grew dark beneath them as they flopped onto the boards, gasping from exhaustion and scare. Bertie let go of the rope, leaving the Nazi to gather it back into a coil and untie the life ring. He ran to Sofie and nearly fell on top of her as he scooped her into a hug. He first thought she was shaking from the scare, but he realized it was her arms from exhaustion.

"I did it," she said. It took a moment for Bertie to realize what she meant. She so rarely talked about her drowned nephew. When he loosened his grip on her, he saw she was quietly crying.

Two of the men crouched to check on Karl, who had finished coughing up a bit of seawater. When they offered their help, Karl back-walked until he knocked into Sofie and Bertie. Bertie brought him into the two of them, part to protect him, part to comfort him. He was not sure he would be particularly good at either.

They all held each other a moment, cold and wet and breathing. The shadow of the Nazi fell upon them. Bertie looked up, squinting against the midday sun. The man stood over them, holding Sofie's shoes in his hands, his three friends not a step behind. The other passengers were already returning to their old places. The entertainment was over.

"Are you all okay?" the Nazi asked. His eyebrows were raised in what appeared to be genuine concern. He placed Sofie's shoes near her and then took a step back again.

Bertie waited until he knew he could not deny him an answer anymore. "Yes." His instinct was to thank the man and his friends, he knew this was the expectation, but he once again resisted it. He immediately worried that would anger them, that it would cause trouble later. He did not know what the best choices were anymore.

The man stood awkwardly now. "Well . . . I'm glad we were here to help." His friends nodded in agreement, all watching over them intently. "Maybe we could all play cards in the next day or so in our quarters. When you've all rested, of course." He lowered his voice. "We have some food and cigarettes."

Bertie gave a grunt of some sort, moving his head somewhere between a nod and a shake. He hoped the man would read him as too preoccupied in the moment, too overcome with relief that his wife and nephew were safe to show proper Deutsch hospitality. But when the man extended his hand nonetheless, he knew he could not ignore it. He looked up again, the man continuing to hold out his hand as his toothy smile returned.

Bertie finally removed his dampened arm from Karl's back to shake his hand. The man beamed. He shook heartily and all Bertie could do was match him. The man closed his smiling lips over his teeth, gave a final nod, and returned with his friends toward their quarters.

The three of them were suddenly, finally left alone.

"They're so nice," Bertie muttered in disbelief. "I can't believe they're so nice. They're like normal, everyday people."

Karl swallowed between his still-heavy breaths. "That's what makes them so terrifying."

25

THEY SPENT THE NEXT FEW DAYS IN AN AWKWARD BALANCE between keeping to themselves and associating with the Nazis just enough to keep them from getting suspicious. They never took them up on their offers for cards or socialization. The Nazi tried to talk with Karl three times after the incident. Every time, Karl shrank away. It was not until Bertie pulled the man aside and explained to him that Karl was painfully shy around strangers that the man finally left him alone. But Bertie would see him sometimes trying to catch Karl's eye, giving a small smile or a motion of apology. Karl always looked away. He continued his lessons with Sofie, the soft, unmelodic tapping of his fingers against the wood.

Karl did not try to talk with the group of women again. When they gathered in their circle, he sat in the farthest corner, alone.

Sofie had been in better spirits since the incident, drying her things as far as she dared in a modesty she pretended she cared about. Karl, however, suffered. The water had soaked his bindings and there was nothing he could do about it. The old fabric took over a day to dry against his skin beneath his sodden clothes. The salt chafed him, and Bertie could tell by the way he winced that he had developed a rash. Every movement rubbed against his raw skin. The moment they could get some privacy in Amerika, they would need to strip him down, rinse him with fresh water, and hope he did not develop an infection.

Bertie was dozing midday, nearly fourteen days since they left Amsterdam. He awoke to a sudden commotion. The sounds of loud talking, exclamations, many feet walking fast. He shot up, looking around for Karl, lest he had somehow gone overboard again. But he and Sofie were getting up from their drawn keys. They followed the rest of the group onto the deck. People were pointing, some smiled, some cried.

The Statue of Liberty was on the horizon. First her torch, then her crown. The midday fog gave way as they got closer. They began to slow, making way for other ships that were coming in from other places. Amid a sea of relief and hope, all Bertie felt was worry. He did not know if they would get in, and even if they did, this world would not be kind to them. It would be a different life of hiding, but still a life of hiding.

An hour passed before they docked. The three of them were quick to grab their suitcases, the urn, and go down the gangway. It was odd being back on solid land. Bertie felt like he was still swaying in time with the boat, and it took him several steps to gain his composure. As they walked further down the plank, as he watched Sofie and Karl have an equally difficult time finding their footing, Bertie suddenly thought about the piano keys Sofie had drawn. How long would it be before they were washed away?

They joined the line that had already formed halfway down the gangway. The Nazis were one family ahead of them.

"Herr Durchdenwald!" the Nazi said, smiling like always. He excused himself as he parted through the family that stood between them. "We would love to keep in touch."

"Oh! Ähm . . ." Bertie had not anticipated this. At first, he was terrified that this man knew his name. But then he remembered he must have read it in his passport. Bertie wondered if he could finally risk being rude now but worried that doing so would somehow put the three of them in danger, after all they had gone through. He did not want to cause any scenes. He did not want to stick out.

The man stood expectantly. "Would you like to give me your address?"

Bertie immediately saw a way out. "I certainly would, only we don't know for certain where we're staying yet."

"Oh, well you could certainly come stay with us. I have some dear friends who have lived here for years."

"No no, that won't be necessary." Bertie held up a palm and gave a pleasant chuckle. He could feel the heat of Karl's presence as the younger man slunk further behind him. "We have a place to stay, we just don't know the address. Our own dear friend is meeting us here."

The Nazi nodded, still smiling. "Of course. Well, let's do this, then." He pulled out a torn and wrinkled piece of paper and penciled something down. "Here. Please do call or visit once you're able."

Bertie took the paper, folded it in half, and shook it gently before both of their faces like it was a prize. "Certainly. That's very hospitable of you." He was proud of the fact that he had yet to thank the man for anything. But it made him worry. How many other Nazis might he associate with and not even know it? How many had he already?

The Nazi smiled wider, gave a wave to all three of them, and then returned to his group. As soon as he turned his back, Bertie ripped up the paper in the smallest pieces he could and let them catch in the sea breeze.

The line moved slowly. But they appreciated this, for they had time to review their strategy. Bertie and Sofie were married, Karl was their nephew on Sofie's side. They had left Deutschland because they loved Amerika and had wanted to flee ever since Hitler came to power. They were just poor farmers who had stayed out of the way, helping people when they could. They had even hidden a Holocaust survivor. They would just not mention when.

"The key will be how we carry ourselves," Sofie said. "I believe if we find a balance, we'll be alright. Not so happy that they think we liked the War, but not so depressed that they don't see us as hard, strong workers. And not so clean as to look like we haven't endured troubles, but not so dirty as to look ill."

"That's the big one," Bertie said, looking at Karl. "If they pull me or you out for a physical examination, we're all in a lot of trouble." His head was still fairly light from the lack of food, from the rationed water. But he patted Karl on the shoulder as best he could. "Do you remember everything?"

Karl did not look over at him. They all knew that Karl had made it this far. But while he could last three weeks on a ship and a ferry, barely moving or speaking, with his chest being bound constantly and shortening his breath and rubbing his irritated skin raw, to now walk and talk and hold himself to full capacity was a bigger challenge.

"Keep my back straight," he said. "Walk with space between my thighs. Speak from my chest, breathe from my belly. End my sentences at a lower octave than a higher one. Shake one's hand harder than is necessary . . ."

He continued to rattle off their lessons, growing quieter and quieter the closer they got to the front of the line. He soon went silent entirely.

A few uniformed men were at the bottom of the gangway, methodically checking papers, asking questions, sometimes pulling people out of line for inspections of either themselves or their luggage. Bertie thought of the flat-cap, as if somehow the officers would know it was something important. He had not yet told Sofie or Karl what he had done, did not know when he should. And what if it was not even Gert's? Was Bertie still justified in what he had done?

"I wonder if Roy is here," Karl said.

"He'll be waiting past the docks if he is," Bertie replied.

Sofie had her eyes fixed to the shrinking line. "I'd be impressed if he was. Just because he'd know when we were leaving doesn't mean he'd know when we were arriving. But like you said, we can just go to his address, right?"

Bertie nodded. He was suddenly stricken with the fear that Roy had died, that he had moved entirely. He did not know what they would do then. He wondered if he should have thrown away the address of the Nazi so easily. He did not know if he, if any of them, would ever consider such an option. No matter how many times he faced it, his desperation seemed to forever leave him ashamed of himself.

They stayed quiet as the line got smaller and smaller. The closer they got to the front, the more he noticed Karl trembling. Karl hugged the urn to his chest, his suitcase dangling from three fingers.

Bertie gently placed a hand upon his shoulder. "One day," he whispered into his ear, "you'll forget that you're supposed to be scared."

He did not know how possible that was. Karl would certainly find solace in their home together, but out in the world, that was a different matter. There would always be fear popping up somewhere at any time. He knew Karl knew this. But his words seemed to calm him nonetheless. Perhaps he knew that while he could never have eternity, he could at least have moments.

They watched as some were let through, others denied, yet others taken away for further inspection. Pockets of uniformed men standing further back yanked rejected people to one side, likely to send them back on the ship they had just disembarked, no matter how much they pleaded or protested. It seemed most people did not have the proper papers, had not been aware that these were no longer the Ellis Island days, or at least hoped mercy would be shown in the circumstances. Some people who were pulled for further inspection were taken directly into a nearby building. Bertie did not know what went on in there. He did not want to find out.

He saw the Nazi and his group reach the front of the line. He could not hear their words, only the sounds of speech. The Nazi was moving crisply and with confidence. When he flashed his red-covered passport, Bertie heard Karl hold his breath. Bertie braced himself, waiting for the scuffle. He suddenly hated that he had not thought to get themselves ahead of the Nazi's group. To present themselves so soon afterward could put ideas in the Amerikans' heads.

But after only a few moments of speaking, each of the Nazi's group was waved through. Their luggage was not inspected, and they had, Bertie was certain, taken the least time of any group so far. Was it simply because their passports were so convincing? Did the Amerikans not know what a red cover meant, even with a swastika? Bertie felt both sick at this notion and hopeful that it meant maybe they could get through easily, too. This country, he decided, was not one with morals you could set your watch to. He did not feel that was something to be proud of.

"Whatever you do," Sofie reminded all three of them as the family before them stepped up. "Don't sneeze, don't cough, don't clear your throat. Watch your feet, don't trip, keep your back straight. We are healthy, we are hard workers."

The family in front of them did not make it through. They were pulled to the side despite their pleas, and suddenly Bertie found himself face-to-face with the Amerikans.

He placed down his suitcase, stood up straight, and clasped his hands before himself. "Hello," he said in the best English he could muster, a smile on his face. "We are man and woman together, and this is the nephew. We thank you for your kind—"

"Papers?" the mustached agent said in English.

"Yes," Bertie said too quickly. All three of them handed over their passports, each thankfully looking travelworn. "We have stamps."

He held his breath. The agent thumbed through each one quickly, almost an insult to the time they had put into making them. But quick was good, quick was helpful. He began to hope that maybe they would make it.

The agent glanced up at the three of them after reviewing the passports, brow furrowed slightly. He went through the passports again. He stopped at one of them, and Bertie's heart dropped. He could not tell which passport the agent was inspecting, nor what it was that snagged his attention. The paper's design? A flaw in the stamp? Or was he that familiar with the citizenship numbers?

"Step over there," he said, pointing. The pointing was unnecessary, as was the request. Uniformed men were already grabbing each of them by the upper arm and firmly escorting them not to the rejected group, not to the luggage inspection, but to the building. Only a handful of people had gone into that building. They had yet to see anyone come back out.

"What's in there?" Karl whispered.

Bertie swallowed. "I don't know."

26

THEY SAT IN A ROW BEFORE AN OLD DESK, THE MAN BEHIND it dressed in a suit rather than a uniform. Bertie did not know what this meant. But he was at least grateful they had not immediately been sent to a holding cell or an examination room. Their suitcases were still beside them. Karl was sitting perfectly straight, the urn clutched in his lap like a hug. He answered most of the questions in his near-perfect English. Bertie contributed when he could. Sofie was largely quiet, knowing the least English of the three of them. It was odd to hear her so quiet. Bertie did not like it.

"Let's go over this again," the man said through a sigh. It was hard to read his tone. He was either bored or frustrated. At them, at the small space, at the aging and windowless white walls, Bertie did not know, but he remembered what he had told Sofie and Karl back in Ulm. This was it. This was the one, singular person they had to convince in order to get through. The country did not matter, nobody else mattered. It was just this one man a desk's length away from them.

The man picked up one of their passports and released it, letting it slap back down onto the desk. "You got your citizenship just a few weeks ago?"

"Yes, sir," Karl said, breathing from his belly. He adjusted an old cap of Gert's upon his head before speaking again. "As soon as the War was over and the Nazis were no longer in control, we knew we could finally flee."

The man tapped the passports with all five of his splayed fingers. "These aren't the highest quality."

"I guess I'm not surprised. There aren't many materials to go around."

"And why would you leave now? The War's over."

Karl risked softening his voice, his eyes downcast as he hugged the urn to his chest. "The Nazis killed our family."

It was quiet after that. Bertie was impressed. Karl not only cut off what remained of that line of questioning but also knocked the man off guard. Maybe even pulled out some sympathy.

"We're looking for strong, red-blooded Americans," the man finally said. It was unclear what exactly his insinuation was.

Karl forced a chuckle. "Who could be more American than us? The Germans that came over before the first World War introduced many things that America has now accepted as its own."

The man seemed vaguely intrigued. "Like what?"

"Hot dogs," Karl said.

"Christmas trees," Bertie said.

"Hamburgers," Karl said.

"Lager," Bertie said.

"Kindergarten," Karl said.

"Mozart," Sofie said. She almost had it.

The man produced a thoughtful grunt. "You don't look like a Christmas tree, so what is it you can contribute?"

"I'm a student of medicine," Karl said without hesitation. He looked young enough for it to be believable.

This could very well be true, that Karl wanted to go into medicine. Bertie did not know. He had never asked. The Amerikan was staring at him now, so Bertie cleared his throat and answered, "Farming."

"We already have enough farmers."

"Oh! Ähm . . . papers, forms . . ." He struggled to think of the right words. He had not been as ready for this as he should have been. "Filing . . . writing . . ."

"Administrative work," Karl said. "He's very good. Very neat, very organized." The man looked skeptical at this dual answer. "He used to do administrative work before he took over the family farm. After . . ." he purposely trailed off, hugging the urn closer.

The man glanced at the urn and shifted in his chair. He looked at Sofie. "And you?"

They all held their breath in the silence that followed. If she could not prove that she knew enough English, they might all get rejected. Bertie chastised himself for not practicing with her on the voyage over.

Her eyes lit up as the word she sought came to her. “Piano,” she announced.

“You play piano?”

“Teach-ing.”

“She’s amazing,” Karl said. “I’m one of her students myself. She’s been teaching me ever since I was little. I assure you, sir, that you won’t find a finer pianist.”

The man leaned back in his chair, the old wood creaking. He laced his fingers upon his chest, sucking on his lips before releasing them in a slight pop. He sat back upright. “Prove it.”

Sofie leaned forward, smiling a little at the thought. “You having piano?”

“Not you,” the man said. He looked at Karl. “You.”

Karl knitted his brow a little. “Pardon?”

“Prove to me that you can play the piano and then I might believe your story.”

“I . . . why?”

“I can’t exactly ask you to perform surgery—” he then pointed at Bertie “—or him to fill out a damned form. Show me how good of a teacher she is. Play for me.”

A dread filled the small room. Karl swallowed, gave a small smile, and said the only thing he could possibly say. “Of course.”

* * *

The man walked them down the long, white hallway until he opened a door that looked like any other. Behind it was a neglected social area. A few thin tables were surrounded by mismatched chairs. An upright piano was in the corner, a beam of dust motes fluttering down before it from the open window. The smell of sea breeze returned.

“After you,” the man said, extending his hand outward. His tone had barely changed.

They set down their suitcases and Karl walked to the piano like an authority. He plinked a few keys without sitting down. He twisted back around, his finger pads still on the piano.

"It's a bit out of tune," he said simply. Bertie had no ear for this and was certain Karl did not, either. But perhaps it would buy them some grace if Karl did not quite hit every note. He sat down. "I shall play for you now."

"Since you love Mozart so much," the man said, "play his 'Alla Turca.'"

This would most assuredly not happen. Sofie held one of her hands over the other, as if to stop from doing it herself. Bertie stiffened and waited. But Karl simply smiled at the man and gave a short nod. He adjusted his weight upon the bench, cleared his throat, and twice snapped his hands outward at the wrists. He placed his fingers upon the keys.

He suddenly brought them back to his lap.

"If I may make a suggestion," he said in his most polite tone. "In honor of American acceptance for German traditions, I would love to offer you one more." He waited for the man to protest. When he did not, Karl twisted around to look at him. "Are you familiar with 'Das Lila Lied'?"

The man frowned slightly. "I am not."

"It's a wonderful song, sir. An empowering song. It's all about pride for who you are and sticking by your family and seeing things through no matter how hard they get." He raised his fist as if to punch him. "To fight and never stop fighting. Very American values, correct?" He waited for the man to answer him.

The man cleared his throat and straightened his back better. "Very American, yes."

Karl gave a happy nod and turned back to the piano. It was only then Bertie realized Karl had never actually gotten the man's blessing. He bit down on the small smile that dared to grace his lips.

Karl adjusted himself once more and brought his hands to the keys. And once more, he retreated to his lap.

"Forgive me," he said. "One moment." He slid his way out from the bench, walked back to their luggage, and picked up Oma and Opa. He came back and set the urn atop the piano, directly at center. "They always listen to me play."

The man said nothing. Bertie swallowed, feeling many thoughts creep up on him at once. He was unsuccessful in shaking them loose.

Karl hunched over the keys. Just as Sofie was about to correct him on instinct, Bertie put a hand to her forearm. They both had the same thought at the same time. Karl had spent more time hunched over outlines on planks than he had sitting upright at a bench. It was best not to alter things now.

Sofie gave Bertie a slight nod and he let her go. She stepped toward Karl and leaned close to his ear, her voice a faint rush of air.

"You are full of passion," she said in Deutsch. She patted his shoulder and resumed her position beside Bertie.

Karl gave one last glance to the urn before taking a breath.

Bertie looked at the urn, too, and then his own suitcase by his feet. It hit him then. He had bounced back and forth about it, but he knew it was true, knew he could no longer escape it. Gert was dead. He would never know exactly what happened to him, or when, or where it had been, or where he rested now. He still did not know for sure if it was even his flatcap in the suitcase, but he now knew what to do. He would indeed burn the hat. He would add the ashes to the urn. If it was Gert, they would finally be together again. If it was not, Oma and Opa would still be glad to comfort whoever it was.

Karl struck the opening chords of "Das Lila Lied." He hit the keys forcefully, with all the passion Sofie reminded him he possessed. Bertie felt transported to their Eldorado days. He felt delight and sadness all at once.

If Gert ever wanted an honor, this would be it. Bertie raised his voice and sang just like he had back at the Eldorado. Sofie joined him. The man, though it was clear he had no ear for the Deutsch language, listened intently. He did not notice when Karl hit a wrong note. Karl continued as if nothing had happened and added his voice to Bertie and Sofie's. They gave the man a performance, not unlike when the ausländers would come into the Eldorado looking for cocaine and easy sex and stories to tell their friends over their next game of cards. As they rounded back to the chorus, Bertie saw one of the man's fingers tapping lightly against his jaw in half-time to the beat. Karl ended in a flourish, his hands prancing upward before he returned them to his lap. He turned. Sofie and Bertie waited. All three of them were out of breath.

The man stayed quiet. His hand was still at his jaw, his finger no longer tapping.

Bertie was not sure what he had expected him to do. Applause felt like a silly expectation. But something would be nice. After all the noise they had just made, the room was choking them in the quiet. Dust motes still lingered in the sunlight.

The man finally brought down his hand, returning it to cross his arms over his chest. "Come with me," he said. His tone was the same as when they had entered.

They walked behind him in a single file, suitcases in hand, the urn securely back in Karl's one-armed hug.

They followed the man back to his office. They sat down without invite, again placing their luggage beside themselves.

The man sighed and walked behind his desk, adjusting his suit jacket as he sat down. He laced his fingers and stared at each of them in turn. After what seemed like a long while, he scooped up all three of their passports with one hand, opened a drawer in his desk, and dumped them inside.

With the sound of the drawer snapping shut, Bertie finally gave up the last of his hope. Sofie's face went ashen. Karl simply looked guilty, as if this was somehow all his fault.

The man pulled out a piece of paper. He hovered his fountain pen over it. "Name?" he said, looking at Bertie. His tone had yet to change. If anything, it had become gruffer.

"Oh! Ähm . . ." He considered lying a moment, to give one last fight as the man took down their names for one punishment or another, to put them in confinement on Ellis Island for months while they checked their stories back in the Soviet occupation of Berlin, but realized it would do no good. If this was it, at least he could say his name one more time, after all the years he could not, confidently and without shame. "Berthold Durchdenwald."

It felt both terrifying and freeing to finally say it again, to once more be seen in this way.

The man looked about to write and then stopped. "Pardon?"

"Berthold Durchdenwald." He felt insulted that after all this, the man had never even bothered to look at their names in their passports.

"Burt-ed Ditch-in-vold?"

Bertie swallowed, keeping himself from glancing at either Karl or Sofie. He was unsure if correcting the man would make him look like he was being difficult. He realized his hands were trembling. He tried to mask the one over the other, pretending he was just giving them a small massage after their long journey.

"Burr-told," he said slowly with a polite smile on his face, "Durch-den-vald."

The man finally wrote something. He kept his eye to his paper. "You're now Burt Jones."

Bertie blinked. He was not sure he had heard correctly. He did not know exactly what he was saying or how the man could have misheard him so poorly. Had he not spoken clearly? He was about to dare to correct him, but suddenly, the realization dawned on him. A small slit of sunlight emerged from the depths of his heart. He swallowed, suddenly feeling lightheaded, suddenly hoping and also afraid to hope.

He tried to keep his tone even, but it came out lighter than he could manage. He fought off the urge to cry. "Yes, sir. Thank you."

The man finished writing and looked back up, jutting his chin impatiently at Karl.

Karl jolted, quickly leaning forward as if he were in school. "Karl Fuchs, sir." He looked equally unsure as to what he should dare feel in this moment. He was distrustful of his own hope.

The man squinted as if he had just been insulted. "That certainly won't do. Carl Fox."

Karl simply nodded and resisted the urge to tell the man that was, indeed, what his surname meant.

The man wrote more words and then pointed his pen at Sofie.

"Sofie Durchden—" She answered immediately, but then stopped, now looking confused. "Sofie . . . Jones?"

The man simply nodded to himself as he wrote down more words. They all sat, waiting for what felt like a long time. Bertie fought the urge with everything he had to lean over and look at the paper. He told himself writing was good. Writing meant paperwork. Paperwork surely was good. It would be easier just to shove them back onto the ship.

"If you please . . ." Karl suddenly said in a small voice.

Bertie felt his stomach drop. The man stopped writing mid-word and slowly lifted his head back up, eyebrows raised.

Karl swallowed. "Would you allow us the name Baumann instead of Jones?"

"And why's that?"

Karl stopped cradling the urn to his chest and held it out slightly with both hands. "They saved people hunted by the Nazis."

The man's face barely changed. But he did indeed scratch out three different places and write something new beside them instead. He pointed his pen at all three of them this time in a sweep, landing on Karl.

"All three of you want Bauman?"

"Yes, sir," said Karl.

"Yes," said Bertie.

"Thank you," said Sofie. She looked the most unsure of what might be happening, lines of worry creasing across her forehead. She was simply following the other two the best she could. Bertie wished he could at least take her hand, but worried doing so would signal something wrong to the man. Why would innocent people need to be comforted right now?

"Health?" the man demanded.

"Us all good, sir," Bertie replied.

This seemed believable enough. With the time they had spent with the man, they had all stood straight. There had not been a single cough or sneeze or sniffle.

The man stared at each of them a moment longer, as if waiting for something. Bertie simply held his breath.

Finally, the man opened up a drawer of his desk, looking suspiciously like the one he had just closed and, like magic, pulled out a sight that made Bertie want to cry all over again. He placed three new little booklets on the desk. Deep, glossy blue with the Amerikan eagle emblazoned on the cover with shiny gold paint. He opened each one in turn and stamped them with a thump so forceful that Karl jumped at the first one. Just a couple dips into the ink pad in between and it was over. It was so quick that Bertie, once again, felt insulted with all the work they had put into making theirs. He wondered what would happen to the ones in his desk, if they would be destroyed or filed away somewhere. He was still certain the man did not believe that they were real.

They remained quiet, afraid to breathe, as the man wrote in each of their names. He punched out a few dotted numbers and gave a few more forceful thumps when he stamped the date into each.

He leaned far over his desk, first in Bertie's direction. Bertie dared to lean over just as far to accept the first passport. He was suddenly afraid this was all still an elaborate prank, a terribly cruel joke. That if he would be so cocky as to accept the offering, to think they had successfully fooled them, he would be met with handcuffs.

But the sleek passport slipped into his hands, unnervingly effortlessly, and then into Sofie's, and then into Karl's, who still held on to the urn with one hand. Bertie quickly flipped through his to look at the information. *Male*, it said. He had finally gotten his transvestite passport.

"Alright then," the man said. His tone had never changed. He either did not know the gift he had just given them or he did not care. "Burt and Sophie Bauman, husband and wife. And Carl Bauman, nephew under your care."

Bertie let out a breath. Sofie clasped her hands together in polite thanks.

"Our best to you, sir," Karl said. "Thank you."

But the man was unmoved, already pointing with his pen at the door. "Take a left soon as you leave, another left at the end of the hallway, and you'll find the doors."

They stood up immediately, thanking him once more each. Bertie's muscles tensed again, however, when he saw a man in a white coat at the end of the hallway, just before the doors, as if guarding them. They had barely gotten there when the doctor swooped down upon each of them, raking his hands through their scalps and shining a light into their mouths. Bertie nearly choked when his fingers pressed against the glands beneath his jawline. He was not sure if he fled after that point or if he had been pushed. But suddenly the three of them were outside. They had made it out through the other end of the building. And suddenly, the air felt very different.

Karl blinked in the sunlight as if they had been shut away for days. He craned his head everywhere at this busy and noisy place called New York, finally looking at Sofie and Bertie. "Did we make it?"

"We made it," Sofie said. She did not seem to quite believe it herself.

Bertie looked at his passport again. *Male*, it still declared.

He suddenly realized he wanted Sofie and Karl to promise him that they would burn him after he died. He did not want to be the next one noticed after death and plastered across the papers for sensation. He wished he could be more fearless, someone who would show his full self without hesitation. But if people could not be kind about it, would not be respectful, then they were not allowed to know. He wondered how many people like him had lived and died undetected. Surely for every one reported, there were ten others who slipped by. Maybe more. It all came down to your luck and your loved ones.

He realized the rare gift he had just been given and how many people would have done what he had done and more to get it. He felt relieved. He felt lucky. He also felt sad.

He noticed the man had spelled their new surname with only one *n*, and his new name of Burt with a *u* instead of a much-preferred *e*. Sofie was with a *ph* and Karl was with a *C*. Bertie had a mix of feelings well up inside him. He was surprised that some of them were bad.

"I'll never get to be Berthold Durchdenwald again," he said.

"And I never got to be Karl Fuchs. Not really."

Bertie was quiet. For the first time, he felt the loss in his heart. It was an ache deep inside. Through all these years, he had believed that one day he could be himself again. He had believed it possible, if only because to not have it would be too cruel. Only now the cruelty was here. This was his life, this would always be his life. To hide. Even when he was showing who he was, they still made him hide.

Sofie was quiet. She slipped an arm through his and gave it a squeeze.

"What do we do now?" Karl asked.

Bertie tucked his new self into his jacket pocket. "We do our best."

27

THEY HAD BARELY MOVED FORWARD BEFORE KARL CAME TO a dead stop. He put down the urn and suitcase and crouched.

"I have something for you." He opened the suitcase and carefully sorted through the clothes. "I didn't want to mention it until we were safely through."

He gently extracted one of Gert's handkerchiefs, tied into a tiny bundle. He placed the bundle in Bertie's hand and gestured for him to open it. Bertie was at a loss as to what Karl could have possibly brought with him, but he did as instructed and carefully unwrapped the bundle. It unfurled to reveal dozens of berries, thick and red. A few still clung to the remnants of asparagus fronds.

"You said these were important, right?" Karl sounded breathless in his need to be helpful. "Now we can plant the seeds and see if we can regrow the same bushes that fed our family for generations."

For the third time that hour, Bertie felt the urge to cry. He wondered if this was a new part of himself or if he was finally feeling more able to release it. He stifled it regardless, remembering they were in public, foreigners in a new world, and this was not a helpful first impression to make.

He cleared his throat and smiled. "It'll take a lot of patience and management to get them properly started, but I'd love to try once we've finally settled."

Karl looked pleased with himself and carefully rewrapped the handkerchief, placing it back into his suitcase.

"It's time," Sofie said simply, gesturing out at the city. She looked worried at everything that waited for them out there. There was too much unknown.

They walked a short way past the building. Throngs of people washed over the piers, speaking a babel of languages cut through with sudden, unaccented English. Several folks frowned at them as they passed by in their good suits and dresses, faces pinched and disapproving. Bertie was suddenly very aware of how much he and Sofie and Karl surely smelled, how poor and dirty they looked. How foreign. In a land of foreigners, they had long stopped being welcomed.

Bertie looked at all the people walking by and was suddenly afraid of wading into such a strong current. Everyone seemed so busy and unfriendly. The buildings were dizzyingly tall, their endless windows reflecting the sun in a harsh glint. People worked in their cages, stacked atop each other, heating and heating until they surely died like ants under a magnifying glass, toiling away in their Sunday best. The paved streets smelled like hot urine. Sound was an assault here. All the familiar noises twisted into an endless aggression, angry shouting, and constant honking.

Despite what Bertie remembered Gert saying so many years ago, this did not feel like Berlin at all.

Bertie looked around. There were too many people, and he was not tall. But then the aggressive seas parted a moment, and through the crowd, far down across a nearby street, was a familiar face. Older, but still familiar.

"Roy?" he called out.

Roy glanced around at the faint sound of his name. His eye landed on him. He smiled big, already looked near tears, and stretched his hand up high so they would not lose each other. "Bertie!"

The river of people closed again, but Bertie could still see Roy's outstretched palm over all the heads. He stood on his toes, craning, trying to find a good way around.

And then he heard Roy call out the most beautiful thing possible. "Gert!"

Bertie's heart swelled. Somewhere in the crowd, Gert was looking for them. Roy was calling him back over. A smile bloomed across Bertie's face, the biggest he could remember since that last Silvester, standing out with them all during the fireworks. He glanced over at Sofie, who looked equally in disbelief.

"He's alive," he said. Without another thought, he charged through the crowd, parting and pushing and shoving, not hearing the angry English shouts and insults. He broke through, his suitcase swaying in his hand.

And although they had met on only two occasions, Bertie barreled into Roy's arms, nearly knocking him over.

Roy held him tight and laughed into his neck. "I'm so glad you're alright, Bertie," he said in English. He finally parted from him and took in a big sigh, like he was releasing so much angst himself, like he could finally be happy again. He looked over Bertie's shoulder expectantly. "Where is he?"

The smile slipped from his face. "Who?"

Sofie and Karl finally caught up with them. The brightness in Roy's eyes showed that he remembered Sofie. But when Karl came into view, his face fell. He looked as if someone had stolen his life back away in an instant.

"Oh." He searched for more words. "I'm . . . I'm sorry. I thought . . ."

They all came to the realization at once. Karl looked horrified. He wrenched the cap off his head in a single swipe, as if this would help. "I'm so sorry, sir," he said quickly in English. "These were the only clothes that fit me."

Roy looked to age another ten years. He tried to give a weak smile to Karl before looking at Bertie. "I'd hoped maybe he fled to you. And your letter . . . it was code . . ." He took the piece of paper from his jacket pocket and unfolded it.

Bertie did not look at it, did not take it. He just let it all wash over him. This unexpected moment of joy suddenly made everything feel so much worse.

Roy finally folded the letter and put it back into his pocket. "I'd really been hoping . . . this whole time . . . just maybe . . ." He swallowed thickly. He glanced back over at Karl and wiped quickly at his eyes, pushing his tone to something sunnier. As if to hold out hope, as if to love someone, was silly. "But what am I saying? I'm very happy to meet you."

He extended his hand, his watery smile too large.

Karl shook his hand awkwardly. "Karl," he said, small, still clutching his hat in his other hand. "I'm pleased to meet you, Roy. I'm sorry it's not under better circumstances. But I thank you for everything you're doing for a stranger."

Roy gave a polite nod and released his hand. He looked ready to cry again. A dull glint around his neck caught Bertie's eye. He pointed, the recognition overwhelming him.

"That necklace. Is that . . . ?"

"Gert's fortune casting from the Silvester fest," Roy said. "He threw it out when we got to his apartment that night, but I dug it out and kept it."

"But why?" It was a silly question. Bertie already knew why. It was the same reason why he would show the flat-cap to him later, to finally admit to Sofie and Karl that he had stolen it. That he had carried it around this whole time like a child's blanket.

Roy gave a slight shrug. "I have so little of him here. Only his toothbrush and a few clothes he forgot to pack from his last trip. A shirt, two ties, a sock I found under the bed. I still have them all." He cupped the lead symbol, looking down at it from its chain. He had pierced it so that it fell in the shape of a dagger. "But this was something he once held in his palm." He closed his fingers around it.

This, then, was all that was left of Gert. At that moment, Bertie realized how quickly Gert and the others, how all of them really, would slip away from memory. His mind flashed to that last night at the Institut, the burning of the archives. He suddenly wanted to scream and never stop. In whose memory would any of them remain?

"What is the date?" he suddenly asked. With everything he had once known gone, he had the need to feel grounded.

"The twenty-fourth of June."

After all they had been through, after all the change they had endured, it was still asparagus season. The final day, but still asparagus season. Bertie decided he would no longer trust time. He could no longer trust many things.

"The Americans," he slipped into Deutsch, for he wanted to

make his words very clear, "I saw them let in Nazis without concern. War-criminal Nazis. Why?"

Roy blanched a little as a few Amerikan heads turned at the sound of the Deutsch. "No German," he whispered, still in English. "Only speak English here, at all times. If Germany comes up, you spit upon the ground. You hate Germany now. Understand?"

Bertie tried to not think in that moment about all the things he loved about Deutschland. Sofie, quiet this whole time as if she already had suspected the rules, simply nodded.

"But the Nazis," Roy continued in English, "yes." He lowered his voice. "The United States has been welcoming them in. They've been seeking them out for recruitment with the government. Mostly spy work and war tactics. I've heard they're terrible at it so far, embarrassingly bad, but they keep inviting them in."

"How?" Bertie could not think of anything more he could sputter out, English or otherwise.

"Because the United States wants to eradicate Communists and homosexuals. And nobody hates Commies and queers more than Nazis." He looked at all three of them, as if sure they did not believe him. "They're getting great pay and benefits."

Karl looked horrified. "Are they at least being watched?"

"Not from what I've heard. Some government agent just knocks on the doors of their houses once a month—"

"They have *houses?*"

Bertie realized many things at once. He realized why their ferry went through the other occupations effortlessly, why their ship was not attacked by the Allies while out in open water. There were valuable Nazis on board, most likely some that had been specifically requested by Amerika to join their ranks. The Allies had known about the ship all along.

He realized why the passport of the Nazi on the ship had looked so real. Because it had been. After everything he, Sofie, and Karl had gone through to leave, to save themselves from people like him, to run to a country that hated them just as much as the one they left— The anger stoked inside of him, a burning inferno. Was this how Karl felt? So much inside of him, churning, the world swallowed whole. But he could never let it out. Not satisfyingly, not effectively, not in any way that would not simply cause more harm toward himself and those he loved. It would only split him open at the ribs.

"Thank you for coming," he said instead, carefully in English.

Roy gave a weak smile. "Every day, all day, since Friday. I wanted to make sure I didn't miss you." He tried once more to wipe away his heart, to make his tone more upbeat. It almost worked. "Come. You must all be so tired and hungry. I don't have much, but we'll make it work. You stay with me as long as you need." He clapped Bertie on the shoulder, sounding now like he was apologizing, as if this were the biggest thing on their minds. "You're gonna hate the beer here."

Bertie could only give his own wan smile.

They walked together in the direction Roy had vaguely indicated. Bertie thought of Gert. He thought of Gebhardt and Karsten and Markus. He thought of Doktor Hirschfeld and Rüdiger and Dora and the Institut, of the Eldorado and his old apartment. He thought of meeting Sofie, of their first night in bed together. He thought of the farm. He thought of Oma and Opa. He thought of Frau Ber. He thought of the nephew Sofie had lost, of the former life Bertie had lost, and the one that Karl never got to taste. He thought of the berries tucked so gently away in Karl's suitcase. He thought of Sofie's parents, believing she had died, had taken her own life, until they were gone themselves. He thought of drinking at the Eldorado, and the many drunken staggers home with Gert. He thought of putting together the schedules of Doktor Hirschfeld. He thought of giving tours. He thought of sitting at his desk, filling out forms for so many transvestites, their faces relieved and hopeful for their futures. He thought of when he met Karl, both the first time and the second. He thought of their last Silvester fest, laughing and joyful with jelly donuts and fortune-telling games, unaware of how their lives would upend in four weeks. He wished he could remember what the last thing he had said to Gert was. He hoped it was something of love.

He thought of Sofie, so quiet this entire time. She was a woman of strength and voice. Yet here she was, silenced. Her English was so poor. He found her hand and squeezed it. He then found Karl's hand, doing the same amid the swinging suitcase.

They had survived. And none of them knew why. None of them felt they deserved it.

"Is it better here?" Bertie asked after they had walked a short way. It was a useless question, a silly question, but he so badly needed to hear something good. "For people like us?"

Roy did not answer. When Bertie glanced sideways to him, he saw the way his lips were pursed, and he did not ask again.

"Perhaps it will get better," Bertie said flatly. "Herr Doktor taught many people, many countries. He put his life into it. He was right here in New York just before the War."

"There is teaching and then there is listening," Roy said quietly.

"So . . . what do we do now?" Karl asked.

Sofie finally opened her mouth. "Live."

Bertie knew she was right, but he was also filled with bad feelings. He worried about moving forward, about putting so much trauma behind him. Because if he put it behind him, he worried that meant putting Gert and all the others behind him, too. All of his community, all of his family, all of his friends. He worried that to smile, to thrive, would be a betrayal to everyone who had died. If he was a good person, if they had meant the world to him, then he was not supposed to move forward. But he knew he had to. For the only other option was death, and after all those who had fallen, after all Gert gave so that Bertie could live, that felt like an even bigger insult to his memory.

Bertie felt it all weigh upon him. They walked slowly, the sunlight peeking through the clouds. It glinted dully against the dagger around Roy's neck.

Bertie gave a dry chuckle, which sounded more like a cough. He spoke in Deutsch, and he did not care. "What a cruelty. One of the last surviving artifacts of our community, of our history, is an omen of death."

Karl shook his head. "History isn't artifacts or pictures or things. History is the people who made them."

Bertie glanced over at him. They all did.

"The history is us," Karl said. "And we'll keep passing it on."

They continued to walk, then. All together.

And they did just that.

Notes from the Author

CORRECTIONS

- There were five Eldorado clubs in Berlin, each gracing slightly different time periods. However, pictures and descriptions were difficult to come by for any of them. While I was able to use outside photographs of the actual location on the corner of Motzstraße and Kalckreuthstraße (Bertie's club), I had to use the one on Elsässerstraße for descriptions of indoors. I decided to merge this mismatch of fact rather than invent something myself.
- The fifth and final issue of the transvestite journal *Das 3. Geschlecht* (The Third Gender/Sex) came out in May 1932. It's unlikely Bertie would've been able to easily purchase it off the newsstand six months later, but I took the liberty here for the sake of flavor. Likewise, any given queer title by that year was subject to tightened censorship laws. Some days you could find some of them on the racks, other days they were taken back down. I decided to have as many of them available to Bertie as possible so readers could get a fuller idea of the expanse of options available up until the recent law changes.
- Some sources say the tours at the Institute for Sexual Science were weekly, others say daily. I went with daily.
- Dr. Magnus Hirschfeld left Germany in 1930 for his multiyear world tour, not 1933. Because this fact would have destroyed the plot's timeline, or have removed any direct interaction with Hirschfeld, I changed the timeline to have him leaving the day of the Institute's attack.
- It's believed the attack upon the Institute of Sexual Science occurred in the morning around 9:30 a.m. and lasted into the evening. For dramatic purposes and to better fit the storyline, I changed the start of the attack to nighttime.
- While Dr. Hirschfeld did have a secretary and assistant, documen-

tation suggests these tasks most likely fell under the guidance of his lover, Karl Giese, who was also the museum's librarian and archivist. For plot reasons, I gave the fictional character of Bertie this role. Giese was described by Christopher Isherwood as "a sturdy peasant youth with a girl's heart." He stayed behind when Hirschfeld went on his world tour. He survived the Institute's attacks unscathed, eventually coming to France to stay with Hirschfeld and Li Shiu Tong, Hirschfeld's second lover who he met during his world tour. After a certain "bathhouse affair," Giese had to quickly relocate to Vienna, then Brno. He died by suicide in 1938 before the Nazis invaded Czechoslovakia. He had played the part of the younger version of the protagonist in Hirschfeld's film *Anders als die Andern* (Different from the Others, 1919).

* This novel is told through the eyes of Bertie, but the reality is that Hirschfeld was a complicated sexologist. To learn more about his messy and tangled relationship to racism, misogyny, and eugenics—and to learn more about his lover and intellectual successor Li Shiu Tong—read *Racism and the Making of Gay Rights* by Dr. Laurie Marhoefer.
* Hirschfeld's canary speech was my own creation. I felt it was an important point to make and it worked into the novel most organically through Hirschfeld.
* The Night of the Long Knives (June 30 to July 2, 1934) took place almost exactly one month *before* the death of President Paul von Hindenburg (August 2, 1934). The attack upon the Institute of Sexual Science was likewise more than a year earlier (May 6, 1933). Hindenburg's death was nonetheless narratively included ahead of these two events in the several sparse pages illustrating Hitler's rise to power in order to complete that picture. Besides that jump in time, all other events are narratively portrayed in the order in which they occurred.
* The Night of the Long Knives (otherwise known as Operation Hummingbird) was primarily intended to purge Ernst Röhm (well known as homosexual) and the Sturmabteilung (SA), also believed

to be notably homosexual. Hitler believed Röhm and his SA were no longer of use and, therefore, now a liability. The degree to which the attacks were motivated by prejudice against Röhm's and the SA's homosexuality is muddy, though this prejudice likely played a part. While Röhm and the SA were considered the primary targets, many of Hitler's other perceived opponents were also targeted; at the time, those were primarily political opponents or LGBTQ+ people. Somewhere between 85 and 1,000 people were murdered during the three days of the Long Knives, and more than 1,000 others were arrested and/or sent to the freshly built Dachau.

* Dora Richter was originally believed to have died during the attack on the Institute. However, it was later found that she'd fled to Karlsbad—now the West Bohemia region of the Czech Republic—and become the owner of a small restaurant. In 1934, she was finally granted a legal name change by the president of Czechoslovakia. She owned her own home, remained unmarried, and eventually moved on to working as a lace maker from home. After 1939, there is no known record of her. The rest of her life is unknown.
* Due to the destruction of documentation and near-complete erasure of gender nonconforming people—both literally and figuratively—Karl's monologue as a trans man surviving the Holocaust is not based on distinct, primary sources. Rather, it's speculation based on heavy research regarding the treatment of (gentile) cishet women, cis queer women, cis queer men, and the intentional fluidity of interpreting and/or upholding Paragraph 175.
* I initially mentioned the punishment for §175 (homosexuality) was six months in jail, while §183 (cross-dressing) was a year. However, when Bertie later talks with Ward about punishment regarding cross-dressing, they discuss the time length of §175 instead. While it's true that America decided to keep the lengthened Nazi punishment of §175 from six months to five years, it's unknown what, if any, changes the Nazis made to §183. I decided to include this discrepancy so readers would further understand how America treated and viewed LGBTQ+ survivors.

* With the evolution of language being what it is, I occasionally took liberties in terms of how "transvestites" were categorized and labeled. At the time, *transvestite* was defined as someone wearing the clothes of the gender "opposite" of them (e.g., a woman wearing men's clothing), and those who engaged in it full-time were "total transvestites," though this term wasn't used regularly in casual conversation. As such, transgender people of the time were defined—and, it would appear, self-defined on some occasions, though not always—in their transvesting based on their sex assigned at birth. Who we would today likely define as a trans man was often defined as a "female transvestite" during the time. I avoided such references when possible, opting for terminology used within the community itself, and changed such references to "male transvestite" when unavoidable in order to prevent confusion and misunderstanding by current-day readers.
  * Please note that (1) the terminology of the time overall wasn't intended to misgender, but rather an attempt to understand and explain to the public in ways they might comprehend, and (2) language has since changed and to now refer to a trans man as "female" is, indeed, an act of misgendering and an insulting practice.
* *Lila* is most often translated as *lavender*, with *purple* being second-most popular, and *lilac* as third. I felt *purple* was too vague, but worried *lavender* would be misconstrued in America with the lesbian community (e.g., Lavender Menace). I chose *lilac* because it felt the most distinct for this story, as well as the most visually similar translation.

FACTS

* While their stories are significantly different than in this novel, the characters of Bertie, Karl, and Gert were named in honor of three of the few known presumed trans masculine and/or intersex individuals

documented to have survived the War: Berthold Buttgereit, Karl M. Baer, and Gerd Katter.

* Berthold Buttgereit (1891–1983) inexplicably survived in plain sight of the Nazis throughout the War, mainly in Cologne, his entire life documented save for an eight-year disappearance from 1942 to 1950. This is a significant time to disappear, and yet I was never able to account for this disappearance. With Dr. Hirschfeld's help, he acquired a "transvestite card" in 1912 and a "transvestite passport/travel pass" in 1918. His "transvestite passport/travel pass" is the only known surviving article of this nature. His "transvestite card" is lost. He acquired a name change in 1920, after over a year of battling the regulations. He soon after sought to marry his girlfriend of eight years but was denied when he presented his birth certificate. He then tried to change his birth certificate, but the outcome of this, and his consequential marriage, are unknown. Save for his name continuing to appear in Cologne's address books until his death, the remainder of his life is largely unknown.
* Karl M. Baer (1885–1956) wrote the semi-fictional book *Aus eines Mannes Mädchenjahren* (*Memoirs of a Man's Maiden Years*) under the pseudonym N. O. Body in 1907, with a foreword by Dr. Hirschfeld. The book was popular enough in its time that copies survived beyond the burning of the Institute's library and the Nazi book bans. With Dr. Hirschfeld's help, he underwent gender confirmation surgery in 1906, the first known person to do so. He had a male birth certificate issued in 1907 and gained the right to marry a woman later that year. He was arrested by the Nazis in 1937. After being interrogated and tortured, he and his wife left for the region of Palestine, where they survived the remainder of the War. He ended up in a throuple with a second woman, his secretary. He began to lose his sight in 1950 and his final six years are unknown.
* Gerd Katter (1910–1995) stayed at the Institute from 1928 to 1932 and was considered a confidante and "valued son" of Hirschfeld.

He was a frequent guest on visits by politicians, doctors, and civil servants and was personally involved with public relations work on homosexuality and transvestism at the Institute. He received a name change and his "transvestite card" in 1928. Much like Buttgereit's "transvestite passport/travel pass," Katter's "transvestite card" is the only known surviving artifact of its kind. He received gender confirmation surgery an undisclosed amount of time later by Dr. Otto Nordmann, who purposely put in an incorrect diagnosis so that Katter's health insurance would cover the operation. Instead of leaving the Institute, Katter continued outreach, especially for young transvestites. It's believed he wanted to become a sexologist himself. Katter began to contact archives in 1945 to try to keep the memory of Hirschfeld, the Institute, and his community alive. He was only successful forty years later, when in 1985, Katter finally donated all of his surviving estate, including his "transvestite card," journals, and other documentation, to Ralf Dose of the Magnus Hirschfeld Society. At Ralf Dose's request, he also wrote an autobiographical document in 1988 about his time at the Institute. Little is known about Katter's experiences or whereabouts from the Nazi era to the end of World War II. He did not discuss it.

- As of this writing, the Eldorado location of Motzstraße and Kalckreuthstraße is an organic grocery store.
- Dr. Magnus Hirschfeld was in the south of France when he heard about the attack on the Institute. It was four days later, during Joseph Goebbels's cleansing by fire, arguably the first documented queer book ban. Hirschfeld and his second lover, Li Shiu Tong, had to sit in a Paris theater to watch his life's work thrown into a pile heads tall, in Berlin's Opernplatz, set ablaze as people circled it in the salute for Hitler. Over twenty thousand books and journals, over thirty-five thousand photographs, thousands of personal clinical files, hundreds of slides, and even the bust of his own likeness that used to greet people as they entered the main building. Everything that had ever been gathered, everything that had ever been learned about the third sex.

Everything they had ever written or created themselves. The primary archive of sexual intermediates for the entire world. Hirschfeld would never return to Germany. Devastated by the loss, he remained exiled, taking to France until his death two years later, on his sixty-seventh birthday. He died in the company of loved ones. For years to come, history books around the world would use the footage of the "cleansing by fire" night to discuss censorship and fascism. But the captions, quite ironically, never mentioned what exactly was being censored and burned.

* Despite the Nazis' attempts to destroy every copy of *Anders als die Andern* (Different from the Others, 1919), fragments of the film were found by happenstance in the Russian Film Archive in Ukraine in the 1970s. It survived by the ingenuity of Dr. Hirschfeld himself, who after the ban on the film took portions of it and scrambled them into his educational documentary, *Gesetze der Liebe* (Laws of Love, 1927). While that documentary was also banned, a single copy had found its way into the Russian Film Archive. After its discovery, the fragmented *Anders als die Andern* was carefully reconstructed by Stefan Drößler, director of Filmmuseum Munich, aided by surviving stills and Hirschfeld's own words describing the plot in one of his yearbooks. In 2019, two more full minutes of runtime were believed to be found, including a transvestite explaining the difference between sexuality and gender. A full copy of the film has yet to be recovered.
* The two buildings of the Institute for Sexual Science were bombed during an air raid on November 22, 1943. The extent of damage was estimated at 84.2 percent. After World War II ended, Dr. Hirschfeld's surviving colleagues were unable to reclaim the Institute's original property, as the postwar courts declared its prior seizure by Nazis legal. In 1950, the ruins were blown up and the rubble cleared away because they constituted a public danger. Despite various efforts to reestablish it after the War, the Institute for Sexual Science fell into oblivion. As of this writing, the site is overgrown with grass.
* At Hirschfeld's death, he willed the Institute's remaining assets to Karl Giese and requested that Li Shiu Tong take care of his personal

effects. In 1993, after Li Shiu Tong's death, a suitcase was discovered in an apartment-block dumpster in Vancouver, Canada, by Adam Smith, a tenant of the building. It included papers, photographs, diaries written in German, and a death mask of a mustachioed man. He did not know exactly what he had but knew it was important, and so he held on to it all, including during a move from Vancouver to Toronto. In 2002, with the continued emergence of the internet, he posted a notice online. It was seen, quite by chance during "one slightly drunken night" by Ralf Dose, director of the Magnus Hirschfeld Society in Berlin. Adam Smith had, indeed, rediscovered and kept safe the words and photographs of Magnus Hirschfeld, including his death mask, piecing together the unknown final years of Hirschfeld's life. Li Shiu Tong had kept to his word up until his own passing, lovingly taking the suitcase and boxes of surviving Institute books with him everywhere he traveled. The boxes of books were eventually found safe in the basement of Li Shiu Tong's younger brother, also collected by Ralf Dose. It's unknown how the suitcase ended up in the dumpster.

* If anybody has any information, documents, or artifacts regarding any of the aforementioned history, please contact the Magnus-Hirschfeld-Gesellschaft e.V. (the Magnus Hirschfeld Society) in Berlin. If you don't have information but would still like to help, please consider a donation, a button for which can currently be found at the bottom of their home page at https://magnus-hirschfeld.de/.

"Das Lila Lied" ("The Lilac Song")

Written by Kurt Schwabach and Mischa Spoliansky (1920)
in honor of Dr. Magnus Hirschfeld

This is the first known documented queer anthem in the colonized world. It includes snark and playful double meanings, such as *schwül*, originally meaning "sultry" or "humid" but also slang in the community for "gay" or "queer." The phrase "we're different from the others" is a direct reference to Dr. Hirschfeld's groundbreaking film of the same name. It's believed additional double meanings are in the song, but most of the slang and cultural references are lost to history.

Was will man nur?	What do they want?
Ist das Kultur	Can this be considered culture
daß jeder Mensch verpönt ist	if everyone is frowned upon
der klug und gut	who is bright and good
jedoch mit Blut	but with a particular kind of blood
von eig'ner Art durchströmt ist	flowing through them
daß g'rade die kategorie	that just this category
vor dem Gesetz verbannt ist	is banned by law
die im Gefühl	which is related in emotions,
bei Lust und Spiel	in pleasure and play,
und in der Art verwandt ist?	and in nature?
Und dennoch sind die Meisten stolz	And still most of us are proud
daß sie von ander'm Holz	to be carved from different wood
Wir sind nun einmal	We just happen
anders als die Andern	to be different from the others
die nur im Gleichschritt	who'd only love
der Moral geliebt	in the lockstep of morality
neugierig erst durch	curiously wandering
tausend Wunder wander	through a thousand wonders

und für die's doch nur das Banale gibt
Wir aber wissen nicht, wie das Gefühl ist
denn wir sind alle
and'rer Welten Kind
Wir lieben nur die lila Nacht, die schwül ist
weil wir ja anders als die Andern sind

but still cling to the trivial
But we don't know that feeling
since we are all children
of different worlds
All we love is the sultry-gay lilac night
because we're different from the others

Wozu die Qual,
uns die Moral der Andern aufzudrängen?
Wir, hört geschwind, sind wie wir sind
selbst wollte man uns hängen
Wer aber denkt
daß man uns hängt
den mßte man beweinen
doch bald, gebt acht
wird über Nacht
auch uns're Sonne scheinen
Dann haben wir das gleiche Recht erstritten
wir leiden nicht mehr, sondern sind gelitten

Why the torment
to force others' morals on us?
Listen up, we are what we are
even if you want to hang us
But we should feel sorry
for those who'd like to hang us
Pay attention, our sun will shine
after this night
Then we will have
our hard-earned rights
We will no longer suffer
but instead suffer tolerance

Wir sind nun einmal
anders als die Andern
die nur im Gleichschritt
der Moral geliebt
neugierig erst durch
tausend Wunder wander
und für die's doch nur das Banale gibt
Wir aber wissen nicht, wie das Gefühl ist
denn wir sind alle
and'rer Welten Kind
Wir lieben nur die lila Nacht, die schwül ist
weil wir ja anders als die Andern sind

We just happen
to be different from the others
who'd only love
in the lockstep of morality
curiously wandering
through a thousand wonders
but still cling to the trivial
But we don't know that feeling
since we are all children
of different worlds
All we love is the sultry-gay lilac night
because we're different from the others

Wir lieben nur die lila Nacht, die schwül ist
weil wir ja anders als die Andern sind

All we love is the sultry-gay lilac night
because we're different from the others

Acknowledgments

Thank you to Counterpoint Press for your enthusiasm, support, and wisdom. Thank you to editor Dan López, editorial assistant Yukiko Tominaga, editor in chief Dan Smetanka, senior managing editor Wah-Ming Chang, copy editor Sarah Lyn Rogers, production manager Olenka Burgess, associate production editor tracy danes, proofreader Barrett Briske, creative director Nicole Caputo, cover designer Farjana Yasmin, head of marketing Rachel Fershleiser, digital marketing manager Ashley Kiedrowski, marketing assistant Alyssa Lo, events manager Lily Philpott, head of publicity Megan Fishmann, and everyone on the editorial, production, marketing, and publicity teams.

Thank you to LGR Literary for your dedication, guidance, and outright refusal to give up on me, especially my agents Mike Nardullo and Sarah Bedingfield, and associate agent Rebecca Rodd.

Thank you to my writing mentors, Michelle Hoover and Samantha Rajaram, as well as the writing community of GrubStreet. Thank you to Suzannah Lutz, Teddy Howland, Shalene Gupta, and Julie Carrick Dalton for the personal support throughout this project. Thank you to both of my therapists. You do important work.

Thank you to Mary Benard and George Grattan, who among many things provided friendship, unwavering support, and a place to sleep and shower when I was in need. I'm so happy we happened to be together when my book deal came in.

Thank you for the support in various ways from Lambda Literary, Tin House, Pitch Wars, Monson Arts, and the Massachusetts Cultural Council.

Thank you for all the research help—both directly and indirectly—from Suzannah Lutz, Teddy Howland, Deborah Good, Jerry Whelan, Kristofer Thomas, Samson Dittrich, Charles Coffland, Dr. Zavier Nunn, Dr. Jane Caplan, Dr. Susan Stryker, Dr. Katie Sutton, Dr. Laurie Marhoefer, Dr. Jack Doyle, and Dr. Rainer Herrn. People act like I uncovered all this history myself, but really all I did was stand on the shoulders of others. We've entered a time when people are finally discussing and researching trans people during the Nazi era, and I welcome the updates, changes, and discoveries that occur beyond my armchair-historian novel.

Thank you to Arnd Rühlmann, Marcos Sullivan, Koboldmaki, and Monika Tirola for the help in the cultural and linguistic subtleties of the English translation for "Das Lila Lied."

An unanticipated shoutout to the language-learning app Duolingo. The pandemic hit the United States just as I was about to start German language classes for the latter stages of my research, and Duolingo ended up providing me access to learning while the country figured out how to do the whole virtual classroom thing. If it weren't for that app, I'd be at least two years behind with this novel.

Thank you to Julie Carrick Dalton, Potato Expert, who excitedly talked to me for hours about growing vegetables, starting with the phrase, "Well you know, here's what *I* would do if *I* were trying to survive on a small farm for years during a major war . . ."

Thank you to Suzannah Lutz for all the website building, publicity brainstorming, and dedication helping get this book noticed.

Thank you to my beta readers Teddy Howland, Samantha Rajaram, John McClure, Katrina Stacey, and Rick Hendrie.

Thank you to the Magnus-Hirschfeld-Gesellschaft e.V. Forschungsstelle zur Geschichte der Sexualwissenschaft (the Magnus Hirschfeld Society Research Center for the History of Sexology) in Berlin. I especially want to express heartfelt thanks to Ralf Dose, cofounder and researcher at the Society since 1982. His level of commitment to uncovering and collecting the history portrayed in this novel is astounding. Almost everything we know is because of the tireless efforts of this man and the Magnus Hirschfeld Society. Thank you, Ralf Dose, and to everyone, both known and unknown, who have given all of their time, energy, and love to reclaiming our history and our ancestry. We owe you more than words can say.

Finally, thank you to the countless queer and trans people who came before me, providing a better world for our communities from active resistance to just plain existing. Whether you're remembered, erased, or lost to history, whether you got to live as yourselves or survived through untruths, you made a difference. Ancestry is the most important thing in this world. As difficult as things can be, we often forget that what we have is because of those who lived before us. This novel was the hardest book I've ever written, and every time I wanted to give up, I thought of you all. I hope I did right by you. That's all I ever wanted.

MILO TODD is a Massachusetts Cultural Council grantee and a Lambda Literary Fellow. His work has appeared in *Slice Magazine* and elsewhere. He is co–editor in chief of *Foglifter Journal* and teaches creative writing to queer and trans adults. Find out more at milotodd.com.